A SINISTER SUBTRACTION

Richard P. Kluft

IPBOOKS.net
International Psychoanalytic Books

International Psychoanalytic Books (IPBooks)
New York • http://www.IPBooks.net

Published by International Psychoanalytic Books (IPBooks)
Queens, New York
Online at: www.IPBooks.net

Book cover design by Kathy Kovacic, Blackthorn Studios

Interior book design by Medlar Publishing Solutions Pvt Ltd., India

www.IPBooks.net

ISBN: 978-1-949093-27-8

DEDICATION

For Phyllis Lile-King, Esq.
"Lawyer Nancy Drew"
Sherlock would have smiled. . .

Donald Nathanson, M.D.
(1936–2017)
Polymath and Friend

Bardin Levavy, Esq.
(1943–2018)
Friend for over seventy years
He could match quotes with Lord Peter Wimsey. . .

and

Those who know far more than they ever wanted to know
about getting up after having been knocked down. . .

CAST OF MAJOR CHARACTERS IN *A SINISTER SUBTRACTION*— IN ALPHABETICAL ORDER

Gillian Bullock – Junior lawyer for plaintiff Travers

Michael Burgoyne – "Maserati Mike," acknowledged super-lawyer and CNN commentator

Christine Cadawalder – Second chair defense lawyer for Hatfield, "Lady Carbon Monoxide"

Beau Chalmers – Governor of Virginia, with a confusing connection to Gordon Travers

Joseph Chaudvent – Expert witness for plaintiff Travers, a man confident in his superiority

Doyle Clifford – a military man with a dislike for domestic criminals

Brett Connery – Second chair defense lawyer for Underwood, victim of an obstructive hoax

Miriam Danziger – Judge in Cross & Cross v. Hatfield, a lady to be reckoned with

Nate Donaldson – Psychiatrist, authority on bullies and bullying, outrageous if provoked

Bruce Fuller – Rising "win at any cost" first chair lawyer for plaintiff Travers
Louis Galvin – Senior attorney, second chair for plaintiff Travers
Linda Gilchrist – "Lawyer Nancy Drew," young attorney for defendant Underwood
Kate Gilchrist – Divorced down and out cancer-survivor, Linda Gilchrist's once jet-set aunt
Robert Hatfield – Psychiatrist sued on the basis of fraudulent charges
Benjamin Jordan – Psychiatrist expert witness for Hatfield and Underwood, can be difficult
Oliver Lasko – Judge in Travers v. Underwood, a ferocious intellect
Barton Laird – Senior senator from Virginia
Melody Jarrett – Traumatized art teacher claiming she was victimized by Gordon Travers
Jonathan Lauder – First chair defense lawyer for Hatfield, formidable friend of Burgoyne
William "Bill" Mackey – First chair defense lawyer for Underwood, hiding two big secrets
Billie Mason – A beautiful, naïve, and frequently revictimized woman
Jay Philips – Psychiatrist defense expert for Underwood, battered, but unbowed
Phoenix – An abandoned mastiff-cross, about to get lucky
Peter Rapier – "Win at all costs" Expert witness for plaintiff Travers
Raymond St. James – Dramatic first chair plaintiffs' lawyer for Cross & Cross
Gordon Travers – Psychologist denying he abused Melody Jarrett and suing Joan Underwood
Joan Underwood – Psychiatrist sued by Gordon Travers for attacking his reputation
Sally Markham Warren – "Savvy Sally," a senior lawyer who steps in to help Linda Gilchrist
Jeff Wilder – Emotionally-explosive senior lawyer who steps in to help Linda Gilchrist

CHAPTER 1

She ran a hand over her hair. A wayward tendril captured and tamed and her Armani suit straightened, she implored her apprehensive gut to run silent, summoned her best professional smile, and knocked.

"Come on in, Linda," said Bill Mackey. Unapologetically aristocratic and old school, the stately senior partner of Mackey Markham & Wilder rose to his feet. He pulled out the particular chair he'd chosen for his young associate and held it for Linda Gilchrist as she settled herself.

Consummate gentleman, celebrated schemer, and subtle strategist, Mackey positioned Linda precisely where she would never have placed herself, directly opposite a tall, slender woman who looked vaguely familiar. *I recognize her from somewhere. . . The dog park? The gym? The nature trail?*

Every associate in the firm dreaded the drill. Every associate flinched in anticipation of what might follow. As soon as he could, Bill would run a manicured hand through his thick steely-gray hair, push his own chair back those few inches that would take him beyond Linda's comfortable field of vision, and direct his full attention to studying her interactions with the poised, attractive mid-30ish woman seated across from her.

Nothing would be said in the presence of the client, but when Bill Mackey offered his feedback, invariably delivered in the kindest possible manner, he would be meticulous, thorough, unflinching, and potentially devastating. At one time or another his perfectionistic mentorship had reduced nearly every young attorney in the firm to tears. Once elevated to the rank of partner, survivors felt obliged to share tales of their own ordeals to prevent promising young associates from submitting their resignations scant moments after Mackey macerations.

You got me last time, Bill. Today, you'll never see me sweat.

"Dr. Underwood, this is Ms. Linda Gilchrist, the colleague I mentioned earlier. Linda, Dr. Underwood is a psychiatrist on staff over at Memorial Hospital. Dr. Underwood, I'd like you to tell Ms. Gilchrist what you just told me."

Dr. Joan Underwood looked up. She pushed her dark, wavy hair away from her face and locked eyes with Linda across the enormous and overbearing rosewood table that dominated what Bill Mackey called The Founders' Room.

"So, you're the one who wrote that law review article on boundary violations in psychotherapy?" Dr. Underwood's voice was almost flat, maybe mildly sarcastic.

She tries for a poker face. What's her tell? Linda wondered.

On the wall behind Joan Underwood, oil portraits of the firm's past luminaries, their expressions stern and forbidding, stood eternal and demanding vigil. Bill Mackey's grandfather and father and other partners past and present, their visages grim and exacting, sat in wordless judgment over the proceedings below.

Linda smiled, swiveled her chair and adjusted her position to remove the venerated and venerable, but threatening, from her field of vision before she studied her interrogator. *The gym! I've seen her at the gym! She lifts a ton!*

Whenever the firm gathered around the Board Room table, Linda found herself imagining that these imposing avatars were actually enthroned upon elevated benches, a regal court overseeing every conversation and decision made beneath their imperious eyes. She couldn't help feeling herself shrinking, becoming magically transformed into a lost little girl in some bizarre and scary mansion, unsure what she was doing or how she got there, wondering if the patent leather Mary Janes on her dangling feet could really touch the deep plush carpet that seemed to grow right out of the floor, and worrying whether her lawyerly manners and legal fingernails would withstand their formidable inspection.

Bill Mackey clipped a pen to the first sheet of a yellow legal pad and slid it down the table's flawless surface. It came to a stop precisely in front of Linda's right hand, her writing hand. *How does he do that?* She claimed the pad. Looking up, she realized that Joan Underwood's intense blue eyes had never left her own. She wanted to check out Bill's face to get some read on his thinking, but Bill had set her up so that any glance in his direction would be obvious and awkward. . . *That would be sweating!*

Now Linda Gilchrist, Esq., and Joan Underwood, M.D., were locked in a world of their own, unsealed, but effectively contained for study under the Mackey microscope.

"Guilty as charged, Dr. Underwood." Without looking away, Linda asked, "Does that have something to do with my being here today, Mr. Mackey?"

"Yes, it does, Linda. Mackey Markham & Wilder has a contract with the malpractice carrier for the American Psychiatric Association. We've been asked to look in to Dr. Underwood's situation."

Linda tried to tear her thoughts away from the skyscrapers of files on her desk, insistent towers of paper threatening to either topple or transform themselves without warning into fusillades of angry calls from overwrought clients and all manner of regal rebukes from impatient partners far above her in the food chain. Probably both. . . Nodding, she directed her full attention to Dr. Joan Underwood, whose remarkably deep blue eyes remained relentlessly fixed on her own.

Most men found Linda distracting. Most women found Linda threatening. But there would be no insecurity or feline jealousy with this Joan Underwood. . . She was her match. . . Maybe more. . .

Linda continued to hold Dr. Underwood's gaze. "How shall we proceed, Mr. Mackey?"

"Dr. Underwood, why don't you give Ms. Gilchrist a brief overview?"

Dr. Underwood nodded, extracted a handwritten sheet of paper from her briefcase, and began.

"Ms. Melody Jarrett is a 34-year-old unmarried art teacher who presented five years ago complaining of. . ."

"Dr. Underwood, my sister Eve is a psychiatrist in Boston. I've got a bunch of doctors in my family. I've heard some of them make case presentations, and that's what you're beginning to do. I don't mean to be rude, but I'm not a psychiatric colleague. I need to start with a different kind of information. What brings us to this conference table today? Why are we here? How can we be of help to you?"

The dark blue eyes looked away for a second. *Is the good doctor actually beginning to show some emotion?* Linda wondered. *Not quite. . .*

Her face still expressionless, Dr. Underwood asked, "Ms. Gilchrist, are you old enough to remember, 'Just the facts, ma'am?'"

"No, and neither are you. But we both probably heard about *Dragnet* and Sgt. Joe Friday from our fathers. Or did I learn that from Mr. Mackey?"

"The callous cruelty of youth," said Mackey. "OK. Let's focus on what we're here to do."

Dr. Underwood shrugged, finally smiled, and began again.

"One year after Melody Jarrett came to me for treatment she began to show signs of Multiple Personality Disorder. . . The new DSM calls it Dissociative Identity Disorder. I knew nothing about that condition. Nobody I knew did, either. So, I tracked down a course given by some experts, read a couple of articles and books, and went ahead. As I worked with her, I consulted some of the folks who'd been teachers in that course.

"A year and a half after that, a personality named Cindy said she had a big secret. I didn't push her. . . There's so much talk about creating false memories. Perhaps I was over-cautious. Half a year after that, this Cindy told me that the psychologist Melody had seen before me—his name is Gordon Travers—molested her during sessions.

"Several more months later still, Melody came in, completely blown away. She told me she'd been having nightmares about this Dr. Travers doing stuff to her in his office, nightmares so vivid that they convinced her it really happened. As a whole person, Melody kept going back and forth about whether or not these things really happened. Some personalities said 'yes,' some said 'no,' and others say everything in between.

"Do I know what really happened? I don't. I mean, I actually believe her, that bad stuff happened, but memory is tricky."

"Believe her?"

Joan Underwood smiled. "Yes. Both ways, all ways. I believed each part was telling its own truth most of the time, but they're drawing from different memory banks, whatever, and from different ways of understanding the world. Basically, I believe there is truth in the sense that something happened that should not have happened.

"While all of this was going on, my husband and I were trying to start our family. I took a couple months off after I gave birth to Adam and Jonathan. After all those years, we had twins.

"This whole motherhood thing caught me by surprise. I couldn't believe how much I loved being a mom. I mean, everything else was fantastic already, but I wanted it all. . . I had a wonderful husband, a great career, real quality of life, and so on, but all. . . That meant a family. So, I started out, 'Oh, well! It's about time to have kids.' But I fooled myself. It meant more than I can put into words."

The tears came. Caught by surprise, Dr. Underwood put a finger to her eyes. She tried to push on, but she couldn't.

"Tissue, please?" A minute passed.

"Sorry. All those years of grinding away. . . If anyone ever tells you medical school is anything but hell, they either have to be a genius, a liar, or a flat-out psychotic. Maybe all three. I got lost in the ordeal. I'd never stopped and caught up with myself, you know, as a person. . . One of those shrinks who understands everyone but herself. Anyway, I took more time than I'd planned before I could tear myself away and go back to work, and then only half time. Actually got into some therapy for myself.

"By the time I caught up with my patients and the docs who were covering my practice, I found out after the fact Melody had filed a complaint against Dr. Travers. I never promoted that. I never even knew she was thinking about it."

"A complaint? But no lawsuit?" asked Linda.

"No. There was some back and forth about the statute of limitations. I don't understand the details."

"That can be confusing. Under most circumstances, malpractice charges have to be filed within two years of the offense. But if the victim of the offense doesn't even know or realize he or she has been victimized until after that period of time has passed, it can be different. In some states that period of two years begins only after the mistreatment has been remembered. I'm pretty new in this state. I'll have to check whether there were any changes in the relevant statutes over the course of your patient's experiences. And then, of course, the battles over the reliability of memory begin."

"Linda, before you joined us," said Mackey, "there was a bill in the state legislature that could have affected lawsuits like this. Ultimately, it went nowhere. It might have been that the lawyers Ms. Jarrett consulted were waiting to see if there would be some change that might affect their client's situation. Circumspection, bad move, or somebody fumbled the ball. . . Who knows?"

"For sure," Dr. Underwood continued, "In any case, I never thought any of this would mean anything to me. I mean, Melody withdrew her complaint. But one thing led to another. Pretty soon word got around, it got into the news, and. . ."

"I'll step in here, Doctor," said Mackey. "Dr. Underwood has been served notice that she is being sued."

"By whom? For what?"

"Dr. Travers. He accuses Dr. Underwood of falling short of the standard of care in her work with Ms. Jarrett. Specifically, he asserts that she created an iatrogenic condition, Dissociative Identity Disorder, and, by means of leading questions, suggested false memories of mistreatment that caused her to believe that Dr. Travers had molested her.

"It goes on from there. Travers alleges that these false accusations, made public, have damaged his professional reputation and practice."

"Pretty derivative. What about standing? People just can't decide to sue someone. They have to have standing, legitimate grounds. . ."

"It's tricky, Linda," said Mackey. "The first wave of false memory lawsuits hit in the early 1990s. That mostly involved patients who retracted their complaints against abusers, and they and the folks they once accused sued the therapists, alleging the memories that had come up in treatment were caused by some other party, usually the therapist.

Now, past the midpoint of the decade, we're seeing third party suits. All over the country folks who claim their parents abused them are preventing their parents from seeing their grandchildren or limiting their access to them. The grandchildren's parents are claiming they want to prevent a replay of what they believe happened to them, whether they can prove it or not. So, some of these alleged abusers, who insist they never did anything wrong, are suing for grandparental rights. Some courts have been granting them standing to sue their children's therapists. They claim those therapists have created false memories that estranged them not only from their children, but their grandchildren as well. But you know all that."

"The so-called 'parental alienation syndrome' once removed, taken back a generation."

"Yes. You know that in some previous cases when patients retracted their allegations against abusers, the people patients once alleged abused them were granted standing as co-plaintiffs. In others, the issue was claiming grandparental rights. So, with prior therapists this creates still another opening wedge for third party lawsuits, and even more litigation thereafter."

"And by implication, more than likely going after punitive damages."

"What do you mean?" asked Dr. Underwood.

Linda was unsure whether to be frank. With no cue from Mackey, she hoped she'd guess right.

"It's a nasty slap on the wrist if the court decides punishment as well as compensation is warranted."

"What does that mean?"

"It can mean three times the basic award for compensation."

"Oh." Dr. Underwood took in a deep breath quickly, let it out slowly.

"Precisely," said Mackey. "And either losing or settling the malpractice suit can prime the pump for other problems."

Dr. Underwood gave Linda a hard look.

"OK. Ms. Gilchrist. You said, 'And then, of course, the battles over the reliability of memory begin.' What's your take on the 'memory wars'?"

"You probably know that subject far better than I. . ."

"But I'm not the one who'll be defending me. What do you know?"

"Fair enough," said Linda. *Fair? Are you kidding me? Pretty darn arrogant, Dr. Underwood! You've just ordered me to run through a minefield!* For a split second she thought of appealing to Bill for relief. . . *But that would be sweating!*

"Long story short. . . Most societies have been patriarchal and the privileges of men, especially powerful men, have been safeguarded. The rights and privileges of women, children, and the weak in general have been given more lip service than true respect. That preserves the traditional patriarchal order and offers protection to the powerful, especially if they transgress against women, children, and the poor.

"There's always been an implicit escape clause to protect the powerful. Once, if a woman complained that her father or priest had abused her, that was unthinkable. So, the devil must have taken the form of the father or priest, or actually taken possession of her, so that she would make such outlandish claims. Declaring the woman must be a witch, or destroying her to drive out some demon, is win-win for the powerful. Save the soul of the woman and destroy a witness against the goodness of the great.

"Jump to Freud's trauma theory. . . Well, it must have been one of those Oedipal fantasies. Jump to the 1950s, and complaints of child abuse. . . Clearly it was easier to attribute all but the most clearly proven instances to children's inability to distinguish between fantasy, imagination, dreams, and reality.

"Twenty years ago, the most prestigious textbook in psychiatry said father-daughter incest occurred once in a million families. Now we know incest and other sexual transgressions are commonplace. But with this new awareness, some feel the pendulum swung too far toward believing the victims. Those folks pump new life into the old arguments and they claim memory research shows the act of remembering is reconstructive, it's not just opening up a reasonably accurate file. They talk about influences that can distort memory, that can lead people to make reports that are not based on events that actually occurred, or that actually occurred but not exactly as they are recalled and reported.

"So, we've got those who attack any recollection of anything that's brought up after being out of awareness as a 'recovered memory,' and assume it is inaccurate in whole or in part. We've got those who insist what victims report should be believed. And we've got folks who question both polar positions and argue that generalizations are unwarranted, that each allegation has to be assessed on its own merits. The folks on either side attack the other side and those in the middle, and as of this moment, in the mid-1990s, it's a real mess. The ones who claim recovered memories are inherently unreliable dominate academia. They accuse their opponents of being unscientific. The ones who are inclined to respect reports are mostly clinicians. They include feminists and victims' rights advocates as well. They argue that the other folks are ivory tower types aloof from reality and what they find in their experiments is not terribly relevant to clinical work or to the true situation of women and children in society. They find the 'scientific' stance unscientific, dismissive, and contemptuous to women and children."

"Where do you stand?"

"With the folks in the middle. There's enough information out there to challenge both extremes. Go skeptical, and it becomes impossible to confront possible perpetrators. Go credulous, and 'innocent until proven guilty' gets turned into 'guilty until proven innocent.' My sympathies. . .

That's one thing. But for law and science I go for honest confusion over arrogant certainty, congenial or not. Fair enough?"

"Fair enough."

Mackey moved his chair back to the table. "Dr. Underwood, you've met our Ms. Gilchrist. Shall I give her the green light to dig in to your situation?"

Once again Dr. Underwood impaled Linda with her striking but merciless deep blue eyes.

"And where, Ms. Gilchrist, would you propose to begin with what Mr. Mackey described as 'digging into my situation'?"

Who the hell does she think she is? Another test from this. . . Linda reigned in her resentment.

"Doctor," Linda replied, "by now you must know that cases like this are awfully complicated. The mental health professions are calling this whole mess 'the memory wars' for good reason. It's incredibly nasty. In litigation, the momentum so far has been toward favoring the plaintiffs accusing therapists of creating false memories. Evidence doesn't support such an extreme swing of the pendulum, but there's blood in the water, and many think that a lot of these cases have been won and lost in the press. Claiming an army of incompetent therapists are responsible for suggesting false memories and creating countless cases of multiple personality comes across powerful, righteous, and sexy to the media. Trying to argue for rational, balanced scholarship is boring. Our media go for the gusto and the best press kit."

"Nasty is news, nice is 'No thank you'?"

"Precisely. So, in addition to studying your situation in depth, I would want to develop a series of overviews from three perspectives. The first would be from the lawyers who are winning the big settlements in cases like this. I wouldn't want to learn about their favorite moves at deposition or in the courtroom. The second would be from the lawyers who've done the best job of defending defendants in similar situations. They probably have battle-tested strategies you won't find written down. Finally, I need to talk with some true experts about patients like Melody Jarrett. For that, I can begin by calling my sister, Eve. One of her mentors was involved in a high-profile case involving DID. Then, I can study your situation in depth from a reasonably knowledgeable perspective and begin to come up with a strategy."

"You don't want to focus on this particular case?"

"Not from the start. Not exclusively. I'd like to minimize the risk of tunnel vision. Sure, I want to understand you and your work, but I can't walk into court and say, 'Dr. Joan Underwood is competent, well trained, conscientious, and hasn't done anything wrong.' The other side will say, 'That's well and good, but because such terrible damage has been done to our client, that doesn't mean a thing. Our client has been hurt. He deserves justice.' Those noble high fallutin' words mean taking everything they can out of your hide. I have to look elsewhere to learn what I would need to know in order to defend you against a skilled plaintiff's attorney. I'd rather study this particular case in depth when I know what the other side's generic points of attack are likely to be, what has been thrown at similar defendants, and that sort of thing. Then I can ask you about the areas they target and help you prepare for the nasty questions you otherwise might hear for the first time when you were being deposed by someone who might be brighter and more experienced than yours truly."

"Since white always moves first," said Dr. Underwood, "you want to know and prepare for their opening gambits?"

"Something like that."

"Sigmund Freud would approve."

"You've got to be kidding."

"Freud used a chess analogy to describe learning psychoanalysis. He said that you could learn the opening moves of chess and the end-game from books and lessons, but how to master the middle game, the majority of the battle, could only be learned by studying the games of the masters. You're talking about needing to know the gambits, how the battles have been fought, and on what points they've been decided."

"Does that make me a Freudian lawyer?"

"To be determined."

"Thanks, Ms. Gilchrist," said Mackey. "I'm sure that you have an unreasonable amount of everything awaiting you back at your desk."

"Right you are, Mr. Mackey."

After Linda left, Bill Mackey scribbled a note. "What did she mean by DID?"

"DID? Acronym for Dissociative Identity Disorder. Psychiatry has its very own alphabet soup, as bad as government agencies, maybe worse. And our DSM just changed Multiple Personality Disorder, MPD, to this DID thing.

"Sorry to force an audition, but since you were thinking of putting her on my team, I needed to be sure. I've seen her at the gym. I was afraid she might be just another pretty face. Don't say what you're thinking, Uncle Bill! She'll do."

CHAPTER 2

Later that day, Bill Mackey called Linda into his office.

"Linda, we still don't know how we're going to approach this case, or who will take first chair. But the senior partners were impressed by your thoughts about how to study some of the major issues. We want you to be part of Dr. Underwood's defense team. In fact, we'd like you to start researching along the lines you proposed."

"Great! If it's OK with you, I'll begin by asking Dr. Underwood whom she'd like to have in her corner."

"Because?"

My God! Am I going to be Mackeyed? "No shortage of becauses, Bill. First, since she's worked hard to learn how to treat this kind of patient, it would be condescending, disrespectful, and dismissive to begin without consulting her. Second, it would risk infantilizing a strong, intelligent client. We'll want to be our active partner in organizing her defense. Not bringing her in from the start would be insulting her at best. At the worst, it risks diminishing her, reducing her to a passive 'take care of me' role. Third, this is new territory to us, and I bet she has a lot to teach us, including the cast of characters. Fourth, it's a really safe way to get a feel of how it will be to work with her as our client, a sense of what she's going to be like to deal with. Fifth, it's also a safe place to begin to educate her about how legal considerations differ from medical. . ."

"If I were a kid, Linda, I'd cry 'TMI! TMI!' Good thinking. I know her family. She's charming, but she's tough, critical, and a bit on the suspicious side. You're right. Disrespect her and you lose her. Go ahead. Call her. See what she has to say."

* * *

"Don't you lawyers have a secret list of super-expert witnesses on every subject under the sun?"

"Yes and no. Yes, we probably can figure out whom to call on to say this, that, or the other thing. Yes, we can choose experts based on what we want our witnesses to say. Some call that kind the 'whores of the court.' They can be useful when you figure the expert witnesses will cancel one another out and you're sure you can out-lawyer the other side. Makes it easy to plan how to go forward.

"And then there are the witnesses who call things as they see them. Some are pretty close to ruthlessly honest and objective. Some may be prejudiced one way or another, and you have to take their biases into account going in. But, starting from their basic attitudes, they're pretty objective, and fair enough."

"Is that a problem?"

"Well, they're not quite as predictable as death and taxes."

"Not quite?"

"Objective people aren't fanatics. They can change their minds. . . One of my professors told us about an expert who evaluated a man and reported he was sane. But when he saw the transcript of what that man said on the stand the day before he was to testify, he said that if he'd evaluated him that day, he would have had to conclude the man was psychotic. He felt obliged to change his opinion."

"What happened?"

"No one was very happy. Another consideration is to get someone local, so the jury doesn't get the idea that what your other experts say isn't just nonsense from some high-priced showboats from far away giving them the old razzle-dazzle."

"So. . . Are you saying you are looking for a mix and match? Including someone you can be sure of, just in case?"

"That's just a general idea. For each individual case, there may be different considerations. Anyway, these choices belong to the big dogs. I want to bring them your ideas. You've taken yourself to school. You've studied the field and the people in it."

"I'm no expert. I've taken a few workshops. I've read some things."

"Well, that puts you way ahead of me. Who would you want in your corner?"

Linda could hear a long sigh.

"Sorry. I still can't believe that this is happening to me."

"This isn't easy. Would you like to talk some other time?"

"It won't be any easier some other time. . . I just want to wake up from this nightmare."

Unreal? Nightmare? What's going on here? No one likes being sued, but that sounds out of character for Miss Calm, Cool, and Collected. . . Linda put aside her curiosity for another time.

"Understood," she said. *I hope that's the only lie I have to tell.*

"OK. But I know you don't."

"*Touché!* But I hope to."

"Don't worry about understanding me, Ms. Gilchrist. Just worry about defending me."

"I don't think. . ."

"Ms. Gilchrist, I don't mean to be unpleasant. I'm a very private person, and I practice a very private profession. I'll take my feelings elsewhere, if I take them anywhere at all. What I've shared with you and Mr. Mackey is as much of myself as I choose to."

"I can respect that."

"OK. One problem is that almost anyone who's anyone in the dissociative disorders field has been attacked, even sued, because there's a lot of difference of opinion out there. What those attacks would mean in court, I don't know.

"I don't know how many of the people I read and took workshops from do any forensic work at all. For example, Betty Keene is brilliant, incredibly effective, and almost everybody falls in love with her, but she won't go anywhere near this kind of thing. Darwin Brody is beyond reproach, and very solid. No one in their right mind wants to go up against him. I called him as soon as I was sued, but in a few months he's going to leave for a sabbatical year in Paris. Matthew Grant is full-time salaried out at Midwest U, and he's not allowed to do outside work. Bob Hatfield is great. He's got a lot of forensic experience. But he's being sued by two families, one using Bruce Fuller, the same big gun they've pulled in to go after me. . ."

Big gun? Bill didn't mention that! I'm so green! I never thought to ask who's on the other side.

As Joan Underwood went over the pros and cons of over a dozen potential experts, Linda felt her neck and shoulders growing tense and tight. She was glad the noise from her gut couldn't be heard over the phone. It seemed that everyone on Joan's list was either unavailable or had something in the past or on the horizon that could be used to attack them, somethings ranging from frivolous to potentially damning.

Usually it was no trouble to find expert witnesses with untarnished reputations. . . But in this crazy field it seemed that a reputation for expertise attracted insults and attacks instead of accolades.

"Why do you think that everyone you consider good is under attack by people who consider them bad?"

"That's complicated. I heard one workshop leader break it down like this. . . Go back twenty years. Psychoanalysts were talking about incest fantasies, not real incest. Textbooks were saying incest occurred in one of a million American families. If a woman insisted she'd been molested by a family member, if she suffered flashbacks of the traumas she reported, or if she heard the voices of her alleged abusers, she usually was diagnosed as a delusional paranoid schizophrenic. Vietnam vets were being diagnosed with character disorders or schizophrenia. They weren't recognized as warriors suffering PTSD. PTSD wasn't even in the diagnostic manual. You see, character disorders don't qualify for benefits, and psychotics get medicine, the cheap fix. No matter where you looked, there was some rationalization that reframed trauma victims as delusional, defective in character, or as people whose memories and allegations you couldn't trust. People seemed determined to find some way to blow off the possibility that these were real victims of real trauma. Kind of like what happens to rape victims."

"Got it. When I was in college a girl in my dorm was raped by three half-drunk jocks, all rich kids. By the time the cops interviewed her, and the high-price defense lawyers tore her apart, she felt she'd been beaten up, humiliated, and stripped bare in public, like she'd been raped all over again, this time in front of the whole world. It destroyed her."

Linda could hear Joan Underwood's long, painful sigh. "Right. Then, a bunch of things gathered momentum around the same time. Feminists found their voices. We learned that about one out of three women experienced some kind of unwanted sexual experience before they were eighteen and that one out of seven stepfathers and one out of twenty biological fathers overstepped some kind of sexual boundary, from minimal to horrible. We learned almost one in ten male therapists had exploited at least one patient. The vets forced us to stop lying to ourselves about the price they paid for serving our country. They bypassed the VA and began to set up clinics staffed by people who had been in 'Nam and knew the truth of their experiences.

"And more and more people started finding and reporting on these multiple personality patients. With them, sometimes the things they reported seemed so extreme that they were hard to believe. And a lot of the early pioneers used hypnosis. In the hypnosis world there was a long history of creating amazing phenomena and changing people's perceptions and beliefs for therapeutic purposes, like leading a person with terrible pain from metastatic cancer to experience the discomfort as a mild and comfortable warmth. There were experiments showing that misleading suggestions could cause errors in recollection. Some big shots jumped in to claim that true multiple personality was rare, nonexistent, or just being created by their therapists, and the same for their memories of abuse, especially anything that came up under hypnosis. They blew off the fact that a lot of recovered memories were pretty accurate.

"So, imagine when some patient comes up with memories of something bad with their mommy or daddy and tells someone besides their therapist about it, or even confronts the people they say abused them!"

"Not good."

"Right! Outrage. . . Usually the accused pitches a fit and goes on the offensive. Loyalty conflicts get stirred up. . . Patients often become uncertain, fearful, or even take back their accusations. They call that 'recanting.' Therapists wind up in court facing the patients they were treating, flanked by their parents, now just one big happy family of plaintiffs."

"And most cases fit that pattern?"

"Yes. So, anyone I mentioned probably is facing a lawsuit, except Betty Keene, Matthew Grant, and Darwin Brody."

"So, no one we can tap is going to come into court without baggage. We can't find anyone who's untouched. Who knows the field best?"

"A guy named Jay Philips."

"You didn't mention him."

"You asked whom I wanted in my corner."

"What's the problem with Jay Philips?"

"How long do you have?"

CHAPTER 3

"Sorry, Linda," said Jim. "Eve is nursing Chloe. She'll call you back as soon as she can."

"Thanks, Jim. Sounds like. . ." But Jim was gone.

The single tear moving drifting down Linda's cheek caught her by surprise. Soon it was not alone. When Linda and her sister Eve were young, they had raised sibling rivalry to an art form. They were both in junior high school when Betty and Arthur Gilchrist sat their "Irish twins" down for a talk.

"You'll be going to different schools next fall," said their father.

The two girls cried, screamed, and begged not to be separated, but Betty held firm. "We won't have bloodshed in the family."

"You have to learn to be people," said Arthur, "not just two wildcats who promise you'll never make war again, and then it's mayhem as usual ten minutes later."

As grown-ups, their rivalries remained tactfully unspoken. But over the last few years, Eve had been fruitful and multiplied while Linda remained childless and frustrated, struggling with nasty, jealous feelings she could barely contain. *I don't know whom I hate more. . . Eve for showing me up one more time, or me for being such a bitchy loser.*

Up in Boston, Eve and Jim were rising stars at Children's Hospital and Mass General respectively, producing bright, beautiful daughters on a predictable two- to three-year cycle.

Hunter Madison, Linda's husband, knew going in that his career would depend upon latching on to the funding streams of more established researchers in his field and winning career development grants until he could call his own shots. The couple had planned to start their family early. By the time Hunter was securely ensconced in the tenure track of a first-line research university, they reasoned, they could afford a nanny and Linda would be free to launch her legal career.

The children. . . They never came, not for lack of trying. One fertility specialist after another, from Harvard all the way down the Atlantic Coast through Columbia to Johns Hopkins, reassured the anxious couple. Nothing was wrong. . . But nothing was happening. Not for year after barren year. For nearly a decade of "meantime," Linda had come to feel that she was no more than a travel-weary caboose at the end of Hunter's meandering train. Their love and their love-life took hit after hit. Moving around, Linda had trouble catching on with first-rate firms. In her private moments she envisioned herself as a scraggly tumbleweed, helpless at the mercy of an unforgiving windstorm. Beyond law review and a prestigious clerkship right out of law school, Linda could never hold the undistinguished employments that came her way long enough to parlay them into something better before they relocated. Years of effort with little to show. . .

Sadder, wiser, but battered, Linda understood that her looks, family connections, and personal presence could open any door, but they could not keep one propped open long enough for someone with her obvious inexperience and hit and run resumé to land the kind of job she wanted.

Desperate, she lay the foundation for Plan B, an academic career. She wrote two scholarly articles. One caught the eye of a young associate at

Mackey Markham & Wilder. It helped Bill Mackey win a major case. As his firm's managing partner, Bill Mackey knew he'd need for someone to fill in for that associate, about to have her first child and take leave. When she informed him that the author whose scholarship he had relied upon was impressive, living nearby, and currently unemployed, he arranged to meet Linda.

Mackey Markham & Wilder's recent hires had been dominated by talented young women. They brought impressive intellectual firepower to the firm. But to Bill Mackey, that translated into a probable dozen or more maternity leaves in the foreseeable future. Bill wanted to bring in a new male associate, but it was clear that Linda would bring more to the firm than any of the dozen men he'd interviewed.

Mackey convinced the senior partners that the pragmatic benefits of hiring Linda, short on experience but ferociously intelligent and a perceptive legal scholar, incurred an appreciable but acceptable risk/benefit ratio.

"She has all the earmarks of a diamond in the rough. I think she could be a great one," he'd argued. "She walks through the door with enough potential to more than repay our assuming the risk of facing a tidal wave of simultaneous pregnancies. Reminds me of Jeff, but easier on the eyes."

"Sexist!" muttered Sally Warren, a third generation Markham and senior partner.

"We could hold out for a dumb man, Sally," said Jeff Wilder, "a cute one, if you'd like."

To the firm's delight and her despair, within weeks Mackey Markham & Wilder was celebrating Linda's hiring as a match made in heaven. Whoever needed some last-minute research or writing, whoever wanted a junior colleague to send to court on short notice for some minor matter, whoever yearned for a competent "can't say no" to stay late to burn the midnight oil. . . they had the factotum of their dreams. Tallying up Linda's billable hours, the bean-counters waxed ecstatic.

Linda Gilchrist, Esq., hid her deepening bitterness behind a dazzling smile and a façade of stunning beauty, powerful intelligence, and graceful charm that quickly endeared her to colleagues and clients alike, all the while inwardly cursing the infernal infertility that left her available 24/7/365.

* * *

"Sorry I couldn't talk before," Eve apologized. "Chloe seems to know if I'm not all there when I nurse her. She fusses, and I feel incredibly guilty. Knowing too much about childhood and development can be a real pain in the neck. Every time I look into the attachment research, I feel so guilty I could cry. I'm always feeling I'm juggling a dozen balls at once and dropping more than I want to admit."

"Three girls. . . You've got your hands full."

"Poor Mom had five of us to handle."

Linda quashed a dozen unattractive emotions and pushed on.

"I hate to bother you, but I really want your input. This is the biggest case they've let me work on. I have to do a good job." She summarized Joan Underwood's situation. "Do you know anything about this MPD/DID thing?"

"Not too much, but maybe more than most. When I was a resident our director of training stepped into a case of mine that was going sour. This poor guy was caught up in a mind control plot to create something like an artificial multiple personality. I had to read up on the real thing. When the same guy talked me into learning hypnosis, I met a lot of people who knew about it. I even took a couple of workshops. All that helped me with the cases I've seen myself."

"You've worked with DID patients?"

"Enough to know I'm not an expert!"

"OK. Let me run a few names by you, and tell me what you think about them as potential expert witnesses. . ."

In a matter of minutes, Linda came to see that Eve's opinions were virtually indistinguishable from Joan Underwood's. "So, everyone loves Betty Keene, everyone respects Darwin Brody and Matthew Grant, and everybody thinks Bob Hatfield is great. But Hatfield's under fire from the same folks we'll be facing."

"Right."

"Who is the expert's expert's expert? Is there one?"

"Well, apart from Keene, Brody, Grant, and Hatfield? There are experts overseas, a real ace at NIMH, plus a guy named Jay Philips. But there's no joy there. Folks from Europe, the Middle East, and down under just don't get the American scene and they're not licensed here. NIMH is going for molecules and genes these days and seems allergic to whole patients. Folks there don't dare go looking for trouble. It's hard as hell as it is to study something controversial on government funding. Jay Philips? He's a sad case."

"When I asked Joan Underwood what the problem was with Jay Philips, she came back with 'How long do you have?'"

"Smart lady. OK. Jay Philips. . . A real pioneer, scientifically, clinically, and by counting the number of arrows in his back. He figured out a lot of things early enough to be pretty far ahead of the curve. That left him isolated, standing with just a handful of others against an incredible backlash. He caught it from all directions. Most of the next wave of pioneers had support from at least a few friendly colleagues. Philips had none of that. He had trouble getting published. When he got published, you'd think that would have brought him respect. No way. Just more intensive attacks. His own university was a hotbed of skepticism. He got passed over for promotion, and then he got dumped. . . Academic assassination. Most people would have backed down. He didn't. He lost just about everything except his private practice.

"So, unless he's at some national or international meeting, he's been a pariah for years. Pretty much a loner. He looks depressed. He's a short, dumpy guy, plain verging on ugly. He fumbles for words. My old director of training insists he's brilliant, a real therapeutic genius. I wouldn't dispute that. But Jay Philips is damaged goods. He can make a lousy impression. Some say he's so miserable that he's hard to be with. But I've heard him discuss cases. He knows more about dissociative disorders than anyone but Grant, Hatfield, Brody, and Keene. In my humble opinion, with all those years of experience, he probably knows even more."

"Your old teacher. . . You keep referring back to him. Does he know about this stuff? What kind of guy is he?"

"Actually, you met him at my wedding. . . Ben Jordan."

"I don't remember him."

"You'll remember his wife, Elani."

"The fashion designer. That woman is unforgettable." Linda remembered Elani Jordan as the most beautiful woman she had ever seen. But her husband?

"Was he a dark-haired guy with a great smile? But not a looker like his wife?"

"Fair description. He knows a lot about dissociative disorders, but his real thing is differential diagnosis. He wrote a paper about identifying DID patients in our residents' clinic. He got called in on that DID serial killer case last year."

"The Catfish Killer? My God! That's the same Ben Jordan? He's famous."

"And none too happy about it. That's him."

"Any problems to worry about?"

"A new chair brought in his own man and replaced him as director of training. He's in private practice now, outside of academia."

"Any lawsuits or things like that?"

"You'll have to ask him. In addition, he's still a pilot in the New Jersey Air Guard."

"He might do. So, you say Philips is an overall expert who might be vulnerable. Jordan is nowhere near as vulnerable, knows a lot. He's solid as an expert on diagnosis, but I couldn't present him as an expert on treatment."

"You could, but he'd say he wasn't. Iffy at best."

"If you were being sued like this, who would you want?"

"Betty Keene, Darwin Brody, and Bob Hatfield or Matthew Grant. But I'd get Jay Philips' help, and keep him in the background. I'm sure he'd have a lot to offer, but I'd keep him out of court."

CHAPTER 4

Every Friday the senior partners of Mackey Markham & Wilder gathered over lunch in the Founders' Room. They reviewed ongoing major cases, screened possible new matters for conflicts of interest, and considered the merits of potential *pro bono* and contingency cases. In the latter, payment depended upon victorious outcomes.

Mackey Markham & Wilder had developed an exceptionally conservative screening process for contingency cases. Conversely, the firm saw itself as a bastion of idealism and took on more *pro bono* cases than most. Sally was inclined toward women's issues, Jeff had strong feelings about disability cases, and Bill Mackey was invested in civil rights concerns.

But even idealists had to eat. . . Some cases tugged on the heartstrings but had questionable legitimacy in the world of law. Others were just plain unwinnable. A number were likely to devour more resources than the firm was prepared to invest. Committing Mackey Markham & Wilder to cases that proved more involved than the partners had bargained for risked dumping hundreds of hours and untold thousands of dollars of the firm's resources down some unforgiving black hole.

The senior partners decided against taking a pretty strong case compromised by a possible conflict of interest. . . A new associate was related to a litigant. After some anguish, they declined another in which the plaintiff seemed too unstable to withstand the stresses litigation would impose upon her. They accepted a pro bono case against a slumlord. Wilder summarized: "It's righteous, and odds are that this bastard will fold once he sees what he's up against."

Potential new cases reviewed, Sally asked for an update on Underwood.

"We're getting a feel for it, Sally. Linda is doing a hell of a job tracking down potential experts, reviewing other cases, and outlining the major issues."

"I heard through the grapevine that Dunham & Brady is bringing Bruce Fuller in on this case. He's got an awesome track record."

"We've got an innocent client."

Jeff Wilder shrugged his shoulders. "OK. But innocent clients lose every day. How do you think we should staff her defense?"

"I don't see Linda Gilchrist as ready to play a major role in the litigation itself," said Mackey. "Strong on the law itself, but a babe in the woods about procedure. But whoever is first chair would be wise to have her on board. She's scary smart. Her scholarship on professional boundary violation cases is well regarded. This is the first major case we'll be doing for the American Psychiatric Association's carrier, and we're going against Lou Galvin, the best Dunham & Brady has got, plus this quote unquote 'superstar' on a winning streak. We should put a couple of pretty experienced folks on it. Someone in this room, and another partner or an experienced associate we're sure is partner quality. Linda Gilchrist can staff it."

"Well, Bill, you have more med mal experience than the rest of us combined," Wilder began.

"But this kind of case is new to me. I don't think I bring anything special to the table. I'd rather pass."

Bill Mackey pass on a case he's brought into the firm? Sally was still formulating a trademark jibe when another partner spoke up.

"I'll be glad to join in, Bill." Eyes turned to Mark Ellsworth, the firm's newest partner.

"No go," said Sally. "Your dad's a psychiatrist, and he's still on staff at Memorial. Remember, Memorial is Underwood's co-defendant."

"Do you think that's a deal-breaker?" Mark queried.

"With all due respect, Mark, Memorial is the biggest hospital in the city. With your dad on staff you might find yourself looking at conflict of interest concerns in any case regarding Memorial."

"Bill, I hear what you're saying," said Wilder. "But you've done the lion's share of the med mal here for twenty years. Let me say what you don't want to hear, Bill. You're the best we've got. I don't remember who usually works those cases with you. We haven't had one in a year or so."

"Bev Czarneki."

Heads shook. Bev Czarnecki was, by consensus, the best young associate the firm had ever hired. But Bev had left Mackey Markham & Wilder to become a professor at Georgetown only a few months before.

Jeff Wilder suggested another name.

"No," said Bill, "his procrastination drives me crazy. He's a good man, but I don't want to contend with his last-minute dramatics on a tough case."

"We're running out of time," said Sally Warren. "Let's all give it thought. Meanwhile, Bill, let Linda get started. You know anyone in the firm will be glad to work with you. Admittedly, some with greater joy than others. I hate to say this, but we've all been asleep at the switch. We have to bring someone else up to speed on med mal. Selecting someone to work with you would be a good way to start."

"Fair enough," Mackey replied. "But let's resolve it now. I think I'll approach Brett Connery. He's a little bit senior for a job that probably won't amount to much, but I want a real gunslinger in the second chair."

Sally shook her head slowly. "Bill, you know he'll come up for partner soon, and he's juggling a lot of big cases."

"True, but I'll ask nicely"

Over the ensuing chuckles, Bill said, "Look. I have to admit I've been feeling kind of tired lately. I'm scheduled to see my doctor in a couple of weeks."

"Hypochondria at the start of trout season, Bill?" asked Sally. "Very suspicious."

"I said I'd be nice, Sally."

"Yes, but that was to be nice to Brett, and I don't recall signing that kind of treaty with you. Look! We want Brett to stay with us."

"What ever happened to the concept of the devil's advocate?" mused Wilder. "Alive and well in Mackey Markham & and Wilder?"

"We all know his quality," said Mackey. "But partnership is an honor. This will remind him he has to earn his keep."

"To drive a grown man wacky. . ." Wilder began.

"Make him work with Bill Mackey," finished Sally with chorus of others. Her momentary wondering about why Bill had tried to transfer the Underwood case and why he might miss the first days of trout season slipped from memory.

CHAPTER 5

Bill Mackey and Brett Connery! Two heavy hitters! We're going all in for this Dr. Underwood! Linda clenched her fists, ashamed of her escalating anger. *The girl who has everything gets everything! And I go under the microscope with the two most demanding workaholics in the firm! My big chance to make a good impression, or go directly to Hell, without passing Go, without collecting $200!*

Swallowing still another gallon or two of resentment with a rage chaser, Linda pushed herself to make a fast start. She placed a call to every expert on her list of potential witnesses and waited by the phone. But come day's end, not a single one had either taken or returned her call. When she felt sweat breaking out on her forehead, Linda threw dignity to the winds and called her sister. A miracle! Eve had just seen her last patient.

"Eve! What am I doing wrong? Why don't they call me back?"

"My God, Linda. I should have thought to tell you. It's the middle of May. I bet they're all at the American Psychiatric Association. I'm usually there, but Chloe's too young. The meetings end Thursday. A lot of them won't be back in their offices till Monday. And then they'll have to catch up. I'd call next Tuesday."

* * *

"No problem," Mackey reassured her. "If they're not there, they're not there. Leave word that you'll call 'em Tuesday."

* * *

Linda wanted to scream, weep and throw everything she could grab. *But I wasn't raised that way!* She wanted to cuddle up with Hunter, rest her head on his chest, and lose herself in his calm, solid strength. But of late Linda's tower of calm, solid strength had become a nervous wreck, resting his own worried head on her lap or her breasts. Hunter was off in Los Angeles, interviewing for the job of his dreams, trying to lay a foundation for their future and bring their Gypsy years to an end. When they finally connected late that night, Hunter overwhelmed her with his excitement before she could say a word.

"They really liked my lecture, and the class I taught was really responsive. Most of the department knew my work, and some of it meshes with their own research. I got along great with the chairman. We actually discussed a tenure track appointment. This could be it, Linda! I love LA. I didn't even want to let myself get my hopes up, but this could be it!"

"Fantastic! I'm so proud of you. That would be great!" *Please God! Let him get something that makes him happy, so my tiny fraction of a life can begin! Please!* She steeled herself to protect Hunter's joy, subduing the powerful "Debbie Downer" within her threatening to burst through her unruffled façade like the Incredible Hulk taking over mild scientist Bruce Banner. Linda Gilchrist, Esq., was one last frazzled nerve away from pouring herself an enormous scotch on the rocks, throwing every exquisite dish in her house against its lovely stone fireplace, or both.

CHAPTER 6

Two pairs of long escalators conveyed unending streams of mental health professionals down to the cavernous exhibition level of the Mid-American Convention Center and back up to street level. The mid-May meetings of the American Psychiatric Association were in full swing, with everyone Linda tried to reach in attendance. At the foot of the down escalator Jay Philips, fresh from an entertaining lecture by Miles Ernest, walked past security into an enormous central hall bordered on both sides and at the rear by segmented floor-to-ceiling moveable beige-gray walls. Beyond these walls corridors, their far sides lined with dozens of doors, gave access to countless conference rooms where concurrent symposia were in progress.

In the exhibition area itself, two dozen multimedia displays in large squares were bordered by long rows of booths. The year before Darwin Brody had quipped, "If it's a big booth or square, it's probably some drug company or for-profit hospital. If it's a small booth, it's probably someone honest, a start-up, or a legitimate scientific publisher."

You nailed it, Darwin! Jay chuckled. Several publishers later, with two books shipped home and a particularly interesting third crammed into his convention tote bag "for the road," an unusually prominent and colorful publisher's display caught his attention. Unprecedented glitz celebrated the Corrigan Press release of *America's Most Dangerous Psychiatrists and Psychologists.*

This I've got to see! Within its pages, the flyleaf promised, preeminent psychiatrist Joseph Chaudvent would present irrefutable arguments that men and women were disgracing their professions and ruining the lives of thousands of patients and their families by suggesting false memories of childhood mistreatment and creating untold legions of iatrogenic multiple personalities. Chaudvent blamed their misadventures on narcissism, ignorance of true science, credulous endorsement of the wild ideas of disturbed patients and unscientific clinicians, and the use of suggestive brainwashing techniques like hypnosis.

He won't have anything good to say about me! The index entry "Philips, J." was followed by dozens of page references. Jay selected one in the middle of the book, and read, "Despite the scientific facade of Dr. Philips' contributions, the subject about which they are written, multiple personality disorder, is *a priori* fraudulent. Therefore, his publications are much ado about nothing, no more than smoke and mirrors. At his best, Philips succeeds in providing us with exceptionally skillful rearrangements of the deck chairs on the *Titanic.*"

"I have a particular fondness for that one," a deep voice boomed from behind Jay, "but a dozen others are equally thought-provoking."

A large hand spun him around. It belonged to a burly bearded bear of man more than half a dozen inches taller than he. Bear Man slid his right arm behind Jay and took a painfully firm grip on Jay's right shoulder.

He called out to an attractive young woman seated behind the book display, "Hey, Sharon! Get some pictures of me with my good buddy and scientific hero, Dr. Jay Philips." He tightened his hold, fixing Jay in place like some unfortunate butterfly or star-cursed beetle impaled on a cruel pin in a museum's display case.

The decorative Sharon smiled, and did as she was ordered.

Twenty feet away, three people left Goliath Pharmaceutical's enormous exhibit and strolled toward the publishers' booths. A tall, broad-shouldered man and his slender elegant wife were walking with a second man, vociferous and still in mid-rant.

"Wrap up your tirade, Ben. Nate! We'll be late for lunch with my sister."

"Easy enough, Liz," said Ben Jordan. "Once more, Goliath is heralding the arrival of the messiah in a molecule! What strange chemical, its time come 'round, slouches toward Madison Avenue to be sold?"

"Don't you dare degrade my favorite poet with clumsy doggerel about big pharma!" said Liz, "I like Yeats! Shame on you, Ben!"

"You tell him, Liz! Poor old fella isn't here to defend himself."

"*Mea culpa!*" Ben raised his hands in mock surrender. "Good grief? What's that ruckus?"

They turned toward the bellow of a loud male voice. A very big man smiled as he restrained a much smaller man, struggling to break away. A young lady with a smile and a camera was taking shot after shot of the proceedings.

"A few more pictures!" shouted the big man. "Smile, Dr. Philips!"

Among his scholarly colleagues, Nate Donaldson's bushy eyebrows and polymath mind had earned him the sobriquet, "Super-Owl." His physical presence commanded a different kind of respect. . . that accorded to a rugby forward. He squared his shoulders and clenched his fists.

"Do you have any idea of the harm people do when they humiliate someone like that? It's cruel. It's destructive. I really hate bullies. Someone ought to. . ."

"Let it go Nate." Liz grabbed her husband's arm. "Oh, no! Ben, his biceps are hard as rocks. Reason with the man."

"Please prevent the woman I love from intervening," Nate muttered. "I hate bullies, but I don't hate them enough to subject them to her wrath."

"Do you really think I can stop him when he's on a crusade? Nate, I know the guy he's messing with. Jay Philips is living proof that no good deed goes unpunished. I'll be glad to step in. . ."

"Benjamin, you can do your diplomatic thing, or kung fu somebody, or climb into your Sopwith Camel or whatever, scramble with Snoopy, and soar off into the wild blue yonder to save the world. This is mine. Please don't let Liz become too upset. She might become violent."

And Super-Owl was off. . .

"Ben, what on earth is he going to do?"

"With him, he's so. . . so whatever he is. There's no way to know."

"I hope he's quick about it. Maybe we can all have dinner after that improv show Goliath Pharmaceuticals is sponsoring tonight. Looks like my guy is. . . Oh, no!"

Nate had already extended his hand to the publisher's rep and drawn her away from where she stood as if he were leading a partner to the dance floor.

"Can I help you?" stammered Sharon.

"No thank you," replied Super-Owl. "I'm beyond help."

"But, please! Come out front here, young lady! Fantastic! Let me take a picture with you and this amazing author in front of these huge, impressive piles of books! I knew some rising stars will be doing a special improvisational comedy show for Goliath Pharmaceuticals later today! I'm sure you have a brilliant career ahead of you, young lady.

"Stand next to the pretty lady, sir! You don't have to let go of your friend. What a pleasure to meet you all before the show and see you warming up! You may say you're doing improv, but really. . . I think you must have at least a few scripted lines to start with. Tell me I'm right!

Who writes your material? So incredibly, so artfully insulting! That takes creative genius!

"And you, sir," he said turning to Jay, "if you are a method actor, I doubt I could survive whatever you did to prepare for your role as a squashed bug. I can't imagine what you drew upon. I just have to shake your hand."

He pumped Jay Philips' hand with flamboyant wild swings. Pulling Jay free of the big man, he turned to address the colleagues and exhibitors beginning to crowd around them.

"Can you believe our good fortune? Three members of the troupe that's performing this evening! They're actually doing street theater right here! Clever! I bet they're testing out their material. On second thought, no! I must be wrong. This isn't for tonight! With all these props, I bet this one's a test skit for some new fake reality show you're marketing for that comedy channel. . ."

"Fake reality? No, you've got this all wrong!" Chaudvent argued. "I'm the author of a new book about dangerous psychiatrists, and he. . ."

"A master! Amazing how adroitly the truly great actors and comedians contrive to stay in role despite all distraction. I remember seeing a bit about this project in *Variety*. . . 'Impossible People'! Yes! That's it! 'Impossible People.' Every week they focus on someone behaving in an impossibly obnoxious manner! You must be playing some professor who thinks he knows more than he does, a man determined to force everyone to think he's the smartest guy in the world. Right? Whoever writes your material. . . Wow! I bet your book is just a great prop! Fake reality, too!"

Nate turned the onlookers as the trio of protagonists stood speechless, their mouths gaping open like carp gasping for oxygen in a stagnant pool. "It's nice when modern comedians respect the classics. We're witnessing an intellectual version of Hans Christian Anderson's 'The Emperor's New Clothes.' Just wait! Pretty soon he'll tell us something.

I'll write it down, and you," Nate hastily scribbled a note and handed it ceremoniously to a distinguished grey-haired psychiatrist standing nearby, "After he speaks, you, sir, can read my predictions aloud. Please! Go ahead, professor."

"This is outrageous!"

"Genius!" applauded Nate.

"I don't know what you're up to, but I'm trying to point out a real problem most people don't understand, and many don't even notice."

"Your last lines are a good first effort, but they need work," said Super Owl. "They don't expand your initial premise quite widely enough. They're too predictable. You'll do better next time, I'm sure."

He turned to man who held his scribbled note. "And, sir, the text you hold in your hands reads?"

The grey-haired man kept a straight face, "Very few will be clever enough to appreciate the wonder and glory of my words."

Nate raised his hands. "And now, a round of applause for these wonderful entertainers! And for Goliath Pharmaceuticals." And those nearby applauded, for any number of reasons, especially their not wanting to admit they had no idea what was going on.

"We look forward to your troupe's performance tonight. Isn't it at 7:00?" He patted Jay on the shoulder. "Well done! Well done!"

Chaudvent bellowed over Nate, "Are you insane? I don't know why you're doing this. I'm not an actor. He's not an actor. I'm not appearing on any TV show called 'Impossible People.' Are you crazy?"

For a moment, Nate's eyes widened. Crestfallen, he lowered his gaze. "Well, then I guess I owe you an apology. But really, I think you'd do great on 'Impossible People.' You mean seriously. . . No one wrote that material? You really were just standing here, spontaneously being that obnoxious, that impossibly rude, and that insulting to this other fellow just because that's what you wanted to do?"

"That's right. I just wrote this book. . ."

"And this other man is a reviewer who trashed you?"

"No. He's never said a word about the book."

"Wow! It's very hard for me to believe this, doctor. . . what is your name?"

"Joseph Chaudvent."

"Well, Dr. Joseph Chaudvent. . . I guess you know that things like what you've been doing and saying are very hurtful. Did you say you had a license? Never mind. Are you going to apologize to the man you insulted?"

"Never! Everything I said in my book is correct."

"That may be. But your behavior is not. And you, sir," he turned to Jay Philips, "Remember it's always good form to punch a bully in the nose, one way or another."

Nate checked his watch.

"Sorry to put us behind schedule, dear," said Nate, taking Liz's hand, "I think we'll still be in time to meet your sister for lunch at the Marseilles. Catch up with you at the improv, Ben."

As Super-Owl and Liz walked away, first one witness to the scene, then another, and finally everyone besides Joseph Chaudvent and the publisher's rep broke into applause. Then the publisher's rep began to clap, until Chaudvent skewered her with a glance that would make a bull shark cower.

"Nate," said Liz, "Did you see what Ben was up to?"

"You mean he wasn't devoting his full attention to my work?"

"No, he was laughing like hell. But I don't think that young lady is going to be very satisfied with the pictures she took."

"He didn't! Wait! Being Ben, of course, he did!"

CHAPTER 7

The improv proved thin comedic gruel compared to dinner with Super-Owl. Ben and Jay were still chuckling as they walked back to their hotel.

"I don't think I've ever laughed so hard," said Jay. "That man is a force of nature. And I can't believe what you did with her camera, but I'm grateful. Hey, Ben. That guy who's walking funny. . . Isn't that Chaudvent?"

"Probably had a few. Jay, if he's out of control, we walk into the restaurant up ahead and call a cab. No reason to let things get nasty."

"I want to talk to you two."

"Coming to take a stroll with us this evening?" Ben asked. "We are honored."

"I didn't like what happened back at the convention hall."

"We didn't either," responded Ben. "What's on your mind?"

"You can't do that kind of thing to me and get away with it."

"Look, I'm sorry if. . ." Jay began.

"You're sorry?" Chaudvent pushed Jay. "Not as sorry as you're going to be."

Ben Jordan cleared his throat.

"Oh! You going to do something about it without that big friend of yours?"

"Dr. Chaudvent," said Jordan, "I've served. I can take care of myself. This is not your night to push people around. Please apologize to Dr. Philips and move on. I'll get you a cab if you'd like."

Chaudvent pushed Ben hard against a streetlight pole. Ben offered no resistance as Chaudvent entrapped him in a bear hug.

"OK, you got that out of your system. Apologize to Dr. Philips and get gone."

"No way."

"Dr. Chaudvent, you've been warned."

"You're nothing, Jordan. I own you."

"OK. Jay, I want to teach you something about bullies. It goes by the numbers. At one, I select my target, the spleen. At two, I make a perfect fist. At three, I focus my aim six inches below the surface of the bully's skin at the selected location. As you can see, I have very little leverage, or breath, right now. So, four, my first blow, from three inches out, will be pure arm and shoulder. That will loosen Dr. Chaudvent up enough for five, a blow from six inches out. I'll be able to put some weight behind that one, 'cause I'll have some room to pivot. That should hurt Dr. Chaudvent a bit more, and set him up for six, a blow from nine inches out with nearly my whole body behind it. That will break Dr. Chaudvent's lower left ribs. Dr. Chaudvent will gasp, let go, and then seven comes from twelve or more inches out with everything I've got. It ruptures Dr. Chaudvent's spleen. Eight, we call for the police and an ambulance to arrest him for assaulting us, and to carry him off to the hospital.

"I'm running out of breath, Dr. C. Ready to release me and apologize to Dr. Philips?"

"You're so full of shit, Jordan. You. . ."

The first blow won Jordan enough space to put serious weight behind the next. A sharp crack. Chaudvent released Jordan and doubled over, grasping his side.

"You bastard! I think you broke my ribs."

"Sorry about that, Jay. I apologize, Dr. Chaudvent. I thought I'd need the third one to do that. Soft target, Jay. So, we arrive all too early at apology or spleen. Your call."

"Damn! I'm out of here."

"Not so fast. You assaulted me. I struck back in self-defense. Try to leave now, and I'll put you on the ground and file a police report."

* * *

"I can't believe he apologized, Ben. And that's the first time I heard a bone crack, except in an OR. I don't know whether to be impressed or appalled."

"Has anyone ever hit you?"

"Sure. . ."

"Did you ever strike back?"

"I've never hit anyone in my whole life."

"Then you're overdue. Letting people push you around doesn't work. It just encourages the next attack. Even if you can't win, make 'em pay."

"My folks are Quakers. Non-violent as it gets. Heck! I'm a conscientious objector."

"Chaudvent led with violence. That's just plain wrong. But you have to consider the cost/benefit ratio, Jay. What higher purpose would be served if I let that jerk beat up on us? He'd walk away cock-sure he could do it again. You've got to make a bully realize it's not worth it. Look at that as good preventive medicine."

"I'm confused. I don't know what to think or feel. No one ever stood up for me when other kids hit me. Not too many stand up for me now when my work gets attacked. In any case, thanks."

"I'll show you how to make a good fist. You should acquire that skill so you don't hurt yourself punching out some bully somewhere down the road."

"I can't imagine myself hitting someone."

"Remember the old condom rule?"

Jay did not. "Go ahead."

"A good fist is a nice thing to have in your wallet in case you get unlucky."

CHAPTER 8

On Tuesday morning Linda reached Ted Billingsly, Chairman of the Department of Psychiatry at SouthEast University School of Medicine.

"Yes, Ms. Gilchrist. I ran into Bill Mackey at the membership dinner at the club over the weekend. He told me to expect your call."

'The club'? There are millions of country clubs and golf clubs around the city and near 'burbs. But I guess for the rainmakers, there's just one, 'The Club,' the right club. Linda remembered a Harvard student she'd dated briefly. . . very briefly. With him it was always "The College," "The Law School," "The Medical School." *As if there were no reason to consider any other institutions in Boston and Cambridge or the immediate galaxy worthy of mention in the same breath!* Little demons bearing snide sarcasms rushed to escape her lips, but memories of her mother's cautionary voice arose to keep her evil imps in check. Whenever Betty Gilchrist led her daughters into a formal diplomatic function or social event, she would drop her voice to a near-whisper, "Party manners, girls!"

"Well, I'm delighted to be speaking to you. Mr. Mackey speaks quite highly of you."

"We go back a long way. Bill just mentioned it. He said you'd fill me in."

* * *

Dr. Billingsly listened to Linda's summary, and posed several thoughtful questions.

"So, Dr. Underwood was practicing within the standard of care. She went out on maternity leave. When she was on leave, somebody either talked her patient into filing a complaint or didn't caution her adequately against filing a complaint about which Dr. Underwood knew nothing until the deed was done. In a criminal case, that's an airtight alibi. But this lawsuit is barely glorified mudslinging. Now this Dr. Travers is complaining that somebody talked about what he is alleged to have done, and claims bad consequences that he attributes to malfeasance by Dr. Underwood? Correct?"

"Yes, sir."

"Ms. Gilchrist, you probably know far better than I that successful malpractice suits have to prove what we call 'The Four Ds': dereliction of duty directly leading to damages. Regardless of the truth or falsehood of what the patient said, and regardless of what Travers may or may not have suffered in terms of damages, I see no evidence of malpractice. Of course, I might have to change my mind if something unanticipated showed up in the depositions, but on the face of it, even if Travers has suffered some damage, there's no evidence to link Dr. Underwood with the other three Ds."

"What about her use of hypnosis?"

"I'm not an expert on that area. But Hatfield and Philips' articles offer pretty good arguments for its usefulness in treating these patients. And even if you buy the arguments over memory distortion,

Dr. Underwood isn't saying she either believes or encouraged her patient to believe in the reality of what she came up with.

"As far as I can see, she's squeaky clean, and Travers should be suing himself. She's Snow White unless someone produces evidence to the contrary. Send over what you've got."

"I'll bring the materials over myself, later today."

CHAPTER 9

Reaching Miles Ernest, psychoanalyst to the stars and frequent talking head, proved a more daunting task. Linda had to keep her line free and await his callback. At 4:00 p.m. Eastern and 1:00 Pacific Coast Daylight Savings Time, the great man got around to her.

"Sorry I couldn't get back to you sooner. I was on the set. . ." Linda tried to let the half-dozen A-list names who seemed to have been in urgent need of Ernest's advice on matters personal and professional go in one ear and out the other, but she couldn't help being impressed. His self-styled apology cum self-promotion completed, Ernest announced, "I have five minutes before I shoot off to the Polo Club."

Dated, but still classy, Linda reflected.

"What do you have for me?"

For you? Linda rushed through her summary.

"I like the case. Send me the files."

"Wonderful! Thank you, Dr. Ernest."

* * *

"Bill, I think I need another lesson in Lawyering 101. We need to talk about experts."

"After what you said in front of Dr. Underwood? You sounded like you could take us all to school. OK. I'll call Brett. Let's get together in an hour."

* * *

Bill is right. I can give a hell of a lecture about experts. I can research them and put together a decent list. But I've never really had to recommend them! I don't want to look like a fool.

Both men rose when Linda entered Bill's spacious corner office.

"The last redoubt of gentlemen! I'm honored."

Brett opened the conversation. "Bill tells me you have some concerns about selecting experts. How can we help you?"

"It's no secret that I've bounced around a lot. I've wound up with more book knowledge than practical experience. I'm getting confused. I want to get some feedback and advice. I don't want to waste time and wind up making a simple-minded presentation to the two of you."

"So far, so good, Linda," said Brett. "Fill us in."

Bill Mackey ran his fingers through his hair and pushed back from his desk. For a split-second Linda let herself wonder, *Is Brett coming up for partnership? Is he being Mackeyed one last time?* Putting her curiosity on hold, Linda came back on task.

"Dr. Billingsly heard me out. He came to a quick decision that if nothing to the contrary comes up in depositions, Dr. Underwood was as pure as the driven snow. He even called her 'Snow White.' My concern is that his thinking and his testimony will be boiler-plated. He already seems to know what he'll say. He could be tripped up if he overlooks the specifics of the case.

"Dr. Ernest shoe-horned me in between more important matters, tried to dazzle me with the names he dropped, and made me summarize the case standing on one foot. I felt like some poor writer making a desperate elevator pitch. Then he delivered an over-the-top commercial for himself and said he liked the case. He sounded like an actor getting revved up for a juicy part."

"Not exactly what you hoped to encounter in objective, clear-thinking experts?"

"Frankly, no!"

Brett smiled. "I wish I'd had that kind of directness when I was younger. I figured, 'If these are supposed to be the experts, this is how experts are.' But what Bill told me you said to Dr. Underwood. . . It's advice you need to remember for yourself.

"We seek out and select experts for a lot of different reasons. Sometimes the considerations that go into figuring out which ones to hire on, how to instruct them for depositions, and how to present them at trial are straight-forward. Sometimes our rhymes and reasons get pretty complicated.

"Have you ever seen *My Fair Lady?* A really good production?"

"Sure. Here and in London."

"Forget London. You may not have noticed that in good American productions, when the curtain goes up, you hear the actors' English accents, but they're pretty mild. As the show goes on, they become more and more English, more characteristically Cockney for some, upper class for others. Gradually, the actors are teaching the audience how to hear and understand their words being pronounced in an increasingly unfamiliar way."

"I never noticed."

"Me neither, but my daughter taught me all about this stuff when she played Liza Doolittle last year in her high school play. We're trying to do the same kind of thing. I'll talk you through a hypothetical line-up.

"We want to start out with someone who talks a language pretty much like everybody talks around here. Ted Billingsly was the first in his family to go to college. He's never lost that common touch. We don't need him to do more than say, 'Sensible folks like you and me, we know this case don't amount to much more than a hill of beans. Let's all go home.'

"Yes, he'll say what he'd say in a billion similar cases, but he can deliver our core message, and he'll do it well. If they try to nail him down, he doesn't know enough of the tricky stuff to trip himself up and stumble over his own feet.

"Miles Ernest? He talks like a pompous show-off, but he works like hell. You nailed him. At heart he's an actor. But we've reviewed transcripts of his testimony in other cases, and the man is a closet tiger. He just likes to make it all look breezy and eloquent. I checked with an old friend who used him. Ernest will put his heart into Joan Underwood's defense. . . Maybe not for the best of reasons, but he'll fight like hell for her, even if he's really fighting to show everyone how wonderful he is. He'll dance along the line between ferocious dedication and shameless exhibitionism with the grace of a Mikhail Baryshnikov.

"You've done a great job of sizing up these two people. We can't help you improve on that except with the local knowledge I added. But maybe this helps you get a clearer picture of what we're trying to achieve. In this hypothetical scenario, Billingsly lays the foundation by making the unfamiliar familiar. He makes the jury comfortable and receptive. Then Ernest grabs the hearts of the jury and gets them to care about Joan Underwood and how she's breaking her back to help her patient. The we bring in the real experts. We put them before a jury mobilized to hear testimony for Dr. Underwood with open minds and open hearts, and they nail down what Billingsly said in the first place, 'This is a tempest in a teapot. Let's all go home.'"

CHAPTER 10

"I spoke to Ben Jordan," said Linda. "He's pleasant and funny. He's thoughtful. He says up front he's not an expert on treating dissociative disorders. I don't think he understands the whole concept of third-party suits. But he's actually treated three DID patients successfully, to complete integration. We could call him an expert, and most would, but he seems to have pretty elevated ideas of it means to be a real 'expert.' I respect his modesty, even if it's false. He wants bucks up front to review the case. He won't promise a thing before he does."

Once again, Brett did all the talking. "So, it's not his first rodeo and he prides himself on his objectivity. Send him the file see what he has to say. If it looks like he could be a good witness for us, we'll pay him a visit."

"Educate me, Brett. Why not get reports from Ernest and Jordan, and prep them just before their depositions?"

"Do you like him? Do you feel safe with him?"

"He seems knowledgeable."

"That's not responsive, Linda. When we put a man in front of a judge and jury, we want more than expertise and authority. We want someone who's calm and collected, but warm. Someone who's not remote, someone the judge and every juror will see as sincere, honest, humble, strong, stable, and friendly. The kind of person you'd want in your life, that you'd trust in a difficult situation. Holding all the cards doesn't mean a thing if we put experts on the stand who bore the jurors, confuse them, turn them off, or even piss them off. . . And an arrogant expert witness can destroy our case in a flash. . . That's especially important here 'cause the other side will present experts who've been on a winning streak so long that they may come on too sure of themselves.

"So. . . Do you like Ben Jordan?"

"It's complicated. He was director of training where my sister Eve did her residency. I met him at Eve's wedding. I remember his wife, Elani, the fashion designer, but I really don't remember him at all. Eve says he helped her out of some serious trouble a few years back. No one will talk about what happened, but my parents talk about him like he walks on water."

"Being married to a glamorous woman doesn't hurt. Star-power by association. So?"

"Brett, I just don't know. I think he holds his cards pretty close to his chest. I'd bet he always has a few jokers in his deck."

"Find a few more names, then. Just in case."

"Slim pickings. Been there, done that."

"Go somewhere else, do something different," said Brett.

Bill Mackey nodded.

CHAPTER 11

Medical malpractice law suits don't go on forever, but for the plaintiffs and defendants, it can feel that way. Attorneys and expert witnesses grow accustomed to the creaky, arthritic pace of the justice machine as it gimps along. They learn to tolerate its interminable delays, its countless reschedulings of depositions and trial dates, and its often-startling indifference to the realities, urgencies, and distresses of the lives of the principals. With experience, they learn to take it all in stride.

But plaintiffs and defendants usually yearn for vindication and closure. All but the jaded, cynical, unusually calm, frankly insane or highly medicated, and those convinced that delays will give them some advantage, live in a state of unnerving anticipation, apprehension, and angst as major portions of their lives, their beings, and their reputations in the eyes of others remain compromised and to all appearances are going nowhere, except perhaps downhill. Entrapped in an often-humiliating paralysis that leaves them feeling miserable and powerless to affect the course of their fates, plaintiffs stew in exasperation. Defendants, doomed to endure their torment in states of enforced passivity, dwindle toward demoralization.

Linda met with Joan Underwood from time to time as she prepared materials for the "big dogs." When they spoke on the phone, nothing seemed amiss. Even in person, for many months Joan Underwood appeared to be cruising above it all, not a single crack in her composure. Linda wondered: *Was Joan's describing her situation as a nightmare a figure of speech, overdramatic talk, or genuine terror that things were veering out of control?* Face to face, Linda looked to Joan's expressive eyes for the tell, but it was Joan's hair that finally began to give her away. Dr. Joan Underwood carried herself with a casual, apparently effortless glamorous elegance. Linda knew first-hand how much work achieving that look could entail. The dark hair that lay always just so began to need barrettes and pins to sustain itself. From time to time it deteriorated into a sloppy pony-tail. Then Joan Underwood became inclined to avoid eye contact, to puncture her quiet stillness by fidgeting with a pencil or fashioning paperclip sculptures. The deep blue eyes that once could sustain a fierce unnerving focus no longer held her gaze.

"Bill, I don't like what I see. This lawsuit is eating Joan Underwood up alive."

Linda found herself entertaining a weird fantasy. . . that some particularly heinous fiend had seized control of a diabolical rheostat and was taking delight in dimming the luminosity of Joan Underwood's spark, wit, and intelligence, reveling in defeating her efforts to hold on to the radiant, vivacious personality that once was hers.

Once more, Linda turned to her sister, Eve.

"I'm getting really scared for her. What's happening?"

"I don't know Joan Underwood, so everything I'll say could be way off target. I have to go with what I've learned along the way from colleagues and continuing medical education courses."

"Doctors have courses about how to handle being sued?"

"You better believe it! Joan Underwood is a proud woman. She's worked hard to get where she is. And now she's facing a death by a thousand cuts. Even if she's tough, confident in her own innocence, and trusts her attorneys and the legal system, it's once accused, always tainted. . ."

"But. . ."

"Look, Linda. Step outside your own profession and slide into Joan Underwood's shoes. Months, maybe years go by. She can't really defend herself. She'd have to break confidentiality and violate medical ethics to do. If she did, she could be sued by both her patient and, on other grounds, by the plaintiff. And speaking of her patient, Melody Jarrett never came back to her. She has no idea what's going on in Melody Jarret's head and what that could mean to her. Plus, it's likely that her colleagues, patients, and potential patients know only that she's been accused of doing something wrong. You know lots of folks are going to figure where there's smoke, there's fire.

"And remember a little fact. . . Very few people notice or read retractions. Underwood's being sued is news. If she's cleared three years later, that's three years of damage followed by a vindication that will never make the news or make the rounds with the same force as the accusations. Her reputation has been compromised, maybe even forever. You know that many, probably most malpractice cases are settled to make them go away rather than litigated down to the end. Insurers find it's cheaper to settle than to fight. Their fiscal prudence means that the matter of guilt or innocence is left just hanging there. An accusation of malpractice is an albatross around Joan Underwood's neck. It could mess her up forever.

"A doctor's good name is precious, Linda. If Joan Underwood feels it's been damaged beyond repair, or that it could be destroyed, she may feel she's looking at professional oblivion. And that can happen.

Yes, you and your firm can do her a world of good. . . But in terms of giving her back everything she may be losing? The best you can do is too little, too late."

"Her reputation is great, Eve, but I hear that Dr. Travers is trashing her to everyone he meets. One of his lawyers is a guy named Bruce Fuller. He's going around all over the country talking about the need to protect victims of bad therapy, including therapists like Dr. Travers."

"Have you considered asking the judge to muzzle that stuff, so the case gets tried in court instead of in the press?"

"Do these cases really get that dirty?"

"From the defendant's perspective, you bet! Try to run a practice when you're being trashed in the papers. It's hard enough when they're singing your praises."

CHAPTER 12

"Bill, Brett, I'd like to run something by you."

"Shoot," said Brett.

"We all know Joan Underwood is under a lot of stress, and if this goes to court, we're still probably a year or two away from that. I'm hearing through the grapevine that Dr. Travers is railing against Dr. Underwood every chance he gets, and I'm holding a series of clippings and transcripts that indicate Mr. Fuller is working up to trying this case in the media, and quoting some other lawyer, a Randolph St. James, who says he's sure Dr. Underwood is no good."

"St. James? Actually, we're going to chat with Judge Lasko later today. It might be instructive for you to come along."

* * *

Brett Connery summarized defense's concerns with a precision and brevity Linda found awesome. Linda had never met the rotund but highly respected Judge Oliver Lasko, who'd been assigned the Underwood case. Lasko's ferocious energy and the agile play of his intellect began to erode her usual aversion to overweight people.

"Got it, Mr. Connery. You are asking me about what appear to be efforts to protect Dr. Travers' reputation at Dr. Underwood's expense, and about Mr. Fuller's playing to the press. But you have a third problem as well."

Bill Mackey nodded.

"Your honor?" asked Brett.

"Bill?" asked Lasko.

Linda flinched. *Is Brett about to be Mackeyed?*

"You never quit, you old. . ." Lasko shrugged. "But we have a lady among us."

"Bill! Make it quick and painless," said Brett.

"His honor may have a few more aces up his sleeve, but I believe that he is referring to the fact that Mr. Fuller carefully attributes most of his negative swipes to Mr. Randolph St. James. Fortunately, he generated a few nasty things on his own before he thought better of it. So, we have to consider that if Fuller is utilizing proxies, our circumstances become more complicated."

"Let me get Lou Galvin on the phone." Judge Lasko dialed a number. "I need to talk to Mr. Galvin. No, later will not do. . . Right now. . . Judge Lasko. . . Sorry to break into your conference, Lou. Now, Lou. . . About Travers v. Underwood. You know how I hate to see my courtroom turned in to a three-ring circus. . . I'm sitting here with the team from Mackey Markham & Wilder. . . They have a few concerns. . . Too many people saying too much about this case. . . Yes, it would be a shame if this situation required some action on my part. . . You're sure you can work things out with these nice folks?. . . I'm sure you can. . .

"Why don't you call me this time tomorrow and tell me about how you all made that happen?. . . Can you three meet Mr. Galvin and Ms. Bullock for a drink at O'Rourke's?"

After a brief silence, he continued, "About 6:30?. . . Galvin needs some time to make a couple calls. He's buying. . . Big dogs don't really need to bark. . . Of course, Lou, that includes the Internet and all those new things I don't know anything about."

* * *

"I don't expect you to believe this," Galvin began, "but Fuller has been taking the lead and calling the shots. I know better than to go public with any case in Oliver Lasko's courtroom."

"I knew you're too savvy to shoot yourself in the foot like that, Lou, but these out-of-towners are used to playing for the headlines."

"We're just the local folks, the bumpkins. Fuller's a hell of a litigator, but I'm beginning to see there are aspects of his strategy that don't show up in the record, things he never discussed with me. Those moves won't fly down here.

"Now, he knows the score. He doesn't like it, but he'll shut up and he'll call off the others who love to see their names in print. I'm meeting with Travers later this evening."

"I don't envy you, Lou."

"Well, better we clean up the mess than leave that job to his honor. Oliver Lasko on a tear? That's a scary thought."

"Amen to that."

CHAPTER 13

SouthEast Medical School's academic buildings surrounded a large grassy quadrangle. Before the trio entered the Department of Psychiatry, Brett turned to Linda.

"Say something nice about Ted Billingsly's office. His wife is an interior decorator." Indeed, Billingsly's office was unusually attractive. Linda rose to the occasion, Billingsly's face lit up, and the interview went along very smoothly. Ted Billingsly would do.

Brett missed the trip to LA when an ongoing matter was rescheduled abruptly. Linda and Bill spent two hours parked in Miles Ernest's lavish waiting room while his decorative secretary offered a series of fatuous excuses for his lateness.

Bill muttered, "Reminds me of a gate agent at the airport." When the great man appeared, he explained that he had been supporting a mentally fragile actress as she went through half a dozen takes of a painful scene that reverberated with some personal tragedies, presenting his inconveniencing them as a praiseworthy achievement.

On the one hand, the celebrated psychoanalyst to the stars seemed to be a corpulent narcissist determined to persuade Linda and Bill to endorse his high opinion of himself. But on the other, Miles Ernest had done his homework. He bombarded them with perceptive questions and insightful comments, placing a pudgy finger on many of the loose ends sure to bedevil the case.

"Can you depend on Melody Jarrett? So many back off or recant. Could she leave your client exposed? What makes this Gordon Travers want to fight? I'm sure that I won't be the only person to tell you that once the complaint was dropped, if he kept his mouth shut, this non-sense wouldn't be all over the place. Something else is going on, and I don't know what that is. And I'm both impressed and concerned that this Dr. Underwood is being portrayed as perfection personified. Beware the client who seems too good to be true. Any chink in her armor, and suddenly everything becomes suspect. Thinking of using Jay Philips? Don't! I repeat, do not use Jay Philips! He's hard to like, easy to attack, and he thinks so long before he opens his mouth that he can look slow-witted."

As they rose to leave, Miles Ernest uttered a final warning, "And I'm not sure you understand exactly what Melody Jarrett is trying to say. Be sure we know what her journals and artwork really mean before this comes to trial."

"Why are you so concerned about Melody Jarrett?" asked Bill.

"Because if Dr. Underwood is as clean as you say, this suit isn't really about her. The source of the pollution may be upstream. Maybe she's caught between Travers and Jarrett. I leave Travers to you. But what do we know for sure about Melody Jarrett, and what does that tell us? I can attest to Underwood's innocence and skill all day, but if it turns out that she was proceeding from a faulty understanding of Jarrett, we may have problems."

As their taxi battled traffic all the way to LAX, Bill turned to Linda. "What do you think?"

"At first, he reminded me of Jabba the Hut. But when he started to address the case itself, he sounded more like Obi Wan. His stark intelligence impresses me."

"Would you like to cross-examine him?"

"No! Not on your life!"

CHAPTER 14

Linda and Brett Connery arrived in Philadelphia mid-morning without Bill Mackey, managing a ticklish negotiation for the firm. Brett Connery was a graduate of Penn Law. When traffic slowed on the notorious Schuylkill Expressway, he exited at South Street, and took their rental on a route that skirted the campuses of University of Pennsylvania and Drexel, coasted through Mantua, and meandered past the Philadelphia Zoo into Fairmont Park. He worked his way over to Belmont and had a nearly straight shot to within one turn from Ben Jordan's office in Bala Cynwyd.

Jordan asked very few questions as Brett reviewed the state of Travers v. Underwood and Memorial Hospital but filled several pages of a yellow Levenger pad with illegible notes.

"Well, Dr. Jordan, what do you think?"

"I don't think. Let me get some more information first."

I don't think! thought Linda, *that's Inspector Maigret's catch-phrase! Most smart alecks run directly to Conan Doyle and "It's a capital offense, Watson, to hypothesize in advance of the facts"! Jordan went somewhere else. Is he a mystery buff?*

"What more would you like to know?"

"I'd like to know what this case is really about."

Linda saw Brett's eyes widen. "I'm sorry. Did you ask me what the case was really about?"

"Yup."

"I don't understand."

"OK, Dr. Jordan. I thought I just told you, but you feel I haven't. Take us to school."

"Brett, may I have a word with you?"

"Just be rude and whisper out loud, Linda."

"Myles Ernest voiced the same concerns."

"I'm sure he did," said Jordan. "Whatever else he is, he's brilliant. Look. . . If things are as you say, this case is a farce. Sounds like there are no grounds for anything. The complaint was dropped. If Travers' reputation is trashed, it's 'cause of his own big mouth. Ernest may not be earnest, but he's a pretty smart cookie. You don't get his kind of rep on BS alone.

"On the basis of what you've told me and my review of the records, I certainly can testify on behalf of Dr. Underwood, assuming nothing unexpected and horrible pops up. But I don't get it. Travers created most of the damage he's complaining about. I've got to think something else is going on."

"Not that we can figure out. Your point is a good one. But we can't find a 'something else.' Our read is that Travers is just an outraged and prickly guy who's thinking he can ride that whole false memory thing to a big payday."

"What are they asking for?"

"Six million with punitive damages."

"Eighteen million. Is that just from Dr. Underwood?"

"You get it. Yes. And the same from Memorial. Dillon & Stein is defending the hospital."

"Shooting to beat that big settlement in LA?"

"I think so. Fuller and St. James teamed up for that one."

"This makes no sense."

"We're hoping the judge and jury sees it that way."

"Sounds like a crusade to me. To take the Holy Land back from the infidels. . . If the Holy Land is a bank, and the infidels are your targets of opportunity."

"That's how Fuller describes it. A holy war against bad therapy," said Linda.

"Ms. Gilchrist, a crusade is a plan, usually Papal, to get European Catholics to kill Middle Eastern Moslems rather than one another, and do it where the collateral damage won't destroy the church and mangle generations of Christians, all the while diverting the nobles from figuring out how to raid the Church's coffers."

"But. . ."

Brett interrupted. "Linda, do you realize that what Dr. Jordan is saying is oversimplified, but pretty close to some historical facts?"

"No. I was taught it was to free the Holy Land."

"That was the secondary gain to be hoped for," said Brett. "So, you think that this case is part of a more complicated strategy?"

"I wouldn't be surprised. I understand there was a lot of fuss in the press, and then it blew over."

"You get extra credit for that one, Doctor," said Brett. "Linda caught wind of it, and we were able to stop them from trying it before the public."

"Uh, Brett. . . first, you and Bill saw it the same time or earlier, and I get no points. My sister Eve warned me about it, and she. . ."

"Is a former student of Dr. Jordan's. Correct, Doctor?"

They continued a while longer, Jordan bombarding them with questions. Finally, he offered a formulation.

"There is no evidence to demonstrate malpractice on the part of Dr. Underwood. She has jumped through every hoop, taken every reasonable precaution and then some, sought expert consultations, and was not around when things went south. But this case is coming up at a moment in time when virtually every case of this sort seems to win, or settles big. It's like that case in Portland, when the doctor wrote in the chart that the patient's memories were spontaneously offered, but were inaccurate and probably manipulative lies. He was sued anyway for inducing those memories, and pressured to settle. It's a legal fashion statement, a fad that's become a powerful wave and taken on a life of its own."

* * *

"I see what you mean, Brett. He's fierce, no-nonsense, sincere, and I'd want him on my side."

"Likeable?"

"Pretty much. But we'll have to be sure to make him look human. That kind of intelligence can be scary."

"You're right. Did you know he played some pro ball?"

"No."

"We were talking about the Phillies when you stepped out for a minute. He's down to earth, and he's got a sense of humor. He'll do fine with a jury."

CHAPTER 15

Bill was still otherwise occupied the next week, when Linda and Brett interviewed Jay Philips in northern New Jersey. He practiced in a suburban professional building across from a park, where a handful of children tossed scraps of bread to a vocal conclave of ducks under the watchful eyes of two nannies.

Jay Philips, M.D., was short, overweight on the way to obese, and no slave to fashion. His office was clean, but its cluttered, pile-strewn decor declared it the lair of a consummate slob.

"Based on what you've seen so far, Dr. Philips, what do you think? What do you think?" asked Brett.

There was a long pause. "Uh. . . This is all you've got so far?"

"So far."

Jay Philips closed his eyes. Just when it seemed he must have fallen asleep, he looked first at Linda, then at Brett, and began to speak, his voice low and slow.

"OK. Dr. Underwood was practicing state of the art therapy methods, and she sought excellent consultation. On the one hand, it doesn't seem like there is anything to sue her for. On the other, that doesn't matter."

"What do you mean, Dr. Philips?"

"I'd imagine you've seen enough nasty SOBs dodge the bullet and enough folks you thought were clean take a bad hit. There are fashions in law, just like anything else. Right now, plaintiffs' false memory accusations are riding high on confirmation bias, granted validity on trivial evidence. That's bad enough, but every time some nonsense suit wins a victory or a settlement, it sets a dangerous precedent. The 'me too' train for Money Land starts to board, and nobody wants to be left on the platform when it pulls away from the station."

After a long pause, he resumed. "I don't see 'The Four Ds.' Unless this Melody Jarrett has some hidden agenda and fed Dr. Underwood a bunch of malarkey to set up a money grab, and Travers is trying to head that off at the pass, I don't get it. Something has this Travers guy riled up. . . 'Cause he'd have been better off expressing his sympathy to Jarrett for her painful confusion and hoping that Underwood could help her find her way out of the woods."

* * *

"Dynamic, he's not," Brett reflected as they headed to Newark airport. "Dynamic, he's not. But he seems solid. Kind of like Ernest. . . no, Jordan, in slow motion. But. . . I can see him turning off a jury. What did you think?"

"Miles Ernest said, 'Don't use Philips,' and he has tons of court experience. I hate to say this, Brett, because it seems so shallow. . . I didn't like him. Short, fat, sloppy people. . . Prejudices aside, I don't think he would go over too well with women, young people, and folks who value fitness and appearance."

"You seemed OK with Judge Lasko."

"Lasko radiates energy and brains. Same with Ernst. You get beyond appearance in a split second. Philips doesn't, and you don't."

CHAPTER 16

The Friday meeting of Mackey Markham & Wilder's senior partners worked through its agenda, finally arriving at Underwood.

"Where do we stand, Bill?" asked Sally. "Is the good doctor still Snow White?"

Bill Mackey did not reply.

"Bill?"

"Oh, sorry, Sally, my mind wandered. You were asking?"

"An update on Underwood. Are you OK, Bill?"

"Just a little tired. TGIF, Sally. We have agreed on three experts, with one maybe. As I mentioned last time, most of the top people are either unavailable or under siege. We need one more sure-fire winner."

"What's the problem with number four?"

"Frankly, he doesn't make a good appearance and he has a lot of baggage. Better as a background consultant. Depositions are just around the corner."

"I don't know whether or not you've seen this, Bill," said Jeff Wilder, "but this Bruce Fuller who's teaming with Lou Galvin's bunch is popping up on CNN and NPR preaching his gospel."

"Anything about our case?"

"No, but a few months back another fella, Randolph something, seemed to be taking shots at Underwood without mentioning any names. I wouldn't be surprised to see Underwood catching some media attention."

"God forbid! Judge Lasko knows. He's cracking down."

CHAPTER 17

Dr. Travers sublet his office from the much larger suite occupying half of the sixth floor of HighPoint Centre. The larger suite was home to Chalmers Brothers Investments and housed the law offices from which Beau Chalmers had practiced before he won the state house.

Defense was surprised to find Governor Chalmers presented for deposition. Bill Mackey had contributed to Chalmers's campaign, and Linda was needed elsewhere. Accordingly, Brett Connery questioned the governor.

"Governor Chalmers, how did you come to rent space to Dr. Travers?"

"Well, my fool of an architect. . . We wound up with useless space just sitting there. Along came Travers. He liked the location, but we had nothing open. Somebody remembered that space, and well, it was no trouble to eliminate one inner door, create a new one in the hall, and erect one interior wall so he'd have a little waiting room. Win-win. We recouped construction costs in a few months, and it's worked out well."

"Had you known Dr. Travers?"

"I'd heard his name. Maybe I'd bumped into him. If so, it didn't register."

"Did you or anyone in your suite hear or notice anything about Dr. Travers that raised concern?"

"No. And I'm sure you can understand. . . I can't have some fool who's messing up subletting space from me. Politics can get pretty damn dirty. Prevention is better than cure."

It was a quick deposition.

* * *

The full team from Mackey Markham & Wilder was on board for Dr. Travers' deposition.

By Dr. Travers' account, Melody Jarrett was an attractive young woman with promising artistic gifts. However, she had horrible nightmares that she confused with reality. Travers was very upset when she left him abruptly and refused to return his calls. He was surprised when someone Melody Jarrett consulted years later passed the word back to him that he had been accused of mistreating her. Apparently, the word was out that he was an unethical practitioner. He learned that she was under the care of a younger psychiatrist, Joan Underwood. When he asked around about her, he'd learned she had become caught up in this faddish recovered memory and dissociative disorder nonsense. He found that the people she had learned from were being sued right and left. As word got back to him that he was being trashed, he decided to take steps to protect himself.

Bill Mackey took the lead.

"Please name every individual who has confirmed to you that something negative was said about you by Dr. Joan Underwood."

"Well, apart from the first one, I really don't remember. The rest fade into the background."

"Please identify the first one who made such a statement to you."

"It is my understanding that such inquiries are protected by attorney-client privilege."

"So, you received this news from your personal attorney?"

"Yes."

"Kindly identify your personal attorney, Dr. Travers."

"Margaret Dedham."

"Where does she practice?"

"She practiced just outside of DC. She passed away last year."

"I'm sorry to hear that. Did someone else take over her practice?"

"Not to my knowledge."

"Please identify every individual by name who is alleged to have said these negative things about you."

"Counselor," said Lou Galvin, "I am instructing my client not to answer that question. It is my belief that information first shared by an attorney in the context of conversation between attorney and client falls within the scope of attorney-client privilege."

"Understood, Lou. But I want to be clear. Dr. Travers, are you saying that you learned each and every allegation from your personal attorney, who is now deceased?"

"That is correct."

"And how did she learn all of this?"

"She was worried for me. She asked if she could engage a detective."

"Did she identify that detective or that agency to you."

"No."

Every one of Bill's inquiries encountered a brick wall or a skillful finesse. Finally, Bill reviewed the opinions Travers had offered, one by one. For each, he asked, "Are there any other observations, facts, thoughts, experiences, or concerns that you took into consideration in forming the opinions that you have expressed here today?"

"None come to mind, sir," answered Dr. Travers.

"At risk of covering old ground again, Dr. Travers, earlier you stated that you have never practiced in Suite 312, HighPoint Centre. Is that correct?"

"Yes."

"What was your previous place of practice, prior to Suite 606?"

"2300 Midvale Avenue, Suite 421."

"And you closed down there when you came to HighPoint?"

"Yes."

"Dr. Travers, are you able to state your income for the year in which Melody Jarrett first came to see you, the year in which she last was your patient, and the last calendar year?"

"No."

"Are you able to produce this information, Dr. Travers?"

"This can be arranged," said Fuller.

Bill Mackey's further lines of questioning produced no additional information.

* * *

Brett Connery struggled to contain himself.

"This case is bullshit! It's built on smoke and mirrors. I bet Lasko throws it out. . ."

"That's not going to happen, Brett," said Bill. "I've already had that conversation with another judge I know. Oliver Lasko inherited this case from Amanda English when she moved up to the Appellate Division. That's before you and Linda got involved. Oliver isn't going to overrule Amanda without exceptionally solid grounds."

"Amanda. . ." muttered Brett.

"I don't get it. What are we talking about?" asked Linda.

"Judge Amanda English. . ." Brett began, but Bill took over.

"Judge Amanda English is an old friend of mine. She's actually a pretty good judge. But she has a flare for the dramatic. She never saw a potential headline case she didn't like."

"She wants to sing with the Supremes," said Brett.

"She is ambitious, Brett. She always was. But if she kept the case and threw it out later, she could do it with a flourish. No matter how it ended, she could make a speech from the bench that could make headlines. Brett, she'd be completely fair. But Amanda does things her way. And before we condemn her, or Oliver, let's remember that we're blowing off steam about nothing. Neither of them knew what we just learned today. We can take this to Judge Lasko, but I think he'll take it under advisement, and let things proceed. The wheels of justice are turning, and he'll trust the process to do what it's supposed to do."

"I have a question, Mr. Mackey," said Linda. "Why did you go over all those areas and ask if there was anything more he wanted to say about them?"

"Brett?" asked Bill.

"Several reasons. First, one set of inquiries may trigger recollections relevant to those asked earlier. Second, how often do we walk away from something and say to ourselves, 'I should have said. . .' You know. Third, just in case the deponent is withholding or lying, if they blow off the follow-up questions, and their deception is uncovered, they have impeached themselves."

"So, it's a kind of question you always want to consider in a deposition," added Bill, "but never in a trial. By the time you get to trial, you are working with materials already in hand. If you ask a question like that in court, you open the door for anything else the other side may want to throw at you that they otherwise could not introduce without running it by the judge. Remember that."

* * *

"That bastard Mackey is as clever as you said, Lou. You can say, 'I told you so.'"

CHAPTER 18

Bill Mackey escorted Melody Jarrett into the Founders Room. Four attorneys rose to their feet. Only the court reporter remained seated. Melody Jarrett's shaking hands clenched a very large pocketbook. It shook visibly as she hid behind it, shielded from waist to neck. She gave a weak smile as Mackey pulled out a chair for her. She quickly drew herself close to the table, put her pocketbook between herself and the world, and crossed her arms over the pocketbook.

She's sitting there like she was naked. The poor girl's spent a lifetime feeling exposed. Gillian Bullock caught Linda's eyes, and rolled her own. Linda responded with a faint nod.

"Ms. Jarrett, Mr. Bruce Fuller, Mr. Louis Galvin, and Ms. Gillian Bullock are here representing Dr. Travers. Mr. Fuller, another attorney for Dr. Galvin, will not be with us today. Mr. Bleier represents Memorial Hospital. Ms. Linda Gilchrist and Mr. Brett Connery are my colleagues. As you know, we represent your former psychiatrist, Dr. Joan Underwood."

* * *

The court reporter introduced, and Melody Jarrett sworn, Bruce Fuller began.

"Ms. Jarrett, while I am sure that Mr. Mackey or others have already spoken to you, and you know what a deposition is and how it usually proceeds, bear with me as I cover the same ground. I will be asking you some questions Also, some of the artwork you produced and presented to Dr. Underwood in the course of your work with her is here, displayed on the table. Each piece will be marked as an exhibit. I will try to be straight-forward and clear, but I may not always succeed in making my meaning plain. If at any time you are confused or don't know how to understand or respond to a question, please don't hesitate to ask me to repeat or restate my question. If you are in doubt about whether or how to respond, please feel free to consult Mr. Mackey or his colleagues. If at any time this situation becomes too uncomfortable, inform Mr. Mackey and we can take a break. I will be asking most of the questions today, but Mr. Galvin or Ms. Bullock may raise an issue from time to time. Mr. Mackey, Ms. Gilchrist, Mr. Connery or Mr. Bleier may request a clarification, raise an objection to something I or other say, or offer you instructions in particular instances. If there is any disagreement about how a particular question is to be handled, that disagreement will be put before His Honor, Judge Lasko, who will be on the bench for this trial.

"Before I begin with my own questions, are there any questions, or concerns on the part of your folks, Mr. Mackey? Very well."

For all his bluster on the lectern, Bruce Fuller had a surprisingly gentle, respectful style. Melody Jarrett was the oldest daughter in a large, dysfunctional blue-collar family. Her skill in drawing won her a scholarship. She was the first and only member of her family to go beyond high school. Melody had worked hard to remain a "good girl." She had broken off relationships when men became demanding or she feared her own emotions were "getting too strong." She had suffered terrible nightmares as far back as she could remember, but when she completed her graduate work and began to teach art in college, things became more difficult. No matter what themes she approached in her own creative work, unwanted scenes of violence and mistreatment appeared on her canvases. For several years she had restricted herself to realistic, profoundly detailed, pencil drawings.

There were times during which she could not concentrate well, when she suffered headaches so severe that she had to cancel her classes. She found things in her possession that she had not recalled acquiring, including clothing she would never have purchased or worn. Worst, her nightmares began to include detailed scenarios involving mistreatment. She had believed she succeeded in preserving her virginity. She felt forced to seek treatment when she awakened one morning in the bed of a man who seemed to know her by a different name. Her family doctor recommended Dr. Gordon Travers.

"And what was your first impression of Dr. Travers?"

"He seemed very kind and caring. He was very interested in me and my situation." Gradually, Dr. Travers became even more kind and supportive.

"He held my hand. He came to sit alongside of me on the couch. He put his arm around me. . ." At first, Melody Jarrett didn't seem to notice the tears welling up in her eyes, slowly making their way down her face.

Bill Mackey offered her a tissue, but Melody Jarrett did not seem to notice his gesture.

"Ms. Jarrett?" he asked.

All at once, Melody Jarrett startled. Her eyes grew wild, looking large as saucers as they raced uncomprehendingly around the room.

"Ms. Jarrett?"

For a moment, Melody Jarrett made eye contact with Bill Mackey and tried to smile, a moment eclipsed almost immediately by a return to that wide-eyed wild expression. She pointed to the pictures on the table. She tried to gather them up.

"Bad men! Bad men!" Melody's voice was child-like, terror driving every sound. She began to tear some pictures in half. When Bill Mackey tried to take hold of her hands, she cringed and began to wail, "Bad men! Bad men!" She pushed him away and sprinted from the room. Her pocketbook sat abandoned, by her chair.

CHAPTER 19

Bill Mackey and Brett Connery assumed that Melody had run to a nearby ladies' room and would return once she recovered her composure. After a few minutes, they sent Linda to look after her. Linda checked every facility in the firm's suite. No Melody! Finally, she touched bases with Billie Mason at the receptionist's desk.

"Ms. Jarrett, Ms. Gilchrist? She was upset. She left in a big hurry."

"Did she say anything to you?"

"She said something, but I don't know if she was talking to me."

"How do you mean?"

"It was like she was talking to herself in this tiny little voice. She kept saying, 'Bad men! Bad men!'"

* * *

"So that's Dissociative Identity Disorder," mused Mackey.

"With all due respect, Mr. Mackey," said Fuller, "perhaps. But perhaps that's great acting or the unfortunate induction of a believed-in role and fantasy by guile or dangerous technique by an inept therapist."

"Is this on the record?" asked the court reporter.

"Yes!" said Fuller and Mackey in unison.

"We might as well adjourn for the day. We're going to have to consult with Judge Lasko," said Galvin.

* * *

Linda was asked to look in on Melody Jarrett. Melody did not answer her telephone. Her car was not parked near her apartment, and no one answered her door. It was ajar. She reached Bill Mackey.

"Don't open the door. I'll call the police."

The patrolman who responded was reluctant to enter the apartment. Linda could hear a curse and snarl through his radio. Ten minutes later a detective was on the scene. The place looked ransacked. Jewelry, money, checkbooks, identity papers, and some toiletries and clothing were gone, but her television, stereo, and electronics, things a thief could turn into quick cash, were still there for the taking.

"Looks like she did a runner or left under duress, ma'am. A crook would have. . . uh. . ."

"Made out like a bandit?"

"You got it."

* * *

"Looks like she bolted, Bill."

"I just spoke to Joan Underwood. She told me that DID patients sometimes have fugues. She suspects Melody couldn't face the pressure, switched and took off. Even if we find her, I'm afraid she may not be stable enough to depose or present as a witness. When I get the police report, I'll talk to Lasko."

"Bill, when you saw how Melody behaved, you said something like you just saw what DID is like. But Fuller came on like it was just one big act for the sake of a big payday. Can you believe how he behaved. . .?"

"Like such a shit? Yes. Remember, we're engaged in an adversarial process. He took the opportunity to place his opinion about this witness and her disorder on the record. Whatever else happens, he'll try to put that before the jury."

"What do you think Judge Lasko will do with all this?"

"If I know Oliver, he'll sit back, and give this situation a while to sort itself out. If it doesn't, he'll work on the principle that 'justice delayed is justice denied.' We may lose Melody Jarrett's testimony, whatever it might have been."

* * *

Underwood's team tried to touch bases with their experts. Only Jay Philips answered Bill Mackey's call.

"The only honest answer is 'I don't know.' But here are a few notions that may be helpful. First, one of those pictures may have been of someone whom she has, or believes she has, reason to fear. You may have witnessed a switch into a personality more in contact with the experience of mistreatment, and/or a flashback. Second, maybe she was overcome by guilt or shame. Most people victimized by someone they feel attached to struggle with the notion that they may have wanted or deserved or somehow caused it, attitudes which abusers often encourage. Or, they may feel so afraid of losing the attachment to the abuser that they act to cancel out the accusation or destroy their own credibility. A third possibility would be some fear of retaliation or punishment from a childhood abuser, the current abuser, or both. A fourth would be a need to defend abusers past and/or present, out of traumatic bonding or shame or guilt over committing a betrayal. A fifth possibility is a combination or all of the above at once, through the simultaneous and largely incompatible reactions of two or more other personalities."

CHAPTER 20

A few weeks later the same attorneys, minus Mr. Bleier, assembled in the Founders' Room at Mackey Markham & Wilder for Joan Underwood's deposition. Memorial Hospital had decided its exposure was minimal. Their attorney was instructed to step back for the moment and liaise with Mackey's team.

"Now, Dr. Underwood," said Fuller, "we've reviewed your curriculum vitae and your professional education. Before we proceed discuss your treatment of Ms. Jarrett, whose whereabouts I gather remain unknown, I would like to ask one further question. Is there or are there any other employment or occupational experience or experiences not specified in that document?"

"Of course."

"Of course? Why haven't you included them in the material you presented to us?"

"I didn't think that my summer jobs and part-time work high school through medical school were relevant."

"They may not be. But we won't know that until we hear about them."

Bill Mackey sat silent as Linda spoke. "Objection! Where are we going with this, Mr. Fuller?"

"Just trying to get a complete picture of how Dr. Underwood became the person she is today."

"Irrelevant. Dr. Underwood, you don't have to answer that question. Let's move on."

"You agree, Mr. Mackey?"

"Yes, I do."

"Fine. Well, I guess we'll let his honor decide the matter."

Linda broke Mackey's rule and glanced toward him, then quickly back and forth around the room. Bill, Brett, and Lou Galvin sat impassive as Fuller scribbled furiously. Gillian Bullock looked around like a bewildered child, then ducked her head and tried to look busy taking notes of her own. Linda turned toward Dr. Underwood. Her lovely smile had drawn as tight as a miser's purse-strings.

Whatever's going on, I'm left in the dark. Joan's face reminds me of something. But I can't place it.

* * *

At the next break, Bill Mackey admitted he was puzzled about Galvin's line of questioning. He tactfully avoided challenging his client's defensive response.

"Joan, do you have any idea of what Fuller is up to?"

"Not at all. I guess I'll try to remember where I waited tables summers up on Martha's Vineyard."

Too breezy! Too darn glib! Linda wanted to scream. *But we have nothing to go on. Why do Bill and Brett seem OK with where matters stand?* Recalling the image of Joan's face, drawn tight with tension, Linda found herself drifting back to a dark summer night more than twenty years before as a memory caught her by surprise. The Gilchrist family was sailing offshore on *Cricket's Caper*, making for Martha's Vineyard. An unpredicted storm seemed to blow up out of nowhere. Within moments their Morgan Out Island 51, no tiny thing, was being tossed about as if Poseidon had declared a vendetta against *Cricket's Caper* and made the Gilchrist family the particular targets of his vindictive wrath.

Mom took the helm. . . a sure sign Dad was worried sick. He wanted the best sailor calling the shots. Even in the face of danger, Betty Gilchrist was a laughing charmer. *Cricket's Caper* was caught by a rogue wave and nearly went over, but Betty brought them upright, taunting the storm as if it were a boring roller-coaster. "That's all you've got?" she'd roared. That's where Linda had seen a beautiful woman's smile suddenly go that tight! Now Linda grasped for the first time what had at stake. . . Her mother knew she was fighting for the lives of her family. . . She tried to calm her children with a brave, defiant front. *Mom was the best, but Mom was afraid she wouldn't win. Whatever's going on, for Joan Underwood, it's life or death!* The terror her mother had shielded her children from with such strength and grace so many years before swept over her. Panic rose up in her chest. Tears threatened to flood her eyes.

Linda excused herself. She made it to the restroom just in time.

CHAPTER 21

Joan Underwood's deposition concluded, Bruce Fuller, Lou Galvin, and Gillian Bullock huddled in a conference room at Dunham & Brady.

"Curious, that reluctance to look into what she did before she became a doctor," said Galvin.

"Sure is," Fuller agreed. His smile grew more lupine, displaying his well-capped teeth to perfection.

Grandma! What big teeth you have! Bullock mused. . . But she controlled herself. "May I assume that Dr. Underwood's testimony suggested a particular line of attack?" she wondered.

"Perhaps, Ms. Bullock. Perhaps."

* * *

After Bruce Fuller sent Gillian Bullock on a pointless errand, he turned to Lou Galvin.

"I have a detective I use when I need to get background information, deep information. I'm going to sic him on Dr. Underwood. I don't think Ms. Bullock would be comfortable with how this man works, but he's the best. I have a gut feeling that there's something about her that doesn't ring true."

"I'm OK with following your intuition, but about Gillian. . ."

"That's intuition, too. I think I'm afraid she might identify too much with the defendant."

"Well, she is pretty caring. Maybe you're right."

CHAPTER 22

It was just past nine that night when Joan Underwood telephoned Bill Mackey.

"Uncle Bill? I'm worried. Galvin is going after every job I've ever had. I can't let him go there. Don't ask. I don't want to talk about it. It could ruin everything. Is there anything you can do?"

"Joan, if I don't know what we're trying to protect you from, it's going to be hard to come up with a good strategy."

"Just know that no matter what, I will refuse to answer."

"OK. We'll try to hold the line, but I'm not sure that we'll be able to keep them at bay. Are you sure we can't. . .?"

The line had gone dead.

* * *

Still later that evening, Linda's escalating misgivings overcame her apprehension about troubling Bill Mackey at home.

"Bill, I'm deeply concerned about Dr. Underwood's refusal to talk about her employment before medical school. Should we be afraid that she's waving a red flag in front of a bull?"

"I think she's solid, Linda. And she's very insistent. I tried to reason with her, but I got nowhere. I'm afraid we're going to have to respect our client's wishes."

"You say 'insistent.' I'm thinking I should switch from 'waving a red flag in front of a bull' to 'bull-headed.' Maybe she's covering over something that terrifies her. Whatever it is, I'm afraid it's going to come back and haunt us. At the least, the jurors may think she thinks she's too good to be bothered by following the rules. At the worst, the judge may charge her with contempt of court. In the middle, if she's evasive, Galvin and Fuller could move to have her declared a hostile witness, and really go after her. That could wind up hurting her career more than the lawsuit itself. This really bothers me. And if she really is terrified under it all, and they somehow push the right button. . . I don't ever want to think about that."

"If this blows up, you have my permission to tell me and the world that you told me so."

CHAPTER 23

After the first hour of late-night talk shows by East Coast time, Bruce Fuller figured Lawrence Cavendish would be surveilling some errant spouse or running up someone's expense account in a posh restaurant where he could rationalize he "had to be." Lawrence Cavendish did not like to be called "Catfish Cavendish" to his face, but accepted, with mock reluctance, that his nasty nickname was a dandy *nom de guerre*. It portrayed him as a relentless bottom dweller and scavenger who would take on anything. . . Not a bad rep for a private eye in LA.

He had decided that his persona would require a demonstration of affluence, but he had yet to decide which *grand cru* would advertise this identity best to cognoscenti and poseurs alike when his cell vibrated softly.

"Cavendish, P.I." he said, loud enough to attract the stunning brunette walking by his table. She looked his way. He stood and pulled out a chair for her. She accepted. "This shouldn't take long," he whispered.

"What?" asked Fuller.

"Nothing. I was just talking to the most beautiful woman within miles, perhaps within light years." That earned an appreciative giggle.

"Joan Underwood, M.D. Everything. I mean everything. ASAP. Details to follow."

"The name means nothing to me. I'll get on it as soon as I can."

"Damn! I need this yesterday."

"You need it yesterday? You should have called me yesterday. And," he smiled across the table, "I am involved in an incredibly important and interesting case at this very minute."

"I need it now."

"Just like that? Brucie, baby! I work for a living. You want magic? Call Penn and Teller."

Catfish rang off, leaving Fuller sputtering. "Now, we were just beginning to get to know one another. Take a look at these vintages. Any favorites?"

"Gee, I don't know. Aren't these wines pretty expensive?"

Catfish held the wine list between them and slowly ran his finger down to the most costly bottle in the column. The young lady noticed where his finger settled, and her eyes opened very, very wide.

Gotta love a pretty deer in the headlights! The bottle isn't worth it, but she is.

"Let's enjoy this one while we talk about dinner." *I am such a pig*, Catfish Cavendish reveled, *Ain't life a bitch*?

CHAPTER 24

"Mr. Burgoyne? It's Ken Schaefer, from CNN. Will you take his call?"

"Got it!"

"Maserati Mike" Burgoyne, occasional legal commentator for CNN and arguably the most expensive lawyer on planet Earth, pressed the blinking button for his outside line. "So, how's my favorite news director this fine day?"

"Mike, have you seen this AP piece on false memory lawsuits? All the papers are running it."

"Not yet."

"I don't have to tell you that since that California case, plaintiffs' attorneys are setting up a cottage industry of suing therapists and claiming that what their patients told them about bad stuff that happened once upon a time was some sort of nonsense the therapists had suggested."

"And that they are accusing therapists of creating a cottage industry of malicious fraud and/or grotesque incompetence by making patients worse and charging them big bucks to get them better, but really making sure they stay sick and paying through the nose forever. . ."

"Well, there's this guy Bruce Fuller. . ."

"Yeah, the plaintiff's attorney in one of the first of those cases to grab the headlines. He's claiming he's on a crusade to clean up bad psychotherapy. He's been holding workshops for plaintiffs' attorneys either involved in false memory lawsuits or just salivating to get in on the goodies. Idealism has proven very, very profitable for Mr. Fuller."

"The last time he gave a talk, he said that these cases were so open and shut that all you have to do is drive a Brinks truck up to the back of the courthouse and tell them how much money to load on board. I got the word that there's one shaping up in Virginia, and Fuller's been brought in to work with a local fellow, Galvin, who's got a pretty good rep in his own right. It's shaping up as a pretty unique situation. It may be a story with long legs. How about you follow it and see if we have anything to go with?"

"What makes it unique?"

"Usually the plaintiff is a patient who claims she's been led down the garden path, plus/minus parents who feel the therapist has made the patient think they've done something wrong, usually sexual abuse. But here the plaintiff is a therapist. He's complaining that the next therapist after him convinced a former patient of his think that he molested her, and wrecked his reputation."

"And why is this story looking so good for us?"

"Because it's got substance and sex. Fuller's already won nearly a dozen cases of these cases in a row. He's pretty damn full of himself. . . Talking like he's the new sheriff, coming in off the range to clean up therapy town. He's aggressive. He's provocative. He oozes testosterone. . . Comes on like he's bent on destroying the defendant. He and others like him are becoming public figures, making the radio talk show rounds and even breaking into TV. On the other side, both the defendant and one of the defense attorneys are sharp, drop-dead gorgeous ladies. Real eye candy. There's real drama and steam here. I can see this turning into a special down the road."

Damn! That professional peeping tom wants me to cover a public rape!

"And you got the word how?"

"Let's just say, from an impeccable source close to this matter."

Mike Burgoyne asked for a moment to think. Swiveling back and forth on his Eames chair, he asked himself, *Who would tip CNN? Who stands to profit? Fuller never met publicity he didn't like, but if his approach didn't fall upon favorable ears, it could backfire on him. No. Not Fuller. Maybe after someone else made contact. . .*

"OK, Ken. First tell me what side Randolph St. James is on."

"Holy shit!"

"Well, I've just run down my short list of self-promoting shrinks who've done pieces for CNN, and guess who came out on top of the list?"

"You should have left out the simple logic. God! You had me blown away."

"You'll have to get blown elsewhere, Ken. I'll take a look. But I've been involved in a couple of cases that turned on memory and memory science. Know going in that what we're going to find is that it's not as simple as Fuller makes it out to be. Give me the docket number of the case, and I'll get started."

"Fuller says that all the science is on his side."

"He called you, too, after St. James? I thought he was smarter than that. I guess he's fuller than I thought. . ."

"He thinks the case is a slam-dunk."

"Don't get sucked in. You've got to know that he's trying to make his case in the media, feeding reporters talking points so they'll approach his opponents from a perspective that discounts in advance any argument they could make."

"What do you mean?"

"Look. If you give reporters, even good reporters, a game plan or even a press kit that provides them with questions and talking points that are going to make them look smart, that teach them how to pepper the other side with 'Have you stopped beating your wife?' questions, you push common sense and reason off center stage. By the time the interviewer gets through with Fuller-generated agenda, the segment is over, and the other side is left looking like a smacked ass no matter what. There is evidence to the contrary, but Fuller works hard to make sure the other side doesn't get a fair hearing. Was it a nice press kit?"

"Go screw yourself! OK. OK. Keep an eye on it. We may send you down for the trial. Nothing goes on the air until the verdict is in. Fair?"

"Fair enough. Who's on the other side?"

"Mackey Markham & Wilder. Old line medium sized firm."

"First chair?"

"Bill Mackey. You know him?"

"We've met. He was a federal prosecutor at the time."

"Any problem there?"

"Not on my side. He may not remember me kindly."

"By the way, Fuller is headlining some conference in Baltimore in a month or two, kind of whipping up his anti-therapist crusade."

Burgoyne pulled up the conference announcement on his computer. "Sponsored by the Family Justice Project. An all-star cast. . . If you want me to consider covering this, I should be there."

"Mike, for that, you'd have to go on your own. I can't afford your life style."

"Ken, if you want to hear the music, you've got to pay the band."

"You're no band. You're a fucking symphony orchestra."

"So, send the New York Philharmonic. I'm sure they'll do a hell of a job. You know my terms."

"By the way, Dr. Hollywood is on the other side."

"Pretty far down my list of titanic egos."

"Why?"

"He's full of himself, but not the other stuff. I've used him."

CHAPTER 25

The senior partners faced a short agenda that week. They declined two iffy "slip and fall" cases, referring them to a former associate who'd gone solo. Jeff updated the others on an unanticipated zoning problem concerning one of the sites Goliath Pharmaceuticals was considering for a new plant. Some issues might have to be discussed with Goliath's home office in Frankfurt. Brett Connery had been stationed in Germany for two years as a JAG. He spoke fluent German. They agreed to send him to Frankfurt should the need arise. Sally convinced her colleagues to take a *pro bono* case for the family of an African-American girl who had been given a scholarship to a ritzy private school on the basis of her athletic abilities, only to find her scholarship threatened when she suffered a season-ending injury. Bill Mackey observed that when the school acquired a full appreciation of the adverse publicity it would suffer and the costs it would incur if matters went to litigation, it would discover that the prompt restoration of the scholarship would one hell of a bargain. His optimistic stance drew skeptical glances. Jeff Wilder summed up the partners' attitudes.

"Righteous. It has my full support. But I think they'll hang tough. We're in for a tough fight."

Finally, Bill Mackey proposed the firm's sending himself and either Brett or Linda to a conference in Baltimore, most of which involved presentations by their adversaries and experts in the Underwood case. Sally and Jeff felt the firm should not invest its own money if the insurers were unwilling to foot the bill. The senior partners held firm even when Bill stated that he considered the matter so crucial that he would fund conference attendance out of his own pocket.

Bill argued no further. He volunteered to take the pro bono case.

* * *

Three hours later. Bill asked the senior partners to meet for five minutes in the Founder's Room. He circulated copies of a fax from the headmaster of the ritzy private school, apologizing for "an unfortunate misunderstanding" about the status of the injured athlete, and offering reassurance that the school would stand behind the young lady until graduation. The case had been resolved with the expenditure of under fifteen minutes of billable time.

"Before the young lady, her family, her headmaster, and I hold a press conference at 6:00, is there anything anyone would like to add?"

"Just as we told you earlier today, Bill," said Sally, "Your proposal to take your team to Baltimore meets with our unanimous approval."

"That's what I thought we'd agreed upon. I'll try to get the insurer to pay us back. I just had to make sure these old ears didn't hear things wrong earlier today."

"What the hell did you do, Bill?" asked Wilder. "What kind of Houdini act. . .?"

"Just plain horse sense. When every generation of your family has sent two daughters to the same school for over a century, and you sit on its board of directors, you may be positioned to apply the principle of Archimedes rather effectively."

"Give me a lever long enough," said Sally.

"And a place on which to stand," said Jeff.

"And I will move the world," Bill concluded. "They're going to take care of her kid sister, too. Have I ever told you how much I love crabs?"

"I'm impressed. I guess horse sense is most effective," said Sally, "if you have the right horse."

CHAPTER 26

Linda took her morning run along Baltimore's Inner Harbor, making mental notes on the restaurants and shops along the way. She tried to convince herself she'd carve out time to visit the National Aquarium, all the while knowing it was wishful thinking. *Not a chance on Mackey Markham & Wilder time!*

"Confronting the Consequences of Voodoo Science: A Workshop for Legal Professionals," had been organized by the Family Justice Project. The FJP represented itself as an advocacy group that stood up for those falsely accused of mistreating children and others. Its supporters portrayed it as a heroic defender of the innocent. Its detractors depicted it as an energetic apologist for perverts and pedophiles, obscuring the truth of their misdeeds. A reasonable middle ground seemed hard to come by.

Standing in the registration line, Linda felt her heart speeding up. *But there's nothing for me to be nervous about! Or is there?*

Until late yesterday afternoon, Linda had been relaxed. Sure, she'd have to be on her toes with Bill, but she knew she was well-prepared and poised to a fault. *Living wherever Dad was posted, I learned to handle just about everything. I'm not going to make a complete fool of myself.*

But then Bill had called. "My doctor says I need the rest and a dozen or so diagnostic procedures. How's that for a paradox? Pretty far over the top for an old guy who's just feeling a little tired and has a touch of anemia." Brett Connery was involved in a high-profile trial that had just begun. And there it was. . . Linda would be off to Baltimore on her own to learn what there was to learn, hammer it into a coherent summary, and pass it along to her seniors.

On site, the vibes were bad. Standing in a registration line that moved along at a snail's pace, Linda picked up snippets from nearby conversations that screamed, *You are in hostile territory!*

"My firm wants in on these cases."

"My niece came home from college and told my sister that my brother-in-law molested her. Some crazy shrink put that nonsense in her head. My sister is a fucking mess. My family wants payback. . . Big time."

"Fuller took home 2.3 million from that last case."

"We've had a few bad years. We're looking to develop some new income streams. . ."

This is no time for nerves, she argued unsuccessfully with her stiffening neck and clenching jaw. *What am I doing here? What have I gotten myself into? I'm not in Kansas anymore! Sure, I can handle this. But, Bill. . . I wish you were here!*

Registration completed, Linda found a quiet place to scan the conference materials and figure out how to wear her cheap nametag without savaging her silk blouse. She pinned her tag to her handbag and began to read.

"Linda? Linda Gilchrist? My God! It's been forever!"

"Beth Berman? This is wonderful! The last time we got together you were clerking at Morgan McGuire for the summer." It felt good to hug an old friend.

"I got lucky. I'm still there. Jonathan, Chris, this is Linda Gilchrist, an old, old friend."

A slender man a little younger than Bill Mackey and a well-dressed woman just a few years older than Beth and Linda turned in her direction. Jonathan Lauder pivoted swiftly, a basketball small forward on a pick and roll, looking for his shot. He radiated a feisty athletic energy, eyes on sharp focus, smile on high beam, and ready for God knows what. *My God! That man's a Jack Russell terrier on two feet!* Christine Cadawalder came about more slowly. *I bet she played field hockey. . . defense.* Her smile took much longer to spread across her features. Her eyes were every bit as intense as her colleague's.

"My old buddy! A real Philadelphia lawyer! I'm impressed."

"As are we," said Jonathan. "What brings you to this workshop, Linda?"

For a moment, Linda hesitated. What she'd heard at registration put her on guard. If Beth and her firm on the other side of one of these cases. . . *I'll trust our friendship and deal with it up front.*

"My firm is defending a psychiatrist accused of creating false memories. I'm here to get a better overall picture of how these things go."

"So are we," said Beth. "But we seem to be a tiny minority. Most of the people here are. . ."

"It's OK to say, 'hot and bothered to cash in on a hot trend while the getting is good'," said Christine.

I never expected that from her! I thought she'd be the calm, quiet one. My God! They're both tigers. How do they survive with one another?

"Sit with us," Christine suggested. "It looks like they're about to begin."

* * *

Anita Ausminder, the Executive Director of the Family Justice Project, greeted the assembled. "On behalf of the Family Justice Project, I would like to welcome you to Baltimore's beautiful Colonial Heritage Inner Harbor Hotel and Conference Center, and to our workshop, aptly entitled 'Confronting the Consequences of Voodoo Science: A Workshop for Legal Professionals.' It is our sincere hope that the knowledge and skills that you acquire this weekend will allow you to save countless individuals and families from the heartbreak and loneliness brought upon them by unskilled and unethical mental health professionals who practice unscientific psychotherapies, psychotherapies that destroy the truths of their patients' histories and their loving relationships with devoted family members they have been misled into mistrusting.

"The mental health professions have failed to police themselves. Too many good people have been left confused and distraught when the children and grandchildren they loved and raised with such dedication and care were turned against them by voodoo science and the therapies derived from unproven and discredited ideas about human behavior. We must be grateful that the legal profession, assisted by those few mental health professionals who hold fast to scientifically informed treatment approaches, is beginning to push back the darkness that has cloaked the unethical atrocities being promoted as medical and psychological therapies.

"It is a pleasure to introduce our keynote speaker, attorney Bruce Fuller of Fuller and Associates. Not only has he pioneered legal approaches to the pursuit of justice that will be of immeasurable comfort to countless families, but he also has proven himself a true champion of justice in the courtroom. Mr. Fuller has brought over a dozen cases to trial in defense of those wounded and betrayed by irresponsible therapists. He has won either a decision or a substantial settlement in every single one. Thanks to him, over ten therapists have been censured by their licensing boards, and two have lost their licenses to practice. Every victory he achieves brings us closer to an era of safe psychotherapy for everyone, treatment that is designed to help, not harm, both those who suffer the anguish of mental illness, and those who love them.

"Bruce Fuller, Esquire, is a hero to everyone who cares about caring and quality in treatment, a man whose name strikes fear into the hearts of incompetent and unethical therapists everywhere, and a wonderful role model to every legal professional in attendance here today. I give you a man whose skill and dedication are always an inspiration. . . Mr. Bruce Fuller!"

On the podium, Bruce Fuller appeared unremarkable, a medium-sized man with medium dark hair. But once he began to speak, Linda could feel his power.

"Thank you, Mrs. Ausminder. It is a pleasure and a privilege to kick off today's meeting. Over the next two days, we will review the recent history of the alarming rise of irrational practices in the mental health professions—How they began, and how they proliferated. We will discuss both the voodoo science that is used to justify their use, the fallacies inherent in their ostensible rhymes and reasons, and the nature of the terrible problems that they cause for patients and their loved ones alike. We will discuss several of the major figures among the many who advocate and practice such outlandish approaches, and why their number includes some of the most dangerous men and women in contemporary psychiatry, psychology, and psychoanalysis. We will show you how a small group of heroic individuals stood tall against this tidal wave of irrationality and began to develop both a literature and a series of laboratory studies designed to restore scientific clarity of thought to the mental health disciplines. We will introduce you to the work of some of the figures who have provided expert witness testimony to confront the charlatans who either believe irrational false statements about child abuse or create false memories of childhood mistreatment with their mindless theories and destructive approaches to treatment. For example, Dr. Joseph Chaudvent and Dr. Peter Rapier will address you. This truly fantastic team that has helped me win either judgments or considerable settlements in over a dozen consecutive cases without a single defeat or failure to exact significant monetary settlements.

"Now, I know that the mention of financial considerations may seem offensive to those of you who've come here to learn how to redress grievances and pursue justice to the fullest extent possible. Like you, I would like to see myself as an idealist. However, for better or for worse, in our society apologies for this type of wrongdoing do not take the form of either admissions of guilt, public censure or humiliation. Nor do they take the form of incarceration. Instead, they take the form of awarding financial compensation to the injured parties.

"And as repugnant as this way of approaching justice may be to many of us, and as unsatisfying as money may be as a compensation to those of us who see this as a matter of right versus wrong, and who want to bring about an era of enlightenment in the mental health sciences and raise the standard of practice to help those in psychological distress, sadly, it proves necessary. You see, there is a need to curb those who do not want to believe truths that they either cannot or will not embrace, a need to rein in people who just will not understand that they need to change their behavior and offer safe, legitimate, and helpful treatment. . . Like it or not, financial disincentives deliver a message that they can understand. Those people who cannot understand true science can understand that their universities will no longer accept the risk of allowing them to continue to teach and practice their nonsense. They can grasp that funding agencies and foundations will reject all of their wrong-headed proposals and deny them support to continue their unscientific work. They can understand employers who fire them because they are not doing what they were being paid to do, and who realize their quackery brings their employers exposure and liability because they can be held responsible for the actions of those under their supervision and oversight. Those in private practice can understand when their malpractice insurers no longer will write policies for them because their way of practicing invites litigation, and when their patients drop out of treatment with them, and when their potential patients are referred elsewhere by colleagues who become aware of the harm they are likely to do to those they might refer.

"When reason fails, financial disincentives become powerful persuaders. Our recent victories allow us to state with confidence that we are approaching a point at which when we intercede on behalf of those harmed by such voodoo therapies and witch-doctor therapists, all parties will realize that almost all of these cases are the same, the legitimate complaints of the truly mistreated. We are reaching the point at which wise jurists and juries will recognize that our arguments are so powerful that all we will need to do is drive a Brinks truck up to the back of the courthouse and tell them to fill it with money, and be quick about it, because we have other unethical therapists we need to either reeducate or drive out of practice.

"That, my friends, is how we, together with all of you, Ms. Ausminder's organization, and all right-thinking people will clean up the sorry state of psychotherapy in America today. Are you with me?"

Cheers and applause broke out. Looking around, Christine, whispered, "At least some polite applause, Jonathan! Let's not make targets of ourselves."

Smiling broadly, Jonathan replied, "Long time since I've been to a revival meeting! Halleluiah!" He looked around, studying the crowd.

"Four rows ahead of us to the far right. Do you see the man in the Harris tweed jacket?"

"My God!" said Beth.

"OK, I'm the ignoramus. Who is he?" asked Linda.

"That, young lady," said Jonathan, "is the living legend himself, Maserati Mike Burgoyne. One of the handful of people in our line of work who's as good as he thinks he is."

"Didn't you go to school with him?" asked Christine.

"I did. We were partners in the moot court competition."

"I guess I don't have to ask which team won," said Linda.

"Beth, you have a smart friend."

"Give it a rest, Jonathan," said Christine, "or I'll start calling you Model T Lauder."

CHAPTER 27

Mike Burgoyne and Jonathan Lauder caught up with one another at the first coffee break. Jonathan stared at Mike's nametag, tented his hands before his face, and made a polite bow.

"Yeah. A press pass! CNN yet!"

"You old bastard! I've seen you on the tube pretending to make sense of things discussing the Catfish Killer and other cases. I hate to admit it, but you do a hell of a good job."

"Thanks. From you, that means a lot. I'd like to catch up with you, but not here at the conference itself. I think I have to keep my distance. How about dinner tonight? As long as we don't discuss current cases. I hate to talk to you this way, Jonathan, but I didn't anticipate running in to any old friends here."

"Understood. Let's make it easier. I'll bring along one of the few people who's never heard of you before. She's an old friend of one of our associates. She probably doesn't know I know this, but my smart phone tells me she's Arthur Gilchrist's daughter."

Mike's eyebrows arched. "Really. Linda Gilchrist is Ambassador Gilchrist's kid? If Diogenes was roaming around with that lantern looking for an honest man, and ran into Arthur Gilchrist, he could have gone home, poured himself a nightcap, and gotten a decent night's sleep. By all means! I'd like to meet her."

* * *

Jonathan got back to Christine before Linda returned.

"Chris, keep this between us. But I'm betting Mike is here because CNN plans to cover the trial this Gilchrist gal is involved in."

"Come on, Jonathan! That's one hell of a stretch. No way you can figure that unless he told you."

"Well, in a way he did. He asked us to join him for dinner tonight, with the proviso we discuss no current cases. I told him we'd bring along the only person in the world who didn't know who he was, and mentioned she was Ambassador Gilchrist's daughter. . . Got it off the net. But he comes back and says, 'Linda Gilchrist is Ambassador Gilchrist's daughter?'"

"And you hadn't mentioned her first name! Wow! Jonathan, you just might be right. Arthur Gilchrist is famous. There are a lot of Gilchrists. But for him to. . . Yeah. Makes sense."

Jonathan's cell vibrated. "Mike's text. . . 'Damn. I got sloppy. You probably figured it all out by now. Be kind and cover my six.' Will do. He'd do it for me. Beth doesn't have to know."

"Do you think Linda's people have figured out what's headed their way?"

"Mike's gone against Bill Mackey twice when Bill was a federal prosecutor, and won. But he says it could have gone the other way both times. We can't expose his slip without compromising him. Gilchrist's firm wouldn't have planned to send a team if they hadn't already figured out they'd be walking into a war zone. They must have gone through the same line of reasoning that we did. They'll know soon enough."

* * *

Everyone worked to keep conversation light at their seafood dinner overlooking the harbor. Travel, the movies, and books provided safe havens. Dessert and coffee was on the table when Christine turned to Mike.

"Jonathan tells me that you share his love for mysteries and thrillers. Me, too. I'm always looking for a new series. Recommendations?"

"Are the rest of you interested?" Mike asked. "I wouldn't want to go off on a tangent and bore the heck out of everybody."

"Please," Linda said. "I love mysteries."

"You know I'm on board, Mike," said Jonathan. "Surprise me."

"OK. We can go around. Let's assume this is a cultured bunch, so Poe and Conan Doyle and Dame Agatha can be assumed. I love LA-based stories, so you can bet I'm good for all the old noir novels, Mike Connelly, and the Kellermans. . ."

Linda and Beth said little, especially when Mike, Jonathan, and Christine went on and on praising Maj Sjowall and Per Wahloo's Martin Beck series. Neither had read most of the European authors they admired.

When they turned to Linda, she was afraid she would seem incredibly naïve.

"I'm still a complete Nancy Drew freak. But I love Tony Hillerman and Batya Gur."

"Yeah," said Jonathan. "Tony Hillerman for sure. But who the heck is Batya Gur? Do you know about him, Mike? Or her?"

"No. I don't."

"I'm one up on you two? Really?" Christine teased. "Batya Gur is a brilliant Israeli writer. She weaves really nuanced and detailed webs that give you the whole modern history of Israel with all its cross currents. She writes long. Sjowall and Wahloo write short. They paint a picture of social issues in Sweden with a few really good commentaries and vignettes. Gur digs up the archeology of everything she says. With her, everything is deep upon deep."

"Funny thing about Nancy Drew," Mike remarked. "Her publishers contracted different folks contracted to write the series from time to time. My wife says Nancy Drew was a modern woman before her time. Quite a role model for bright gals with minds of their own, zipping along in her little blue roadster or convertible, depending on the fashion of the moment. And what do you pick up from Gur?"

"Everything is so complicated in Gur," said Linda. "She can send me racing back to Nancy Drew!"

"Well," said Mike, "I'll take a look at her stuff. Complications are where we live. Long book? Maybe for the flight back to LA?"

Christine beat Linda to the punch. "Probably better for Baltimore to Sydney or Tokyo."

"I love a challenge," said Mike.

"I'll let Mikey do it," said Jonathan.

CHAPTER 28

Jonathan, Christine, and Mike left halfway through the last afternoon.

"OK. We've seen the elephant," said Mike. "I get the idea."

* * *

Linda and Beth shared an early dinner just before they headed out.

"So, you folks are defending Bob Hatfield. I've read his work."

"I can't imagine how this litigation is being allowed to go forward. It makes no sense. There seems to be some concentrated effort to take down the leaders of the dissociative disorders field, and these battles are so damn bitter that people are calling them 'the memory wars.' I mean, I know there's a lot of bad therapy out there. Hell, there's a lot of bad sushi out there. But pushing the idea that it's some epidemic sounds like an effort to score points and win cases in the press.

"You never know how a trial will go. That St. James guy who talked yesterday is coming into town to buttress the locals. They plan to put Bublekopf, Chaudvent, and Rapier on the stand as experts, along with the new chairman at the U. I forget his name."

"Dr. Farrier. He threw my sister's mentor out of a job. My sister never uses foul language unless she's driving with me or the rest of the brood, but she goes ballistic at the mention of his name. Who are you going to present for Hatfield?"

"We have Marius Defoe, chair down in South Carolina, I think. He's very matter of fact testimony-wise, but very congenial. You know. . . that Southern charm. He's one of the few academic higher-ups who's actually treated a few cases. We're bringing in Edward Frelinghuysen from Chicago. I haven't met him, but Christine describes him as a cross between Bacchus and Albert Einstein. I have no idea what that means. We've called but haven't finalized with Ben Jordan. He's local. . . an expert on diagnosis. We hope he'll balance off Farrier."

"He's the guy that Farrier sacked."

"Yeah, but he got a lot of press and street creds in that Catfish Killer case a little while back. Maybe he'll enjoy knocking Farrier down a peg? And, we've got Matthew Grant on retainer for this trial."

"Matthew Grant? Two of our experts said he's incredibly knowledgeable, but works in a department that doesn't allow outside work."

"That changed two months ago. His department discovered some new programs were underbudgeted. They forced full-timers into a practice plan. Now they have to generate more of their salary by direct service."

"Can they do that?"

"Good question. Some folks told them to stick it and walked. Others decided to go with the flow. Matthew Grant wants to stay. He's taking on a couple forensic cases."

"What is he like to work with?"

"Jonathan described him as calm, cool, collected, and competent."

"My team may want to call him in. Would that be a problem?"

"I doubt it. He's eager to make enough on a couple of forensic cases to preserve his time for what he really wants to do."

CHAPTER 29

"Sure. If Matthew Grant is available, grab him," said Ben. "He's done one of the few studies following DID patients' response to treatment. There are two more pluses. He's written good articles on diagnosis, and his patients actually get well. He knows the treatment side inside out. You might not need me or Jay."

"He has no track record in court. We can't take the risk of relying on an unproven witness. I think we'll wind up going in heavy on the experts but not presenting everyone. Would you take that personally?"

"No. But other people might. Jay Philips always winds up getting the shaft. I hope you don't wind up cutting him loose. See you in a few days."

* * *

Neither the plaintiff's nor the defendant's attorneys had a Philadelphia connection. At Linda's suggestion, they arranged to make use of the downtown conference facilities of Jonathan Lauder's firm, Morgan McGuire.

Over his years at the U, Ben Jordan had developed profound respect for the uncanny intuitive judgement of his office manager, Sheila Conlan. When Farrier, the new chairman of psychiatry, insisted on bringing his own secretary and selecting a director of residency training who shared his perspectives, she and Ben Jordan were on notice. Sheila had been the secretary, executive assistant, and unofficial eyes and ears of the previous two chairmen. Ben, the director of training for over a decade, became expendable and inconvenient. When Ben left, he hired Sheila.

Sheila arrived at the reception area of Morgan McGuire toward the end of the lunch hour, ostensibly waiting to deliver a manila envelope of confidential material to Ben Jordan. She sat quietly, listening as the attorneys assembled. When Jonathan greeted them and escorted them back toward a conference room, Sheila placed a call.

"What's your read, Sheila?"

"Machiavelli, Charley Brown, and a lost little girl who wishes she was somewhere else."

"Why did I bother to go to medical school?"

"To make your mommy happy? They're waiting for you."

CHAPTER 30

The court stenographer positioned a panoramic microphone in the center of the table and plugged her stenotype and tape recorder into outlets near the end of the table closest to the door.

Bill Mackey held out a chair for Linda to the reporter's right.

"Dr. Jordan, why don't you sit between Ms. Gilchrist and me, right in front of the microphone?" Brett Connery placed himself to Mackey's right. Lou Galvin took a chair to the reporter's left. Bruce Fuller stationed himself directly across from Ben. Gillian Bullock sat beyond Fuller, closer in than Brett Connery.

The men chatted aimlessly about golf while the stenographer completed her preparations. Finding no opening in the conversation, Linda and Gillian Bullock exchanged a smile of understanding. . . Linda struggled to contain the dozen gut-level snarky gender-relevant resentments that clamored for expression, but her appreciation of another plain truth helped her keep her peace. Today, she and Gillian Bullock were mere junior associates. . . barely more than bystanders, along for the ride and learning the ropes while the big kids played for real.

The stenographer looked around the table. The six lawyers seemed distracted, the men on the links and the women in worlds of their own.

"Folks," said Ben, "I think we're holding up the wheels of progress."

* * *

Fuller wasted little time reviewing Ben's credentials until he asked,

"Can you tell us why you are no longer Director of Training in the Department of Psychiatry at the U?"

"The new chairman brought along his own man to fill that post."

"Did you appeal. . . Strike that. Did you protest?"

"No. He was brought in to move the department in a different direction. I spent ten years developing the training program he decided to replace. I would not have been comfortable working within his vision of how things should be. There was nothing to discuss."

"Was this a smooth or acrimonious departure?"

"Both. But it was the right decision for both of us."

"Did you find it difficult?"

"Of course. But not as difficult as it would have been if I had stayed and tried to work under uncomfortable circumstances."

"He wanted to improve your program?"

"No. He wanted to change it."

Fuller moved on to Ben's scholarship and clinical experience.

"What is your experience with Dissociative Identity Disorder?"

"I have seen about three dozen cases. I have treated three to integration."

"And currently?"

"I don't answer questions about my patients in any detail. I don't answer questions about my current patients at all."

"Mr. Mackey, will you instruct your expert to answer my inquiry?"

Bill Mackey sat, silent, pensive.

"Mr. Mackey? Mr. Mackey?"

"Dr. Jordan," asked Bill, "Do you realize that Mr. Fuller is entitled to ask that question?"

"I believe that he believes that he is."

"Do you realize that he may present this matter to the judge overseeing this case and ask for an order to compel your testimony?"

"Yes."

"Mr. Fuller, it is clear that Dr. Jordan regards this as an ethical matter. You will have to approach the judge. Would you like a brief recess in order to be able to do so?"

"At the next break. Now, Dr. Jordan, I'd like to direct your attention to the book I am holding, entitled *America's Most Dangerous Psychiatrists and Psychologists*. It was written by Dr. Joseph Chaudvent. It is receiving a tremendous amount of interest and acclaim. Are you aware of this book?"

"Yes."

"Have you read it?"

"Yes."

"Have you formed an opinion of Dr. Chaudvent's book?"

"Yes."

Fuller locked his eyes on Ben's. He searched Ben's face for a tell. Finding none, he moved forward.

"Do you agree with Dr. Chaudvent's assertion that Professor Bublekopf's research demonstrates that recovered memories of abuse are almost invariably untrustworthy?"

"No."

"Do you appreciate that many eminent authorities would hold a different opinion?"

"Yes."

"Do you agree with Dr. Chaudvent's assertion that Dissociative Identity Disorder is an iatrogenic disorder, an artifact of inept clinical work?"

"No."

"Do you appreciate that many eminent authorities would hold a different opinion?"

"Yes."

"Do you agree with Dr. Chaudvent that Dr. Philips' studies on the treatment of dissociative disorders are deeply flawed?"

"No."

"Do you appreciate that many eminent authorities would hold a different opinion?"

"Yes."

"But Dr. Jordan, surely you agree that his reports are anecdotal, that there is no established treatment protocol, and no formal control group?"

"Yes, no, and yes."

"I'm going to object. Nonresponsive."

Bill Mackey intervened. "With all due respect, Mr. Fuller. . . You asked three questions and you got three answers."

Fuller tented his fingers and consulted the ceiling. "Very well, Mr. Mackey. Objection withdrawn. Would you read back my question?"

The question repeated, Fuller began, "Sorry, Dr. Jordan. My question was unduly complex. I got what I deserved. You are asserting that Dr. Philips followed a protocol?"

"Yes. The plan of treatment outlined in his 1985 article."

"Do you consider it appropriate to rely on work that is without strict diagnostic criteria and a control group?"

"Yes, until. . ."

"Thank you, Dr. Jordan."

"Mr. Fuller, I believe that you interrupted Dr. Jordan's reply."

"I asked a yes or no question and got a yes or no response. Dr. Jordan has stated under oath that it is appropriate to rely on work that is without either strict criteria or a control group."

"Perhaps you should ask Dr. Jordan if he believes that his response was complete."

"Very well. If I interrupted your response, please continue."

"Until more sophisticated studies become available, these are the best we have."

"You consider that ethical?"

"Yes, sir. On several grounds. First, the diagnostic criteria changed several times during the period of time these patients were diagnosed and treated. Requiring conformity with criteria that did not exist at the time many of the patients were diagnosed would be remarkable, indeed. Second, comparing the outcome of those treated in this series with the untreated patients in a 1984 series, the treated group did better at a statistically significant level. That's my statistical work, not Philips'. Third, the alternative to using the information at hand, however imperfect, is leaving these patients undiagnosed, and/or untreated, or to take a guess about something else that might work. Those courses of action would be unethical under the circumstances."

"Why not wait for solid research findings?"

"Several years to obtain a funding grant, more to obtain a series of suitable patients and controls, studying a treatment that takes 5–10 years as often as not. . . . Most patients with a serious and devastating mental disorder with a high rate of suicide can't wait 15–20 years for their doctors to decide what to do. . ."

CHAPTER 31

After a break, Fuller took Ben through Dr. Underwood's evaluation and treatment of Melody Jarrett.

"Many authorities dispute the existence of Dissociative Identity Disorder except as an artifact of poor treatment. Yet Dr. Underwood made this diagnosis. What findings lead you to believe that this diagnosis was represented a real disorder?"

"The patient manifested all of the phenomena required by the diagnostic criteria."

"What findings cause you to consider that these phenomena were real?"

"She observed them."

"Is it possible that Dr. Underwood saw what she had suggested into existence?"

"Most things are possible, Mr. Fuller. But I would consider that quite unlikely in this instance. In any case, the *Diagnostic and Statistical Manual* is phenomenological. The phenomena were there."

"What facts lead you to offer that opinion?"

"First, they emerged spontaneously. They were only elicited by design later, when Dr. Underwood decided to document her findings further by administering Steinberg's *SCID-D-R*."

"But, Doctor, is there not a risk of suggesting those findings by administering the *SCID-D-R*, which I will state for the record is an acronym for Steinberg's *Structured Clinical Interview for DSM-IV Dissociative Disorders, Revised*?"

"Do you mean, Mr. Fuller, a risk of suggesting into existence for the first time what was not already there, and might have been triggered by the administration of the test? Or do you mean a risk of suggesting into existence what was already there, and was what had led to the decision to administer the test? You have me confused."

"Thank you, Doctor."

Bill Mackey spoke. "Mr. Fuller, I believe that you interrupted Dr. Jordan's initial answer."

"Did I? Please go on, Doctor."

"Second, the symptoms of the disorder had been noticed by several previous mental health professionals who documented them, but did not make a dissociative disorder diagnosis. They have been reported for over a decade prior to Ms. Jarrett's treatment by Dr. Underwood."

"But they did not make this fraudulent diagnosis, did they?"

Brett Connery spoke for the first time. "Off the record?"

Fuller agreed for plaintiff's team.

"Mr. Fuller, you are becoming argumentative. Could you rephrase that query?"

Fuller's face turned red, but his voice held steady.

"Thank you, Mr. Connery. I strongly disagree with your remark. But rather than debate the depth of your mischaracterization and burden the judge, and in the interests of moving this process along, I will withdraw the question.

"On the record. I withdraw my previous question. Dr. Jordan, would I be accurate if I stated that previous mental health professionals who documented phenomena you indicate are associated with the diagnosis of Dissociative Identity Disorder nonetheless declined to make that diagnosis?"

"Yes."

"Do you consider their failure to do so a mark against them?"

"I cannot answer that question in a 'yes or no' manner, Mr. Fuller."

"What prevents you from doing so?"

"Mr. Fuller, I do not know those clinicians. I have not interviewed them. Their reports do not address many important concerns. It is possible that they shared your stance that the condition does not exist. It is possible that they did not have a full understanding of the condition. It is possible that they had never seen a case before, and either were unsure what the condition actually looked like or did not want to take the risk of making a diagnosis they could not be completely comfortable in making. It is possible that they feared that by making the diagnosis they might become targets of litigation and face the pleasure of encountering you or someone like you in an adversarial situation. But I cannot testify that a possibility is a fact. I respectfully reiterate that I am unable to answer the original question as it was asked."

"Very well. Moving along, your report indicated that you found no fault with the treatment plan Dr. Underwood implemented. Does that remain your opinion?"

"Yes."

"And Dr. Underwood relied on the work of Dr. Philips?"

"Yes. Among others."

"Others?"

"Drs. Brody, Grant, Bublekopf, and Rapier."

"Drs. Rapier and Bublekopf are authorities who disagree with the others you named. Both are expert witness I have called upon to testify against her. Is that correct?"

"Yes sir. As she indicated, she was careful to study different and opposing points of view for balance. She really did her homework."

"And you find nothing to fault in her work?"

"No. Her work followed the guidelines of the International Society for the Study of Multiple Personality and Dissociation."

"And you accept those guidelines?"

"I respect them as reasonable."

"And you accept her validation of Melody Jarrett's memories as accurate?"

"I found nothing in the record to demonstrate that she expressed such sentiments to the patient."

"Don't you think that it would have been appropriate for her to caution Ms. Jarrett about the fallibility of human memory?"

"She did."

"Don't you believe the standard of care requires such cautions be stated each time a memory is elicited or processed?"

"What is your name?"

"What do you mean, 'What is your name?'"

"I want to be sure that you remember who you are. I hope you are not impersonating. . ."

"Dr. Jordan," said Bill Mackey, "Please respect the decorum of the situation. I'm sure that Mr. Fuller knows who he is." Mackey looked to the ceiling, his eyes twinkling. He struggled to contain a chuckle, "And he understands that you are saying it is as ridiculous to go through those warnings time after time as it would be to readminister your oath to tell the truth in advance of asking every single question."

"Objection!"

"I will withdraw my comments. Dr. Jordan. Kindly reply to Mr. Fuller in a more straightforward manner."

"My apologies, Mr. Fuller. I should have spoken more plainly. I should have said that to do so would be as unwieldy and superfluous as having the reporter readminister the oath to me prior to my making any answer to any question."

"Off the record!" said Fuller. "You get a point there, Bill. I won't even protest that you were leading the witness. Pretty slick. On the record.

"Dr. Jordan. Kindly explain for the record why you seem relatively unconcerned about the type of cautions I have been inquiring about, cautions that are paramount concerns of many distinguished scholars."

Mackey and Connery looked up and studied Fuller's face. Fuller had morphed from humorous geniality into a poker-faced absence of expression. Linda found herself wondering, *Why such an open question? All the others have been more or less focused?*

"I will do my best, Mr. Fuller. Psychotherapy is dedicated to the alleviation of human suffering. We work to help our patients deal with problematic experiences, thoughts, relationships, and feelings. We try to help them cope with what they cannot change, to help them take a good look at their problematic issues, behaviors, symptoms, and dynamics and work to change what they can. We practice a healing art.

"We are not optimally trained or equipped to discover historical truth. To anticipate what might be your next question, information from documentation, eye witnesses, and concerned others is rarely available, and when it is, often it is suspect. If you expect an honest answer from alleged abusers or witnesses of alleged abuses, you are expecting confessions from those who might stand to lose by making candid admissions, whose own memories could be challenged, and whose recollection and interpretation of facts may seem very different from their different perspectives. We help patients find narratives that makes sense, that represent their truths and offer them a foundation for understanding themselves in the world."

"Do you not think that it is important to know the truth before proceeding?"

"That is rarely possible. Even when allegations are confirmed, in my experience those confirmations usually come up only years after therapy has begun. Philips has done good research about that."

CHAPTER 32

"Mr. Fuller, Dr. Jordan," said Lou Galvin, "I'm going to need a break about here."

Once Lou Galvin had collected Bruce Fuller and Gillian Bullock in the hall, he voiced his concerns.

"Bruce, this Jordan is looking like a problem for us. The more things you ask him about, the more we're tipping our hand. Connery is taking reams of notes, and you can bet he's dissecting our strategy. Same for Gilchrist. You don't know her, but she's a demon researcher. It's clear that Jordan really knows this literature inside and out. He has no respect for anyone's reputation. . . He does his own statistics to check things out. He chews up everything from everyone. He's already made it clear that he's ready to defend Dr. Underwood's work, and that it's not hard to guess that he'll take personal pleasure in dismembering our man Chaudvent, if he gets a chance."

"I wish I could disagree with you, Lou. I guess you noticed that after he trashed Chaudvent on Philips, I kept away from Chaudvent's stuff. I don't think we'll continue much further."

"Excuse me," said Bullock. "Either now, or sometime, help me understand why you're saying that. We come all the way here, and we don't make full use of our time?"

"Good question," Fuller replied. "We're deposing Jordan to anticipate his testimony, to tie him down to facts he may mess up or contradict later on. But when you depose someone in detail, you may take the risk of revealing your strategy, showing him how we may be trying to impeach him later on. Show your hand too openly, and the other team and the witness can see you coming and set up a good ambush. You also take a chance that if the witness is extremely persuasive on a number of points, the judge may be inclined to see that witness as especially credible. Jordan's supposed to be a clinician. But he has a real grasp of what the research really says, not what grant-chasers want you to believe it says. Like you said, Lou, he's unaffected by what other people say it says, and he's a career teacher. He's an expert at communicating ideas clearly to all sorts of people. We could anticipate what Billingsly, Ernest, and Philips might say. But this Jordan is a wild card. He'll be a very dangerous witness unless he can be provoked into shooting off his mouth, and pretty much guaranteed to be convincing unless he can be discredited."

"So, we might gain a step by cutting down what he gets a chance to present to the jury?"

"Right. We can't stop his direct testimony, but we can try to minimize the importance of what he says by making it ho-hum, treating it on cross as if it's no big deal, and not giving him an extra chance to impress the judge."

"Aiming for 'Yeah, but so what?'"

"You've got a smart girl here, Lou! Let's go and finish this thing."

The "girl's" face turned red. . . Not from embarrassment.

* * *

"Just a few more questions, Dr. Jordan. Looking back on your review of Dr. Underwood's diagnosis and treatment of Ms. Melody Jarrett, and the opinions you have stated, I want to leave here confident that I have understood you as well as I possibly can. With regard to how Dr. Underwood made the diagnosis of Dissociative Identity Disorder in Ms. Jarrett, are there any other facts, observations, or concerns that you took into consideration in forming the opinions that you have expressed here today about her diagnostic efforts and conclusions?"

"Not that come to mind, Mr. Fuller."

Fuller made similar inquiries about a number of other subjects and received similar replies. He turned to Galvin and Bullock, who shook their heads "No."

"Thank you, Dr. Jordan. Ms. Gilchrist, Mr. Connery, Mr. Mackey. . . That's it for us."

"That's it for today?" Mackey inquired.

"I think so. Dr. Jordan was concise and to the point."

As the lawyers arranged for the distribution of copies of Jordan's testimony and his right to review and correct the text with the court reporter, Brett Connery turned to Ben.

"When we were talking before, it came up that you'd played a little ball, Dr. Jordan."

"A little. That's right. Came up the end of one season with Detroit. I still go down to spring training for a week every year. . . Assistant hitting coach."

"Every boy's dream. They gave you quite a moniker, didn't they?"

"Yep."

"What do you mean?" asked Galvin.

"My God!" said Fuller. "Are you the famous. . . I should say the infamous. . . Flash Jordan?"

"Was."

"Damn!"

* * *

"What happened?" asked Bill Mackey. "You were supposed to be the next phenom."

"Fell in love, went to Israel, joined the IDF."

"Quite a loss!"

"Hell, no! We're still married."

"That's not the answer I expected. But that wasn't the dep we expected," said Brett.

"I don't get it," said Linda. "It's like they just wanted to get it over."

"Put yourself in their shoes," Brett challenged, "and what do you get?"

"Unhelpful cost/benefit ratio?"

"Spell it out."

"If I read this correctly, there's something going on that makes them worried about what Jordan might say about Chaudvent, and there's something about the way Jordan goes about things that makes them uncomfortable. . ."

"And?"

"In the normal course of reviewing Jordan's report and likely topics on direct, there would be no real reason to question Dr. Jordan about the research plaintiff's experts will rely upon. They're used to bulldozing opposition experts. They were checking out Jordan for two reasons. First, they sense bad blood between Jordan and Chaudvent and between Jordan and Farrier. They wanted to see if they could get a rise out of him. They failed with Chaudvent and they failed with that fracas at the U. Then, they got a pretty clear picture that if they try to use their favorite research to trap Jordan, it may backfire. And they let Jordan say some things about their experts' credibility that could come back and haunt them."

"Well done, Linda. That Fuller is clever. Now he knows that Jordan has Chaudvent's number. He sees he'll have to protect Chaudvent from

Jordan. He's learned he can't count on provoking Jordan on the stand. And, he found that he has to make sure that Jordan won't be allowed to put anything more on the record to make his experts look bad."

"And I thought depositions were to find out what the other side has. . ."

"And you were right. But 'what the other side has' is a lot more than the facts and opinions put in evidence. They knew what to expect from our other witnesses. They needed to know what to expect from Jordan."

"I had another thought," said Linda. "What if our client comes out looking like Snow White? That leaves the only person who slandered the plaintiff as the plaintiff himself. No one else said a bad word to anyone else. Is that what you were setting up, Dr. Jordan?"

Brett turned to Jordan. "Dr. Jordan, you've got to avoid playing Lone Ranger. Why didn't you tell us this little plan of action?"

"Would you believe it didn't come together until he started questioning me? I'm here about diagnosis. Suddenly, he's questioning me about treatment and research. When you guys didn't pull the plug, I went with it."

Bill Mackey seemed to withdraw into himself for a long moment.

"Are you OK, Bill?" Brett asked.

"No. I'm not. Jordan has a point. We were asleep at the switch. But even though we bungled it, it worked in our favor."

Brett gave a sigh of relief. "The next time you decide to meditate, Bill, give us fair warning."

Brett turned to Ben. "Dr. Jordan, you are full of surprises. Lawyers don't like surprises. So, before I get embarrassed or terrified again, what's with you and Chaudvent?"

"That obvious?"

"Yeah." He turned to Bill and Linda, "Obvious?" They shook their heads, "No."

"He attacked me, I defended myself."

"Scientific argument?"

"Street fight."

"Does it bear on this case?"

"Maybe. He attacked me because I was between him and Jay Philips."

"Oh, shit!" said Linda. "Oops! Sorry."

"Who won?" asked Bill Mackey.

CHAPTER 33

Two nights before Jay Philips' deposition, Bruce Fuller received an unexpected call.

"Mr. Fuller, it's Vinnie."

"How's my favorite private eye?"

Vinnie Testaverde knew better than to tangle with Fuller's nonsense. He knew he was number two, or even lower, on Fuller's food chain.

"This may be nothing, but you said to let you know if anything came up about any of the folks involved in that Underwood case. Like I said, it might be nothin'. But I've been tracking a few more folks than you listed, jus' on general principles, you know?"

"OK, you slimy bastard! Stop running up your fee. What have you got?"

"It's about Jay Philips. . ."

When he hung up with Vinnie, Bruce Fuller pulled out a new legal pad and began to write.

* * *

Jay Philips' deposition was taken in the conference room of a small local law firm in his own office building. Bruce Fuller and Gillian Bullock represented Dr. Travers, while Brett Connery and Linda Gilchrist were there for Dr. Underwood. Dr. Philips had placed the available medical records and copies of a number of Melody Jarrett's drawings in front of him.

Fuller began with a brief review of Jay's background and education before moving on to Jay's hospital privileges and faculty appointments.

Jay Philips' initial responses were calm and contained, but within minutes he became tense, fidgety, and distraught. He seemed to lose focus.

"You have been on the faculty of some very fine medical schools in the past. Are you currently on the faculty of any medical school?"

"No."

"Have you applied for any faculty positions recently?"

"Yes."

"Despite your many scholarly publications, did they decline your application or applications?"

"Yes."

Fuller took Philips through his dismissal from the paid academic staff of one school, and from the voluntary teaching staff of a second.

"Dr. Philips, were you given any explanation for these actions?"

"Yes."

"Could you state those explanations?"

"I was told that major figures on both faculties did not agree with my thinking about trauma, memory, and the dissociative disorders."

Sweat broke out on Jay Philips' forehead. Bruce Fuller remained silent as Jay mopped his forehead.

"Yes, it is very painful to be rejected and repudiated by those you wish would give you their respect. Do you need a break, Dr. Philips?"

Jay started to speak, but words would not come. He shook his head "No."

"Let the record show that the deponent has nodded his head 'No.' Dr. Philips, in a deposition, it is important for every reply to be spoken aloud so that the court reporter can document it. Although you have indicated that you do not need a break, I am requesting one on my own initiative. If you are having difficulty speaking or otherwise uncomfortable, we will be glad to reschedule this deposition."

Brett and Linda shepherded Jay to a private alcove.

"Dr. Philips, I'm getting worried about you. Are you really OK? It's not a good idea to continue if you are unwell."

"I-I didn't sleep well l-last night. It will pa-pass. L-Let me get a drink of water."

"Dr. Philips?" said Linda.

"Sometimes I stammer. Bear with me." Jay walked to a restroom, tripping slightly as he walked. Brett caught Linda's eyes. "Oh, shit!" he muttered. "Oh, shit!"

* * *

"Back on the record," said Fuller, "and hoping you are feeling better."

Philips said nothing.

"I'd like to move on, if we may, to your observations on the treatment of Melody Jarrett by Dr. Joan Underwood. You have reviewed the case?"

"Y-yes."

"Was it your opinion, your professional opinion, that the care rendered to Ms. Melody Jarrett by Dr. Joan Underwood met or exceeded the standard of care for the treatment of her psychiatric disorders?"

"Yes."

Fuller asked a dozen questions about specific aspects of the treatment. In each instance, Philips approved of Dr. Underwood's efforts.

"Dr. Underwood appears to have been highly influenced by your contributions to this field. Is that correct?"

"Yes."

"So, we would not be surprised to find you voicing such approval, because doing so defends and asserts the rightness of your ideas, and is quite self-serving?"

"Objection!" said Brett.

"Grounds, counselor?"

"Improper form, provocative and argumentative. I am instructing my client not to answer this question."

"I disagree with your characterization of my remarks, but in the interests of completing this deposition expeditiously and with due decorum, I will withdraw my inquiry."

Fuller sighed with overdone drama. He turned to another yellow pad, zebraed with questions penned in bold, broad black strokes.

"Dr. Philips. I am trying to ascertain your own insights into the regard in which your work is held by your colleagues. I would like to read you the names of several medical schools whose departments of psychiatry are held in high regard. I would like you to tell me the names of the professors at each school who endorse and support your work, whether in whole or in part, whether they are clinicians or researchers. Rather than repeat the entire inquiry for each institution, I hope it will be acceptable for me to simply read off the schools' names, one at a time, and give you an opportunity to respond. I have not included any schools with which any of the co-authors of your papers are affiliated. May I begin?"

Jay Philips was perspiring heavily. He looked up at Bruce Fuller, and then away from him, toward the floor, then up to Brett Connery.

"I'd like a moment to confer with Dr. Philips," said Brett. "Dr. Philips, Ms. Gilchrist, let's go out in the hall."

Once in the hall, Brett turned to Jay.

"Dr. Philips, I'm getting worried. Are you all right?"

Philips nodded.

"I don't know enough about academic infighting to know how to advise you to handle this."

"M-most people are either confused by all this ruckus or don't give a damn. You know almost everyone in the field has been attacked, and not too many people want to hang out with a living target. I know a lot more people value my work than are comfortable saying so. I know there are lot of places where you get a lot of crap if you make dissociative disorder diagnoses besides Depersonalization Disorder, and even more where recovered memories of abuse are always considered suspect, if not wrong, from the get-go. And I don't know what people think unless they communicate it to me in one way or another. Plus, there is no way I could list the names of all of the medical schools in the country, let alone know who is where. And a lot of the folks in the field are Ph.D. psychologists."

"Got it," said Brett.

* * *

"Mr. Fuller, my client has advised me that the only available honest responses to your inquiries that he can produce will consist largely of repetitions of the words, 'I don't know.' Feel free to proceed."

"Very well, Mr. Connery.

"Dr. Philips. Rather than expend unnecessary time and effort, I will ask you to affirm the essence of Mr. Connery's explanations of your stance, because he cannot answer my questions for you. Is it true, as a generalization, that you are unable to go down a list of America's medical schools, exclusive of those with which your co-authors are or have been affiliated, and indicate the members of their faculties of psychiatry who endorse your work and your treatment methods?"

"Yes."

"Now, moving in another direction, would you be able to indicate which of those schools have faculty members who are critical of your work?"

"Only in terms of those who have published critical articles, and only then after a literature search."

"Nonresponsive."

"Mr. Fuller is correct, Dr. Philips. He asked a yes or no question. If you can answer it as asked, please do so."

"The answer is no."

"Would you be surprised if I told you that the number is not inconsiderable?"

"I'm sorry, Mr. Fuller. I have no way of knowing what you mean by 'not inconsiderable.'"

Jay Philips was sweating again. He mopped his brow. He took off his glasses to wipe them, but his handkerchief was so wet. . . Brett offered Jay his own.

"Good point. Strike the question.

"To continue. . . It seems that despite your rather determined efforts to communicate your point of view, it remains quite unclear whether more than a handful of individuals have endorsed them. That kind of rejection must be very painful."

Jay seemed to be blinking back some tears.

"Final question. Dr. Philips, how does your family. . . Ooops! Sorry. I owe an apology to all present, especially to Dr. Philips. That's from another matter. I don't know why it is mixed up with the Underwood file. Reporter, kindly strike that question. I feel like such a fool.

"Hmm. Thank you, Dr. Philips. I think that will be it for today. We can stop here."

CHAPTER 34

Brett and Linda conferred briefly with Jay Philips, who hung his head and made only the briefest replies to their questions. The little man seemed to be sinking into despair. Finally, Brett said, "Well, we had a rough day, Dr. Philips. They really got after you. I can't imagine what they were trying to achieve. They didn't learn a thing."

Walking to their rental car, Brett Connery began to open his mouth as if he were going to speak, only to shake his head and remain silent. Finally, he managed, "Whatever he's got, I think I'm catching it." They trudged in silence.

As he turned the key in the rental's ignition, Brett finally broke the silence.

"I don't get it."

"I don't either," Linda confessed. "That whole thing was so weird! I don't have any idea what happened back there."

"Without raising his voice, without breaking the rules, though he bent them with ingenuity, Bruce Fuller launched a barely disguised *Blitzkrieg*. Anyone who reads that dep could come away thinking that Jay Philips is a total outsider, a complete loser without a friend in the world. And Philips, who's supposed to be indestructible, looked like he lost it. The man was sweating like a pig. He was tearing up over and over again. Fuller was delivering a message: 'I'll take you through the bowels of every humiliating rejection you've ever faced'. And we have to take that 'slip' at the end as a warning. He's up to dirty tricks."

"But he was so different with Dr. Jordan. . ."

"True, but Boy Scout Lou Galvin was there to keep him in check. Dealing with Jordan. . . Jordan stays cool under pressure. No. Fuller saw he was actually losing ground with Jordan, and Jordan's hard to attack, except for?"

"I don't know."

"Yes, you do. You just haven't realized it. Jordan relies on Philips' work."

"You mean, discredit Philips as a beachhead for impugning the testimony of everyone who's cited him?"

"Uh-huh. And that includes everyone we've got, from Billingsly to Ernst and on. . ."

"OK. I can see that strategy. Now that you tell me. But what about Philips himself?"

"He's toast. I don't know what's going on, but I'm afraid Philips has gone to pieces, Fuller has his number, or both. He's toast. I'll think it over, but if it were my call, I'd cut my losses and just pay him for services rendered."

"That would be kicking Philips when he's down."

"Don't think I don't know it. And I'm not one of those lawyers who loves to play the hard-ass. But our duty is to our client, Joan Underwood. Every decision we make has to be based on what serves Joan Underwood best."

"I'm not happy."

"We don't get paid to be happy. We get paid to make Joan Underwood, M.D., less unhappy."

"Look! In the park. That's Philips sitting by the pond, isn't it?"

"God! Not even the ducks. . . He looks like the loneliest man in the world. Maybe he is."

* * *

Bruce Fuller congratulated himself. He wanted to boast about the "dark ops" moves he was making behind the backs of his co-counsels and experts. But. . . that would be telling. His celebration would have to be very private indeed.

"This was a good day for us. I could use a drink, Gillian. Are you OK to drive us back to the airport?"

"I think I can handle that burdensome responsibility."

"I know. I remember how frustrated I felt when I was in your shoes. You prepare just as if you were the first chair, you imagine how you'd handle the situation, how you'd do this and that. . . and then you sit on your hands. Sometimes you admire the first chair, and sometimes you wonder, how could he be so dense? And if the first chair makes a sudden change of course, you're caught leaning in the wrong direction, and you're wondering 'Who's on first?' Plus, at times you get treated like a lackey when the big dogs get a little full of themselves. Like now."

"Thanks."

"Like I said, I remember."

"It's more than getting caught leaning the wrong way. I'd like to say something that at least sounds smart, but I'm so lost I feel like I fell down some rabbit-hole. Or maybe into a worm-hole. . . What is happening?"

"Ah! It is not what is happening, grasshopper. It is what I am working to make happen."

"A strategy?"

"Precisely. Our system of law is based on adversarial processes. It's the great-great-great grandchild of trial by combat."

"You mean. My God! You were trying to destroy Dr. Philips?"

"Close. To defeat him, to at least weaken him. More like the picadors and bandoleros do a job on the bull to set things up for the matador. I didn't need to hear him go on and on about Underwood. Underwood followed his treatment recommendations, so his answers about treatment would be predictable. If this goes to trial, I want him to walk into court already intimidated, knowing that he and his work are completely disrespected, and knowing in his heart that he'll be facing public humiliation in front of people who already know he's admitted that hardly anyone who's anyone buys his nonsense."

"But hasn't he. . ."

"Yeah. He's tough. I actually admire the little SOB. But he's taken so many hits that he's battle-weary, punchy. He had a bad day, but I think he sees that he can't take much more. Maybe he knows he's going to crack if he keeps getting hit. And today, we saw him flinch. That's worth celebrating."

"But we'd reviewed your line of questioning. And you went in a completely different direction."

"That comes with experience, and intuition. A little bit down the road, and you'll be bewildering some young associate yourself," said Fuller. As Gillian's eyes widened with amazement, Bruce Fuller savored his favorite beverage long before they reached the bar. . . an ambrosial sip of the admiration of an attractive woman. He felt the first stirrings of carnal temptation. . . *Down, boy! Can't afford a mess.*

CHAPTER 35

Shocked, numb, moist-eyed, and sweat-stained, Jay Philips was amazed that he'd made it back to his office. The small wet spots on his shirt and slacks caught him by surprise. *I didn't know I was crying! I didn't even feel the tears. I made a fool of myself!*

When he finally managed to drag himself to his feet, his body felt stuck in slow motion. He picked up the bagged lunch he couldn't eat the day before, and never would. He shuffled across the street and found a bench by the pond. *Might as well feed the ducks. Why is it so hard to walk? Did I have a silent MI? Am I just waiting to fall over? Am I dying? I woke up today thinking my life was over. Then I convinced myself that maybe, just maybe, I could prove to myself that I still. . . But Travers' lawyers treated me like a useless piece of shit. . . Underwood's? What good were they? What's left of me?*

Going after me in a deposition? They usually save that for the trial. . . It's got to mean something. Throw me off balance? Make me look bad? Get a chance to put all that crap on the record? They did a darn good job of making me feel like a loser.

It's almost as if they knew my life was coming apart! Like they knew there was blood in the water. . . That last remark. Ooops? I doubt it.

Jay's feathered fan club rushed through the water to inspect his offerings. One or two bites, a few sharp quacks, and they turned away. *Even the ducks have given up on me. . . Fruit of the poisonous shrink? Smart birds! If it's connected to me, it can't be good.*

Jay put his fingers to his forehead. He pressed as hard as he could, and began to rub his brow in two widening circles. *I knew I was losing her. I knew my life was circling the drain. But I never thought things would end this way. And I never thought anything could break me. It was only a year ago. . .*

* * *

They were 23 when she took him to her special place, Sea Street Beach, where she spent the happiest days of her childhood. They were 25 when they wed, 48 years ago. But now the legs that once raced toward the sand, the tiny hands that happily carried a red pail and shovel, the strong and supple arms of the lover who pulled him along. . . Time brought unwanted gifts: an unsteady gait, and clumsy knotted fingers. Their golden wedding anniversary was two years away. . . If they made it.

Just last summer they decided against driving straight through to the Cape. It made sense to break their journey. After all, before going north, they'd dipped south from New Jersey to visit her sister's family in Maryland, so they faced a much longer drive. Jay took the first shift, from south of Baltimore to the Vince Lombardi Service Area on the New Jersey Turnpike, just before New York City. There she took over to complete the first leg of their trip, to a hotel in Connecticut. She was at the wheel when they reached their exit. At the foot of the ramp off 95, they had to make a left turn across a divided four-lane road.

"That's our left," he said.

She began to cross the road and stopped.

"I don't see a left."

"It's there. Keep going another few feet."

Cars were coming off the interstate, their drivers already anticipating the turn. Motorists screeched to a halt behind them or whizzed by, swerving to avoid a collision. Their car was blocking traffic on the two near lanes before the barrier dividing the road they had to cross. Horns began to blare.

She started to turn toward the second of the two near lanes, into oncoming traffic.

"No! Jesus! No! You'll get us killed! Straight! Keep going straight!"

"Don't yell at me. I still don't see any other turn."

A shock of air rocked their car back and forth as another car barely missed them.

"Go straight!"

"Stop screaming! I don't see. . ."

"Go straight! For the love of God! Go!"

She crept a few feet forward, and finally began a painfully slow turn onto the other side of the divided road. Their car shivered as a van missed them by inches.

"You don't have to yell at me!"

"Let's get there alive, in one piece!" *My God! I'm shaking!*

At the hotel, he'd overheard her on the phone, complaining about him to someone. He'd come to think of her finding fault with him as part of their bed-time ritual.

But now things were changing, from bad to worse. Her complaints took on a more accusatory tone, and maybe, just maybe, her memory was beginning to slip. So much of their life was just a predictable routine. . . Things just kept on keeping on. But watching her face a new situation in a new place? For the first time Jay realized his wife might not be as together as he'd thought.

He took a quick walk. *I'm losing her. Whether she's losing it or just wants to be rid of me. . . The only woman who ever. . .* His eyes filled. Sadness and guilt fought with frustration and shame. *Our friends are dying right and left. I can't lose her! The only woman who loved me enough to build a life with me. . . Not a perfect life. . . No way! But ours! And I'm losing her, bit by bit.*

It was late. . . Time to face the unwelcome night of an unwanted day that left him torn to shreds, powerless to evade the grim vision of an already crumbling future slowly, no, rapidly falling apart. He fingered the smooth anonymous surface of his magnetized room key.

Good lord! What's our room number?

* * *

And then this this summer, this woman, so brittle, so bitter, so critical, and so much a part of his life, someone he feared was on the way to needing help and care, had reared up, slapped him with a divorce suit, and emptied out their house while he was undergoing a colonoscopy less than 72 hours ago. She'd left him groggy and unaccompanied at the imaging center, forced to fend for himself. Later he'd discover she'd raced to catch a flight to Las Vegas and a quickie divorce. Before day's end, he would learn that while he was coming out of anesthesia, he had signed a form he'd thought was related to identifying the possessions he was retrieving from his locker. In fact, it was an agreement not to contest her divorce. That was Monday. He was served with papers on Wednesday. Now it was Thursday.

* * *

Jay looked up. Across the pond, the ducks were chasing what must have been better bread crusts thrown by three commercial-cute little girls in bright shorts and tops while a pretty soccer mom read a paperback. A teenage couple sat close together on a bench, their young love full of promise, theirs just beginning as he had to steel himself to face what could no longer be changed, and truly begin to mourn the love he'd thought would last forever.

An unwelcome thought invaded his mind. *Did Fuller know what's been happening to me? Was he playing some nasty mind game with that 'Ooops!', designed to break me, to get me so shook up I'll fumble even more than usual? No,* he tried to reassure himself. *That's paranoid thinking. . . That could never be. . . Or could it?*

CHAPTER 36

The die was cast. Linda drew the dirty work.

"We still want your expertise on board, Dr. Philips, but. . ."

"What does that mean?"

Linda had rehearsed her next move over and over, drawing on the all the savvy and advice Bill Mackey and Brett Connery had offered. Everyone had seemed to think it would work, except her sister, Eve.

"I don't get it. All three of you are lying to yourselves. You're trying to talk yourselves into what you want to believe. Jay Philips will see through that in a millisecond. So would any fifth-grader. And you'll have hurt his feelings in a really horrible way," said Eve. "Awful! It's a bonehead move. Just tell him the plain truth. Cut out the bullshit and treat him with respect."

Linda did what she was told to do. She took her best shot.

"We are looking for you to be an additional expert witness who's been deposed, but whom we may or may not present. Someone with special wisdom who can go over every minute of testimony and advise us day by day about where things seem to be headed."

"So, you want to pick my brain without having to endure my charm and be tainted by my stellar reputation. Will I be allowed take a walk outside after dark? Off leash? No thanks."

"Dr. Philips!"

* * *

"Dr. Jordan? Bill Mackey here. I hate to impose, but I'm facing a dilemma and I need to tap your wisdom."

"What can I do for you?"

"We've brought Matthew Grant on board."

"He's a good man. I didn't know he did forensic work."

"I'm glad you vouch for him. But that's not the problem. Linda Gilchrist called Dr. Philips to discuss revising his role in Dr. Underwood's defense."

"No way that went well."

"I'll ask you to explain how you knew that some other time. But the immediate crisis is that our Ms. Gilchrist seems to have touched a raw nerve. Dr. Philips hung up on her."

Ben swallowed *Good for him!* and gave a loud sigh. "OK. What are you asking of me?"

"Well, I'd like some advice. We have to decide whether to cut him loose and pay him for services rendered, or try to restore our relationship with him."

"I can't begin to help you decide on your strategy. But I can give you some advice that may help you make a decision."

"I'd like to hear it."

"If you don't have Agatha Christie's *The Third Girl* at hand, get ahold of it immediately and read the first several chapters. I'll be by the phone."

* * *

One hour later Bill Mackey called again. “Thanks,” he said. Then he called Linda Gilchrist and instructed her to rearrange her schedule for the next day.

CHAPTER 37

Around 2:30 the next afternoon, Jay Philips was fighting the lethargy of an after-lunch low. He walked out into what he expected would be an empty waiting room, with nothing more on his mind than a coffee run. The woman who rose from one of his well-worn chairs was a knock-out. . . Blond, athletic, dressed to kill, and considerably taller than he. . . The kind of woman who had never given him a moment's consideration when he was a younger man, and never would. Her cornflower blue eyes glittered a bit too much. *She's almost in tears!*

It took him a moment to realize that he was face-to-face with Linda Gilchrist. *My God! The day of that deposition I was so messed up. . . I must have been looking at the floor. I hardly remember her. . . But I remember the floor.*

In turn, Linda beheld a short, balding, non-descript man, over-weight, in rumpled slacks, a shapeless jacket and a poorly-matched out of fashion tie, eyes wide with surprise behind smudged, thick, dark-framed glasses.

"Can I help you?"

"Dr. Philips. I came to apologize." She handed him her card. "Linda Gilchrist from Mackey Markham & Wilder."

"Ah yes, I remember. Wasn't it something about playing the title role in *The Elephant Man*? Have you come to fit my head for a burlap sack?"

Linda took a deep breath. "I'm so sorry. My legal colleagues advised me on how to put things and either I made a mess or it or maybe our whole approach was off base. My sister's a psychiatrist. . . She's met you, by the way. . . She warned me you'd see that approach as one hell of an insult and chew me a new one."

"Not Eve Gilchrist, by any chance?"

"Yes. She's my sister."

"Hell of a clinician, that Eve. Consider your new one chewed. Lucky you. . . The shit flowed downhill. Let's get some coffee and have a very frank and uncomfortable conversation."

* * *

They took seats at the local Starbucks, and Linda began.

"So, Mr. Mackey, my boss, called Dr. Jordan. He told him to read the beginning of an Agatha Christie book, *The Third Girl.* Do you know it?"

"Yeah, I know it. Ben Jordan devours mysteries. He's crazy about Hercule Poirot. I've read all Christie's stuff, too. For different reasons. Do you know why I read Agatha Christie?"

"I guess it's not just 'cause you like mysteries. . . Right?"

"Right. In 1926 Agatha Christie disappeared for 11 days. She'd had it with her husband's screwing around. He fell in love with this other lady who was nuts for golf like he was. She pulled a disappearing act to bring him in line, or payback, I guess. Who knows? She left her car and some things in a place and a way that suggested something awful had taken place.

"Well, it backfired. She snuck off to a swanky hotel and registered under the last name of hubby's mistress. She figured she'd be found in a couple of days and either shock hubby into good behavior or at least take a piece out of his hide. But nobody found her. Well, actually, a number of people did, but. . . Remember, it was a different era. People recognized her, but they respected her privacy and held their tongues. They didn't rat her out. Wouldn't be proper, you know? Suicide or foul play was considered. Some thought it was some kind of publicity stunt. Her dashing husband, not the brightest of men, hypothesized she was suffering amnesia.

"So, for a week and a half, police and volunteers were searching for her all over the UK. Finally, some guys playing in the band at the hotel who'd recognized her thought they really had to call the cops. Enter the police. They brought her husband to the scene. It was an awful mess. Her husband, probably in order to save face and hide his affair, kept up the amnesia hypothesis. Agatha Christie was mortified. Everything had blown up in her face. She compounded the mess by accepting hubby's nonsense and doubling down. Claimed she'd been in an alternate personality, one with the mistress's family name. She never recovered from the scandal of her husband's betrayal, their divorce, and the disgrace surrounding this episode. She even left it out of her autobiography. Spent most of the rest of her life in relative isolation. Her books contain dozens of references to amnesia, to one person passing for another, disguises, and all sorts of trickery, and you can see how the poor woman keeps looking for a happy ending."

"How do you mean?"

"You've read some Christie? Putting aside the maudlin stuff Dame Agatha wrote under a pseudonym, have you ever noticed how often Poirot takes as much interest in bringing young lovers together as he does in solving crimes?"

"No. I never did."

"Well, Agatha Christie was preoccupied with love, and with how to cope with her betrayal. She got a double dose, courtesy of both of her husbands. She was brought up at home by an imaginative mother and spent a lot of time in fantasy play. She always handled her imagination better than her reality. An Israeli researcher I know would call her a pathological daydreamer. She's a case study of normal dissociation going out of control and intruding into reality testing."

"So, back to why I'm here. . ."

"Patience. In *The Third Girl*, a young woman comes to the great Hercule Poirot for help. But she at first glance the famous detective is no more an old, short, round, unimpressive, weirdly-dressed foreigner, not in the best of shape, and she walks out. Poirot suffers a brief existential crisis. He wonders whether he's over-the-hill, whether time has passed him by. Whether he's stayed too long at the fair and that in fact, no one has any confidence in him any more. . . . With some sense slapped back into him, he rises to the occasion. Usual ingenious ending.

"Ms. Gilchrist, whether I'm too beat up, too weird, or too over-the-hill is your firm's call. Frankly, your opinion and your colleagues' opinions mean nothing to me. If I conducted myself in accord with what other people's think of me, I would have shot myself after making a public confession of charlatanism and social unacceptability. All I ask from those who consider me a useless piece of shit is a modicum of tact and courtesy. And if that isn't freely given, I'll take it."

"So I've learned."

"Why are we sitting here?"

Linda looked toward a clock on the wall. "Do you have another patient?"

"What I have is irrelevant. What you have is ten minutes, max."

"Then I won't waste any time with further apologies. Bluntly, your deposition performance called into question how you would do in front of a jury."

"Understood."

"When Matthew Grant became available, we wanted to bring him on board."

"Understood."

"We're too heavy with experts. You know that sometimes in mid-trial an attorney will decide that the jury is getting overloaded, and cancel the appearance of a first-rate expert out of fear that the jury will get bored, lose interest, resent spending still more time in court. . . You know."

"Understood."

"Mr. Mackey is not sure whether he will want to present you as a witness during the trial. We'll have to see how that goes. But he wants you on scene to review every day's testimony in order to help us plan for the next step. Before you react, consider. . ."

"That's a hell of a big nut. Witness fees for one or two days vs. maybe two weeks at the same rate. Is he sure?"

"He's sure."

"Well, I'm not that difficult an ogre. Put soft rags, clean water, and cockroach-free porridge in my cell, and, for your sister's sake, I may say yes."

CHAPTER 38

"We've been friends since high school, Bill. I wish I were in as good shape as you are. I really can't find anything but a little anemia. All your other lab studies are perfect. Your calcium is higher than last time, but it's still within the range of normal. In all likelihood the iron and vitamins will fix you up, if you slow down a bit and let yourself recharge your batteries. Neither one of us is getting any younger."

"I don't see you slowing down any, Charley."

"We doctors are great when it comes to lying to ourselves. We talk a good game, but we're like signposts, Bill. We point you in the right direction, but we don't always move down the right road ourselves."

"OK. I'll take the pills. I'll come in for shots. My wife told me to ask this. What kind of anemia do I have?"

"Well, I'm not quite sure. Lots of common kinds you can tell just looking at the cells under the microscope. But your cells look fine. We'll check your lab studies in a month and see where you are. In all likelihood your anemia will be better, you'll have more oxygen getting where it needs to go, and you'll be feeling just fine."

After Bill Mackey left Charley Williams' office, his secretary buzzed.

"Dr. Williams? Ms. Pierce is next. Examining room three."

"Connie, please walk back and tell her I'll be there in five minutes. I have to look over the Mackey chart."

Charley Williams was a worrier. The odds were that Bill Mackey was strong as a horse, that some transient something had knocked down his blood count; it would rebound, and Charley would never know why. Bill Mackey's blood cells were not smaller than normal, or larger than normal. That argued against low iron or common major vitamin deficiencies. But countless legions of things can lower a blood count. *Let's wait and see. It's probably nothing.* The old medical school adage cautioning against jumping to exotic diagnoses consoled him: *When you hear hoofbeats in the hall, don't assume it's a zebra.*

Bill's calcium level bothered him. Higher than last time, but still within normal limits. Charley glanced toward his office copy of Harrison's *Textbook of Internal Medicine*. Parathyroid? Something wrong in the bone? *If those heme studies don't bounce back. . . We'll see next time.*

* * *

"I've been feeling a little off," Bill Mackey told his old college roommate, "but my doctor thinks I'll be back to myself real soon. I'm still thinking I should let someone else handle the case."

"Glad to hear it, Bill. I hear you, I see the complications, and you might be right. But you know she won't consider anyone else, and you know how hard-headed she can be. There's no one else we'd trust as much. I hate to burden you with this, Bill. But I'm begging."

"I hear you. I just hope when this is all over. . . Ah! What can I say? Brett Connery and our young associate Linda Gilchrist are first rate."

"She made a good impression, and you vouch for Connery. Bill, we trust you."

After Bill Mackey said good-bye to his old friend, he sat a few minutes in silence.

"Is something wrong, Bill?" asked his wife. "You look like. . . Well, I don't know."

"Just something upsetting about one of our new cases. Nothing we can't deal with. Just a little messier than I thought."

"Why don't you ask Sally or Jeff to handle it. Charley says he thinks things will turn around, but until they do. . ."

"I'm on top of it. They are not. It's nothing too demanding, just unexpected."

"Promise?"

"Promise."

Bill Mackey could still count the times he had lied to his wife of forty years on the fingers of one hand. But this burden he could not share. *I've had hundreds of cases where more was at stake for the client. I've never had a case where more was at stake for me.*

CHAPTER 39

"I'm beginning to get a feel for depositions, but there's still so much I have to learn. I'd like to go to Philadelphia and observe some of the Hatfield trial, especially the beginning. There's a lot to learn about these false memory lawsuits."

"My first thought," said Bill Mackey, "is that since you've already taken that workshop, your going to Philadelphia costs us more billable hours and outgoing expense than I can justify. It seems to offer us very little in exchange."

"Bill, you and Brett both know I don't have much courtroom experience. Hardly any. And I'm not likely to get much more between now and the Underwood trial, at which I imagine most of the time I'll be sitting there like a bump on a log. If I don't know how things work in the real world, anything I might try to contribute might be off-base or worse.

"My ignorance could compromise my usefulness to you and Brett, and to our client. I want to see how a case like this develops. I want to see these folks in action. I'll take vacation time and pay my own way. My friend Beth tells me that they've just empaneled a jury for Bob Hatfield's trial. Then there's the weekend. Opening arguments begin

Monday. Both the plaintiff's attorney and Jonathan Lauder are famous for their opening arguments. I want to be there."

"What about my opening arguments?"

"I hear they're terrific, but you cut my orders. I've never seen you in action. I'm too young to go to the grown-ups' movies without permission."

Bill sat quietly for a moment. He looked out the window, sighed, and looked to Brett, who met his glance with a surprisingly gentle smile.

"You know, Linda," said Bill. "You're right. You've been such an incredible workhorse that we've failed to mentor you about litigation. It's all your fault, though. You're the best legal researcher we've ever had. It's almost painful to let you step away from what makes our lives easier and remember you're also here to build a career of your own. Go. You're covered. Any problem with that, Brett?"

"None whatsoever."

"But I. . ."

"Get out of here," said Brett, "before the big guy changes his mind and we chain you to your desk. Scoot!"

CHAPTER 40

Linda made her way to Philadelphia's City Hall. Bypassing the elevators, she took the wide stairways to the third floor. She found herself facing a central atrium. With no directory in sight, she made a mental coin toss, and turned right into a rogue wave of lawyers, litigants, city workers, and courtroom personnel.

Almost every man in the place is checking me out! Did I just walk into a pig farm? Linda cursed the color rising to her cheeks, knowing it made her even more appealing to the opposite sex. She turned away from everyone who approached her and refused to ask anyone for directions. She had worked her way almost 360 degrees around the central atrium before she located Judge Danziger's courtroom immediately to the left of the stairway she had taken.

An attractive African-American woman carrying a Gucci briefcase arrived at the courtroom door at the same moment.

"Chill, sister. I see the steam rising out of your ears. Once they've seen you a few times they calm down. . . a little."

"Thanks. Is that typical of Philadelphia men?"

"Not all of them act like drunken Eagles' fans. . . But almost."

"Are you here for the Hatfield trial?"

"Sort of. I'm a summer intern at Morgan McGuire. Half the summer interns at the downtown firms are coming to see Randolph St. James and Jonathan Lauder make their opening arguments. Serena Clark."

"Linda Gilchrist. You? A summer intern? You're kidding."

"Don't let the Gucci fool you. I'm just a plebe around here. Law is my second time around. I was a nurse at Jefferson. I married a doctor. A few kids later I was ready to go back to work, but I didn't like where I saw my profession going. Looked around, applied to law school, and here I am. You?"

"Up from Virginia. My firm has a case like this. . ." They heard a surge of loud noise.

"That's probably the second tidal wave, the summer interns. Let's get the good seats. The ones that aren't broken."

As they settled themselves, Linda asked, "Before we have to be quiet, do you know why this case is being tried here? Hatfield doesn't practice in Philadelphia."

"Christine and Jonathan aren't sure, but they have three ideas. First, the plaintiff is from here, and well-connected, while Hatfield has no local connections. Since he spoke to her and did some phone sessions after she returned from his program, the court held that action could be brought in either location. Second, Philly is known as a plaintiff's town. . . And generous. Third, Hatfield is stuck here alone over a thousand miles from his family and friends. Maybe they figure that will soften him up and he'll be ready to concede to a big settlement and go home."

"What do you think will happen?"

"Let me quote that great sage, Mr. T. 'I pity the fool who underestimates Jonathan and Christine.'"

"Met them a while back. That good?"

"You tell me this afternoon. You tell me."

* * *

Between overhearing the last-minute discussions between Judge Miriam Danziger and the attorneys and the discrete whispers of her new friend, Serena Clark, Linda managed to pick out the major players. In turn, she filled in Serena on the individuals she recognized from Baltimore.

Randolph St. James, the out of town malpractice specialist, stood to make the plaintiff's opening argument. At the plaintiff's table, Rex Singer, the plaintiff's local attorney, sat at the end closest to the center aisle, with co-plaintiff Noreen Cross at his side. Her father, a multimillionaire and decorated military hero, sat alongside his daughter. Beyond him, Renée Widmark, a rising star, completed the plaintiffs' side. At the defendant's table, Jonathan sat directly across the aisle from Rex Singer. He and Christine flanked Robert Hatfield, with Beth alongside Christine at the far end. Seamus O'Sullivan, Hatfield's personal attorney, sat among those observing the trial.

Anita Ausminder, the Executive Director of the Family Justice Project, planted herself in the center of the first row of the audience and folded her arms across her chest. A cadaverously pale and thin man who looked like an undertaker and might have been her husband sat by her side. Linda recognized several of the FJP board members from Baltimore. They all seemed very excited.

"They've been after Hatfield and Philips for years. They even said so on their website," said Serena.

"They're so revved up. Like sharks at a feeding frenzy."

"They're hoping that this courtroom turns into the Colosseum, and Emperor Danziger goes 'thumbs down.'"

CHAPTER 41

Randolph St. James wore a perfectly tailored suit that screamed Saville Row. Randolph St. James wore a Turnbull and Asser tie worth more than many suits. Randolph St. James wore Alfred Sargent shoes custom crafted to grace his nimble feet. Randolph St. James wore an attitude a powerful prince might adopt to persuade a conclave of Christian noblemen to gather and arm their fiefdoms from serf to knight and march on Jerusalem to reclaim it from its Islamic occupiers.

Linda watched in awe as member after member of the jury seemed to fall under his spell, swept along by his rhetoric, embracing St. James' narrative of the case. . . One juror, a second, and then a third began to nod their assent with every point he made. It was if each and every individual was becoming deeply engaged in a profound and personal relationship with Randolph St. James.

In spite herself, Linda felt herself yielding to Randolph St. James's arguments as he told the sad story of Bob Hatfield's patient, Noreen Cross. He explained how Noreen had first sought help for anxiety and depression, but failed to respond to treatment. Neither psychotherapy or medications brought relief. As the years passed, Noreen's despair grew deeper and more profound. Finally, she was referred for electroconvulsive treatment, "shock treatment."

Midway through her second series of treatments, Noreen's memory for recent events became hazy. She began to suffer horrible nightmares. . . A man in uniform was dragging a little girl into a room and mistreating her. As her post-shock confusion cleared, a systematic year-by-year review of her memory revealed memory gaps. Some encompassed whole years of her childhood. Whenever psychiatrists had tried to inquire about the missing time, Noreen dissolved into tears. She insisted that she did not know why she was crying. Several specialists down the road one interviewer noticed that Noreen's description of her childhood life at home with her parents was very different from the account she had given to earlier interviewers. Noreen seemed agitated and confused. When he asked her what the matter was, she denied being "Noreen," and claimed to have a different name. She asked, "Who are you? Where am I? What am I doing here?" A few consultations later Noreen Cross found herself admitted to the dissociative disorders program directed by Bob Hatfield. While there, far from her ostensibly devoted parents, she claimed that her father had violated her from childhood through her college years.

"And there, in an atmosphere that encouraged patients to distrust and defame those who loved them the most and whom they once had loved the most," said St. James, "where every patient's memory was contaminated day in, day out by the tainted memories of others subjected to the same misleading influences, confabulations germinated and were pushed to full flower. Under the expert misdirection of Robert Hatfield, Ms. Cross had come to believe that her father had raped her for the better part of two decades, and that the peaceful and loving façade of her family was no more than the camouflage for a chamber of untold horrors."

St. James summarized the scientific literature that he believed confirmed his assertions and attacked those who did not share his interpretation of its findings. He spoke with the fervor of a Grand Inquisitor challenging the misguided beliefs of the heretics he was entitled (Nay! Obligated!) to burn at the stake in order to save their immortal souls.

"And look what harm these thoughtless people have imposed on solid, salt of the earth, American families! In one family, the daughter's despair has been deepened, her mind twisted and befuddled, and her relationships with her loved ones thrown into disrepair. And further, her father, a decorated military hero and the chairman of the board of a major business enterprise, has been so tormented and humiliated by unfounded and false allegations that he has suffered the loss of his ability to enjoy the intimacy of the marital bed. Both he and his wife have suffered a painful and anguishing loss of consortium."

St. James pulled an expensive silk square from the breast pocket of his suit, and touched it to his eyes. His body heaved as if he were stifling a sob. When he began to speak again, his cheeks were stained with tears.

"The man whose family and personal life Dr. Robert Hatfield destroyed is a member of what we call our greatest generation. And how has he been rewarded as he enters the golden years he so much deserves to enjoy? A charlatan who is sitting in this courtroom today destroys his daughter's mental health, rips apart the family he loved so much, and destroys his peace of mind and the sanctity of his marital bed. . ." Two jurors were wiping their eyes.

This man is amazing! He's winning their hearts! No! He's won their hearts! Linda shot a glance at Jonathan, who seemed completely relaxed and unperturbed. Christine sat comfortably, taking notes, writing at a steady pace, detached from the turmoil and angst that flooded the courtroom.

As St. James moved toward his sober, sad, finale, he offered several exhibits. The first was a picture of the plaintiffs' family, all smiles, in front of the lovely family home in which the patient had spent her formative years. The second showed the patient, her husband, and two young children from before her difficulties began. The third was a photograph of her father shaking hands with General Eisenhower as Field Marshall Montgomery beamed approval. The fourth depicted her father in full dress uniform, his chest covered with medals. St. James enumerated every single honor. He described the criteria for earning each award, and explained in detail the actions of the plaintiff that had merited his receiving such recognition. He asked the jury to bring justice to the patient and her father, and to send a powerful message of reprimand and warning to every therapist in the world who practices the same hurtful brand of malpractice as Robert Hatfield.

"To that man," St. James looked toward the defense table and pointed. "To that man seated at the defendant's table between attorney Lauder and attorney Cadawalder."

Bob Hatfield! For the first time Linda realized she had been so focused on the attorneys that she hadn't really studied the man. The object of St. James's scorn and derision was a calm and relaxed man in a blue pinstriped suit. He seemed thoroughly focused and attentive. When St. James had pointed at him, Hatfield met St. James' gaze with no change of expression.

"The court will take a ten-minute break before the opening statement by the defense," said the judge.

"All rise!" cried the bailiff.

* * *

Jonathan stretched and smiled as he arose from his chair. He and Christine escorted Bob Hatfield out of the court to a place where they could speak privately, leaving Beth to watch over their things. She caught Linda's eye and shrugged.

"Go for it, Beth," said Serena, "I've got you covered."

"Thanks. I had a second cup of coffee and I'm ready to burst."

"That St. James puts on quite a show. It looked like he got a lot of the jurors leaning his way."

"Pleasure before business. I really have to go."

A few minutes later a much-relieved Beth followed up. "You haven't been in the courtroom that much, Linda. Easy come, easy go. Sure, he's good. Sure, he's got them in the palm of his hand. But at this level, they're all big dogs. Every one of them can do you some real damage. They're not likely to shoot themselves in the foot or throw their clients under the bus with some bush-league blunder.

"But for my money, St. James is the weakest of the power players. He's got great style and panache, and a pretty face, but he pumps up a little into a lot. He's famous for winning a couple of these cases, but if you look closely, he only got pretty small damages or settlements. . . chump change. 'Cause these are contingency cases, he probably lost money on one, maybe both. The other guy, Rex Singer? He's one of the best in town. He takes pride in being a bastard. He's the guy we love to hate. I'd never want to face him.

"Jonathan is a pit bull with a smile, and I'll deny what I'm about to say if you say I said this, but my nickname for Christine is Lady Carbon Monoxide. Colorless, odorless, basically undetectable. . . But she's a killer. Could be the baddest in the room. Remember what I said, and that I never said it."

* * *

"You have heard Mr. St. James describe his efforts in the matter before you as a crusade," Jonathan Lauder began. "You have heard him describe the charges filed against Dr. Robert Hatfield as a noble quest to right a number of terrible wrongs. In less formal language, to force the mental health professions to clean up their acts to avoid inflicting injustices and atrocities upon distressed individuals and their families.

"You have heard Dr. Hatfield's patient described as an unfortunate woman victimized by deviations from scientifically-based treatments in an irrational and hurtful therapeutic approach, the infliction of a false diagnosis upon her, and the induction of horrible and inaccurate memories of father-daughter incest as the artifacts of terrible therapeutic interventions. You have heard that the suggestion of things that never really happened were part of a sinister effort to transform an affluent but unfortunate family into a cash cow to enrich Dr. Hatfield and the program he directs.

"We will outline for you a very different perspective on the established and undisputed facts in this case. We will not try to convince you that research about apples can be applied directly to matters concerning oranges. Instead, we will argue that research shows what it shows, however well or imperfectly, but may not apply to the understanding of other topics under other circumstances. We will present for your consideration some simple factual materials. It will be up to you, the ladies and gentlemen of the jury, to determine which way of putting them together makes the most sense."

Jonathan reviewed the main points in the history of Hatfield's patient, and observed, "Mr. St. James asks you to determine that Dr. Hatfield created an iatrogenic condition, Dissociative Identity Disorder, and further encouraged the confabulation of false memories of father-daughter incest. Further, he asks you to determine that upset over learning of such accusation brought impotence upon the patient's father, a man of stellar achievement both in the service of his country and in the world of business. Please hear me clearly. There is no question that General Merrill Cross is a true American hero. His deserves our gratitude for his distinguished service to our country. His military career has been outstanding. He was decorated for valor in two wars. For this, he has earned his nation's honor and respect. But he also deserves to have his testimony studied with the same respect for truth and justice that we would bring to our consideration of the words of a far less distinguished individual. Equality before the law is a crucial foundation of the American system of justice."

Jonathan reviewed and challenged what St. James had insisted was established science. His remarks were surprisingly brief. Linda turned to Serena with a quizzical expression that asked 'Why?' Pulling a yellow legal pad from her briefcase, Serena wrote, *I don't know*.

"You have heard Mr. St. James' account of Dr. Hatfield's work, and its consequences. You have heard mine. Now, I would like to review for you what happened after Dr. Hatfield's patient returned from his program to her own home. Ms. Cadawalder is setting up a series of draped easels. Defense exhibits 19–26 are enlargements of pages from the diary of Dr. Hatfield's patient. Defense exhibit 27 is an enlargement of a page from the treatment records of this individual on Dr. Hatfield's unit. Defense exhibits 28–31. . ."

"Objection!" shouted Rex Singer. "Your honor! I insist that you reconsider the admissibility of this evidence, and the overly dramatic and misleading way defense counsel is attempting to present it!"

"He won't give up," Serena whispered. "This was argued before jury selection."

"I didn't think you could object in advance."

"You can't!"

"Counsel will approach the bench."

When the six lawyers stood before the Judge Miriam Danziger, she smiled sweetly. "Mr. Singer. We know one another very well. I knew you would try to reopen what already has been resolved, and you knew how I would respond. This discussion is over. In fact, it has been over for some time. Rex, you don't need a crystal ball to know where any further outbursts will take you."

"Yes, your honor."

"They are very close friends," whispered Serena. "They play this out every time he appears before her. It's a set piece."

"Resuming, your honor. . . When Dr. Hatfield's patient was discharged from his program, it was under rather difficult circumstances. Her insurance had expired. She appealed to both her husband and her parents for financial support to continue her stay. After a series of conversations that stretched over nearly a full month, they all declined.

"At this point, Dr. Hatfield's patient severed her contacts with her parents and her husband, left the hospital, went back to her home town, and took a short-term lease on a two-bedroom garden apartment. She felt alone, terrified, and uncertain about her circumstances and future. No dissociative disorder experts could take her into their practices on such short notice, so she stayed in daily supportive telephone contact with Dr. Hatfield.

"Exhibit 19 is an enlargement of the patient's diary entry shortly after she moved into her apartment. It reads, 'Thank God for Dr. Hatfield. My family won't talk to me anymore. Dr. Hatfield checks in on me every day. He's trying to find me a therapist around here.'

"Exhibit 28, which was labeled as such when we were discussing the matters referred to by her honor, depicts the garden apartment complex in which Ms. Cross was living. You can see that it is situated just behind a strip mall that sits right along a highway.

"Exhibit 20, also from Ms. Cross's diary, is dated three days after the first. It reads, 'I've met two people who are supposed to know about treating people like me. Compared to Dr. H. . . I miss him so much.'"

After presenting two more similar pages, Jonathan moved in a new direction.

"Exhibit 23 is dated two weeks after Ms. Cross moved into the apartment complex depicted above. Ms. Cross writes, 'I thought my money would last longer. Things are so expensive. I don't know what I'm going to do. Dr. H. can't help me with this!!!'

"Exhibit 25 is dated two weeks later still. 'Money almost gone. I gave in and called my parents. They will help me out if I go to some meeting with them. I guess I'll have to go.' Exhibit 26 is dated a month later. It reads, 'After the meeting, my father told me that the people at the meeting were telling the truth, that all my memories about him are false. He promised that if I let myself learn the truth, they'll be glad to take care of me.'

"Exhibit 27, dated the following day, states as follows: 'Mom and Dad are going to take care of me! I have decided to sue Dr. Hatfield for all the hurt he has caused to me and my parents. Tomorrow Mom and Dad are going to take me out to find a better place to live.'"

Jonathan moved toward a still-covered larger item on an easel. "Exhibit 29. . ."

Singer leapt to his feet. "Objection, your honor! Irrelevant and inflammatory!"

Judge Danziger squared her petite shoulders and stared Singer down.

"Withdrawn, your honor."

"Please proceed, Mr. Lauder."

"Yes, your honor. My colleague will now remove the cover from Exhibit 29."

Jonathan stood silent for several seconds, allowing the jury to study a very large picture of a beautiful modern MacMansion on a carefully landscaped seaside double lot. "That's quite a house!" He paused. "Yep, quite a house!" He read the realtor's description from its website and advertisements. "That little insert in the corner that's hard to see? That's a picture of an in-ground swimming pool around back. Offered at

2.3 million and sold for 2.1 million. An agreement of sale was reached, and earnest money put down one week after Ms. Cross and her parents went out looking for more suitable accommodations for their daughter. This property was purchased for Ms. Noreen Cross, who has returned to using her maiden name, by General Merrill Cross.

"The day of settlement Ms. Cross's mail was redirected to the address of this home, where she now resides, alone. This series of facts, ladies and gentlemen of the jury, suggest a rather different understanding of why we are here today. We will ask you to consider an alternative to Mr. St. James's assertions, which we will show are inaccurate and erroneous. In any case, they are basically irrelevant.

"We will demonstrate not only that the allegations made against Dr. Hatfield are unreasonable and without foundation, but also that this case really begins with an argument over money and ends with the use of money to resolve that argument and a subsequent painful rift in the Cross family. Ms. Cross made no complaints against Dr. Hatfield until she ran out of money. Then, she was led to understand that if she repudiated her misgivings about her father, her family would unite around her, help fund her divorce, and support her in comfort in a style that most people could only dream of enjoying. How many of us could afford such a wonderful place, right there on the shore in a very desirable community?"

"Objection!"

"Grounds, Mr. Singer?" asked Danziger.

"Withdrawn, your honor."

"This is not a case about bad therapy or the sullying of the reputation of a military hero. This is not about a moral crusade based the loss of consortium. We will present evidence that indicates that Mr. Cross has been impotent since a prostatectomy twelve years ago. We will present evidence, demonstrated in Exhibit 29, that Dr. Hatfield documented his concerns that Ms. Cross's accusations against her father were an angry reaction to his refusing her money to continue her stay in Dr. Hatfield's program. Dr. Hatfield charted his reservations about their veracity.

"No matter what befell Ms. Cross, and I have no reason to doubt that she suffered some misfortunes in her childhood, this is a case about money. This is a case about a woman going from a modest apartment behind a strip mall on a busy highway to a luxurious seaside mansion, and about a man who for some reason feels driven to spend a great deal of money to resolve a family matter, and would like to recoup that investment by suing for such a large sum of money that even a modest judgment or settlement in his favor would both cover legal expenses and balance his books."

Jonathan paused, and took the large picture of Ms. Cross's new home from the easel on which it was displayed, and slowly walked it from one end of the jury box to the other, repeating slowly and softly, "Nice house! Nice house!"

Midway through Jonathan's walk, several jurors had begun to shake their heads. Two started to giggle. Finally, one man in the front row said "Damn!" right out loud, slapped his thigh, and began to chuckle.

"Objection!" shouted Singer.

"Order!" cried Judge Danziger. But it was too late. . .

Singer was on his feet. "Plaintiff's counsel requests a brief recess, your honor."

"Actually, this seems like a good time to break for lunch. Mr. Lauder, can you estimate how much longer you will require to complete your opening argument?"

"About twenty minutes, your honor."

"As much as I would prefer to have the opening arguments completed before breaking for lunch, I am going to honor plaintiff's request. I'm afraid that an interruption plus the remainder of Mr. Lauder's argument would push the jurors' lunch break back too far."

CHAPTER 42

Linda and Serena joined the Morgan McGuire team two short blocks from City Hall at LLR, more formally Litigators' Luscious Repasts, a Philadelphia institution catering to the legal professions. Its featured dishes were named for prominent Center City firms or legal terms. Half sandwiches and smaller salads were designated "pro se" portions. Christine, Serena, and Beth ordered a salad called "Fruit of the Poisonous Tree." On a whim, Linda opted for the Morgan McGuire, LLR's take on a corned beef special. Jonathan merely pointed to an item on the menu. Christine smiled and shook her head.

"OK, Jonathan," said Beth. "What did you order?"

"Symbolism. Just symbolism. But our shrink, Dr. Hatfield, who chose to dine with Mr. O'Sullivan, might call it sublimation."

When their orders arrived, Jonathan growled and tore an enormous chunk from his sandwich. Christine couldn't keep a straight face. The three younger women looked to her, but Madame Carbon Monoxide would say no more than "Symbolism. And maybe that other thing, too."

Linda took another look at the menu.

"I'm impressed!" she said.

"O.K., Little Miss Research," said Christine. "What's your take on the big dog's, I mean, senior counsel's, selection?"

"Is that OK with you, Jonathan?"

"Sure. Let's see what you've come up with."

"Well, I can see you've got roast beef and turkey in your sandwich. The droplets that fell on your plate when you took that first big bite look like Russian dressing. The turkey and roast beef combo shows up in two things on the menu, but only one includes Russian dressing. So. . . I think you ordered the Schwartz, Kelly, Lombardi, and Stein."

"So far so good."

"Rex Singer is a senior partner at that firm."

"Ergo?"

"You are announcing your intentions of eating them for lunch. . . Symbolically, of course."

"Outstanding! Perfect, in fact, but for one detail." He held up his sandwich. "This is dessert. We ate them for lunch before we left the courtroom."

"I'm confused," said Serena.

"Time will tell."

* * *

Rex Singer met them in the hallway outside Judge Danziger's courtroom.

"Jonathan, we'd like a word with your team and with Mr. O'Sullivan."

* * *

Linda watched as the attorneys engaged in an intricate minuet, repeatedly stepping out of Judge Danziger's chambers, walking their clients into the hall to consult with them, escorting them back into the courtroom, and returning to the judge's chambers.

Did they reach a settlement?

Finally, attorneys, clients, and jurors were seated in their places. The bailiff cried, "All rise!" Judge Danziger spoke briefly before asking the litigants to state whether or not they accepted the terms of the proposed settlement.

Both plaintiffs, father and daughter, shell-shocked, downcast, but still scowling defiantly, muttered their assent. The attorneys for Hatfield's hospital agreed, their tone just short of euphoric. Hatfield himself took so long to respond that Judge Danziger inquired a second time. For the first time that day, Bob Hatfield dropped his calm veneer. He stared at St. James with undisguised contempt, gave Singer a quizzical glance. He shrugged, nodded to O'Sullivan, and turned to Judge Danziger with a crooked smile.

"Yes, your honor."

"I want to be sure that you are actually in agreement with this settlement."

"Your honor, I prefer to fight things out to the finish. But I realized early on that I'm no expert on law, and that my attorneys have earned my respect and trust. I accept their advice to accept the proposed settlement."

Judge Danziger turned to the jury. "Ladies and gentlemen of the jury, the opposing parties have reached a settlement in this matter. The court is grateful for your participation and your service. You are dismissed."

* * *

"Beth sends her apologies," said Serena. "They're taking Hatfield out for a drink. It's time to decompress. Hatfield needs it. That may take a while. I'm so glad they included me in the conference. It was amazing. St. James wanted to keep on going, but Singer convinced him and the plaintiffs that once the jury started laughing, it was all over. At first the plaintiffs didn't want to believe their credibility was shot, but finally General Cross realized they were looking at a long, expensive trial that could cost them big with the odds against them. That, the general understood. They came in asking for 13.5 million. They leave with half a million, damn cheap for a case like this. Barely covers expenses and legal fees to date, and sure doesn't pay off that house on the beach.

"Compared to convincing Hatfield to settle, the other stuff was easy. O'Sullivan did the grunt work. Giving up does not compute for that man. He knows he did the smart thing, but Christine is sure he'll kick himself for the rest of his life."

CHAPTER 43

"So, what did you learn in the cradle of liberty?"

"You mean apart from the bullet-points I just listed? A few things, Bill. First, in getting the first crack at presenting what they refer to as 'the science of the case,' the plaintiff's lawyers had a great advantage. St. James presented an enormous cognitive load to the jury, and it wasn't easy material. The man was masterful. By the time defense presented its alternative. . . Let me say it this way. . . The jurors had been nodding along with St. James, but their eyes seemed to glaze over when Lauder began to give his own science pitch. I think he saw them phasing out and cut it short. At best, the jury will be measuring the defense against the plaintiff's presentation. I never realized before that defense's opening arguments just won't be heard for themselves, for what they are. . . No matter what I was taught, they won't enjoy an autonomy of their own. But if defense dwells on knocking down plaintiff's arguments without establishing a credible version of its own, it will sound like nitpicky complaining or pathetic attacks against rational arguments. So, we not only need to anticipate plaintiff's strong points and weak points, but we may have to seize upon any new issues that we see floating by for the first time. We'll have to do some juggling without arguing so much science that we turn them off, make them lose sight of the case, or both.

"Second, it will be important to establish whether or not the alleged damages actually have occurred, and whether or not the complaints of damages come from a source other than those alleged to be the victims. Lauder killed them by making their case look like a money grab. I'm remembering that three of our experts wondered what our case was really about.

"Third, and I never appreciated this before. . . while St. James played to the jury's emotions by urging them to feel what he wanted them to feel, and he seemed to succeed with a lot of them, Lauder evoked the jury's emotions without telling them what to feel and got them all. I mean, both men modeled the responses they hoped to evoke in the jury. St. James might have been an actor in a Victorian melodrama, and Lauder, I don't know, kind of got you to think along with him, 'Damn! Sure looks like they got away with a fast one,' and, 'Man! I could never afford a house like that. . .' Implying 'Screw those crooks!'"

"Well, Linda, this Lauder fella just took me to school. Reminds me of someone I'd rather forget. Let's see if we can get a transcript to study. Write up your notes more formally on our letterhead. I'll send them around under your name, with Brett's and mine below yours in that order. Money well spent, but it doesn't hurt to prove it, and to make a statement. Well done!"

From a man stingy with his compliments and given to restrained understatement, this was high praise. Linda smiled and rose to leave. Just before she reached Mackey's door, he spoke again.

"Don't open the door yet, Linda. What I am about to say cannot go beyond Brett, Jeff, Sally, and yourself. I feel better, but not back to the way I'd like to feel. If I don't perk up soon my doctor wants me to get a first-rate check-up. Since it's hard to keep secrets in this town,

I'm going to be heading to Boston or the Mayo Clinic to see some super-doctors and keep it confidential. If I have to make a trip like that, in my absence, Brett will call the shots. If you can't reach him, and that could be because he has some trials coming up, go to Sally."

"And if I can't reach Sally?"

"Only Sally. She knows how to keep her mouth shut."

CHAPTER 44

"Sore subject. Now that we've got Matthew Grant on board, I don't know what we're going to do about this Jay Philips. Eve, I ran up there and made a fool of myself bringing him back on board. He's old. In the deposition, he hesitated forever before he answered the simplest question. It's easy to find articles that make him look bad. If I present him to a jury, I could wind up having to defend him instead of Dr. Underwood. Yet when I went to see him, he was different. And when Bill reached him for a quick read on Jarrett, he was brilliant. How can I be sure which Jay Philips we'll have on the stand? One multiple personality per case is more than enough."

"You asked me to tell you who's the best, Linda. He is. But appearing as an expert witness is a whole different thing. It's not the same skill set. When it comes to how he would look to a jury. . . That's something I can't tell you. If he really did that poorly in his deposition, you may not want him for the trial itself. But you listed him as a witness. His deposition is already on the record, even if you don't put him on the stand. You have your local professor with all the credentials and respect and almost no direct experience with dissociative patients, Ernest to put on a show, Jordan to attest to the accuracy of the diagnosis Underwood made and comment on memory research, and Grant to comment on her approach to treatment. Jordan can talk about treatment, but everything he's written defers to Philips. And then there's Philips. You should be OK."

"But we're still worried about Philips. I can't help feeling that Philips is broken. I'm afraid the other side will tear him to pieces."

"I've seen a lot of people try."

"And?"

"Bloodied but unbowed. He's taken shit for 30 years without cracking. All you have to worry about is whether he is the right person for your strategy."

"I wish I felt better about him. He always makes me think of some old basset hound, abandoned half-dead in a garbage bag outside a shelter. . . a decrepit mess that no one in their right mind would take home and love. . . a broken, mangy mutt almost begging to be put out of his misery."

"Let me ask you something. When you went up to see Philips, how did he handle the situation."

"Well, I got the dirty job of telling him about his more limited role on the phone, and he hung up on me."

"What? That's not like Jay."

"When we talked, he launched into what seemed to be a self-hating rant. But now that I think of it, at the end, in his own weird way, he was telling us to stick it where the sun don't shine. He made me feel awful. I'm beginning to wonder whether he turned self-depreciation into an incredibly powerful counterattack. But I'm not sure what to say to the rest of the team."

* * *

"Thanks for taking my call, Dr. Jordan."

"No problem. What's up, Linda?"

"I've been thinking about Dr. Philips. . . and worrying."

"Too old, too messed up, too beat up, too easy to trash, too stumbling, too plain, too overweight, too poorly-dressed? Shall I stop there or go on?"

"Yes. I don't know whether I could have made myself say all that out loud, but yes."

"So, you're afraid the jury will size him up as a loser?"

"I'm afraid he'll be ineffective on direct, and a sitting duck on cross."

"Linda, I can't tell you that you're wrong. I don't know a thing about juries and jury selection. I know Jay and his work are rock solid. But I see your point. . . If his appearance and demeanor are off-putting, they'll seem to confirm whatever crap is thrown at him, and you might have a problem. I imagine it's pretty damn hard to present an expert witness in whom you've lost confidence. Attractive, he's not. But I would never underestimate Jay."

CHAPTER 45

"Jay Philips may know everything," said Brett, "but he acts like he's been run over by a truck, and just can't walk without staggering. I don't see how we can dump him after begging him to stay on board, but I'm not sure we can use him except in an advisory role. I'm afraid we'll have to hold our course, eat the loss, and use this Matthew Grant instead."

"Is this all from Linda Gilchrist?" asked Sally.

"No. We both met him, and we both were at that deposition. He was a lost soul. I share her misgivings. If you'd heard it from me first, I would have put things a lot stronger. We've gone back and forth about this man. Then, we committed to him. He was a mess at deposition, not so much in what he said, but in how he expressed himself and how he appeared. The other side asked for a recess. Then they announced that they saw no need to depose him any further."

"What?" Jeff shook his head. "You mean they left him basically undeposed?"

"Essentially."

"How did he respond?"

"I'm not sure. We arranged to obtain transcripts. We talked a bit in our car. When we drove out of the parking lot, we saw him sitting on a bench in a park across the street, all hunched over. He looked pathetic, like the loneliest man in the world."

"I guess we need Grant. And I agree we keep Philips, but for another reason. Whatever's going on, we can't have him mumbling around, talking about this case. We have to keep connected. If we make a show of having him around to advise us for their big guns, that's just a few days. We won't run up that bad a bill."

"It's funny," Brett concluded. "On the flight back, Linda was quiet for a long time. Then she asked me what I thought it meant that they didn't really depose Philips. I told her that I really didn't understand. But I thought it might be gamesmanship. They figured they felt they had something on him, and they knew what he'd say, so they used the opportunity to mess with his head, to tell him he's so old, so dismissible, so intellectually bankrupt that he just isn't worth the effort. You only punt a deposition if you're sure there's nothing there you want to know."

"Ouch!"

"What Linda said was kind of interesting, though. She said, 'Brett, doesn't that mean if Philips comes up with something they hadn't figured on, they won't know it until it comes out of his mouth during his direct examination?' She's right, but that's like looking through a warehouse of shit 'cause you want to find the pretty pony."

"Let's ask Bill how he wants to play this."

Bill was in court. When they shared their concerns, he recommended that all concerned parties read the first few chapters of Agatha Christie's *The Third Girl.*

* * *

"This whole thing about Philips' deposition still just doesn't make sense," Bill said to Brett and Jeff and Sally. "Let me call Galvin."

A few minutes later, they gathered in Bill's office.

"He confirms the decision. I told him I would send a written offer to reconsider. He told me he will reply with a written confirmation of the decision. He says that Fuller doesn't see Jay Philips as a substantial asset to our case."

"At least everyone on both sides agree on something!" said Jeff.

"With a caveat," said Brett. "Like Linda said, that gives us an ace in the hole. It may amount to nothing, but maybe. . . maybe. . ."

"An ace? Hell, no. Maybe a deuce." Jeff replied.

"With all due respect, Jeff, sometimes deuces are wild," said Sally. "No disrespect to you, Brett and Jeff, or to Linda, but I'll go with Bill and Agatha."

* * *

"By the way, if Burgoyne comes down for CNN, how should I handle dealing with him?" asked Linda.

"I would imagine that any show of familiarity would risk some complications or problems," said Bill. "Give him a call. He's as savvy as they come. Sadly, I have reason to know."

CHAPTER 46

"Governor, you asked me to keep an eye on the Underwood case. They're talking about using Dr. Philips as a consultant only. They have some new expert they've hired. It looks like they'll keep Philips in reserve or something like that, not for the trial."

"Good work, Billie. I can't put you on salary yet, but just wait a few days. Then, if you go down to that dress place you like, that Lenore's, you'll find enough credit in your account to have some real fun."

"Oh, I don't think it means anything, but a lot of the girls are talking about Mr. Mackey."

"Oh?"

"They're saying he doesn't look too well."

"Do you notice anything yourself, Billie?"

"No."

"I'll go with your judgment, Billie. You're a smart one."

The Governor turned to his brother.

"Mackey must be sick. Little Miss Perky-Tits can walk across the street and give a dozen men whiplash, but she's dumb as dirt. If she jumped out a window, she'd take a few hours to reach the ground."

"What do you mean?"

"She'd have to stop to ask directions. More than once," he sighed.

"Mackey Markham & Wilder is as good as any big city firm. And Bill Mackey is the best of the bunch. Back in the day, we both were federal prosecutors in New York. I worked under him for a couple of years before he went back to the family firm. He doesn't make noise, but you don't want to tangle with him."

"What does that mean to us?"

"Their team might lose their starting quarterback the day before the Super Bowl. They'll have to go to the bench."

CHAPTER 47

Months passed. Fuller and St. James combined for still another victory. Melody Jarrett was not to be found. The possibility of settlement was explored. Plaintiff demanded more than defendants' insurers were willing to consider. Finally, negotiations broke down. The trial of Travers v. Underwood and Memorial Hospital would become a reality.

When the actual trial date arrived, a jury was empaneled with unanticipated speed. Gillian Bullock, Bruce Fuller, and Lou Galvin sat in a conference room at Dunham and Brady reviewing what they had learned about the jurors.

"What do you think, Gillian?" asked Lou.

"All in all, I think it's a pretty good group. I wish we could have gotten rid of the foreman from that construction company, though. . ."

Fuller's cell chimed. Galvin and Bullock watched his eyes widen as he took notes.

"Really? Catfish, you're the best. Write your report and send it tonight. No! It can't wait. We'll need the details to work out our strategy. ASAP!

"My team outdid itself!" Fuller crowed. "Lennie Testaverde got the dirt on Philips. When I deposed him, I knew that his wife just dumped him a couple days before. That was great! We shattered him. Knocking him down was like shooting fish in a barrel. And now Catfish Cavendish pulled one hell of a rabbit out of the hat! Dr. Underwood has some dirty laundry. Very dirty. This should stop her team in its tracks. If we play it right, we'll have a slam-dunk for sure!"

He summarized Cavendish's findings. "Pure dynamite!"

Bullock's face went pale. Galvin's insides begin to squirm. He studied the ceiling, struggling to find the right words to implore the Lord for guidance. *I don't like this! Not one bit!*

Galvin excused himself. He barely made it to the men's room before his gut exploded. *What did my doctor call it? Irritable bowel syndrome?* Washing up, he saw his face in the mirror, gone grey and haggard. He tried to remind himself that they owed their client the best possible case they could present. This argument offered little consolation. Back in the conference room, Galvin couldn't match his words to Fuller's triumphant mood.

"Yes. It's dynamite and more. But we're past the deadline for depositions, and I don't know how we can persuade Judge Lasko to let this stuff in."

"Great minds think alike. Of course, we don't have a chance. That won't stop us. Let me worry about how to get this in. I've figured out a few approaches already, and I'll keep looking for more."

"Legitimate approaches?"

"Every last one!" said Fuller, crossing his fingers as he lied, just like he had since grade school.

Hours later, Fuller placed a call to a man more akin to his own way of thinking than Lou Galvin would ever be.

"Peter? How would you like to become known as a world-class detective? You wouldn't mind? Details to follow."

That Galvin has a ramrod up his ass. I can't let his Boy Scout mentality mess up my case. But if we play this right, Mr. Squeaky Clean can block for the real ball-carriers.

CHAPTER 48

A senior gate agent passed the word to the lead flight attendant greeting passengers boarding an evening flight to DC.

"A woman who's boarding with the next group. . . Red Hermes scarf, diamond earrings. Snooty, classy clothes, messy hair. Seat 23b. Charlotte almost stopped her, but she wasn't quite sure. I'm not sure either. But keep an eye on her. She could be trouble."

"Pudge" Weston, one of those lovely ladies whose nickname expressed others' envy of her willowy figure, was a take-charge tiger on her way to a commercial pilot's license and the cockpit. Her cabin crew turned to her at the first sign of trouble. She spoke softly to a senior attendant.

"Sue, call out the seat numbers as they board."

Sue gave a curt nod.

"17A, by the window, sir. Have a great flight." Three passengers later, "Seat 23b, on the aisle, to your right. . ."

Pudge took stock. 23b was as advertised. She steadied herself on each headrest she passed. When 23b tried to lift her carry-on into overhead storage, she fell back into 23c across the aisle. Her carry-on crashed to the floor.

"I've got it, Sue."

"Got your back."

Sue is such a treasure! Pudge approached 23b with an easy smile on her face.

"Let me help you, ma'am. It can be tricky to keep your balance when you're. . ."

"Drunk?"

"I was going to say, 'when you are holding something heavy above your head,' but that, too."

"You're sniffing me. I should have had vodka. I get so nervous, flying. You know?"

First Pudge, and then both women turned their gaze toward the carry-on. It was leaking. Some small container had broken. Its contents smelled like bourbon.

"You seem like a very nice lady having a very bad day."

"Well, you're half right!"

"You're very easy to like, and I don't want to make things worse for you."

"You're throwing me off the plane?"

"I'd rather not have to go that way."

"You look like you wouldn't need any help."

"Affirmative."

"Just as well. I wouldn't want to fly on an airline that would have me as a passenger."

"Anyone who loves Groucho Marx is a friend of mine," said Pudge. 23b pulled herself together and left like a lady.

"Any baggage?" she asked at the ramp.

"More than you can imagine, but none that I checked."

Pudge offered up a quick prayer for 23b. Her childhood religious training not withstanding, she wished the wrath of hell upon whomever had reduced 23b to the wreck she escorted off her plane.

* * *

23b staggered to the hotel shuttle stop. The hotel whose shuttle she chose had room for her.

Yeah. I should have gone for vodka. Time to make a change in my life.

Once in her room, she ordered three dry vodka martinis up.

* * *

Late the next morning, 23b rented a car at the nearest agency. The young man behind the desk went speechless.

"I've never met a princess before."

"Not even in Disney World?"

"Yeah, but I mean. . . Wow!"

"Sorry, that was a mistake. I never use that card in the States."

"Oh, I see. Well, an honor to meet you. . . Catherine von Grosseschenkle?"

"That's not much easier to deal with."

"How long will you need this vehicle?"

"Probably a week or so."

"We have the best long-term rates."

Catherine von Grosseschenkle smiled, took the keys to a Toyota, and started to drive. She had no particular destination in mind. Perhaps Boston. Perhaps Richmond. Perhaps Cannes. Perhaps a concrete embankment. . .

CHAPTER 49

The opening arguments were powerful, but predictable. Bruce Fuller began with a vigorous critique of the epidemic of "voodoo therapy" sweeping through the mental health professions. He bemoaned the gross neglect of science and fact that encouraged therapists to believe unproven accusations of abuse, often made against those nearest and dearest to the patient. Linda passed Bill Mackey and Brett Connery a note: "Boiler-plated from what he and St. James said in Baltimore." Then he turned to Dr. Underwood's treatment of Melody Jarrett, and reviewed the allegations that had emerged in the course of that treatment.

"We do not know, and we may never know, why Ms. Jarrett left the care of Dr. Travers and began to work with Dr. Underwood. Unfortunately, Ms. Jarrett is not available for further examination. But even if she were, her memory was probably altered permanently by Dr. Underwood. She might not be able to recall events clearly or accurately. Nonetheless, one thing is certain. Ms. Jarrett was under treatment with Dr. Underwood for almost four years before she uttered a word of criticism or blame against Dr. Travers.

"Think of these simple facts. First, memory is not fixed in stone, it is not a permanent record of the past, waiting to be replayed upon request.

Second, research shows that memory can be distorted by suggestion. In fact, Dr. Bublekopf will attest that her research has demonstrated that adults can be talked into believing in so-called memories of things that have never occurred. Third, Dr. Underwood had nearly four years with Melody Jarrett before Ms. Jarrett first mentioned that anything might have been amiss in her treatment with Dr. Travers. Nearly four years in which Underwood's direct actions and her spoken and unspoken beliefs may have worked their influence.

"Fourth, Dr. Underwood studied with and based her treatment upon the teachings of a group of clinicians whose work was not well-regarded within the mainstream mental health community and is still considered marginal today. Instead of following the lead of the majority of those within the mental health professions, she showed poor judgment in the path she chose to follow, treating Ms. Jarrett for a condition that does not exist, thereby imperiling Ms. Jarrett and those who might be influenced by Ms. Jarrett's responses to her questionable judgment.

"And fifth, when Melody Jarrett began to produce these unfortunate misunderstandings of her experiences with Dr. Travers, she did not confront their self-evident falsehood. . ."

* * *

After a break, Bill Mackey opened the defense.

". . .Ladies and gentlemen of the jury. In order to demonstrate that malpractice has occurred, four things must be demonstrated. Lawyers speak of a duty to a patient, a breeching of that duty in providing treatment below the standard of care for the condition or conditions suffered by that patient, damages being caused, and the breeching of the standard of care being the direct cause of those damages. Physicians refer to these factors as 'The Four Ds.' Those making the accusation must demonstrate that there has 1) been a Dereliction of 2) Duty 3) Directly leading to 4) Damages. These are two professions' ways of saying the same thing.

"We will show that Dr. Joan Underwood demonstrated diligence rather than dereliction of duty in her work with Ms. Melody Jarrett. She sought education and consultation in support of her efforts. She did so out of a sense of professional responsibility, spending thousands in the effort to better educate herself to better serve Ms. Jarrett.

"Mr. Fuller and his colleagues will argue that in diagnosing and treating Multiple Personality Disorder, now renamed Dissociative Identity Disorder, Dr. Underwood allied herself with those who follow a school of thought that is not within the mainstream. Our witnesses will explain to you that the opinion Mr. Fuller promotes was more common decades ago, but this is no longer the case. The American Psychiatric Association had a chance to declare this condition was unreal and remove it from its latest diagnostic manual, but it did not. It simply changed its name.

"Yes, there are two schools of thought about this condition, but a clinician cannot be considered to be committing malpractice if he or she is diligent in his or her application of either acknowledged approach. Mr. Fuller accuses Dr. Underwood of following one school of thought rather than another. That is not a legitimate basis for an accusation of malpractice. In fact, all progress in medicine requires making room for emerging ideas and new findings. If one approach, and only one approach, were declared legitimate, difference of opinion and the possibility of innovative advances would be driven out of the art and science of medicine.

"We will argue, and demonstrate convincingly, that Dr. Travers' accusation that Dr. Underwood followed a recognized school of thought with which he disagrees, and that Dr. Underwood did so in a competent manner, is exculpatory. That is, her diligence and competence proclaim her innocence. Dr. Underwood had a duty to Melody Jarrett, and she fulfilled it by treating her to the best of her ability. She did not have any duty to Dr. Travers. . . Not by any conventional definition of duty under the law. Admittedly, this definition is being explored and expanded. But the duty Dr. Underwood owed to Dr. Travers was to refrain from taking any step that might unjustly compromise him in the eyes of his patients, his colleagues, and the public at large. And since while under her care Ms. Jarrett went back and forth about what she alleged had occurred, sometimes claiming mistreatment, and sometimes denying mistreatment had occurred, Underwood concluded that she had no grounds on which to report Dr. Travers to any state or professional body. Her restraint demonstrates her fulfillment of her duty to Dr. Travers. Many would argue that she should have reported him. In fact, she sought consultation without naming Dr. Travers to the consultant, and that consultant agreed with her conclusion.

"It follows from what I have just said that Dr. Underwood's actions never concerned themselves directly with Dr. Travers' professional or personal life. Thus far, I have addressed three of 'The Four Ds,' and indicated that they do not apply in this matter. That leads us to the fourth of 'The Four Ds.' Dr. Travers admitted in deposition that his practice has been full or almost full over the period of time extending from before he began his work with Ms. Jarrett to the present, now nearly six years after she left his practice. His income tax records demonstrate that his income has risen slowly but steadily over that period of time.

"In the absence of any of the prerequisites for determining that malpractice has occurred, we are confident that you will find that the counts raised against Dr. Underwood and the co-defendant, Memorial Hospital, are misguided, or, simply put, just plain wrong."

CHAPTER 50

On the witness stand, Gordon Travers was a portrait of confused wounded innocence. Bruce Fuller took him through his work with Melody Jarrett. According to Travers, Melody Jarrett had made vague allusions to some childhood sexual abuse, but they had little substance. He feared encouraging false memories if he pursued or explored them in any depth. He had seen no signs of dissociation, only possible hints he feared encouraging into an iatrogenic set of symptoms. He cited the work of Chaudvent, Rapier, Bublekopf, and Humboldt to explain his rationale.

He explained that he was often puzzled by Melody Jarrett's drawings. Certainly, he recognized her very realistic picture of him, and appreciated the quality and clarity of her depiction of others, whoever they were. He had never considered her depictions of sordid events in an office-like setting relevant to their work together, because they usually included a window, and for many years his office had been windowless. He explained that he had invested in original landscapes by local artists to "open up the space." Although his office was somewhat claustrophobic, the price had been right, and HighPoint Centre was very convenient. As his practice grew, he felt he could afford better. He was on a waiting list for the next available small office suite with the blessing of windows. "For now," he reflected, "I practice in a room without a view."

He thought that his relationship with Melody Jarrett was warm and mutually respectful. He was not sure why she had left treatment with him. He wondered if she was having trouble paying his fee, and was too embarrassed to request a reduction, which he would have been glad to consider.

Bill Mackey found no way around Travers' wall of apparent unknowing. The Mackey Markham & Wilder team had protested Dr. Travers' withholding the information Travers stated had prompted the lawsuit. After a month of consideration, Judge Lasko had decided against compelling any revelations. "Mr. Mackey, this case was in the media before it was a case. Dozens of stories quote Randolph St. James's using it as an example of injuring the reputation of a clinician before the suit was actually filed. I agree that you have made a good argument, but the combination of an asserted attorney-client privilege that cannot be disproven and the fact that the horse was already out of the barn makes tracking back the original leaks impossible, and probably irrelevant. When Travers filed, he was already in the news."

The most Bill Mackey had been able to do on cross was to cast severe doubt upon any and all allegations that Gordon Travers had suffered financial damages as a result of whatever negative publicity had occurred.

"The newspaper accounts that mentioned you were all, with two exceptions, published in newspapers from cities over 800 miles away. Is that correct?"

"I don't know, sir. My attorneys have kept track of things like that."

"Do you generally attract clients from that distance?"

"No, sir."

"And do I recall correctly that your income has risen steadily year after year?"

"Marginally, sir, but yes."

* * *

The first expert witness for the plaintiff, Diane Bublekopf, made an excellent appearance. Her illustrious career and numerous honors were reviewed. Bruce Fuller questioned her about the scientific literature on memory, hypnosis, and Dissociative Identity Disorder. She handled every question with becoming modesty. She stated with conviction that memory was not an accurate recording of past experience, but a mélange of information of uncertain veracity put together in response to inquiries by the mind's mechanisms for retrieving its contents. In effect, a recalled memory was a reconstructed phenomenon, subject to countless influences, inaccuracies, and the like. For something to be reported as a memory, she explained, whatever gave rise to it had to be registered in the mind, retained in the mind, and retrieved from the mind. Everything that is registered does not represent an actual autobiographical event. . . It could come from imagination, the media, someone's suggestion, or many other sources. Mental content was not preserved in a pristine state. It was not immune from the influence of other mental content, or from other sources of input. And when it was retrieved, it was subject to the influence of how and in what context it came to the surface.

"Memory of traumatic events cannot be assumed to represent actual events as opposed to imagined or suggested ones. For that reason, and because therapists' attitudes, beliefs, and techniques might suggest that some things that never had happened were likely to have occurred, recovered memories are always suspect."

She regarded all recollection of experiences that had not always been within conscious awareness suspect and unreliable, by their very nature. Therapy, she asserted, should focus on problems of living, and avoid exploring the past, which can rarely be reconstructed with accuracy. While she could not comment on Dr. Underwood's work as a therapist because she herself was a researcher, she felt comfortable asserting that any therapy that did not disregard potentially unreliable memories and focus on real, tangible, problems of living was unscientific and possibly dangerous.

In deposition, Bublekopf had conceded that Fairweather's research did suggest false memories of painful childhood experiences, like upsetting medical treatments, had not proven possible to reproduce with reliability in research settings. At trial she again made this concession to Mackey, but on re-direct Fuller had demonstrated that the quantity of studies demonstrating the possibility of memory distortion was considerable, and helped her assert that a small number of studies could not counterbalance them.

On re-cross, Bill Mackey forced the witness to acknowledge that since it was not inconceivable that false memories of good events were possible, and Fairweather's research was well-regarded, perhaps her global statements might require some modification. However, by demeanor and composure under fire, Bublekopf was a strong witness for Travers' side.

CHAPTER 51

"Where is Brett?" Linda asked.

"He just got a message run down from the office. Something urgent. He'll be back soon," Bill replied.

* * *

From his fresh, confident, and relaxed demeanor, it was hard to believe that Dr. Joseph Chaudvent was nearing the end of many long and stressful hours on the witness stand. Bruce Fuller had begun his direct examination with a skillful review of Dr. Chaudvent's many honors and recognitions, somehow keeping the jury fascinated with a cavalcade of Chaudvent's accomplishments he presented in detail before changing course and investing equal time in summarizing Chaudvent's major publications. Well over an hour was spent celebrating Dr. Chaudvent's stature. Next, he gathered himself to fire off another salvo of bravura accolades.

"Is it true, Dr. Chaudvent, that when Professor Horace Tzimmis of the Harvard Medical School introduced your invited lecture at last year's meetings of the American Psychiatric Association, he described you as an exemplar of excellence in psychiatry?"

"His words were very kind. . . Yes."

"And you were delivering the Strecker Lecture, were you not?"

"Yes, I was."

"Doctor, would you explain to the jury the qualifications for being nominated for what I believe is recognized as one of the most prestigious awards in American psychiatry?"

"I don't know that I should. . ."

"I appreciate your modesty, doctor, but I must remind you that you are under oath."

Chaudvent shrugged. "Well, if I must." He paused.

That's his first false step, Bill Mackey wrote to Linda. *He's shown his Achilles' heel.* She nodded an understanding she did not grasp.

"To be nominated for the Strecker Award, you must have made significant contributions to the field, and still be under 50 years of age at the time the award would be made. The recipient is chosen by a panel of full professors of psychiatry."

"So, it declares the recipient to be what a sportscaster would describe as a future hall of famer, a superstar of the mental health sciences."

Chaudvent tried for a modest smile but overshot in the direction of a smirk.

So, he's an egotist. Probably they all are. What on earth can Bill make of that?

"Is it true that Professor Tzimmis said, 'Dr. Chaudvent's work, like Dr. Bublekopf's, demonstrates that either alone or when asked under hypnosis, leading questions could affect the accuracy with which previously memorized lists of words were recalled. Particular styles of inquiry could result in confabulations, reports including words not included in studied lists of words as if they had been part of them. Chaudvent's social-psychological theory of enhanced confabulation under hypnosis, still being documented, is widely endorsed by other of high attainment.'?"

"Yes."

Dr. Chaudvent was encouraged to state his position in the world of hypnosis research and scholarship. He was asked to give a definition of hypnosis. He modestly allowed that although he knew as much about hypnosis as anyone else, and possibly more because of his extensive research efforts, no one, he explained, could really understand hypnosis, or could offer a definitive definition.

Building upon the foundations of Chaudvent's elevated stature and world-wide prestige, Fuller erected a grander edifice still, reviewing major academic psychiatrists' and psychologists' enthusiastic reception of his recent masterpiece, *America's Most Dangerous Psychiatrists and Psychologists*, especially his scathing denunciations of those misguided enough to believe that Dissociative Identity Disorder was a legitimate psychiatric condition, or that what appeared to be memories of long forgotten mistreatments that emerged during their therapies might actually be related to historical events. Dr. Chaudvent observed that on the basis of the theories he elaborated in his book, the use of hypnosis in patients with memory difficulties virtually guaranteed the production of inaccurate accounts. From this, it was a hop, skip, and jump to finding fault with nearly every aspect of Dr. Underwood's diagnostic and therapeutic efforts on behalf of Melody Jarrett. Underwood had accepted the reality of an unreal mental condition, Dissociative Identity Disorder, and utilized hypnosis. Next, under Fuller's guidance, Dr. Chaudvent issued scathing indictments of the experts who would testify on her behalf. He indicated that their publications were so wrong-headed and unscientific that they did not merit reading.

"As a result, it is my opinion, to a degree of medical certainty, that Ms. Jarrett never actually suffered Dissociative Identity Disorder, and certainly never was assaulted by Dr. Travers. Those memories of assaults by Dr. Travers were confabulated, produced in response to leading questions of a suggestive nature made by Dr. Underwood, many of which were made to a suggestible patient in trance, which is known to further heighten suggestibility."

A few more inquiries about particular details of Dr. Underwood's treatment of Melody Jarrett, and the direct examination of Dr. Joseph Chaudvent came to an end.

* * *

"Thank you for your learned testimony, Dr. Chaudvent," said Bill Mackey as he began his cross-examination.

"If I may summarize, you have given testimony to the effect that there is no such thing as Dissociative Identity Disorder. Is that correct?"

"Yes," replied Chaudvent.

"Further, you have testified that if Ms. Melody Jarrett suffered from something that resembled this condition, that something would have been an iatrogenic artifact of Dr. Underwood's mistreatment of Ms. Jarrett. Is that correct?"

"That is correct."

"Your testimony went on to attribute Ms. Jarrett's report of sexual assault by Dr. Travers as inaccurate, false, and due directly to leading and suggestive inquiries by Dr. Underwood, probably related to her use of hypnosis. Have I followed your argument accurately?"

"Yes, you have."

"In addition, you have stated that no one understands hypnosis better than you, but that no one truly understands hypnosis. Is that correct?"

"Yes. Unfortunately, the first part of that, sounds immodest. But I believe I know as much about that subject as anyone."

"And are there others who share your level of understanding?"

"Yes. Professor Humboldt and Professor Rivers, for example."

"But even you, along with Professors Humboldt and Rivers, those who understand hypnosis best, really don't understand hypnosis. Correct?"

"Yes, sir."

"Thank you, Dr. Chaudvent." Bill Mackey wiped the sweat off his brow. He took a sip of water and a deep breath. He shot a quick smile to Linda, and continued.

"Your honor, Plaintiff's counsel has stated and Dr. Chaudvent has testified that Dr. Chaudvent is here today to give expert testimony in connection with two subjects. The first of these subjects is Dissociative Identity Disorder, a condition that he believes does not exist. His replies to inquiries both at deposition and in this courtroom demonstrate that after learning the attitudes of those who accept the condition's existence, he has not taken steps to acquaint himself with their literature in depth. The second of these subjects, hypnosis, is one that he asserts, under oath, that neither he nor anyone else is able to understand in depth.

"One cannot purport to be an expert in a subject that one does not know or a subject one does not understand. I move to strike this witness. He does not know the literature in the one field in which he is put forward as an expert, and with regard to the other, if it cannot be understood, and an alleged expert is put forward as an expert on the basis of superior knowledge and understanding, we face a problem. We must contend with the simple fact that it is impossible to have superior knowledge when the subject of that knowledge is not understood, and the relevance of what is offered as expertise cannot be demonstrated as fulfilling objective and satisfying criteria for presentation as scientific knowledge. By his deposition statements, repeated here, he affirms that he has not mastered the literature of the dissociative disorders field. By his testimony here today, Dr. Chaudvent has demonstrated that he is a well-spoken skeptic, but not an expert. Dr. Chaudvent has stated that the other area of his purported expertise is beyond understanding. I submit that Dr. Chaudvent is not an expert in the areas in which he is scheduled to appear as an expert witness. I request he be stricken as a witness. I am prepared to present to your Honor and plaintiff's counsel a precedent, the judicial disqualification of another expert who offered the same type of non-testimony, an expert mentioned by this witness as sharing his perspectives."

"Objection, your honor!" shouted Fuller. "Dr. Chaudvent enjoys the highest regard among his academic colleagues. He is widely published. His book, *Dangerous Psychiatrists. . .*"

Judge Lasko pushed his glasses back on his nose, tapped his pen noiselessly, and tented his fingers. His eyes seemed focused on some point far beyond the courthouse walls. When he finally spoke, his voice was soft and mild.

"Counsels, I believe that I need to ask Dr. Chaudvent a number of questions before I can make an informed ruling. Do any of you have any problems with my doing so?" No objections were raised.

"Dr. Chaudvent, in the research you did for your book, did you read any of Hatfield's papers on dissociative identity disorder and its treatment?"

"Yes, your honor."

"How many of them did you read?"

"His first."

"No more?"

"No, your honor. He was writing about phenomena that are caused by unskilled and unscrupulous therapists. The condition those phenomena are linked to are unnatural and unreal. It would have been a waste of my time."

"And the contributions of the others you stated were, in your opinion, not well founded?"

"The same, your honor. Once I saw where they were going, studying their unscientific musings would not have helped me to understand things in greater depth."

"Does the same apply to the work of Dr. Philips?"

"Especially the work of Dr. Philips."

"And the work of Dr. Jordan?"

"His one relevant paper is good. I cannot fault it except that the cases he diagnosed as DID came to him with the phenomena already created by others. He should have stated that."

"And you determined that how?"

"Because the condition is iatrogenic, it had to have been created by those who had treated them previously."

"So, if I understand you correctly, Dr. Chaudvent, you have been offering opinions about work published in peer-reviewed scientific publications, the contents of which cannot be known to you because you have neither read them nor studied them. Have I understood you correctly?"

"Yes, your honor, but. . ." The crack of the gavel was loud and clear.

"Thank you, Dr. Chaudvent. You may step down. Mr. Fuller, you may present your next witness."

"Your honor!" Fuller tried to shake off Gillian Bullock, who had reached across Galvin and was pulling at his sleeve.

"Mr. Fuller, your witness has stated, under oath, that he lacks the very expertise that would qualify him to appear as an expert before this court."

Fuller pushed Bullock's hand away, and shot to his feet, "With all due respect, your honor! This strikes to the core of the plaintiff's argument. We are entitled to counter and invalidate the arguments presented by the experts called by defense. . ."

"Before you say another word, Mr. Fuller, you are indeed free to represent your client to the best of your ability. You are bound by the ethics of your profession to do so. But in my court, you will be obliged to do so within proper bounds, and without the assistance of an expert who has invalidated himself."

"But, your honor. . ."

Judge Lasko's voice had been mild. The retort of his gavel was jarringly sharp, surprisingly loud, and conveyed and unmistakable message.

"Next witness, gentlemen."

"Your honor, there is no precedent. . ."

"Gentlemen, I am not proceeding on the basis of my imagination. I came across the case to which Mr. Mackey refers and to which, in all likelihood, Ms. Bullock was trying to call to your attention. If you wish to debate this point further, I will expect your written arguments by tomorrow at 9:00 a.m. I will not repeat myself. Please call your next witness."

Gillian Bullock passed them a note. Galvin sighed. Fuller slapped the table, shook his head, and rose slowly.

"Ms. Bullock, Mr. Galvin, and I apologize for unnecessarily delaying these proceedings, your honor. I spoke out of turn. On reflection, we accept and concur with your honor's decision. May we request a brief break to explain the situation to Dr. Chaudvent? Also, we had not anticipated presenting our next witness today. We may have difficulty in doing so, but we will try our best to locate Dr. Rapier."

"Anything from you, Mr. Mackey?" Bill Mackey sat drenched in sweat, his hands over his abdomen.

"Mr. Mackey?"

"Sorry, your honor. Nothing."

"Are you unwell, Mr. Mackey?"

"Nothing that won't pass, your honor." To Linda, he whispered, "Well done, Ms. Research."

* * *

Chaudvent paced back and forth, his face suddenly gone blotchy with patches of angry red. "What the hell just happened in there? That son of a bitch Mackey and that asshole Lasko made me look like an idiot."

"Keep your voice down."

Bill Mackey slowly made his way past them, toward the men's room.

"Feel better, Bill," said Galvin.

"Thanks, Lou." They waited until Mackey passed.

"Now," Fuller began, "here's the score. . . Wait! Is Gilchrist gone?"

"She scooted out before Bill. Ladies' room."

"OK. Don't waste time griping about Judge Lasko. We underestimated him. We should have taken your concerns more seriously, Ms. Bullock. You warned us. Joe, a couple years ago there was a case in the military system, overseas. It involved hypnosis, memory, and DID. Dr. Humboldt presented the same points you made on direct. Nobody was worried about the guys on the other side. They were all young JAGs, just out of law school. Their experts were nobodies."

"Humboldt never mentioned any such case."

"You'd think no one could make Humboldt look bad, right? Worldwide, he's one of the biggest names in psychiatry and psychology."

"Yeah. Number one. What happened?"

"The youngest JAG there took Humboldt on a tour of Humboldt's greatest contributions. . ."

"On cross?"

"On cross. He crafted his questions very cleverly to justify reviewing certain aspects of the direct. He encouraged Humboldt to say more. Humboldt became expansive. He offered some opinions that went beyond what he could prove. Once he got Humboldt on a roll, Humboldt started firing off one authoritative opinion after another. He must have sounded like he was the Pope sitting on the throne at St. Peter's."

"No one knows more than Humboldt."

"Just a green, wet-behind-the ears JAG who didn't know enough to be intimidated. He got Humboldt to the point of saying he knew as much about the topics he covered on the cross as anyone. And then the kid asked a few slightly different questions, and Humboldt offered his opinions, remarking that nobody really understood those matters completely. The JAG doubled back and got Humboldt to admit that most of the statements he made were opinions about the topics he said no one really understood. Just when Humboldt thought the JAG had bought into the idea that Humboldt was the world's greatest authority on everything, the JAG turned to the panel of judges and asked them to dismiss Humboldt as an expert witness because he was supposed to be an expert, but he had just testified that major points of his testimony were based on unproven opinions and speculations."

"No one would. . ."

"In thirty seconds, Humboldt was off the stand. Dr. B., if you ever tell someone you know as much or more about something than anyone else, you better be sure you're not swearing that no one, including you, understands the subject."

"I can explain. . ."

"Dr. Chaudvent, Judge Lasko is a conscientious jurist. By his criteria, your disdain for the topics and authors you were commenting about meant you hadn't studied them objectively. It's a real blow to be disqualified. . ."

"That's going to be on my record forever!"

"I'm sorry about that. You and I have worked together a dozen times and we have more cases on the horizon. Usually they go as smooth as silk. You state your credentials and your opinions, and the other side sounds pretty weak by comparison. Nobody's ever called out one of my witnesses before. We just took a wuppin'. I'll do my best to cover your butt, but you have some homework to do and some crow to eat."

Once Chaudvent had muttered his way out of earshot, Fuller turned to Galvin.

"We're going to have to pull out all the stops on this one."

"I don't like where that will take us," said Galvin.

"Where do you think we'd be if the jury were deliberating today?"

"I hear you. I still don't like it."

"Can't say as I blame you. But this is one of those times when investing in a top-flight PI gave us an incredible ace in the hole. Dr. Rapier will live up to his name. . . He has that real killer instinct. When we go in there, we're going to spend as much time as we can on Rapier's CV. Meanwhile, have Bullock print out all the papers Lasko asked about. We may have to ask Rapier to burn the midnight oil.

"And we may have to do that ourselves. We have to outmaneuver the defense and make them make us present the new information, virtually get them to beg us to clobber them. We have to find a way to get them to open the door. I've figured out six approaches, but I don't think any of them will fool Bill Mackey. . . If he's well enough to be in court. If he's not, we can use them, but we'll need to figure out something so simple it won't even be noticed, like pulling a fool's mate on someone just beginning to learn chess. . . We may just have to pull a few strings."

"What do you have in mind?" asked Galvin.

"Nothing really. Just exercising my imagination."

CHAPTER 52

Judge Lasko called the five lawyers before the bench.

"Mr. Galvin, Mr. Fuller, Ms. Bullock. . . How have you decided to proceed?"

"Dr. Rapier has a long and illustrious CV," said Galvin. "With Dr. Chaudvent out of the picture, we'll probably spend the rest of the day laying the foundation for his expert opinion and begin with that testimony tomorrow morning."

"3:30 on a Thursday afternoon, Mr. Galvin. I take it that you anticipate that will take the rest of the day?"

"Most likely, your honor," said Fuller.

"Very well. Let's get started."

"Mr. Mackey, where is Mr. Connery."

"An emergency, your honor. We expect him back soon." Bill Mackey wiped his brow, but new beads of perspiration broke out in a moment. Back at their table, Linda was concerned.

"Bill? Are you OK?"

"I think I can hang in there, but why don't you step out and call Brett, just in case? I don't understand why he's not here."

Linda left the courtroom as quickly as she could. *No loss missing Rapier's swearing in, spelling out his name, and regurgitating his academic appointments.*

It seemed both Brett and his secretary were away for the moment. Billie Mason, a pool secretary both admired for her gravity-defying bust and feared for her cringe-worthy errors and *faux pas*, took the call.

Once Sally had offered to make Billie Linda's personal secretary. "A secretary of your own, Linda!" Sally coaxed, "Who wouldn't want that?"

"If I accepted that offer, Sally, I wouldn't deserve to work here."

Sally collapsed into her chair so hard she almost flipped backward. Once she recovered her composure, she forced herself to muster a ferocious expression.

"Take a note to yourself, Ms. Gilchrist. Never, never, never again are you to make a senior partner piss her pants."

But today, Linda had to deal with Billie, "I'll leave two messages, Ms. Gilchrist, one for Brett, and one for his secretary. What should I tell them? The same for both?"

Exerting self-control reminded Linda that biting one's tongue is a better metaphor than course of action. She returned to the courtroom and whispered her report. Bill looked at his watch. He wrote "15 minutes for that?" on a yellow pad. Linda wrote back, "Billie Mason." Bill grimaced and nodded.

A few minutes later, Bill suddenly put his hand to his mouth.

Judge Lasko broke in to the testimony.

"Counselor?"

"Your honor, I believe I will have to excuse myself. We are reviewing Dr. Rapier's career and work, which was covered in deposition. If you please, Ms. Gilchrist will carry on. Mr. Connery has been called. He should be *en route*."

Fuller had walked back to the plaintiff's table.

"Damn shame this didn't happen when we could run with it," he whispered.

"Damn shame it's happening at all," Galvin whispered back. "Bill Mackey is a good man."

* * *

"Charley, I'm in trouble. That first treatment just slowed me down a little. The second. . ."

"Can I assume that you've tried to keep going full-tilt right through the chemotherapy?"

"You can beat me up tomorrow, Charley. What's happening to me?"

"I'm not sure. You made it home? Stay put. I'm about to make my first house call in a million years, you irascible son of a bitch!"

CHAPTER 53

Bruce Fuller called Dr. Peter Rapier, shooting him a meaningful glance as he walked to the stand. Rapier returned an almost imperceptible nod.

Fuller had planned to go light on Rapier's CV for fear of overkill. But after Chaudvent had crashed and burned, Fuller reasoned Rapier would be at risk if he faced cross before girding himself against a similar assault from Bill Mackey. He set about embellishing Rapier's credentials enough to fill (and kill) the rest of the day.

Linda and Dr. Joan Underwood sat together at the defense table, an empty chair to either side. Joan tried to look like she wasn't terrified. Linda tried to look like she knew what she was doing. While he was exacting in his command of his courtroom, Oliver Lasko was a kind man. He pushed aside a very unobjective surge of pity. *My God! Two orphans in the storm!*

CHAPTER 54

"And then they sent me back to pull articles for Rapier. They told me to study them myself. Looks like a long day's journey into a really boring night."

Gillian and Gilbert, Gil and Gill had been a pair since high school. Gill tried to hold an attentive, sympathetic expression, but couldn't hold back a chuckle.

"What's so funny? We got clobbered."

"Sorry. I appreciate the O'Neill reference, but this is my turf. Chaudvent is right out of Greek Tragedy."

"How do you mean?"

"A flawed character sets the stage for an act of arrogant pride, *hubris*. and Fate takes over and kicks butt."

"I love you, Socrates, but put that in words I understand, or I break out the hemlock."

"Sure. Act like you're too big for your britches and something will take you down a peg or knock your block off. These days, Greek gods being hard to come by, we make do with just plain folks you just pushed too far or fed too much shit."

"Greek tragedy sounds more impressive when you make it seem so lofty and obscure."

"It had street creds then. It still does."

CHAPTER 55

"No. I couldn't reach Brett either, Linda. According to his little Eliza Doolittle, his wife is on her way to her sister's. She and her sisters are sleeping over with friends till Sunday night. That's odd, but I doubt it's a problem."

"What about you, Bill? You've got me worried."

"Nothing big. My second chemo. . ."

"Chemo! Bill. That sounds pretty serious."

"They think they caught it in time. Heck, the first treatment didn't faze me. I think I just had a bad day."

Linda had listened to enough doctor talk in her time to know how often patients tolerate a first round of some treatment only to have a strong reaction to the next. "It's a race, or a war of attrition, Linda," Eve's husband Jim Cabot explained. "All these drugs for cancer are bad-ass. You wish you could pick them 'cause they're nice and safe and don't do anything we don't want them to do. But really, they go about trashing the body's cells, especially those that have a rapid turnover. And because some knock out particular cancer cells faster than other fast-growing cells, like blood and the lining of the gut, we use them to go after cancer. But they're almost always doing damage to cells we'd like to protect, but can only protect so far. Sometimes we don't see the impact on other systems right off, but we usually have to deal with them along the way."

Linda was appalled that Bill hadn't kept her and Brett informed about his health problems, but she held her tongue. *The last man in the world I'd expect would pull this stupid machismo! Men! Arrgh!!!*

"This caught me by surprise, Linda. I feel like a damn fool. I've never missed a day of work except for when I broke a leg rock-climbing. Damn! I see I've never faced growing older of getting sick. I never had to. And now I've made a real mess of things. Early to bed. I'm sure I'll see you and Brett in court tomorrow."

CHAPTER 56

Come morning, Linda found herself alone at the defense table. Dr. Underwood arrived a few minutes later. *Bill! Brett! Where are you?*

Linda moved for a delay. Judge Lasko denied her motion. Fuller moved for a mistrial.

"If defense is unable to continue, I will have to entertain Mr. Fuller's argument. Ms. Gilchrist, may I suggest that we take a brief break to allow you to consider your options?"

"Thank you, your honor. I was about to request an opportunity to consult with my firm."

A partner conferred with her. Bill Mackey was probably delayed because he felt ill, but no one could believe the old warhorse wouldn't make it to court. No one knew where Brett Connery was, but he was as reliable as a Swiss watch. He would be there momentarily. In any case, once made, Judge Lasko's decisions were carved in marble. He would not relent. Certainly, Fuller's examination of Rapier would be extensive and prolonged. They instructed Linda to continue, and sent Phil Weinstein, another associate, to head for court and keep them informed.

As Bruce Fuller's direct examination of Peter Rapier continued, a huge wave of terror swept over Linda. She felt caught in a rip current beyond her strength to fight, carrying her where she did not want to go. Bruce Fuller and Peter Rapier were a smooth and well-practiced courtroom team. Worse, the Peter Rapier on the stand today was not the Peter Rapier she had seen deposed and had been prepared to encounter in court.

This Peter Rapier came across as charming, intelligent, and well-spoken, although visibly fatigued.

"Yesterday evening you informed me that the opinions that you will offer today may differ in some respects from those you expressed in your deposition," said Fuller. "Will you clarify these differences for the court before we proceed any further. To as great an extent as possible, I want everyone involved in the matter before the court to be on the same page."

"Yes, sir. My bottom-line opinions and conclusions remain unchanged. I continue to find fault with many aspects of Dr. Underwood's work with Ms. Jarrett. Nor does my revised thinking affect opinions I have offered in other similar cases. But I have reached the embarrassing conclusion that some of my extremely negative assessments of the work of those with whom I disagree on principle were overstated and require revision.

"While I continue to believe that most cases of Dissociative Identity Disorder are iatrogenic, my re-reading of the literature, both classic and the more recent contributions of Grant and Philips, convinces me that actual cases do exist that cannot be considered iatrogenic, although I remain unconvinced that such instances are commonplace rather than rare. Further, the iatrogenic worsening of these cases, even those deemed legitimate, is a strong likelihood. Likewise, the work of Frelinghuysen and his colleagues, and I should state that Jay Philips is among them, convince me that in some instances recovered memories have proven accurate. Again, I am not convinced that such instances are common, but I find that the more black and white position on these matters that I have held in the recent past requires some revision."

"Anything further?"

"No. I believe that covers it. Humbling realizations, but I guess we all live and learn."

Dr. Rapier's critiques of Dr. Underwood were stated mildly, without the slightest departure from objective demeanor. Predictably, he asserted that Dr. Underwood's patient did not have legitimate DID. Dr. Underwood's work, he maintained, fell below the standard of practice and had caused confabulated false memories that were unfavorable to Dr. Travers.

Fuller was quickly approaching the end of his direct, and no help from Mackey Markham & Wilder was on the scene. Linda's heart began to race. Before terror paralyzed her completely, she sent Phil Weinstein to scream for help.

Linda was granted a brief recess that came to an end all too quickly. Now the transformed and newly formidable Dr. Rapier was Linda's witness. Back at the firm, they had studied Rapier's testimony in a dozen cases. As a rule, his testimonies were brash, abrasive, and arrogant. Now, the Underwood team's diligent preparations suddenly became irrelevant. His new humble, reasonable, and circumspect demeanor disarmed the plan of attack they had devised.

Linda steeled herself to avoid looking toward the door. She pushed Rapier, trying to get him to contradict or overextend himself, but this surprisingly modest Peter Rapier thwarted her at every turn. Linda could feel herself becoming weary, struggling to contain her exasperation. Rapier was scoring points for Travers, mitigating the impact of Chaudvent's fall from grace, and she was unable to turn the tide.

Toward the end of her cross, with fatigue setting in, and still no help in sight, the question Bill Mackey had taught her to ask at the end of every deposition popped into her mind.

"Are there any other matters that you took into consideration in forming the opinions that you have expressed here today?"

Judge Lasko's eyes opened wide, his eyebrows shooting skyward. Mike Burgoyne had been slouching in his seat, barely paying attention, fighting off the urge to fall asleep. Now he snapped bolt upright. *No! My God! No! She didn't say that!* Maserati Mike leaned forward. *That's blood in the water!*

Rapier glanced toward Fuller and Galvin. Fuller nodded. He passed a terse note to Galvin and Bullock. "We're in!!!"

"Yes," Rapier began. "Three other matters caused me considerable misgivings. First, I took the opportunity to visit HighPoint Centre, where the office in which the offenses supposedly committed by Dr. Travers are alleged to have occurred. I walked around. I noticed that the trees were very well groomed and trimmed. None stood over 20–25 feet tall. When I went inside, I found that there was no suite identified as Suite 312. I walked all around the third floor several times and asked a few people I ran into."

Linda felt a cold chill of shock before the panic set in. "Objection, your honor! Move to strike. This information was not presented in this witness's deposition."

Galvin rose, "Your honor, Ms. Gilchrist opened the door when she asked the witness if there were any other considerations he took into account."

Judge Lasko tented his fingers and pursed his lips. Both attorneys stood quietly as the seconds passed. Finally, he sighed.

"I'm afraid that Mr. Galvin is correct, Ms. Gilchrist. Proceed, Ms. Gilchrist."

"But your honor. . ."

"Ms. Gilchrist, try your case. Nothing new was introduced by the plaintiff during the direct examination of the witness. You opened the door. The plaintiff's counsels did not. Please proceed."

Linda's mind raced, then stopped short, completely blank. She leaned on the defense table for a moment before she pulled herself together. *Good Lord! I did the right thing in the wrong place! It was the right question for a deposition! Never for cross examination in court!*

Maserati Mike Burgoyne winced. *She knows she made a mistake, but she still doesn't see what's coming.* Mike had broken dozens of opponents with legal sleight-of-hand. But Linda Gilchrist hadn't been outlawyered. She was just so green she'd shot herself in the foot with a howitzer. Fuller had his "fool's mate" without trying.

"In a deposition," Mike heard himself lecturing law students, "You try to get every bit of information you can in deposition. In a trial, you work with the information that has been developed. You never give the other side a chance to hit you with information you don't already know. With very rare exceptions, you only ask the questions to which you already know the answers." *If I were Galvin or Fuller, I'd feel that blood lust. I'd move in for the kill. Where the hell is her backup? This is just plain wrong! Bill Mackey is too savvy for this. Where's Connery? Somebody fumbled the ball. How did this rookie get thrown into the deep end of the pool. . .?*

"I'm sorry, Dr. Rapier. Please continue."

"Thank you, counselor. So, I learned that we have been talking about a series of sexual assaults that are alleged to have occurred in a suite that does not exist. Dr. Travers conducted his practice in a suite on the sixth floor for years before Ms. Jarrett became his patient. Her drawings show trees topping off almost at window level. She could not have seen anything like that from his sixth-floor office even if it had a window. Taken together, these facts cast doubt upon the accuracy of the accusations against Dr. Travers."

"Thank you, Dr. Rapier. . ."

"Your honor," Galvin rose. "I believe that Ms. Gilchrist has inadvertently interrupted Dr. Rapier's testimony."

Is this payback for the Jordan deposition? Linda dared to hope.

Bad to worse! One stupid question and I've ruined everything! I'm such an idiot! Linda pulled herself back to the courtroom.

"I'm sorry, Dr. Rapier. Were you about to say anything more?"

"Yes. Second. . . Although this case concerns alleged misconduct by Dr. Travers, misconduct I doubt ever took place, as I studied the drawings made by the patient, I was struck that despite her allegations of mistreatment by Dr. Travers, the patient's drawings and her answers to questions about her drawings in her depositions seem to refer to several different men, not a single perpetrator. It is my professional opinion that the patient is depicting and identifying not one, but a number of men, as perpetrators. She is not available to describe the actions of the man or men she alleges have harmed her, nor state which drawing represents her alleged perpetrator, nor affirm what location her drawings represent. I cannot consider her representations in these drawings to depict accurate memories with regard to the defendant.

"Third, and I say this with great regret and discomfort. . . I have concluded that I cannot trust Dr. Underwood's clinical judgment and I am forced to question her accuracy, and, sadly, her honesty as well."

Linda sat wordless and red-faced, her mind frozen, unable to react.

"To continue, during her deposition, Dr. Underwood had refused to answer questions about her employment prior to becoming a physician. Her curriculum vitae states that she had graduated college at age 25, and medical school four years later. Twenty-five is not an inordinately old age for college graduation, but it raises the question of how to account for several years more than the usual four. I also noticed that she had won a National Science Fair Award as a high school student for her project on antibiotic resistance in e. coli bacteria. She was a senior, probably 17 or 18. When I looked up the NSF winners for that range of years, I could not find her current name. The project with that subject of research was presented by a young woman named Veronica Fairbanks. In the picture of Veronica Fairbanks receiving her award, she looks like a younger Dr. Joan Underwood.

"In my explorations, I found that Veronica Fairbanks left Bryn Mawr College for Hollywood after her sophomore year. . ."

Linda glanced to her right. Dr. Underwood's expression remained composed, but her eyes were full. Her chest rose and fell quickly. *My God! She's hyperventilating! Is she going to panic?*

At the plaintiff's table Lou Galvin felt a wave of terror. Was Rapier so tired after a near all-nighter that he had presented the detective's work as his own? Did he know he'd overstated Travers tenancy in suite 606? Would his sensational testimony disguise the gaffes? Or, were there no gaffes at all? Had his co-counsel and his go-to expert witness conspired to pull off an obscene deception?

"Veronica Fairbanks was a beautiful young woman. Her story is all too familiar. She came to Hollywood. A famous agent said he could make her a star. She became caught up in the Hollywood party scene, had a series of brief affairs with famous leading men, got into drugs and not the kind of modeling she'd hoped for. She had some encounters with the police that made all the scandal sheets. She was allowed to sign into a psychiatric institution in lieu of facing criminal prosecution.

"Upon her release, she found nude pictures of herself in a *Playboy* feature entitled 'The Girls of Hollywood.' She had no recall of posing for them. She attempted suicide and was hospitalized again, this time on the East coast. For all practical purposes, Veronica Fairbanks vanished from the face of the earth.

"A year later, a woman named Joan Underwood began her junior year at Bryn Mawr. Although there was no record of her having spent her first two years there under that name, a transcript of two years of courses and grades identical to that of Veronica Fairbanks was found in her records."

"How did you learn all of this information?"

"After giving my deposition I read over other deposition transcripts. I began to get a gut feeling something didn't add up. I started with the science fair. Once I found her name, I began to dig. I got some helpful hints from a colleague in LA who works with a lot of celebrities. I found almost everything on the internet and in copies of old Hollywood scandal sheets. Mr. Fuller provided me with copies of the Bryn Mawr transcripts. I don't know how he obtained them."

Fuller nodded. *Bad start, good recovery! I can make that story work.*

"It seems that Dr. Joan Underwood, then Veronica Fairbanks, went out to Hollywood to become a star and found herself falling into a fast-paced lifestyle that she couldn't handle. I suspect but cannot state as a fact that predators both exploited her and encouraged her to think that what I call exploitation were steps that would promote her career. I have no idea what was going on in her mind.

"In any case, she suffered at least two major breakdowns, two prolonged episodes of severe mental illness. . . When she recovered and went on with her life, it is my professional opinion that the experiences of her past stayed with her.

"In her work with Ms. Jarrett, she believed she found a woman who came to her after a breakdown and hospitalization. Ms. Jarrett is a woman who stated she had suffered exploitation, and then reported further exploitations she recalled vaguely at first, but gradually recalled in more and more detail, with confabulations that included Dr. Travers.

"I do not know what Ms. Jarrett actually experienced. And she is not available to tell us. But I cannot disregard the facts that we do know about what happened to Veronica Fairbanks/Dr. Joan Underwood. And we do know that what she found in this patient has much in common with her own sad story. In my professional opinion, Dr. Joan Underwood saw herself in Ms. Jarrett, and inadvertently influenced her to think that she had endured experiences like her own. I believe that Ms. Jarrett's recollections of mistreatment by Dr. Travers and unspecified others were suggested to her by Dr. Underwood, without Dr. Underwood's conscious intent to do so. They are unfortunate and toxic fabrications, and nothing more. Given that, her use of suggestive techniques such as hypnosis may or may not have intensified the problems she was already in the process of creating."

"Thank you, Dr. Rapier," said Linda, half fearing she was falling into some surrealistic rabbit hole that would lead her somewhere deep under the earth, and half wishing for that very kind of subterranean escape. "In view of the testimony just presented, Your Honor, I request a few minutes to consult with my client."

"Court will be in recess for ten minutes."

As the bailiff led the jury out, Linda turned to her client. Dr. Joan Underwood. sat immobile, her eyes wide open and unblinking.

"Joan?"

There was no answer.

"Joan?"

A single blink, a single tear. Nothing more. Joan Underwood, M.D., sat catatonic, sealed off in a world of her own, withdrawn from a terrifying nightmare suddenly transformed into an intolerable reality.

CHAPTER 57

Judge Oliver Lasko met with the lawyers in chambers. His usually pale round face was nearing crimson. Sitting in his well-worn leather chair behind a battered desk piled high with briefs, tomes, and transcripts, his plump and usually relaxed body seemed pumped so tense and tight that all Linda could think of was a cartoon bomb ready to explode.

And the burning fuse. . . I guess that's me.

"Your honor, my client has been transported to the emergency ward of North Forks General. . ."

"That's all the way across the city, Ms. Gilchrist!"

"True, your honor. But Dr. Underwood is on staff at Memorial."

"Are you convinced that her, uh, state, is real?"

"That's not within my range of expertise, your honor. Yes, there were psychiatrists right at hand, but they were all involved in the matter before this court. Dr. Underwood's own doctor is *en route* to North Fork General."

"Do plaintiff's counsels have anything to say about this situation?"

"Your honor," Galvin began, "we are mindful that this trial must be very stressful for someone as fragile and vulnerable as Dr. Underwood. Whatever is best for her is agreeable to plaintiff's counsel."

"Ms. Gilchrist?"

"Your honor, I am unable to consult with my client about the matters raised in Dr. Rapier's testimony until she recovers from this acute and hopefully short-lived episode. Accordingly, I am unprepared to proceed with cross-examination. I respectfully request that defense be permitted to defer cross-examination until I can actually consult with my client."

Judge Lasko drummed his short sausage-like fingers on his desk for a moment and shook his head.

"Ms. Gilchrist. Surely you know that a delay of cross-examination is generally considered in the worst interests of justice. Memories fade quickly. Other information comes or is brought to the attention of all parties, so that the memories of those involved are not necessarily as they were when the cross began. Permitting delayed cross-examination is often attacked as judicial misconduct."

"May I speak, your honor?" asked Fuller.

"Go ahead, counselor."

"Plaintiff's counsels are painfully aware we have played a part, however inadvertently, in imposing this dilemma upon the court. We will not oppose a reasonable delay to accommodate the interests of justice, and to spare all concerned the burden of a mistrial and starting over. That said, we cannot offer this accommodation without noting the costs involved in inconveniencing our expert witness and paying for his remaining on site."

"Ms. Gilchrist?"

"Mr. Fuller's graciousness is appreciated, as is his pragmatism. I am not in a position to make such a decision for the partners of Mackey Markham & Wilder, but I will convey this request to the firm as soon as circumstances permit."

"Very well. Does the plaintiff have any additional witnesses to present?"

“No, your honor.”

“Is defense ready to proceed?”

“No, your honor. Dr. Underwood is not in any shape to testify.”

“What about your expert witnesses?”

“I don’t know, your honor. I hadn’t anticipating presenting them before Dr. Underwood. . .”

“Well, we all are going to have to roll with the punches. You have fifteen minutes to reorganize your case.”

“Your honor!”

“Please don’t try my patience, Ms. Gilchrist. I hope you realize that I’m cutting you a lot of slack because Bill Mackey is out of action.” He sighed loudly. “Before we resume, I have some thoughts to share with all of you.

“I don’t like what I see happening in this court. Mr. Fuller, Mr. Galvin, Ms. Bullock. You were within your rights to sandbag a much younger and less experienced attorney. But I find both the way you went about it and the kind of vile and scurrilous material you threw at Dr. Underwood in open court reprehensible. Your skill in doing so was impressive. . . So impressive that it is all the more disgusting that you failed to exercise it in the pursuit of other lines of evidence and proceed with greater decorum. I doubt you did yourselves any favors with the jury. Any further such displays and ambushes will be dealt with in a manner you will find uncomfortable.”

“And you, Ms. Gilchrist. . . I have to assume that Bill Mackey’s sudden unavailability deprived you of assistance that might have protected you from making many of the errors you have been led into making and provided the kind of support someone like yourself could use in a trial like this. Please consult a more senior member of your firm over the weekend. No! Immediately! Brett Connery is listed as co-counsel.

Where was he today? Bill Mackey. . . I'll talk to him personally. You and your firm are one short step away from legal malpractice.

"I'm not pleased with any of you. You are forcing this circus toward mistrial. We've got Mike Burgoyne in the courtroom for CNN, a man who could out-lawyer the bunch of you without breaking a sweat. CNN will be breathing down our necks. If CNN does a show on this trial, every last one of us is going to look like a complete fool. Shape up!"

CHAPTER 58

"I'm sorry, Linda," said Bill's wife. "He collapsed and never made it home. He's in the emergency ward at Memorial. His doctor thinks the chemo is catching up with him. Bill can't keep anything down. They've admitted him for IVs. His doctor told me to bring in some things for him. I'm just about to leave for the hospital. He can't talk to anyone. Isn't Brett Connery there with you?"

Linda allowed herself a moment of hope. Brett Connery, Bill's second chair and relief pitcher, if needed, was a rising star. He must have been called out on some urgent matter late the day before. He had not come in to the office that morning. Where was he? Bill had said nothing more about his absence, so she had assumed all was well.

OK! I'll call Brett, and he'll make it right. For a few delirious moments, Linda let herself slide into a princess fantasy from dollhouse days. Her hero would come to her rescue. He would charge into the fray, rescue her, and they would live happily ever after. Brilliant, affable, powerful, and calm, Brett Connery was well cast to become her perfect white knight. . . *But I'm not in my playhouse. I'm not Princess Barbie any more. I stand on my own two feet! Why am I acting like some wimpy damsel in distress?* The unwelcome answer slapped her in the face far too fast.

Because I've never been so scared and completely over my head. . . Not once in my entire life.

When Linda's first call went to voice mail, she bypassed Billie and asked the firm's operator to reach Connery.

"I'm sorry, Ms. Gilchrist. Brett left last night for Germany. He's taking depositions in Frankfurt Monday and Tuesday of next week."

No! No! A wave of terror buckled Linda knees. She twisted just in time to slam her back against the wall and plant her heels. One slipped. The other held. She wiggled her big toes, pumping the blood in her rubbery legs back into circulation.

Brett was supposed to be on call, ready to help out if Bill went down. *What went wrong?*

"Why is Brett in Germany? We're in the middle of a trial."

"Oh, Bill Mackey said it would be OK. Goliath Pharmaceuticals is building a plant out on the highway to manufacture Ultraxene. They bought Ultraxene from a Swiss firm. Now, a German company is challenging the Swiss firm's right to sell it. They claim it was developed in a joint venture. And Brett is fluent in German. I guess they have a lot of confidence in you, Ms. Gilchrist."

Something is very, very wrong, Linda fretted. *This makes no sense. Bill would never. . .*

* * *

Linda could not connect with Phil Weinstein or any of the other attorneys. The secretaries she reached promised to get back to her. She left a message for Sally.

Linda soldiered on alone. She consoled herself that her shaking body could not be seen over the phone. Ted Billingsly, M.D., Professor and

Chairman of the Department of Psychiatry at SouthEast University's School of Medicine, was as mild and affable as always.

"Sure, Linda. I can get there is a few minutes. It's already nearly four on a Friday afternoon. You won't even have time to get though my CV today, and I can review my notes over the weekend."

"Great! But there's something that came up in the last hour or so that I think you have to know." Linda summarized the testimony of the final prosecution witness and waited for Dr. Billingsly's reply. A full minute passed.

"Dr. Billingsly?"

"Ms. Gilchrist, I regret to say that this new information makes it impossible for me to testify to the opinions I outlined in my reports to you and in my deposition. Dr. Underwood's credibility has been undermined beyond repair. If I come into court today, I'll be forced to make a fool of myself or take a position supporting the plaintiff. I am sorry to hear that Mr. Mackey is not doing well. Please give him my warmest regards and assure him my wife and I will be praying for his recovery."

* * *

Linda reached her celebrity expert, Miles Ernest, M.D., renowned "psychoanalyst of the stars." He had just checked into the best suite of the best hotel in town.

"Well! Hello, Linda. What time would you like to get together to review the situation?"

"Dr. Ernest, is there any chance that you could appear in court in a few minutes? Your hotel is only a block away."

"Wait a minute, Linda. You have to be joking. I just got here twenty minutes ago. I haven't even unpacked."

"There have been some unexpected developments," Linda began. "And worse still, Ted Billingsly has withdrawn."

"May I ask why?"

Linda ached to dodge or finesse the question, but she knew Galvin and Fuller would destroy Ernest if he were blindsided. "To be frank, Dr. Ernest, Dr. Billingsly felt he could no longer serve as a witness for the defense." She explained what had occurred.

This time, the silence was just as crushing, but far shorter.

"Ms. Gilchrist, I don't think I can help you. Strike me from your witness list. If you present me, you will not be doing your client a service."

"But. . ."

"Ms. Gilchrist, I'm out of here. I'll forward a bill for services to date."

CHAPTER 59

"I'm sorry, Ms. Gilchrist. I have strict orders not to interrupt this meeting. No! No exceptions. That's what Mr. Wilder said."

"At least take this message. . ."

"I'll take the message, Ms. Gilchrist. And I will hand it to anyone who steps out, or a senior partner when the meeting breaks up. I had to block Mr. Weinstein from barging in on them. I'm sorry. Mr. Wilder was very insistent."

* * *

The only other defense expert already in town was the man Miles Ernest had warned her not to present, the man Wilder described as a decrepit basset hound waiting to put out of its misery. But the cavalry had not come over the hill. . . Linda had to forge ahead and hope for the best. . . *Like dying on the spot!*

Linda had no trouble using Bill Mackey's questions for Jay Philips' direct examination. Most lawyers wrote longhand on yellow legal pads. Bill Mackey's notes were typed in large print, his handwritten changes clearly legible. Channeling Bill Mackey to the best of her ability,

Linda got through Philips' qualifications and contributions without a hitch. Unlike the prosecution witnesses, Jay Philips had no long list of awards and recognitions, only a handful from a scientific society for the study of dissociation. By comparison, his career seemed obscure, his honors paltry.

Worse still, his answers stumbled, were punctuated with long pauses, and often seemed to wander. Linda found herself thinking of one of the family's pet dogs that never quite got housebroken. The five Gilchrist girls had been told it was sent to live out its life on a beautiful farm.

As Linda took Jay through a review of his contributions to the scientific literature, Jay Philips quickly demonstrated another problematic tendency. . . *TMI. Too much information! He's boring them to death.* For a moment she contemplated interrupting her own witness or asking him for a break and telling him to get to the point, but she couldn't quite figure out how to do it.

CHAPTER 60

There was a juror request for a break early in Dr. Philips' testimony. Linda ran to call Mackey Markham & Wilder. The meeting had ended. She ran the secretarial gauntlet. Jeff Wilder progressed from friendly to ice-cold to volcanically enraged in under a minute.

"So, Bill couldn't make it in? He told you to go right ahead?"

"He thought this would be an uncomplicated day of routine boiler-plated testimony, and that I could handle it."

"Routine boiler-plated testimony, eh? And now this. . ." Linda held the phone a foot away from her ear. Linda visualized Jeff Wilder's eyes bulging, his mouth gaping so wide that she could see every single capped tooth, his face going from red to purple, and the veins on his forehead and neck engorging into ugly bloated worms of disgust.

"What the fuck are you telling me, Linda? Our squeaky-clean client turns out to be some psycho stripper/porn star who didn't even know her patient was just plain nuts, or full of it, or both? And she melted down right in court? How did you and Bill cruise into this trial without knowing Joan Underwood's tits are all over *Playboy*, and that Travers fucked his patient, if he ever fucked his patient, in some never-never land you can't prove ever existed? And now, this stumblebum bozo you almost struck from the witness list is the only game in town, and he's pissing off the judge and putting the jury to sleep? This doesn't look good for anyone. Fix it!"

"I could really use some advice here, Jeff. Bill is out of action and I just learned that Brett is probably in Germany."

All Linda could hear was muffled sounds. Wilder must have put his hand over the phone's speaker.

"Advice? I have no idea how things could have gone so bad so fast. Nobody knows what's going on with Connery? None of this makes sense. No one here is prepared to step into this mess. This pile of shit is yours until we figure out how to do some damage control. Clean it up or give strong consideration to finding another line of work. That's my fucking advice!"

Sally Warren's voice came on the line. She was a Markham, another third-generation member of the firm.

"That's a little over the top, Jeff. Linda! You don't have to be told that this is turning into a disaster. We didn't hire you thinking you'd never find yourself in a jam. We hired you, like we hire everyone, because we have confidence that you can think yourself out of a jam. Yes, we're angry. Yes, we're confused. Yes, we're disappointed. But yes, we think you can find a way through this. You enjoy my complete trust and confidence. One of us will be right there. Go get 'em!"

"Yes, ma'am."

* * *

"You were too nice, Sally. Mackey Markham & Wilder is going to look like moron central. We're going to take a hit on this one."

Sally sighed before she turned to Jeff. "I have no idea what is going on. I guess Bill tried to keep too many secrets and keep on going, but he ran out of steam. It boggles my mind that Brett is off to Germany and none of us knew anything about it. Two senior people and God knows how many others screwed up. Or did they? All I know is that fair or not, unless she pulls a miracle out of you know where, I'll be ready to strangle that perfect little golden-haired debutante princess with my own hands. Even if she does, I still might."

"Gloves and a garrote, Sally. Don't let her stupid mistakes tempt you to make one of your own. I don't know how I can break this to Bill. He thinks that girl walks on water. I can't understand why you were so nice to her."

"Two points, Jeff. First, my psychology major daughter tells me that positive reinforcement works better than shaming or criticism. Second, we didn't even know Bill was getting sick. Hell, this must have caught Bill by surprise. We didn't take incoming calls all afternoon. We didn't know Bill left word he was getting sick. We wanted all hands on deck for that presentation to Bronson Automotive. We gave orders we were not to be interrupted, and we pulled it off just right. While we were focused on getting a big chunk of new business for the firm, this whole situation fell between the cracks. Did you know Brett had gone to Germany in the middle of a trial?"

"No! This whole thing about some patent problem with Ultraxene is a shocker. I've never heard a thing about it. Goliath's people said nothing about it, and frankly, we're not the right firm to handle an international patent dispute. I'd call Goliath, but it's late evening there."

He tried to reach Brett's secretary, but Billie Mason answered.

"My God! Brett gave her the rest of the day off!"

"Shit!" Sally stood up and threw a few things into her briefcase. "If things go badly and this Underwood woman turns on us for legal malpractice, or if Judge Lasko raises holy hell, putting Linda Gilchrist on the altar as a sacrificial lamb won't help us. In fact, that would probably hurt us. She won't be the one in the cross hairs. . . We all will. We need to get someone down there right now."

"Sally, I'm getting a real bad feeling about this. Better we both go."

CHAPTER 61

In the blessed solitude of a rarely used stairwell, Linda struggled to review her diminishing options. *I'm down from four expert witnesses and a consultant to two experts I trust and a walking disaster. I have to live through today. But maybe I can put someone credible on the stand, and keep him there long enough to put some distance between today and this mess going to the jury. . .*

That's it! If I can postpone completing Philips' testimony, maybe I'll never need to come back to him. I'll survive today and start Jordan on Monday morning. Clean reputation, still serving his country, and the man who married Elani!

I don't believe this! My first witness runs away like a scalded cat, my second drops the case like a hot potato, the third is off on some mission, and the fourth is on an ocean liner somewhere in the middle of the Atlantic. I can't get him till Tuesday. And there's no way Lasko will grant a continuance at this point. I'll have to put that clown back on the stand and watch Fuller and Galvin tear what's left of my client, my case, and my career to shreds.

Linda made a quick stop at the ladies' room. Washing up, she could barely believe that the trembling hands before her were her own. Looking up at the mirror, she saw no trace of the confident, take-charge woman who had walked into Judge Lasko's court at nine o'clock that morning. In her place stood a rattled, shaking creature whose once-chic coiffure was disheveled mess, whose eyes welled over with tears, whose face was a wreck screaming out for major repair, and whose usually nimble fingers were taking minutes to do what she had done in seconds several times a day for a dozen years. *I'm a walking disaster! All I need now is spinach between my teeth and a trail of toilet paper stuck to my heel!* She checked for both, just to be sure.

CHAPTER 62

Sally Markham chatted briefly with Linda in a warm, friendly manner while Jeff Wilder paced back and forth, his face overrun by a legion of foul emotions.

"We are looking at a bad situation. We will try to help you deal with your problem witness, and then sit down and see what we can do about the disaster you described."

Sally and Jeff took Jay Philips aside.

"Dr. Philips," began Sally, "Ms. Gilchrist is the counsel of record. She will continue the direct examination. She has shared with us the thought that it might be helpful if you answered her inquiries in a somewhat different manner. Before I make any suggestions, I'm wondering if you have any thoughts about her concerns?"

Jay Philips looked off, away from Sally. After several seconds of silence, he spoke.

"Uh. . ."

Jeff Wilder clapped one hand to his forehead.

"Dr. Philips?"

"Uh. . . Ms. M-Markham?"

"Yes."

"Ms. Markham, d-did I s-stall l-long enough f-for y-you to g-get h-here?"

"You ss-ly little s-son-of-a-bitch!"

"I do stammer sometimes. I do talk too much sometimes. I am too intellectual. . . all the time. Ms. Gilchrist needed to play for time, and I didn't think she had enough courtroom savvy to pull it off. Bumbling was the only card I had, so I played it."

Sally turned to Jeff. "I'm still with Bill and Agatha."

"What?" from Wilder.

"It's something, Mr. Wilder," said Jay Philips, "about short, dumpy, little old nobodies."

"Next," said Sally, taking command, "Quick, Linda! Occupations of the jurors. Now!"

* * *

Every small city has them. . . A few of its superstar kids who come home and make their careers where they began. "Savvy Sally" Markham could have gone anywhere. But she married Bud Warren, her high school sweetheart. She practiced law as Sarah Markham Warren, and raised a fine family. The depth and power of her strengths were generally unknown and underappreciated outside her firm. For years, "Ask Sally" was an imperative in handling every difficult case Mackey Markham & Wilder encountered. Linda had yet to witness Sally Warren in action.

Sally looked off for ten seconds. She took a legal pad and printed ten questions, her hand moving so rapidly that Linda, Jeff, and Jay were stunned.

"Linda, you tell me Dr. Philips has been trashed by three successive plaintiff's experts. He has conducted himself like a stumblebum, today. . . Hopefully, mostly for show. This is your game plan for rehabilitating your witness. Use it, or. . . How shall I put this. . . or else."

"I don't understand where these questions lead."

"In this unusual instance, all the better. Beautiful wide-eyed confusion will get the jury interested. You are perplexed about the attacks on him. Then. . . Utter a silent prayer, and toss the ball to Philips."

As Linda walked toward the courtroom, Wilder put his hand on Sally's shoulder to slow her pace. "My God, Sally! A 'Hail Mary' is desperate enough! Are you really calling. . ."

"A 'Hail Jay'? Unless you've got a better idea. . ."

* * *

Back in court, Linda Gilchrist completed the lines of inquiry Bill Mackey had prepared.

"So, in due time, Dr. Philips, you will testify that Dr. Joan Underwood's work with Ms. Melody Jarrett satisfied or excelled the standards of care, and you have no significant criticisms of her efforts. Is that correct?"

"Yes. She not only read the literature. She pursued advanced education and obtained expert consultation on more than one occasion. That demonstrated exceptional diligence and deep concern for her patient."

Here we go again! TMI! Out of Mackey materials, Now Sally's confusing and unsettling lines of inquiry stared up at her from a yellow legal pad. She shot a glance to Sally, who smiled encouragement. *Here goes nothing*. Linda shrugged, and hauled out her most dazzling smile. She let her eyes widen and her jaw relax, knowingly assuming a mask of youthful vulnerability she'd fought to leave behind her.

Sally held her own smile still while her mind raced, planning several moves in advance. But despite her efforts, five words intruded over and over, the five words she'd withheld from Linda Gilchrist and surreptitiously whispered to Jay Philips: "Three teachers, one a professor."

"Before moving on to ask you about those opinions, Dr. Philips. I would like you to address another matter for a few minutes, because I would like the court to be able to place those important observations in context.

"The court has heard from prior witnesses presented on behalf of the plaintiff, Dr. Travers. A number of them have been quite critical of you and your work. They have described your work in uncomplimentary terms, one even likening your approach to science as resembling a particularly skillful rearrangement of the deck chairs on the deck of the Titanic. . ."

"Yes, those are the words of Joseph Chaudvent. I'd expected to see him here today." A titter ran through the onlookers. Three jurors snickered. *That's how Jonathan Lauder got his argument going! Is Sally. . .?* There was no time to reflect.

"Yes, Dr. Philips. Those words come from Dr. Chaudvent. But he is one of many who have attacked you. Please explain to the jury how you understand the fact that so many distinguished scholars have disagreed with you so intensely, so profoundly."

Linda pushed on, wondering why Sally demanded she ask, "Do you think that they are just stupid, less intelligent than you, and can't understand you?"

"Oh, no! I don't know for sure, but I would imagine that they are all exceptionally intelligent, for all I know, more intelligent than I. But as every parent arguing over privileges with a teen-ager and every educator from kindergarten through post-graduate education knows, it's not so much the brain-power of the participants in an argument. . . It's whether they are arguing from the same premises or different premises, with one pattern of reasoning, or another. Lots of us have kids smarter than we are, but when they try to talk us into letting them borrow the family car because they just wrecked theirs, but that's in the past because they haven't had an accident since then, we have to remember that they crashed their car just last week and have been grounded since, so their recent clean record means nothing. We know that given their premises, their opinions, even if they can argue rings around us, are a big problem. We can't allow the eloquence of their efforts to persuade us.

"Now, the same thing happens in science, but when you argue with a scientist or scholar, their opinions and the arguments that flow from them seem so impressive that it is hard to know if you are hearing something that is true, or this year's model of the Emperor's New Clothes.

"Those who attack my work start from the premise that I must be wrong because my ideas are not the same as theirs. On that basis, it is easy for an opinion to generate a notion, and, since that opinion generated that notion, those who share that opinion are quick to elevate that notion of what might possibly be the case into a likelihood, and then into a probability, and then into something they believe is the truth. And that can happen very easily, because facts can become irrelevant."

"How does a fact become irrelevant?"

"There are dozens of ways to bypass a fact. In arguments you often find that each side has either omitted or rationalized away the possible importance of facts that would appear to challenge its perspective. They make the best argument they can. That's great for politics or litigation, but it's lousy for science."

Linda found Sally had anticipated Philips' answer.

"So, you are saying that at times brilliant people who have explored one line of reasoning with meticulous scholarship can be just plain dead wrong?"

"Sometimes. Two very smart fellows thought so. A guy unlike his name, 'cause his name was Boring, pointed out that in every generation some of the most brilliant psychologists oppose one another, and both prove to be wrong, 'cause the truth is a combination of both/and rather than either/or, or some mixture or compromise somewhere between. Kuhn, who wrote *The Structure of Scientific Revolutions*, pointed out that people who organize their thinking around different models, different paradigms, can look at the same set of facts and come to radically different resolutions. It is as if they live in different worlds. You just can't talk a Red Sox fan into rooting for the Yankees."

Linda took the next step. "And have you seen any evidence of this thinking problem in the material of the records and depositions and exhibits pertaining to the case under consideration by this court?"

"Yes."

Yes! thought Sally. *Yes! Yes! Yes!*

"Objection!" shouted Fuller. "Your honor, this witness has not made any such representation in his deposition or testimony to date!"

"Ms. Gilchrist?"

"Your honor, I do not know for certain to which materials Dr. Philips is alluding. May I inquire?"

"Mr. Fuller?"

"Objection withdrawn for the moment."

Linda asked, "Dr. Philips, would you kindly clarify to the court how you formed the basis of your assertion?"

"Certainly. An excellent example can be found toward the end of the deposition of Ms. Melody Jarrett, in the opinions voiced by Messrs. Fuller and Mackey."

"Your honor, since that deposition is a marked exhibit, accessible to all, may I ask Dr. Philips to read it aloud?"

"That won't be necessary, your Honor," said Fuller.

"Actually, Mr. Fuller, I am curious to understand this more clearly, and the jury cannot be asked to tolerate obscurity when a matter can be brought into the light and clarified. Please proceed."

Linda handed Jay Philips the Jarrett deposition.

"Here we are. Ms. Jarrett had suddenly demonstrated some very different behavior and ran out of the room, screaming. The court reporter was still at work.

"Mr. Mackey remarked, 'So that's Dissociative Identity Disorder.' Then Mr. Fuller spoke, and said, 'With all due respect, Mr. Mackey, perhaps. But perhaps that's great acting or the unfortunate induction of a believed in role and fantasy by guile or dangerous technique by an inept therapist.'

"If two distinguished and experienced lawyers, officers of the court, could bear eye witness to the identical incident and immediately offer completely different and mutually incompatible understandings of what they observed, it does not take a brilliant mind to appreciate that the perceptions of Messrs. Mackey and Fuller were not completely objective. The perception of each man was influenced by preconceptions about how to understand his encounters with certain phenomena.

"So, since you all have seen that both Mr. Fuller and Mr. Mackey are exceptionally intelligent men, and came to different opinions just like that, it may be easier to understand why those who come to my work with a respect for its subject matter may come away feeling that I have made a worthwhile contribution, and those who approach it assuming it is nonsense about nonsense, or even open-minded people who approach my work having been taught it is nonsense about nonsense, will have a hard time finding any value at all in whatever I write."

* * *

"The hour is late," said Judge Lasko. "We'll adjourn for the day. Have a good weekend one and all, and we will resume Dr. Philips's direct examination come Monday morning."

Linda was beginning to gather her things. She looked back toward Sally and Jeff. They were smiling. *Sally is a genius. Her questions actually had made Jay Philips look good.*

"Strong ending for a catastrophic day," said Wilder. "I'm sorry for losing it, Linda. You made a rookie mistake, and it cost us big. But if we'd been doing our jobs, that never would have happened. Bill's sick. Brett's God knows where. We should have kept someone outside that meeting just in case. We'll fix that. But now, we have a client to defend. We have to talk."

CHAPTER 63

"We're on the case until Bill is on his feet again, Brett shows up, or both. Bill has asked us to stay with it for him," said Jeff Wilder, back in the Founders' Room. "It's like there's something personal he can't talk about, but this case is breaking his heart. It happens from time to time, and he'll never say why. That's Bill. OK. To work.

"Sally and I will spend the weekend getting up to speed. But we really have to coach you rather than take over. The good part is that most of the hardest work, except for closing, is over. The bad part is the same thing. The way I see it, if the jury were polled Thursday, the verdict would have gone our way after Bill contained Bublekopf and demolished Chaudvent. But if the jury were polled today, it would go the other way. Rehabilitating Philips just gets him back to baseline. And from what I hear, there's no telling what that man will be like when he shows up on Monday. I'm afraid Fuller's going to chop him up into little bits. . . I know, Sally. You're still with Bill and Agatha, but that man worries me. And now that we've begun with him, we'll have to finish with him. Fuller is just chomping on the bit. He looks like he can taste blood. . ."

Linda held her tongue. *Yes, Jay finished strong. But was that because Sally was pulling the strings.*

Jeff voiced Linda's feelings.

"Philips finished strong, but Sally. . ."

"Before you say what we can guess you are going to say, let me point out two things. First, Dr. Philips answered the questions that way without being coached. Second, some of the best questions were Linda's ad libs. The key thing here, Jeff, is that our Linda Gilchrist and this Jay Philips are not old rhinoceroses like you and me. Both are tender souls who do best when either option one, they are treated with respect, or option two, when they rear up and insist on being treated with respect. It is now your task, Ms. Gilchrist, to refute any attribution of a need for option one, and understand that law is adversarial. Gear up for option two. Now, Joan Underwood is circling the drain. Let's see what we can do for her. . ."

"OK, Sally. But what did you tell Philips?"

"No big deal. 'Three teachers, one a professor'. . . There were three educators in the jury, two in the front row. They get Philips. When they started to lean forward and nod with his argument, the others saw Philips was someone to contend with. Common sense."

Linda smiled, and tried to look determined and resolute. *That's common sense? I am so far out of her league it's pathetic!* It took every bit of effort Linda could muster to restrain herself. She still wanted to run out of the Founders Room, find a cave in some primeval forest, and roll a big rock to block its entrance forever.

CHAPTER 64

Linda would have to deal with Jay Philips. The thought of being seen by the others involved in the Underwood case was too painful for Linda to bear. With Hunter away, she decided to meet with the man she did not like in the relative safety of her home study. *Linda Gilchrist and Jay Philips*, she mused, *a classic loser on loser slough.*

Sure, with Sally and Jeff studying the Underwood file she would be protected from making a complete fool of herself come Monday. But first she had to survive the weekend, and push herself to find something, anything, to contribute to Joan Underwood's defense. She had to demonstrate to her client, her firm, and herself that she had something to offer besides stunning good looks and colossal simple-minded blunders. *My God! I'm turning into a better-educated Billie Mason!*

Jay needed some time to make a few calls and wash up. Linda asked him for his favorite Chinese dishes, ordered take-out and promised to pick him up at his hotel.

"I'll be in a blue Miata convertible."

"Pretty woman in a little blue car? You must have grown up on Nancy Drew."

Am I that transparent? Linda mused. *An evening with Jay Philips. . . He already makes me uncomfortable and he's sooo difficult to be with. I really don't like him. And he has my number! He'll read me like a book.*

CHAPTER 65

"What's going on, Jay? I'm out here in California with the Guard. I just picked up some frantic messages from Linda Gilchrist begging me to get back there ASAP. What's happening?"

"Bill Mackey got sick. This Brett fella is God knows where. That left Linda Gilchrist alone. She stumbled into some legal trap that opened the door for them to bring up some new information that tore Joan Underwood to shreds. She had a catatonic meltdown."

"I hope there's a special place in hell for people who do things like that."

"Who do you mean? The people who nearly destroyed her then, or the people who just may have destroyed her now?"

"I don't play favorites. Where are her compadres? What about Mackey and the other guy?"

"Mackey's chemotherapy got to him. He tried to carry on, but he's sick as a dog and had to leave."

"And Connery wasn't there to help?"

"Don't ask me how, but he wound up in Germany."

"I don't get it. This whole thing smells bad. I was afraid there was something weird going on from the get-go. How's Linda doing?"

"Looks like she took a hit. . ."

Jay overheard a voice on Ben's end shout, "Colonel Jordan! Colonel Jordan! T minus zero two!"

"Food for thought. Nearly indigestible. . . Gotta go."

Charlie Foxtrot for sure! Jordan raged. *Nothing I can do about it. Or is there?*

CHAPTER 66

Jay Philips had changed into crisp chinos and a sports shirt. He carried a small attaché case. But Jay was still Jay. Linda had a visceral dislike of overweight and out-of-shape people. Whenever her prejudices came through loud and strong, she hated herself. . . for at least a second or two. *All cleaned up and he's still a paunchy runt couch potato!* Jay Philips' smile of greeting flattened to straight line. *He saw it in my face!*

They swung by the Golden Fortune, Linda's go-to Chinese place. Jay took the bag for her. As they got out of the car, Linda noticed that one of the dishes had leaked all over Jay's lap. *I cannot even imagine what it must be like to be that man!* Jay said nothing until they were in Linda's kitchen.

"Do you have a towel I could use?"

"I'm sorry. I wish I had something around here that might fit you."

"I wouldn't imagine you have anything around in the short and squat department. Tell you what. . . Let me rinse things out and lend me a hair drier. If I stand around the island while I eat, I'll probably be fit for furniture by fortune cookie time."

* * *

Jay Philips was exceptionally well-read and well-informed. He shared Burgoyne, Cadawalder, and Lauder's admiration for Sjowall and Wahloo, and left Linda with a host of new mystery writers to explore. He really did like Agatha Christie, after all. Linda was shocked to discover that his company was painless, even pleasant.

"But those Swedish writers are so depressing. . . How many brilliant, depressed, lonely drunks with lousy relationships. . ." Too late, she realized what she was saying and tried for a saver. Jay Philips' wry smile told her the horse was already out of the barn, galloping toward the horizon.

"But they are great writers. . ."

With Jay finally sitting on a folded bath towel, they began to work their way through the Underwood case, trying to anticipate what Monday's examination and cross-examination would entail.

"Rapier's kinder, gentler approach to the science and clinical stuff went over well," Jay observed.

"Yes, it did. But I'm not sure what the jurors will take away from his testimony."

"Linda, can I speak freely?"

"Just talk. Right now, I'd like to run away from anything else that might make me feel more foolish than I feel already."

"OK. I don't know what the jury is going to do with what Rapier said about Dr. Underwood. Not much we can do with that tonight except understand that it is completely irrelevant."

"Irrelevant?"

"Completely. If Joan Underwood had all the experiences Rapier reeled off, and if every detail about that room situation is like he said. . ."

"Yes?"

"Do these things prove that Dr. Travers is not guilty of mistreating Melody Jarrett?"

"Well, no."

"Let me spell this out. Rapier's arguments describe a possible scenario. Like I said in court, that something is possible doesn't mean it is probable. Nor if it seems probable does it mean that it is so. Nor does it mean that even if it we decide it is so, that it offers a full and comprehensive explanation that exonerates Travers."

"I want to believe you. But spell it out."

"OK. Let's agree that it is possible that all the individual facts Rapier put before the jury are true. Does that mean that the only conclusion to be drawn from them is the one he drew?"

"How so?"

"Suppose Dr. Underwood identified with Melody Jarrett and had strong feelings about their shared kinds of experience. One out of three American women have been exposed to an unwanted sexual event before age 18. One out of eight has been raped or will be raped. I forget which. That means that given a female treating a female, the odds that a female victim of sexual abuse who is being treated by a female therapist who herself is a survivor of some unwanted sexual experience are pretty significant, and the same for a rape survivor's being treated by a survivor of rape. What Rapier is playing up as some egregious situation is actually a sad commonplace. We assume the possibility that the therapist's personal experiences may have some impact upon how she experiences her patient's situation, but the literature is not bulging with reports to substantiate that it clouds their judgments in any predictable way rather than makes them feel bad and have a flashback or nightmare or a dozen. It goes on from there. I'll provide you with a bunch of things like this you can use.

"But here's the main point. You have a client to defend. Whether you believe her or not, that fact is irrevocable. You and Bill Mackey came up with a defense, along with that other guy, Mr. Somewhere-in-Germany. The senior partners who swooped in can hold your hand and wipe your nose and rebraid your pig-tails, but they won't really know the case. What do you know that no one else knows?"

"I believe her." The words were out of Linda's mouth before she'd had time to reflect. "I knew she was holding back on something, and I warned Bill. He told me that if the case blew up, I could say I told him so."

"Not much consolation. So where does that leave us?"

Us? I could get to like you, Dr. Philips!

"OK. Remember, I'm just a rookie, and a rookie off to a very bad start. I see two things I have to do. First, I have to present Dr. Underwood's defense in a way that says, 'Let's try the case before us. . . Not some scientific squabbles or the defendant's personal history.' Second, I have to try to find out what really happened and where it really happened. I guess I have to take a look at that office building. And on a weekend, with no permission to go snooping."

"If you'd like, I'll be glad to give you a hand."

The doorbell interrupted.

"It must be Jane. That new puppy of hers is always running away. I can't imagine anyone else who'd drop this late. Excuse me."

Linda opened her door slowly. The first person she saw was her neighbor Jane, a pert brunette with what was usually a sweet, unperturbable face. Not tonight. She said no more than "Linda," before looking up and to her right. Opening the door more widely, a very tall uniformed policeman came into view. He looked to his right and down. Opening the door completely, Linda saw a slender woman looking down at her feet. She wore expensive but disheveled clothing. The blond color of her dirty hair was growing out. Her fingernail polish was chipped.

"Aunt Kate?"

"Guilty as charged, Linda."

"You know this individual, Ms. Gilchrist?"

"Yes, she's my aunt."

"She didn't remember your exact address, Linda. I'm sorry, but when she kept on knocking on the door and screaming for you, I thought I'd better. . ."

"No problem, Jane. I'd've done the same."

"Are you comfortable in taking care of this woman, Ms. Gilchrist? We can take her elsewhere, if you'd prefer."

"No, I'll take care of her. Thank you, officer. I'm sorry, Jane. Is there anything else we need to take care of?"

"No," Jane began, but the officer interrupted.

"Actually, Ms. Gilchrist, are you willing to take responsibility for the damage to your neighbor's lawn? Otherwise, I'll have to file charges."

"Damages?" asked Kate.

Linda pushed past the trio. A Toyota Corolla was covering half of the flower beds along Jane's side of their shared driveway.

"It was dark. I lost my glasses."

The officer looked toward the top of Kate's head. Her glasses were pushed up, over her forehead.

"She passed the breathalyzer test. She's just exhausted. She's out on her feet."

"My God! Jane, I'm so sorry," said Linda. "I really don't know what to say. Please, just call your lawn guy and send us the bill."

Once inside, Kate protested, "You should have let me take care of this myself, Linda!"

"Another time, Aunt Kate."

Kate raised her voice. "Don't treat me like a child!"

An unexpected voice intruded. "She's treating you like an adult who's not at her best. Let her help you. If you want to be treated like a child, that can be arranged."

"And who the hell are you?"

"Someone who doesn't give a flying damn about what garbage you say, but who's willing to help Linda help you."

"I don't care what you say, you fucking bastard!"

"Good. We have something in common. Truce?"

Kate laughed in spite of herself. "OK, Sir Knight. Oh boy, what a winner! If you plan to rescue me from myself, at least state your intentions. And I want to know. . . Are you married, separated, divorced, celibate, gay. . .? What?"

"Was married, was divorced, and now nowhere on your list."

"What, then?"

"Widowed."

"What?" said Linda. "I didn't know that."

"No one asked."

"When I hired you, your CV said you were married!"

"Things change."

"I don't understand," said Linda.

"Let it go for now, Linda," said Kate. "If it were something normal, you'd get it."

"I don't. . ."

"Your aunt is pretty swift."

"Thank you, kind sir. You are?"

"Jay Philips. I'm here being prepped for my testimony on Monday."

"Excellent. I'm here because when I came home from cancer surgery my husband announced he was trading me in for a new model and that I'd be living alone."

"What?"

"I haven't told people yet. I put on a good front for a few weeks, and then. . . I don't know. I started to fly all over trying to go to places where I've been happy. Then I realized, I was happy there because I. . ."

"Was with him," Jay provided.

"Right. And fuck you for your merciless accuracy, no longer Kind Sir!"

"Sorry. I apologize."

"Don't. For all people say about how great accurate empathy is, sometimes a person wishes the empathy was off target, that somehow they could dodge the pain of someone seeing their shame. One day I'm this lucky rich bitch in the skinny jeans, living the life, hanging with the beautiful people, and everybody envying me right and left. . . And yes, I'm shallow and self-centered enough to know I loved every second of it. The next, my doctor tells me I have breast cancer, and does tests that tell me she'd better take both. Rudy is mister loving super-husband until I come home. He helps me get settled, introduces me to a nurse he's hired, and tells me it's all over. Found himself some new arm-candy. Tells me he's always had someone on the side, but now he's found the love of his life. He's believing the lies he tells himself, just like always. It used to be charming, but it lost its magic long ago. What's your story, Sir Knight?"

"Funny."

"Funny?"

"Not the story, just that someone would actually ask."

"That's hard to believe. . ." Linda began.

"No, it isn't, Linda," said Jay. "Sometimes people just don't get seen as people. Just as what people think of them."

Kate looked hard at Jay.

"You might not believe it to see me now, but until this year I was just this person people either wanted, envied, or wanted to be. Only a handful of people ever bothered to consider who I was instead of what I was. So, I'm guess you're saying that not too many people stop to see who you are. I had something going for me that let people define me by that something. You're not as superficial as I am, and what people admire in you doesn't get you much attention day by day, like the things I lived on. Sounds pretty damn lonely."

Jay tried to hide his feelings. He failed.

"And fuck you for your merciless accuracy, not so Gentle Lady."

"I don't believe you two!" said Linda.

"Let me re-park your car. Then your niece and I have to finish the work we were doing."

Linda settled Kate in her guest room. Jay parked Kate's car and brought up her luggage.

When Linda rejoined Jay, she tried to explain Aunt Kate.

"I'm sorry. She kept it to herself when she needed all the support in the world. I don't think my mother knows. . . Uncle Rudy. . . He's some kind of prince. . . He and Aunt Kate were the golden people. I always thought they were like Fred and Ginger, dancing through a dream, protected and untouchable, living a glamourous life beyond the reach of all but the favored few. They had no kids by choice. Their whole life was running from one big party to the next.

"Dr. Philips. Back to you. I've had enough surprises for a lifetime, and I don't want to go into court and have even more. Sorry to be so blunt, but what is going on with you?"

"Three days before my deposition, my wife left me. Went to Vegas for a quickie divorce. Once it was final, she throws in my face that she had been cheating on me all along with an old boyfriend. The love of her life. His wife had died and they decided to get together. I mean, the divorce, that was awful. To discover my marriage was a charade, no more than a sham. . . devastating.

"But that was just the beginning. Last Monday I got a call from one of her friends asking me why I never showed up for her funeral. I never even knew she'd died. I had no idea what was going on. I called my children. My daughters didn't call back. My son told me that my mother and her Romeo died in an auto accident. There was this place, a turn where she got confused last summer. She was at the wheel and she made the same mistake she made with me in the same place with lover-boy, and they got t-boned. When I asked why I hadn't been told about the funeral, he said that she had told the kids that if anything happened to her, I was not to be told."

"My God!"

"The next day, I got a letter by Federal Express. My son said that my ex and her lover-boy had sat down with my kids and told them they were his children with her, not mine. That was earlier this week. Here we are on Friday. Nothing more to be said."

"My God. . ." said Kate.

"I wish I could think of something to say, Jay."

"Same for me, Linda."

* * *

By 11:00 Linda and Jay were both cross-eyed with fatigue and frustration.

"Time to call it a night," Linda yawned. "Let me go upstairs and get my sweater. I want to leave top down when I drive you back. Believe it or not, that helps me clear my mind.

"No matter what we've talked over, this whole thing makes no sense. How could she have given such an incredibly detailed description of that room? How could she have drawn that sketch of Dr. Travers that captures his face like a photograph?"

"Vivid details don't mean truth. That's just a common misconception."

"But Dr. Billingsly and Dr. Ernest believed they did. . ."

"And they ran like scalded cats the moment the road got rocky. Look. . . Billingsley's classy, prominent, respected, and well connected.

He was your local guy, the one everyone knows and respects. You chose him because if someone everybody in town thinks is OK gets behind something folks might have a hard time believing, his credibility would make it easier for a jury to handle some very controversial issues than if outsiders brought it up first. Ernest covers his butt.

"Look. When something is surrounded by strong differences of opinion, polarized differences of opinion, the truth can get lost in the middle. Let's not waste time speculating and fretting instead of thinking. You say your client is Snow White. She's a nice lady who's fucked up. Her patient is another nice lady who's fucked up. The way her patient is fucked up, through no fault of her own, she is on the brink of torpedoing your fucked up but probably innocent client. For what it's worth, I believe you."

"So?"

"So? If we're trying to save Snow White, it's 'Heigh-ho, heigh-ho, it's off to work we go.'"

Linda raised an eyebrow. "Are you Doc?"

"Maybe, when we figure this out."

"And me?"

"Until we make some sense of this mess, we're both Dopey."

* * *

A minute later, Kate came down the stairs to Linda's home office.

"Linda sat down on her bed for a second and went out like a light. I'm sure she'll wake up in a few minutes."

"Maybe I should call a cab."

"Give her a few minutes. If she's not down, I'll wake her. I could use a drink. What about you? Linda and Hunter are into single malts."

"Sure. Anything. Neat, please."

Kate returned with two glasses. They contained the same amount of Scotch, but Jay noticed a liquid film up one side of Kate's glass, leading right up to a faint touch of lipstick.

"Better times," she toasted, holding up her glass.

"That wouldn't take much," Jay chuckled, touching his glass to her own. He took a small sip, savoring it. "Pretty good stuff. What are you serving?"

"Monkey Shoulder. About the best of the blends. I like it more than the first few single malts I found. Part Glenfiddich."

"So, who are you, Kate? I hate to think of anyone just in terms of their. . ."

"Misadventures?"

"I would have said, misfortunes."

"I'm just an empty shell that used to be extremely rich, attractive, and desirable. I'm still rich, though."

"Please don't talk about yourself that way."

"Why not? That's my reality." Kate took a massive swig. When she lowered her glass, its contents were gone.

"Maybe you've deceived yourself about that so long that you really believe it."

"Linda said you're some super-smart shrink. Don't try to psychoanalyze me."

"Too late."

"Look. It was a good ride. I enjoyed it."

"Let's grant that."

"I don't want to talk about me. Tell me about you. Or are you afraid to let your guard down?" Kate looked at her glass. "I'm due for a refill."

"Kate, I think you need to get Linda, or I have to get a cab."

"Are you afraid of me? Or maybe I repel you and every other man. . . Oh, shit! I spilled my drink. I'll be right back."

"Kate. I'm going to tell you something. Take it or leave it. At a gut level, I think you may be an absolutely fascinating woman. But that's a woman you're afraid to be. What you tell me is the real you is the you think you've lost to cancer and getting older. I understand what you're saying. But without question, if you took care of yourself, you'd still be, though that term disgusts me, a fantastic package. I don't doubt that a while back you were a gloriously beautiful woman by any standards. And you will be again. But the package isn't the person.

"I know what it's like to be judged by your appearance. If you said that you would ever have gone out with someone like me when you had confidence in yourself as a package, we'd both know you were lying. I've spent a lifetime watching beautiful women react to me and people like me. We don't make the grade. But I'm more than a short, overweight, plain guy who's considered a quack in more than a few quarters, and even if no one else on this Goddamn planet knows that, I do.

"In a few months you'll get off your ass, get some help with your depression, get some reconstructive surgery, and be dazzling to everyone but queers and pedophiles. But if you don't try to face the person you can be, you'll be playing 'Beat the Clock' until you run out of time and space, and you'll die never knowing who you were or could have been."

"You have a hell of a lot of nerve to say something like that to me!"

"Sorry you can't take a compliment. I've tried to tell you you're more than you think, and you don't know what to do with it. I'm out of here."

"Let me call you a taxi! Let me call Linda! If you go, what can I say?"

"Tell her my allergies acted up."

"Allergies? What are you allergic to?"

"Masochistic self-loathing and bullshit. You deserve to treat yourself better than that."

CHAPTER 67

Linda rose early, made herself a pot of coffee, and got to work reviewing the Underwood files. She was desperate to find some hint, some clue, some loose end that had eluded her till now and might inspire a new strategy for the defense. . . and redeem her.

Before she poured her second cup, she decided to check on Kate. The guest room was empty. *No big deal. Kate is a big girl. Maybe she's taken a walk. Maybe she's out early, trying to repair Jane's flowerbeds.* An uncanny feeling sent Linda racing back up the stairs. Not a wrinkle on the guest room bed! No one had slept there. *No! Something is wrong! Where is Kate? How did Philips get back to his hotel?*

Our family is so full of drunks! Eve remembers so much more than I do. Mom and Dad drank so much before they sobered up. Mom was happy, pleasant, even delightful when she was drunk. Dad? Completely unpredictable. I'm sure that's why Eve's a shrink.

She found Kate sitting on the grass in her yard, staring at the rosebushes Linda and Hunter nursed so lovingly.

"Kate. Are you OK?"

"That I don't know. But I do know my life is out of control, and that bastard Philips made me look at myself just long enough to. . . I don't know."

"I'm going to get you some help. Today."

"You have this big case to get ready."

"First things first."

Linda called her father at the American embassy in Beijing. "No, Dad. I don't think she told anyone in the family about either the cancer or the divorce. I think there's a drinking problem."

"Stay by the phone."

Eight minutes later, the phone rang. "My name is Phyllis. I'll be there in an hour to talk to Kate and take her to a meeting."

"But. . ."

"I don't know who your father is, but when I get a call from the Chairman of the General Services Board of AA asking me to reach out to a person in need, even I understand someone big is calling in a favor."

"I'm sorry if my father. . ."

"Stop right there. Whoever Kate is, whatever Kate is. . . I once was Kate."

* * *

"That woman from AA should be coming by in fifteen minutes. I hope you'll follow through."

"Uh-huh. I'd guess Jay Philips about 5′6 or 7 and 180–185," said Kate. "Does that seem right?"

"I guess. Why?"

"Just thinking. Do you think he picks out his own clothes?"

"Whoever does, Kate, I'm sure the fashion police have a warrant for their arrest. What are you up to?"

"Nothing. Just thinking."

"Right."

"Linda, you know I've been in love with myself all my life. But I've become a person I can't live with. These days, I'm not liking myself very much. Your mom and dad were pretty good drinkers, and they got their acts together. You probably wouldn't know a thing about sibling rivalry. . ."

"Right." *Touché*, Linda winced.

"Right. . . And if you think I'll let your mom, my big sister Betty, make it look like she can do something I can't do. . . I can't live with that!"

"So, you'll go to AA to prove you're as strong as my mom? What about telling Uncle Rudy to screw himself?"

"OK, that too, though I've done a pretty good job of that already. I'd rather say that than. . . Enough said."

"You're entitled to have a secret motivation or two. Or at least to think that you do."

"Is it that transparent?"

"Oh, Kate! You just met him. Half the world thinks he's a certified loser. He's smart and gutsy. Beyond that, I don't know what anyone would see in him. I wish I felt better about that guy."

"Linda, you don't know what it's like for someone who had it all to become a member of the league of the walking wounded. I hope you never know."

CHAPTER 68

Phyllis Shea proved to be a woman in her 50's with short brown hair, an infectious grin, and a knack for hiding a few extra pounds with flair and style.

"Pleased to meet you, Kate."

"Likewise, Phyllis. Nice of you to come over like this."

"We're a community of people helping one another. You seem to qualify for membership."

"I'm being granted membership in a whole bunch of societies I never planned to join. OK. I'll try this. What do I have to do?"

"First, let me get to know you a little. . ."

Phyllis got to the heart of the matter with lightning speed, frightening speed.

"May I speak freely?" she asked.

"I'll risk it."

"I'd call your ex a pig, but I'm kind of fond of pigs. Let's see. . . Does ass-hole seem to fit the fellow?"

"But isn't it always a two-way thing?"

"What did you do to make the marriage fail?"

"Uh. . . I grew older and had a double mastectomy."

"You sleazy bitch! Your moral failings appall me! If I were a guy, I'd've left you too. Imagine your letting him down that way! You know what Oscar Wilde would have said?"

"You've got to be kidding me."

"No. He would have said that 'To lose one breast may be considered a misfortune, but to lose two? That seems downright careless!'"

It took Kate a few seconds to push through the shock, before her giggle exploded into a laughing jag that swept over both of them. Finally, Kate caught her breath.

"You know, Phyllis. . . I really thought I was so far down I'd never laugh again. When you walked in here, I said to myself, 'Now, I think that's a classy lady.' But I never figured you for a comedienne."

"My audiences didn't figure me for one either, so I came home and made a graceful transition from a coke-head failure in cheap nightclubs into a drunken mediocrity teaching in underfunded public schools. But I finally got sober."

"It's funny. You're funny. And I won't take back that classy lady comment. But when I hear you talk, you sound like someone else I met last night. Someone who got to see the worst of me."

"Another classy lady?"

"Not quite. Let me get my things, and lead on."

"If you let me lead on, you're in for more than a meeting."

"Oh, well. . ."

CHAPTER 69

Forest fires broke out in the area of the planned Air Guard exercises. Ben's mission was scrubbed. His crew was ordered to get some sleep, refuel, and return to base. He contacted Linda Gilchrist to review where matters stood. Then, he made a second call, and a third.

* * *

"Nate? I'm going need to make someone think I'm a sitting duck."

"Be yourself. That should do the trick."

"It's a Charlie Foxtrot situation. This will be in front of a bunch of people, but my real targets are some folks who're gonna try to make me look bad."

"Charlie Foxtrot?"

"Air Force lingo for 'cluster fuck.'"

"Drop your shoulders, look down and away, and think of your most embarrassing moment to get some red in your face. You might even nod your head slowly side to side once or twice."

"Shame?"

"Yeah. Like you're afraid of the world's judgment, like the only outstanding things about you are your shortcomings. I can get you started with a list of the top two hundred, if that would help."

"You are the master. Thanks."

"And what has someone done to earn such special attention?"

"It's a matter of malevolent bullying. Not fit for your delicate ears."

"I don't envy your prey."

CHAPTER 70

After talking to Ben, Linda checked in with Jeff Wilder and Sally Warren. Both senior partners were up early, bringing themselves up to speed on Underwood. Linda told them she would be tracking down a few loose ends, preparing for Monday's completion of Jay Philips' direct, and making notes to prep Ben Jordan.

Linda drove her little blue Miata convertible over to Jay Philips' hotel. She noticed Jay winced as he walked over to her car. . . *My God! Did he walk all the way back to his hotel?* Neither said a word about the events of the previous evening.

HighPoint Centre was a boxy, unimaginative office building set back from the street behind a generous parking area. The parking lot was nearly empty. They spent a few minutes studying the directory. Financial groups, insurance companies, small law firms, and charitable organizations predominated, with a sprinkling of psychotherapists and medical specialists. No Suite 312 appeared in the directory.

"Well, Linda. What's our plan?"

"To wander around until we come up with one. The governor's law firm has offices here. So does the investment company he started."

"Does that mean anything?"

"I don't know."

They started at the highest floor, the sixth. The entrance to the governor's firms was immediately opposite the elevator. They walked the halls on every level over and over. Finally, they stood at the exact spot where Melody Jarrett insisted Dr. Travers' office had been.

The wall was smooth, the carpet undisturbed, and the vinyl cove base ran continuously between the doors of the suites on both sides of the entire length of the hall. Linda tapped the wall up to, through, and beyond where the suite was supposed to be. Jay watched with intense concentration. He said nothing.

"This is crazy. Dr. Underwood was sure Melody Jarrett was telling the truth. I was sure Dr. Underwood was telling the truth. Now I don't know what to think. You may not think much of Dr. Billingsly, but around here. . . Our senior partners think he's the man. When he withdrew, he might as well have said that he was switching sides."

"If he had some knowledge and some balls, he would have known that memory for gist is better than memories for details. Everybody looks for the details as proof one way or the other and tries to knock down an argument if there are discrepancies. But the main thing is the gist, that someone who shouldn't have done something did something. He should have shrugged his shoulders and said, 'Whatever room it happened in, it shouldn't have happened.' When he bailed out, he knocked your entire strategy out of whack, and the judge was so angry that he pushed you to present me, and left the jurors with the impression he has no respect for you."

"Where is Sherlock Holmes when you need him?"

"In the absence of tangible evidence to study, you'd do better with Hercule Poirot and his little grey cells."

"You mean just sitting and thinking?"

"How can you collect and study evidence until you know what to look for and where?"

"I guess you're right. In the absence of an armchair, I'm sitting down."

They sat on the floor in silence, staring at where the mysterious room 312 was supposed to be. A man walked down the hall.

"Can I help you," he asked. "Are you waiting for someone?"

"No," said Jay.

"Well, actually, we are," said Linda. She stood up and straightened herself out. "We're waiting for the mailman."

"The mailman?"

"The mailman. I'm Linda Gilchrist, an attorney over at Mackey Markham & Wilder. My firm sent a very important message to the wrong address by mistake. Well. . . I made the mistake, and it could cost me my job. I have to catch up with the mailman and see if I can talk him into helping me out here."

"Not a chance."

"I know, but I've got to try. When does he deliver mail on Saturdays?"

"Maybe an hour, hour and a half from now."

"Well, I guess I'll be sitting downstairs for a while, waiting and praying."

"Well, good luck. And you?"

"I'm her father," said Jay. "Along for moral support."

* * *

They parked themselves on a bench near the front door. Fifteen minutes passed. Linda tried to think out loud. She became increasingly irritated when Jay Philips seemed to be completely inattentive.

"You're not listening to a word I'm saying!"

"Right! I'm listening to my little gray cells. They are singing a crazy song. I'll be back in 15 minutes."

Linda shrugged, and waved her hand listlessly. Jay tried to say something to lift her spirits, but came up empty. "Be right back." Jay walked the halls of the third floor, looking toward the juncture of the walls and the floor. Then he walked up the stairs to the sixth floor and made a circuit of every other floor except the ground level. Something bothered him, but he couldn't put a finger on it. He climbed back up to the sixth floor, and made the same circuits, floor after floor.

"Come with me, Linda. Let's take a walk. I get the weird feeling that there's something there, but I'm missing it."

I don't believe this! So much in the balance, and he wants to walk around in circles! Oh, my God! A lifetime of gracious courtesy took over. Linda was surprised to hear herself saying, "Lead on, MacPhilips!"

"Indeed! Lay on, MacGilchrist, and damned be she who first cries 'Hold! enough!'"

"You just needing to be obsessive about Shakespeare?"

"About everything. But we're talking about going to war. . ."

"Give me a hand."

Jay pulled Linda to her feet. They walked the halls again. Then again.

"OK. At first, I thought you were crazy. Now I'm not sure. One more time."

They passed a ground floor door labeled "Maintenance."

"Wait!" Linda kneeled, and ran her hands along the wall right over the cove base near the door.

"What? That's just a scuff or scrape."

"It's on both sides of the door."

"So? Probably folks park some cart near the door to get supplies and get careless."

"Let's do a survey on scuffs and scrapes. Count the total number and see if any break through the wall covering."

The sixth floor's cove bases yielded some four dozen scuffs. There were a few on the walls, and one tear opposite the elevator. The fifth, over sixty scuffs on the cove bases, several scuffs and scrapes on the walls, and two tears near a suite being prepared for a new occupant. The fourth floor had about fifty scuffs on the cove bases, half a dozen conspicuous scuffs and scrapes, and a tear in the wall near the elevator.

"Happens all the time," said Jay, pointing to the tear. "Stuff happens when people move in or out or get furniture deliveries."

"Skip the third floor. We'll come back."

The second floor was much the same. They climbed to the third floor.

Two voices spoke at once. "What are we looking for?" They laughed.

"Holmes would say. . ." Jay began.

"Let's just do this."

They worked in silence, pausing only to exchange quizzical glances.

"Twenty scuffs on the cove base, and only a handful on the wall, only one on the wall where Melody Jarrett had situated Suite 312."

"What do you think, Linda?"

"Same as you, Jay. The cove base on this floor is probably newer than the cove base on the other floors, and I suspect that the wall covering along this hall is not as old as the wall covering on the rest of the floor, and the other floors."

"Since you are such a lady, I'll say this for both of us. Holy shit!"

Jay closed his eyes. Now Linda knew better than to suspect inattention. Was he like Poirot? *Are those little gray cells singing to Jay Philips?* She closed her own eyes, just in time to be jolted by Jay's voice.

"Can I borrow your car for a few minutes? I promise to be back in before the mailman is due."

"What are you up to?"

"You'll see."

"Have you ever driven a car like mine?"

"Why, Ms. Gilchrist! At times I wonder if you consider me completely incompetent?"

"Have you?"

"No! Squat, ugly, old people are not allowed to drive trendy convertibles. I'll probably get a ticket for being uncool."

He was gone before Linda could find something to say. *He sees right through me! I'm looking down on him and he takes me to the woodshed. That little bastard! Am I learning something pretty ugly about myself?*

Linda stared at the wall where suite 312 should have been. Jay Philips was not the kind of hero she would call upon to help her hold the line, to help her find her way out of a diabolical maze that threatened Joan Underwood with the imminent destruction of her life. . . And to rescue her from the likely demise of her own career. Worse, no matter how careful she had tried to be, Jay Philips knew that she looked down on him, would never respond to him as a man, and considered him a pathetic last resort, no more than cannon fodder to be thrown into the breach until the real cavalry charged over the hill.

Linda's mother Betty was born rich, a renowned beauty with a natural grace and savoir faire that disguised an awesome intellect. She charmed heads of state wherever she and her diplomat husband were stationed. But she had never minced words with her five striking daughters. "Yes, your looks and presence will open almost any doors for you. But once you walk in through that door, if your character doesn't match the package, you'll never be taken seriously as a person." Alone with Linda, Betty had added, "Sometimes I worry that you think that all the wonderful things about you make you better than other people." Linda argued, but she knew her mother was right. And now she needed the help of someone who'd picked up on her attitude, a man who had had more than his fill of people like her treating him with contempt.

Linda waited in squirming discomfort, reviewing a lifetime of looking down her nose at people less bright, less gifted, less socially adroit, and less attractive than herself.

* * *

As Jay Philips started to drive away, he couldn't help reacting to the block-like ugliness of the HighPoint Centre. *If I were a building, I'd be HighPoint Centre.* The trees planted around it were meticulously groomed, but their placements in symmetrical rows interrupted by equivalent rectangles of manicured grass were stiflingly unimaginative, cookie-cutter identical with one exception. Driving around the building toward the street, a single flaw in its otherwise stifling symmetry caught his eye. One tree in one rectangle was several feet shorter than the others. It was groomed not so much for what someone believed was a pleasing shape as much as to preserve every straggling inch of its height. Jay used the small camera that was his constant companion to photograph HighPoint Centre from every angle and point of the compass.

On his return, he anchored a ball of twine at one end of the building and marked the cord when he reached the other. Then he anchored it once again at one end of the building and walked it to the place where the shorter tree stood, unaffected by Jay's racing ratiocinations. He marked the spot on his cord.

Jay had noticed that there was a window in the middle and at the end of each hall. When he reentered the building, he went to the sixth floor and worked his way down. He photographed the trees as they appeared from every available window on every floor.

“Town and Country Hardware, eh? And Quick Pix, that one hour developing place?” said Linda. “You’re late. What’s in those bags?”

“Film and. . . Wait! Just a minute. . . What’s that?”

They heard someone humming and singing a Beach Boys classic. A mailman turned a corner and began to make his way down the hall where they stood. Absorbed in his task, he was almost upon them before he looked up, startled to see them.

“Shit! Sorry. I didn’t think anyone else was around.”

“We should have spoken up,” said Linda, “but you seemed so busy and I like the Beach Boys. I didn’t want to interrupt.”

“No harm done. Can I help you?”

“Well, I don’t know. I’m a lawyer over at Mackey Markham & Wilder.”

“Yeah. Not on my route.”

“I know. Now, please don’t laugh. I sent some really important papers over to a client in this building. Or at least I thought I did. Just before I left the office yesterday, I was wishing my secretary a good weekend, and I saw those papers on her desk. I nearly died. We figured out she must have sent some other important papers there instead, and those papers are very, very confidential. If I can’t straighten things out, I’m afraid I’ve made such a bad mistake that I could be fired.”

“Well, I’d be breaking federal laws if I let you take some mail that’s not addressed to you, but maybe I can let you know if it’s actually here for them.”

“You’re a lifesaver! Thanks! Even if I have to camp out here till Monday morning, it’s a small price to pay.”

“OK. Who’d you send the letter to?”

“Dr. Travers.”

“But he’s in 606.”

“My God! We sent it to 312. What a mess this is!”

“I wish you were the only one. This happens every month or so.”

"What do you mean?"

"It's the craziest thing. Mail keeps coming to 312. . . sometimes to the doctor, usually just to "Occupant." But there's no Suite 312. I keep taking it up to 606 and telling the doctor to let people know his real address. It's changed at the Post Office, but they keep on coming, and every now and then one slips by."

"So, he doesn't have an office in 312 at all?"

"No. No one does. It ain't there."

"Who's in that suite?"

"There is no 312. If there were, and things were numbered the way the other rooms are numbered here, it would be right where we are, between 310 and 314."

"Could he be in one of those?"

"No. 310 is Burr & Weinstein. They're accountants. 314 was unoccupied for a while. Then, last year Midtown Ophthalmology Associates moved in. Nice folks. Gave me a break on my glasses."

"Who was there before?"

"Beau Chalmers Legal and Financial Associates."

"The governor!"

"Yep. His firm moved to the top floor when he bought the building. Suite 600 and a bunch of others."

"So, you keep getting mail for a suite that doesn't exist?" asked Jay. "And somebody gives my poor daughter some bum address, and now her ass is on the line? How long you been on this route?"

"Dad!"

"I'm your father and this is a mess. Be quiet." He shook his head. "Kids! Little kids, little problems. Big kids, big problems. I got every right to bitch."

"I'm with you on that one, mister. Let's see. I been on this route three years, give or take."

"Just check if there's a letter from her law firm to any place here, and we'll figure out what we need to do."

"That's a big job."

"Bullshit! I bet you're a careful guy. You sorted the mail. If there was something for that suite that isn't there, you'd've put it aside. But, no insult meant, she's my kid. If I walk with you while you make your deliveries and you take a quick look at each bunch just in case something got in the wrong pile or whatever, my kid has a chance to figure out how to make things right, and no skin off your butt. Right?"

"That'll take some time."

"How many kids you got?"

"OK. I get it. Let's go."

Linda spoke up. "Hey. Just a crazy idea. But do the superintendents have a mailbox here?"

"No more."

"Isn't Randy Jones the sup?

"Never heard that name. Interior Services Corp. handles this building, and a lot of others around here. No super on site here since Elijah Springfield."

"Elijah was here a long time, I bet."

"I guess. I never met him. Heard a lot about that big dog of his, though. No one took him in. He still hangs around the building.

"Do you ever get mail for Mr. Springfield and have to forward it?"

"Matter of fact, yeah. Mostly catalogs for seeds and fishing stuff."

"Any idea of where he is these days?"

"I don't know how to say this. He drowned out on Willow Lake a few years back. Some freak boating accident."

"Sorry to hear about that. Lousy luck! OK, kiddo. Let's not hold the man up."

"Dad, would you mind walking with him? There's something else I've got to do or I'll be in trouble about two things instead of one by Monday morning."

* * *

As Linda walked away, the mailman took Jay's measure.

"Yeah!" Jay preempted. "She takes after her mother. She had the looks and the brains."

"I hope my kid turns out as good."

"And has a better secretary!"

The two men chatted aimlessly as the mailman made his rounds.

"Nothing here. Sorry."

"What can I say? My kid's too trusting. Not a bastard like her old man. Thirty years a foreman. Construction in New Jersey. Ya gotta check everybody all the time, right? Thanks. She's tougher than she looks. She'll land on her feet."

Jay texted a message for Linda, "No evidence your letter reached this building at all. I'm going to play a hunch. Later."

* * *

Linda stopped by the local post office. No one there had known Elijah Springfield. Back at HighPoint Centre, she saw a Federal Express deliveryman pushing a cart of packages into the building.

"Hi! Even Saturdays? Is this building on your usual route?"

"Yeah, for years now."

"I was trying to find Dr. Travers' office. I thought he was here, in this building."

"Yeah."

"I thought he was in suite 312, but there is no suite 312."

"Nope. No 312."

"But I was sure he had an office here."

"Not on this floor. Up on the sixth."

"Do you ever have any problems delivering his mail?"

"No, not me. But a few years back, some of us and the mail carriers had problems. When the regulars were on vacation, some of the subs would wander around with stuff for 312, and some would ask me about it if we ran into one another. Usually junk mail, you know? Catalogs, advertisements, y'know? The old mailman told me that lot of stuff came with the 312 address. Doc Travers said it was an old mistake that he just gave up trying to get right, 'cause it was just stuff from mailing lists, and wasn't worth the effort. So, I been on this route 5 years. First couple years, after he told me, I'd bring anything marked 312 to 606. But nothing for 312 for years now. Jeez! Did something important get lost?"

"No problem. I'm just trying to find the man. One of his patients drew a picture of him. She wanted him to have it when she passed. I'm the lawyer representing her estate."

"Something valuable?"

"I doubt it. Probably sentimental. But it meant something to her to be sure he got it, and my job is to make sure that what she left behind goes where she wants it to go. I feel so stupid. I assumed that the addresses on her will were still valid. Wow! I hope that's the only silly mistake I made with this estate. Thanks."

CHAPTER 71

"OK, Dr. Philips. Why did you have to run out to a hardware store?"

"Well, what have we got? What are the facts that we really have?"

"Besides my gut feeling that Jarrett was honest, and that Underwood is innocent? Less wear and tear on the third floor and dead mail."

"Good start. What else?"

"Nothing."

"Nothing? What about the fact that the mailman and FedEx guy gave you different dates for mail problems with 312?"

"I don't get it. What does that mean to you?"

"I'm not sure, but I think it means a bug-out."

"A bug-out?"

"Like somebody moved out quickly and changed their FedEx address ASAP because that can be tracked. For every damn piece of mail delivered, you have a pretty good idea what happened. Regular mail. . . didn't get around to that till later. Sloppy. But no trace."

"Pretty thin. . ."

"Well, true. But you remember, Sherlock, 'When you have eliminated the impossible, whatever remains, however improbable, must be the truth.' And there's something else. I'll tell you after I've checked it out."

"So?"

"If we start with the assumption that Jarrett and Underwood are telling the truth as best they can, there must be a way to make this make sense. Let's unwrap our new toys."

"A stud-finder? What's a stud finder?"

"It's a little doodad that tells us what's beneath the surface. It shows us where you can find the studs, the uprights and cross. I'll omit the usual stud jokes."

"It looks like some phaser thing from Star Trek."

"I didn't know you spoke nerd. Curious!" Jay held the "phaser" against the wall. "Calibrating," he said. He moved the stud finder across the surface of the wall where they suspected Suite 312 had been. Nothing.

"Does that crazy thing even work?"

"You're asking me? Oh! Here's something. But, but it's. . . Something is wrong. I'm looking for a big piece of wood, every 18 inches or so. Here's another, around three feet further along. I don't get it."

Jay tried another wall. He found nothing.

"Shit! I'm calling the SOB who sold me this piece of crap!" He rang the hardware store. "You sold me this stud finder, and it doesn't show any studs at. . ." Jay's face went vermillion. "Thanks. I feel like a horse's ass. I don't even know how to apologize. Sorry I got bent out of shape."

"You look. . . Well, I don't know."

"I made a stupid mistake, and he let me down gently. I went looking for studs, right? Well, I was assuming that they were wood. . . That's the way it is in almost all houses. That's residential. But I just learned that in commercial properties, studs are almost always steel."

"My God! I sure didn't know that."

"We better stick to our day jobs.'

Jay switched the stud finder to the setting for finding metal. He started scanning the wall across from the troublesome site that just might be Suite 312.

Now he found steel studs every 18 inches or so. They seemed a little different near the doors. He switched back to wood settings.

"What are you doing?"

"At doors they usually they put a piece of wood on both sides, and sometimes the top. Makes it easier to hang the door. Yep!"

Jay crossed back to the suspect wall, switched to the metal settings, and recalibrated the stud finder.

"By the way, they call the wood thingy the 'buck.' Studs, bucks. . . May I assume that you can handle this testosterone-drenched vocabulary without recourse to sexual politics?"

"Don't press your luck, Buster! So, what does all this mean?"

"Wait a minute. Not done yet." Jay picked a place halfway between the bucks and ran the stud detector slowly up the wall. "I'm too short. We need a few more inches. You'll have to do this, Linda. Let me turn on the sound."

Linda started at her waist. The stud finder was silent until Linda's arm was extended above her head. "Something's there!"

"OK. Move it to your right till it stops beeping." The stud-finder sang its song until the place where Jay had found the upright buck. "Now, all the way to the left. Same stopping point."

When the noise stopped at the left upright buck, Linda asked, "What do we have? What does this mean?"

"Wait!" Jay instructed. He cut two lengths of twine to extend from the floor to where Linda had found the horizontal buck, and another to cover the length between the uprights.

"What?"

"Wait! Now, do the sweeps the same way with the stud finder set for metal."

"There's a metal cross piece just above the buck!"

"Wait!" Jay unwrapped a roll of blue painters' tape. He cut two lengths the same as the twine that measured the vertical bucks up to the cross buck.

"Fix them in place from the ends of the horizontal piece to the floor. Then, stretch this third length between them at the top."

"OK! What next?"

"Maybe we take some pictures?"

CHAPTER 72

Back at Linda's after a stop at Quick Pix, they reviewed their findings again and again. One exterior photograph caught Jay's attention.

"Damn! I missed something! Look at this. At ground level. What is that?"

"I have no idea," Linda responded.

Phyllis had asked an AA friend to handle the disasters that were Kate's hair and nails. When Kate finally made her appearance, she was more her usual self, and just back from another meeting.

"What happened to you, Aunt Kate? You look. . ."

"Well-groomed, but like shit? Did anyone ever tell you that beginning to face yourself sucks? What are you two up to? What's that? A dog door?"

"My God! That connects with what the FedEx guy said. The old custodian, Elijah something," said Linda, "had a big dog. Scared everyone silly."

"Well, that fits. I don't know how that helps us, though." Jay excused himself for a moment.

"What have you two been up to? Can I help?"

"Thanks, but I don't think so," said Linda. She gave Kate a brief summary of where things stood.

"And then one office suite went missing. . . Now, that's a sinister subtraction!"

CHAPTER 73

Sunday afternoon Linda, Jay, and Kate drove back to HighPoint Centre. They repeated and videotaped Jay's first sets of measurements measures with cord and measuring the cord lengths themselves. That allowed them to state dimensions clearly in yards, feet, and inches. Then, they walked up to the small panel they had discussed the night before.

Jay pushed at the panel. It swung in with a rasping creak. "I think you're right, Kate. I wish we could take a look inside."

"No way!" said Linda. "Completely illegal. And I don't see any way to get a search warrant. What could we say?"

* * *

When they returned to Linda's home, Jay and Linda poured over their findings. Kate occupied herself leafing through Linda's law books. After dinner, Kate told them Phyllis had recommended she attend another meeting that evening to hear a particularly good speaker, but could not accompany her. Linda had misgivings, but Kate reassured her she'd be safe going alone.

"It's at the Presbyterian church, just a mile or two from here. . ."

* * *

Kate drove past the Presbyterian church and beyond to HighPoint Centre. She did not park. Instead, she cruised around, periodically returning to its parking lot. When it was quite dark, she drove into a McDonalds and bought a dozen Big Macs and one large Coke. She stopped at a 24-hour chain pharmacy and bought an extension cord. Kate saw no sign of human activity, but she thought she saw furtive signs of motion under the trees near the building.

Kate took a sip of her Coke, extracted a single Big Mac from her trove, unwrapped it, pushed the dog door open, and underhanded the Big Mac through the dog door as hard as she could. Within seconds, there was a bark, followed by the unmistakable sound of a big dog snarfing down her offering. She tossed another unwrapped Big Mac through the dog door. . . more snarfing.

A few seconds later a dark, massive head pushed the dog door half open. Its eyes fixed on Kate, it took a few steps toward her. Then it growled, turned, and disappeared back through the door.

"I'd like to report a problem with a dog," Kate told the police dispatcher. "No. It is not an emergency."

Twenty minutes later, a patrol car appeared.

"Dog problem, lady?"

Kate explained that she had seen a pack of dogs enter the dog door. "I don't know if they are OK, or if they're tearing the place apart."

The officer called in. He listened silently for over a minute.

"Geez, Sarge! This place belongs to the governor? What should I do?"

"What's going on?"

"Just a minute, Sarge. OK to tell her? Out animal control people are with a surveillance team, staking out a possible dog-fight."

"Maybe I can help. I picked up some stuff for a late-night snack, and my daughter asked me to pick up an extension cord so I can charge my phone in her guest room. Not enough plugs. I'm good with dogs. If your sergeant says it's OK, how about I try to lure the dogs out with a burger, and make a leash out of the cord?"

"My sergeant says he can't ask you to do that, ma'am. There are risks."

"But your sergeant won't stop me, will he?" Kate prepared a slip-noose, propped the dog door half-open with one leg, and plopped two Big Macs two feet from the opening. Within seconds, the head of a dog with Mastiff blood peeked out. Unable to push the door completely open, the dog crawled on its belly till it could grab the first Big Mac, pushing his head through Kate's noose as it claimed its meal. Kate patted the dog's head as she let it finish the second burger. Then she moved the leg that held the dog door partly open, and gently pulled the dog toward her, scratching its head and murmuring gently.

"There may be more dogs in there." Kate threw another burger inside. There was no response. "Should I go it and check? I bet I can get through the dog door."

"My sergeant says no."

"Tell him that come Monday morning, the Governor is going to find a Big Mac swarming with insects and tempting rats, mice, and racoons from all over, and he just might find the Hound of the Baskervilles and his friends waiting to say hello. My guess is that that gives you probable cause."

The officer laughed. "Sarge says that works for him, but you go in with my helmet, vest, and baton."

"I'd be safer with a Big Mac and a flashlight."

"OK, lady. That, too."

Kate prepared herself. The sealed-off super's room was dusty. It smelled of hound. Cobwebs abounded but only above waist-level. *Dogs must have knocked them down.* There was a mail slot in the door that once had been the super's entrance to the inner corridors. Underneath the slot was a scattered pile of dusty mail.

Under the beam of the policeman's torch, she read the addresses on the top half dozen. *Linda needs to know! How can I. . .?*

"You OK in there, lady?"

Kate picked up the Big Mac she'd thrown in before entering. She rubbed it all over the pile of mail.

"Everything is OK. But that Big Mac is all over everything. I guess I should have thrown a plain burger, but I didn't have one handy. I'll have to clean up a little to make sure I don't leave a picnic for the bugs and rats a picnic and an unhappy politician for you. How's my new friend?"

"A hell of a lot less nervous than I am!"

* * *

Kate followed the officer to his precinct. She called Linda before she wrote out the report the sergeant requested.

Phyllis met Linda and Jay at the station. Linda was frantic, convinced that Kate was really under arrest for driving under the influence. They found Kate and the sergeant swapping favorite "secret ingredients" for their barbecue recipes. A massive Mastiff-like dog on an extension-cord leash slept peacefully on the floor alongside Kate.

"Do you want this mail covered with. . . whatever?" Kate asked the sergeant.

"Let's take a look. . . occupant, occupant, occupant. . . Nah."

"I'll get rid of it for you."

* * *

Back at their cars, Linda asked, "Why are you carrying that trash around?"

"I like McDonalds," said Phyllis.

"This trash is solid gold. I'll show you later. Thanks, Phyllis."

"A pleasure to be completely useless. See you tomorrow. What are you going to call your new friend?"

"Well, in the spirit of new beginnings, what about 'Phoenix'? These days I'm all about rising from the ashes. How do you like that, Phoenix? Good boy!"

"I'll take those things for you," said Jay, reaching for Kate's bag of "trash" and her bag of Big Macs.

In a flash, Phoenix leapt at Jay. He went down hard.

"He must have been worried that Dr. Philips was getting between him and his Big Macs and the woman he loves. Oh, my God! He's out cold. And that wrist. . ."

Kate knelt down at Jay's side. "Jay? Jay? You're right, Phyllis! Go back in the station and have them call an ambulance. Someone else has to rise from the dead."

CHAPTER 74

Very early Monday morning, Kate drove her much-abused Toyota Corolla rental to Memorial Hospital. She brought a number of packages to Jay Philips' room.

"But. . ."

"Turnabout is fair play. You told me you weren't prepared to accept my refusal to treat myself with respect. That got me thinking. . ."

"I can't accept all of this. . ."

"So, pay me back some day."

"It won't fit. . ."

"I wouldn't be so sure. I checked out your stuff at my niece's place, and corrected for how badly it fit you. Bribed the tailor to rush. You can't walk into court again looking like you grabbed the first things you saw in a thrift shop. If you have no self-respect, it kills your credibility. Somebody told me that. Quite recently, I believe."

"But. . ."

"No matter what you say, time to face the fact that what you've been going through has nearly destroyed you. I don't know what you're going to decide to do with yourself. But someone has to do for you what you started doing for me, or I won't be the only one who drives a rental car into a flower bed. Alcoholism and cancer didn't break me. Rejection made me a broken alcoholic with her boobs gone. When the person you've built your life around kicks you into the gutter, that can turn anybody inside out."

Jay's face went red. He tried to head off the tears with a blink. It didn't work. He tried to look away. Whenever he looked back at Kate, she stared him down. She made no attempt to wipe away the tears of her own.

"Well," Jay blew his nose, quite clumsily. "You're right. I thought that no matter how much crap I took, I could handle it. My heart was in my family and the handful of people who respected my work."

"Like you said on Friday?"

"I guess I was fooling myself."

"You can't afford that sort of nonsense. When you walk around broadcasting whatever it is, you're broadcasting. . . You make anyone who cares anything about you want to slap some sense into you."

"Luckily, no one gives a damn. . ."

There was a loud noise. Kate turned on her heel and left the room, leaving Jay Philips with a red mark in the shape of her right hand on his left cheek, and a silly grin all over his face.

* * *

When his orthopedic surgeon checked on him, he started when he saw the hand-shaped red mark, fading but unmistakable. "Well, you're good to go. Here's a copy of your films. Uh. . ." He pointed.

"Someone took it upon herself to slap some sense into me."

"Dog bite, concussion, broken arm, and her? Now you've got yourself slapped by a beautiful blonde? You shrinks!" He turned to walk out just as the neurologist came into the room.

"What the hell happened to you?"

"A blonde," shot the orthopod, waving from the door. The neurologist shook his head and smirked.

"What?" asked Jay.

"From my perspective as a neurologist, she should have kicked you in the nuts. With another blow to the head, I'll have to check you again in a couple of hours before we let you go."

CHAPTER 75

Ben Jordan and another man closed the door of Bill Mackey's corner office. They shook hands. The other man turned back into Bill's office. Then, checking that the halls were clear, he escorted a pale and shaky Bill Mackey toward a service elevator while Ben made his way down the hall to Linda's cluttered cubby-hole.

"I expected you here ten minutes ago, Dr. Jordan. Time is tight."

"I stopped in on Mr. Mackey. Sorry."

"I didn't know he was back at work for sure. What's this all about?"

"He's not back at work. He's gone home already. Anything more is privileged. Here I am."

"Everybody's got secrets. Why do I feel so damn screwed?"

"Good reality testing? This secret isn't mine to share, but it would meet with your approval. Let's move on."

"OK. We reviewed your testimony last night. We went over the likely challenges. Turns out Dr. Philips is still in the emergency ward at Memorial. We'll be starting with you first thing unless we have some sort of ruckus with plaintiff's attorneys. But I reached them first thing, and Galvin has no problems. Have any questions or concerns cross your mind since we spoke?"

"What happened to Jay Philips?"

"It's a long story, but my aunt befriended a stray mutt that looks like a mastiff from hell. When Philips reached out to carry some packages for her, the dog, his name is Phoenix, by the way, must have thought he was a threat and half tore him apart."

"That poor bastard. . . Shit. Fill me in later. But for now, sure. . . I had hundreds of questions, but I thought most of them through. What I've got left over are just a couple of questions and a request."

"Go ahead."

"First, tell me something about the personalities of the folks on the other side, and tell me who is likely to do the cross. You don't have to tell me anything about the ringer. He's become quite a celebrity. Just the locals."

Linda filled him in on Lou Galvin.

"But what about Gillian Bullock? I saw her name as well."

"She did a few minor depositions. She's just a gofer. Like I was supposed to be till Bill got sick. I don't know a thing about her."

"Yet here you are carrying the case. If you don't think of her as a significant force, just like you, you're setting yourself up to get blindsided again."

Linda folded her arms across her chest. "I don't think so."

"Those depositions. You've observed her. What impression did she make?"

"She was competent."

"May I speak freely?"

"Here, yes. On the stand, no."

"You've taken some hits. You're angry and depressed. But I think you've got some fight left. When you say someone like you can be blown off, you're either looking down on her or projecting your own self-hatred on her. If she's someone like you, she can rise to the occasion, step in for the first chair, and torpedo your little rowboat. Respect her, respect yourself, or your lawyering and my testimony ain't worth shit."

"I hear you. But I think she's just there for errands and to show that a smart young woman wouldn't automatically side with me and Dr. Underwood."

"Your call. You heard my read. You know I think this whole mess is a deeper and stinkier cesspool than your firm realizes. Now, I am going to make one request of you. It's unreasonable, but I just spoke with your Mr. Mackey. . . When you ask me about my military experience in Israel, which you will, push until I refuse to answer, and then drop it."

"But. . ."

"Like a hot potato."

Oh, no! Another Joan Underwood? Or is he as devious as Eve tells me, always playing to get an edge? But if Bill Mackey says so. . .

"And wasn't there a second question?"

Jeff Wilder stepped through the door.

"Hello, Linda. I was listening in. If Dr. Jordan is as quick as we hope he is, his second question would be compound-complex: 'Why the hell did Mackey Markham & Wilder let a junior attorney like yourself, however gifted and competent, get left out there to hang in the breeze?' 'How did Brett Connery wind up in Germany?' And the answer is, damned if I know, but Bill Mackey told me to find out. Until we do, I'll be sitting in as second chair. Linda, I don't know this case well, but Dr. Jordan might be right. I smell a rat. Linda, let me say this again. I owe you an apology for going after you the way I did. It's clear at this point that someone had to be working very hard to put you and the rest of us this far behind the eight ball. Anything else, Dr. Jordan?"

"Yeah. Why do you suppose plaintiff's counsel did such a weird deposition on Jay Philips?"

"I really don't know," said Linda.

"Nor do I," said Jeff, "but I think it was more gamesmanship than legal strategy. They probably sized up Philips as down and out. They figured treating him as if he were meaningless and insignificant might trip him up if he became a witness of record at the trial. I hope they guessed wrong."

"I'd bet good money that they were tracking him leading up to the deposition and knew about his wife's filing for divorce. They were trying to break him."

CHAPTER 76

After the attorneys met with Judge Lasko, it was agreed to allow Jeff Wilder to assume second chair pending the return of either Bill Mackey or Brett Connery, and that contrary to usual practice, either Wilder or Linda Gilchrist might speak for the defense. Linda informed the court that Dr. Philips remained under neurological observation at Memorial Hospital.

"His broken arm has been set. That's not the problem. Dr. Philips also suffered a blow to the head. He was unconscious for a brief period of time. The doctors at Memorial doctors kept him under observation overnight. A neurologist will check him out later this morning. Dr. Philips will inform us of his availability as soon as he is cleared. If it please the court, your honor, in order to avoid wasting the time of the court, we'll begin with our next witness, Dr. Benjamin Jordan."

"First things first, Ms. Gilchrist. Where is Mr. Mackey?"

"Ill, your honor."

"And Mr. Connery?"

"I have been told that his is awaiting a return flight from Frankfurt, but the first flight he can get for sure is tomorrow. He has placed himself on standby for every flight today. Mr. Wilder is with me today, and

Ms. Warren may join us later in the day, depending on what transpires in Judge Wellner's courtroom."

Judge Lasko sighed. "I'm sure everyone's best wishes are with Mr. Mackey. Mr. Galvin, Mr. Fuller, Ms. Bullock? Any problems?"

"None your honor," said Galvin. "Plaintiffs join your honor in wishing the best for Mr. Mackey, and for Dr. Philips as well."

"Please proceed."

* * *

Linda's direct examination of Benjamin Jordan, M.D., Ph.D., went smoothly. She established his credentials and background, reviewing his education, certifications, work experience, American military service, and professional publications. Jeff Wilder sat immobile, save for an occasional nod.

"Dr. Jordan, I have just read you the titles of three articles. In the two articles about memory issues, you are a co-author with Drs. Frelinghuysen, Archer, and Philips, in different combinations. Is that correct?"

"Yes."

"Would you summarize the main points of those articles?"

"Certainly. In one, we reviewed clinical evidence from over fifty studies that demonstrated that some patient accounts of past traumatic experiences that had appeared banished from memory, and then reentered conscious awareness, could actually be documented as accurate or inaccurate. Recovery of accurate information long absent from conscious recall was demonstrated, along with instances that combined accurate and confabulated elements, and rare occasions in which the so-called memories could be invalidated, in whole or in part."

"Would you please define confabulation, Dr. Jordan?"

"Confabulation occurs when subjects or patients imagine or guess at what might have occurred and present such accounts as their believed-in historical experience."

"Is confabulation an attempt to deceive?"

"Possibly at some level in some cases, but it also occurs without conscious intent and in some organic brain diseases. It's more readily understood as the mind's attempt to fill in the gaps, to achieve coherence, in an attempt to understand or explain. Since memory isn't a videotape recorder, it's possible that even accurate recalls of historical autobiographic events contain some confabulated elements, but such confabulation usually pertains to details, not to the main gist of the experiences described."

"Are recovered memories more or less accurate than memories of things we always recalled?"

"The only study out there that tried to compare confirmation rates, by Dalenberg, found equal percentages of confirmations in recovered and always available memories."

"Is it more likely that a person will confabulate memories of abuse than other kinds of memories?"

"That gets us into that second article, looking carefully at some of the research studies. The literature is clear that subjects can be led to endorse inaccurate recollections. However, these studies generally regard minor details of items in a list. It's relatively straightforward to convince someone to say that the shoes a person wore in a taped sequence were blue instead of red, but the odds against convincing someone that an unlikely large animal, like an elephant, appeared in such a tape are astronomical. Further, replications of those studies indicate that subjects may be more persuaded to make an inaccurate report than convinced of the historical truth of the inaccurate recalls, because when the questions are asked in a way that lets the subject answer 'I don't know' instead of being pressured to choose for or against the experimenter's fake hints, the percentage of subjects following the misdirection crashes. Also, the literature shows that while it is possible to induce reports of false memories of mundane things in the normal range of experience in about a quarter of subjects, like a fearful separation from their parents, the attempts to deliberately induce memories of a traumatic experience, like an intrusive medical procedure, are pretty much complete failures. That allows us to infer that it is generally far less easy to suggest false memories of mistreatment, or to persuade subjects to make such reports, than some have alleged. It's impressive how subjects will follow experimenters' suggestions because they are authority figures, or those they are trying to please, and folks assume their experiment has altered memory rather than demonstrated the power of interpersonal influence."

"So, the second article is a critical examination of the research advocating the dismissal of any information that was not always available in memory?"

"Yes. In brief, the meaningfulness of that research has been overstated and must be understood as unconvincing. The authors start by observing inaccurate recall is possible, especially for simple word lists and details, go on to talk as if inaccurate recollections of far more complex traumatic event were probable, and offer advices that seem to argue that inaccurate recall is inevitable. My co-authors and I concluded that a dismissive attitude toward so-called 'recovered memory' is unjustified and that accurate recovered memory is possible. But most of the time you never know. It's unusual to have objective documentation or confirmatory witnesses who don't have a stake in saying something to point one way or another."

"'Witnesses who don't have a stake'? What do you mean?"

"Very often persons identified as witnesses to mistreatments would be incriminating themselves if they acknowledged they saw or did what they saw or did. They might be admitting to shameful actions or to failing to stop shameful actions. They might fear admissions may bring retributions. Their efforts to defend themselves may render what they report far from objective and unbiased."

"Your third article is entitled 'Nineteenth Century Syndromes: Alive, Well and Confusing Our Residents as We Near the Millennium.' This is the only one of your articles that directly addresses Multiple Personality Disorder, now Dissociative Identity Disorder, correct?"

"Yes."

"What were your findings?"

"I reviewed the records of patients at the residents' clinic at a Philadelphia academic hospital who had presented diagnostic difficulties over the prior ten years. Among them were a dozen patients, ten women and two men, who proved to have Dissociative Identity Disorder. I discussed how their presenting symptoms had suggested they suffered more commonplace conditions like schizophrenia, bipolar disorders, partial complex seizures, or borderline personality disorder, and how their diagnoses were clarified."

* * *

A few minutes later, Linda questioned Ben Jordan about his military service.

"Dr. Jordan, have you served in any branch of the military?"

"Yes. I have spent twenty years in the New Jersey Air Guard."

"Please describe your duties and your rank."

"I hold the rank of Colonel. I am a senior pilot in the New Jersey Air Guard. My crew and I fly a C-141 Starlifter, a large aircraft that can be configured either for heavy cargo or to carry over 100 troops."

"And you last flew when?"

"Last weekend."

"Prior to joining the New Jersey Air Guard, did you have any earlier military experience?"

"Yes. When I lived in Israel, I served in the Israel Defense Forces."

Linda heard a chair scrape against the floor. Jeff Wilder sat erect in his chair, leaned forward slowly and fixed his eyes on the witness.

"Please describe your rank and duties during this service."

"I held the rank of Lieutenant. I had several rather diverse assignments."

"Could you describe those assignments?"

"Some were classified. I'd rather not discuss that period of my life."

"Dr. Jordan, let me ask again. Can you tell us anything about your service there? For example, did you serve as a doctor?"

"No, I did not serve as a physician. I'd rather not discuss that period of my life."

"Very well, Dr. Jordan, we'll move on."

Jeff Wilder began to stand, then sat back in his chair. *That must be a Bill Mackey move. But what the hell is this all about?*

* * *

Linda Gilchrist led Ben Jordan through Joan Underwood's efforts to diagnose and treat Melody Jarrett slowly and methodically.

"What did you conclude as a result of your study of these materials and of a videotape of Melody Jarrett demonstrating several of her personalities?"

"I concluded that her diagnostic evaluation was done thoroughly and thoughtfully, and that her diagnostic impression was consistent with the phenomena she observed and elicited on inquiry, both in the psychiatric interview, the screening measure she used, and the structured clinical interview that she administered."

"Did you find any shortcomings in her diagnostic efforts?"

"No."

"Do you believe that Melody Jarrett suffered Dissociative Identity Disorder?"

"Yes."

"Did you form any opinion on the basis of the videotaped materials?"

"No."

"That's all I have, your honor."

"Your witness, Mr. Galvin," said Judge Lasko.

"Thank you, your honor," said a mild voice that did not belong to Mr. Galvin or Mr. Fuller.

Gillian Bullock, Esq., rose from the seat at which she had remained immobile and silent since the first moments of jury selection.

"Good morning, Dr. Jordan. I am Gillian Bullock. Along with Mr. Galvin and Mr. Fuller, I represent the plaintiff, Dr. Travers."

"Good morning, Ms. Bullock."

Linda tried to maintain her composure. Galvin's and Fuller's subtle smirks confirmed her worst fears. A second Pearl Harbor, and everyone knew she'd been fooled again. *And Ben Jordan warned me. Why don't I listen?* But she knew. *One more senior man telling me he knows more than me. I didn't want to hear it. I screwed up again!* Jeff Wilder passed her a note, *Easy, Tiger. Sit up straight.*

My God! I must be broadcasting my idiocy!

"Dr. Jordan, I am going to do my best to avoid trying the patience of all present by going over your given testimony again. There are only a few points that I would like to explore in greater detail. If you find that my shifting rapidly from topic to topic is confusing, please let me know and I'll slow down."

"I appreciate that, Ms. Bullock."

"Dr. Jordan, you expressed a positive opinion of Dr. Underwood's approach to diagnosing Dissociative Identity Disorder, did you not?"

"I did."

"Please tell the court how one goes about diagnosing a condition that does not exist."

Linda glanced toward the plaintiff's table. Fuller, Galvin, and Dr. Travers were leaning forward, completely focused on Jordan.

"Diagnoses represent our best efforts at putting together a set of phenomena and test results that characterize findings in a particular group of patients. They are always subject to revision as we learn more, as ideas change, and sometimes as scientific and professional politics change. Since recorded history began, philosophers, theologists, and those of us in the more Johnny-come-lately disciplines of psychiatry, anthropology, psychology, and sociology. . ."

"I don't think you are answering my question, Dr. Jordan. Shall I have it read back to you?"

"Fine."

The question reread, Jordan continued, "Folks in a lot of disciplines have had a shot at describing mental illnesses. Long. . ."

"Your honor, would you please instruct the witness to answer the question?"

Judge Lasko tented his fingers. "I have to admit that I'm not sure where you are going."

"Your honor. . ." Linda was on her feet.

"Calm down, counselor. Dr. Jordan, why are you taking us through history?"

"Your honor, I am trying to answer Ms. Bullock's question. She has embedded an invalid statement within her question. Therefore, part of my response must address that invalid statement."

"Make it simple, Dr. Jordan."

"Yes, your honor. Conditions in which one entity takes over executive control of the body and mind from another have been known since antiquity. They occur in most studied societies, probably in all. Bourguignon is the classic reference. Ellenberger's text demonstrates the same structure in pre-scientific possession syndromes, contemporary endemic and culture-bound possession syndromes, and their expression in more secular societies, which we now call Dissociative Identity Disorder. These conditions have been with us since Biblical times and before. They are found in all or nearly all known cultures. Many of their diagnostic features have been reported for millennia."

Bullock stood. "Your honor, Dr. Jordan's assertions are absurd. This condition is almost always a modern iatrogenic artifact, a red flag telling one and all that something has gone very, very wrong."

"May Dr. Jordan continue?" asked Linda.

"Dr. Jordan," said Judge Lasko. "Are you prepared to substantiate your last statements?"

"Of course. The bibliography of that 'Nineteenth Century Syndromes' article is a good start. . ."

"I object, your honor! Dr. Jordan is taking us into mythology. The first cases are fairly modern. These cases have been created and so-called cures have been effected only in recent history."

"May Dr. Jordan complete his answer?"

"Good idea," said the judge, shooting a glance to the plaintiff's table. "Let's be a little more circumspect about these objections, Ms. Bullock."

"Dr. Jordan," said Ms. Bullock. "Can you point us to the first recorded instance of the successful treatment of this condition?"

"Certainly. Take a look at that book alongside the witness stand. Open it to Mark 5:1–20, but especially 9. You can find it in Luke also, but I forget the cite."

"It's in the Bible?" asked Lasko.

"Yes. And the individual committing what Ms. Bullock would call the creation and so-called cure of the condition is Jesus Christ. That is why I took you through history. The same constellation of symptoms, as phenomena, have been reported throughout history but described and explained from many different perspectives.

"So, to complete my answer, I think it would be pretentious for me to do more than note, with respect, the successful cures attributed to Jesus Christ. It would be both arrogant and meaningless to speculate whether Jesus Christ's interventions measured up to the standards of practice of his era. However, I do not have any reservations about stating that Dr. Underwood's diagnosis was consistent with current diagnostic criteria and standards of practice, and in my medical judgment, was accurate."

Bullock looked over to the plaintiff's table, where the two senior counsels were studiously scrutinizing the wooden tabletop. She soldiered on.

"To what extent did you rely on the score of the DES, the Dissociative Experiences Scale?"

"Hard to say. I was looking to see how all the information fit together."

"Can you answer the question I asked?"

"I'm sorry. I thought I did."

"Your honor, I request permission to treat Dr. Jordan as a hostile witness."

"Gentlemen and ladies, please approach the bench."

* * *

Judge Lasko leaned forward and whispered. "This is a court of law. Ms. Bullock, Mr. Galvin, Mr. Fuller, I am becoming more concerned about hostile attorneys than hostile witnesses. Every one of you knows, or should know, that some subjects and some witnesses are more difficult than others. Let's continue."

* * *

"Dr. Jordan, as you know, the DES is a subjective test. It is easy for someone to give false answers. My inquiry was designed to inquire to what extent you relied on the score of this test in forming your opinion."

"Very little. It is a screening test, easily monkeyed with, just as you say. It is not a diagnostic instrument. However, there are certain findings apart from the score itself that have diagnostic relevance. Dissociative Identity Disorder patients who complete the test honestly have at least some score in all, or all or but one queries."

"All but one? Why would one be an exception?"

"One question concerns driving. Not everyone drives."

"To what extent did you rely on the *Structured Clinical Interview for the DSM-IV Dissociative Disorders—Revised*, which is usually called the SCID-D-R interview."

"I considered it important. And Melody Jarrett received top scores in all five areas."

"Doesn't this instrument suggest the very symptoms about which it inquires?"

"No."

"Dr. Jordan, let me turn to another matter. Many eminent authorities state, and there is research to back their statements, that suggestions from therapists can lead to patients' developing and believing false memories."

"I'm sure that can happen, but there is no reason to assert that such happenings are commonplace. There is no research to that effect, only statements of opinion."

"But Dr. Jordan, is it not true that Dr. Bublekopf has demonstrated how easy it is to induce false memories."

"No."

"The most preeminent mental health scientists in the nation endorse her findings. But not Dr. Jordan?"

"Objection! Argumentative."

"Withdrawn. Dr. Jordan, do you have problems endorsing Dr. Bublekopf's landmark studies."

"Yes."

Linda held her breath. *Is Jordan taking over the line of questioning? He couldn't be. But if Gillian Bullock doesn't stick to what she knows, she just might open the wrong door. Eve warned me he's a warrior.*

"Can you explain your rather unusual view?"

"Certainly, counselor."

She bought it!

"Bublekopf demonstrated that false memories of a commonplace childhood experience could be suggested to certain subjects if influence were exerted by a number of conspirators over a period of time. Let's leave aside for the moment that fact that what Bublekopf's collaborators suggested was unlike intentionally inflicted trauma. About one fourth of Bublekopf's subjects accepted suggestions to endorse a false memory."

"And does that not prove that false memories can be induced?"

"Sure. But false memories of what? First, none of those suggested false memories related to intentionally-inflicted trauma. Fairweather's research efforts to suggest false memories of medical trauma, much closer to painful harm to intimate areas of the body, were completely unsuccessful. But second, bear in mind that under a quarter of Bublekopf's subjects took the suggestions. So, if you want to bet on something that may occur less than a quarter of the time, and forget about failures to follow the misleading suggestions, something that occurs over three quarters of the time, then you are wagering that something that occurs about one time out of four is more likely than occurs about three times out of four. If that is how your team's logic works, Ms. Bullock, I would like to play poker with all of you."

Some jurors chuckled. Fuller rose to object. Seeing Judge Lasko stifle a laugh with a hand over his mouth, he sat down without uttering a word.

Galvin rose. "May we request a comfort break, your honor?"

"A prudent thought, counselor. Jurors? About time? I see a lot of vigorous nods."

* * *

When Ms. Bullock approached Ben Jordan after the break, she carried a different pad and asked different types of questions. She literally raced through her inquiries about Jordan's assessment of Dr. Underwood's clinical work. Wilder passed Linda a note. "They want to get Jordan off the stand. They must think he's hurting their case."

Midway through Gillian Bullock's cross, a pale, haunted Joan Underwood quietly entered the court and took her place at the defense table. Linda was so intent on following the Bullock's cross that it took a while before she noticed her client and reached over to squeeze her hand. Joan Underwood tried to summon a smile. She couldn't make that happen.

Jordan has been a good witness for us, Linda wrote. She passed her note to Underwood, who seemed not to notice.

"Just a few more questions, Dr. Jordan. I noticed that when Ms. Gilchrist asked you about your military service in Israel, you declined to give a detailed answer."

Wilder leaned forward, his body suddenly drawn tense as a bowstring. Mike Burgoyne dropped his notepad.

"That is correct." Ben let his body slump. He picked a spot on the floor seven feet to the right of Gillian Bullock. He clenched his teeth and imagined killing Fuller, Chaudvent, and Rapier. His face grew crimson. He shook his head.

"I would like to pursue this in more detail. During the course of this trial we have already encountered the unfortunate consequences of a witness's refusal to be forthcoming. Must we go through this exercise again?"

"Your honor. . ." Linda rose.

"Ms. Gilchrist," Judge Lasko broke in, "Dr. Jordan is under oath. He placed his hand on the same Bible he referred to in his testimony and swore to tell the truth, the whole truth, and nothing but the truth. He knows that."

Ben Jordan nodded slowly. He turned his head still further away from Gillian Bullock. *Here we go, Super Owl!*

Gillian Bullock put her hands on her hips. She favored Jordan with the kind of smile a dominant lioness would give to an antelope she had downed as her pride began to devour the terrified beast before it had breathed its last. In the same moment Ben Jordan seemed to be both a sailor trying to lift an anchor from the seabed and the anchor itself. He appeared to be having trouble slowly raising his eyes from the floor, to be in serious pain as he pulled himself erect. He shook his head, and began to speak.

"Of course, your honor."

Jordan turned to the jury and looked directly at two older male jurors sitting alongside one another in the second row of the jury box.

"When you go to war you see and do and experience a lot of things you'd rather forget. Those things come back to us, to some of us more than others. Every time I have to talk about that time of my life I think of my men, especially the ones who never made it home. . . Excuse me." He took out a handkerchief. "Not very dignified, it is? I lost men. I killed men. I was wounded more than once. One operation went bad and I was captured. Bad things happened for over a week. I was in and out of the hospital for 14 months before I could get around again like a normal human being.

"I was very young and very stupid. I'm told Dr. Underwood wanted to be a movie star, and it didn't work out. It blew up in her face. Well, I wanted to be some James Bond kind of guy, and that blew up in mine. Yeah, I was so stupid I'm embarrassed to remember it, let alone to tell you. And I was good at what I did, very good. But the enemy was good too. I'm damn. . . sorry, darn lucky I survived. I got a lot of medals that don't mean a thing. If you've been there, any 'there,' you know lot of the best you served with never made it home. Happens.

"That's my service history and why I don't like to talk about it. And it will probably come back and haunt me in the middle of the night tonight and for the next few nights. And a lot of men and women who served would tell you the same thing."

Linda saw three men and one woman nodding. *One older man's cheeks were wet. Was that Bill's ploy? To use Jordan to rehabilitate Underwood? Damn!*

Linda turned to her client. Joan Underwood was staring intently at the fists clenched tightly in her lap.

Gillian Bullock rushed Ben Jordan off the stand.

Judge Lasko looked to Jeff Wilder, who looked to Linda Gilchrist.

"Ms. Gilchrist?"

"One moment, your honor." Linda leaned over to Joan Underwood and whispered, "Are you ready to resume the cross?"

"As ready as I'll ever be. Yes."

Joan Underwood relaxed her hands, gently flexed and unflexed her fingers, and looked up at Linda. The Dr. Joan Underwood who locked on to Linda's eyes was a very different woman from any Joan Lockwood that she had seen before. She was not the cool, contained, and often glacial professional Linda had come to know. Nor was she the suddenly softer person who melted and glowed when she talked about her children. Nor was she the pathetic crushed creature of Friday afternoon, reduced to tearful immobility. For a terrible moment Linda remembered looking in the mirror only days before, overwhelmed by the almost unrecognizable shattered wreck whose unfocused eyes stared back at who she thought she was. With caring people all around her and drawing on every ounce of her strength, she had come back. She let herself hope Dr. Underwood had done the same.

"Your honor, Dr. Underwood is here, and ready if there is further cross-examination."

"And will Dr. Philips be available thereafter?"

Linda turned to Jeff, who held up a note and nodded. "Yes, your honor."

Galvin and Fuller conversed briefly before Galvin rose. "No further cross for this witness, your honor."

Judge Lasko looked to Linda.

"Redirect, your honor."

"Are you sure, Ms. Gilchrist?"

"Yes, your honor."

As Joan Underwood passed behind Linda on her way toward the witness stand, Linda heard a soft whisper, "You said you wouldn't lie to me again. What number was that?"

Joan Underwood's shoulders were squared. The wonderfully soft, almost seductive sway of her walk was no more. *If I didn't know better, I'd think. . . That couldn't be. She's walking like some martial artist? Those fists. . . Was she gathering Chi?*

Uttering up a brief silent prayer, Linda rose and approached her transformed client.

"Dr. Underwood, I would like to ask you a few questions about your experiences prior to studying medicine. May I do so?"

"Of course."

"Last week, Dr. Rapier produced some surprising new information. Would you like to add anything to what he put before the court?"

"Dr. Rapier is a pig, but he was very much on target, and has been very helpful to me."

"Objection!" shouted Fuller.

"I'm under oath, Mr. Fuller."

"I'll sustain your objection, Mr. Fuller," said Judge Lasko, "but please remember what you were told on Friday. And let me caution you, Dr. Underwood. No matter how distraught. . ."

"Your honor, some things need be said only once. It is my intent to respect the dignity of the court."

"Please continue, Dr. Underwood," said Linda, "bearing in mind Judge Lasko's instructions."

"Of course. Unfortunately, everything Dr. Rapier said about that time in my life, however and wherever he obtained that information, is true. When I said he had helped me, I meant it. Living with the secrets of my past has been an incredible burden. I thought they would kill me if they ever came out. Now I realize they probably would have killed me if I kept them in.

"When I was a much younger woman, I was considered exceptionally beautiful. Everyone was telling me I should become a model, or go to Hollywood and be a movie star. The truth is that I was a very beautiful nerd. I worked summers on the Cape, Nantucket, Martha's Vineyard. I loved those places. And I dated a lot of really neat, really rich guys. Some had families in show business. One guy's big brother was a producer. Somehow, I got caught up in the dream of being a movie star before I ever figured out whether it was my dream or something other people were putting into my head. At the end of the summer after my sophomore year I went out to LA with appointments to meet with some people and see what Hollywood was all about.

"Two weeks later I had an agent and I was going to A-list parties. In a month I was being chased by movie stars I used to dream about, the same guys whose pictures I had on my bedroom wall. I was living a dream, but most of it wasn't my dream. I took a leave of absence from Bryn Mawr and moved to LA. I made every stupid mistake a young girl could make short of escorting, prostitution, and porn. When I realized what was happening to me, I went more than a little crazy. When I got back on my feet, my agent told me that there were pictures of me coming out in magazines. And yes, they included *Playboy*. I don't even remember doing most of those shoots! I thought I was trapped in a nightmare that would never go away.

"I couldn't live with the shame. I couldn't face my parents. I knew where to get pills. I collected what I thought was enough, and I tried to kill myself. Another failure. I wound up in a different hospital where I really got some help, good help. I was too weak to go on with my real name. Funny, my real name, Veronica Fairbanks, really sounds like a movie star name.

"I chose a new name. I wanted Jane, for 'plain Jane,' but I have an aunt Jane. So, I became Joan—close enough, and no one in my family's ever had that name. I picked Underwood because that's where I wanted my past to be. Under the wood of a coffin, the coffin of a past I wanted to kill. I hated to change my name. I know it hurt my parents, but they understood. They supported me completely.

"I wanted to be able to help other people the way I'd been helped. Sounds corny, but that's why I decided to become a psychiatrist. I had a boyfriend in high school. We broke up when we went off to college, but we never forgot one another. I told him everything. He's my husband now. Together we've made our peace with the truth of my life, then, now, and for tomorrow."

Joan Underwood looked toward Linda Gilchrist and nodded.

"No further questions."

"Recross?"

Fuller rose. "Very briefly, your honor. Dr. Underwood, do you realize that as upsetting as Dr. Rapier's testimony may have been, it was tendered in the interest of pursuing justice?"

"I'm sorry. Could you ask that again without the subjunctive?"

"Your honor, would you instruct. . ."

Linda broke in. "I object, your honor. Everyone in this court bore witness to the devastating impact of Dr. Rapier's testimony. I support Dr. Underwood's request. There was nothing iffy or conditional about the upset that was caused. Describing it in this manner is an insult to both Dr. Underwood and the intelligence of the court."

"Sustained."

"Nothing further."

Dr. Underwood returned to the defense table.

"How are you feeling?"

"Worried."

"About what?"

"About whether you'll defend my husband when he tries to kill those bastards. I can't believe Jordan said what he said." Dr. Underwood looked away for a moment. "I bet he's a hell of a fisherman."

"My sister says he is. Why?"

"He seems to have a weird knack of selecting just the right bait, and casting to just the right place."

"Will you be back after lunch?"

"Sure. Why?"

"It could prove interesting."

"Oh?"

"My turn for secrets."

Dr. Joan Underwood smiled, a warm, beautiful, relaxed smile Linda had never seen before. "Well, after all this, I guess you're entitled."

CHAPTER 77

Jay Philips, M.D., took the stand. He wore a dark grey pinstriped suit, a light blue shirt, and a regimental-style burgundy tie. His posture was uncharacteristically erect.

"Before we begin, Dr. Philips," Judge Lasko inquired, "The court wishes to be assured that you feel prepared to proceed."

"I've had better days, your Honor, and I'm looking forward to a rest. But I'm good to go. And before we begin, I apologize for my appearance here last Friday. As you know, your honor, I had no prior notice that I would be asked to testify that day. I was not dressed in a manner that respected the dignity of the court and these proceedings."

* * *

Linda Gilchrist's direct examination of Jay Philips moved along smoothly.

"We've already reviewed your credentials and your contributions to the psychiatric literature, Dr. Philips. Now I'd like to direct your attention to the problems that Melody Jarrett suffered when she presented to Dr. Joan Underwood, and the treatment rendered to her by Dr. Underwood. . ."

Linda led Jay through the same areas she'd covered with Jordan. She ran her eyes up and down the yellow legal pad on which she had written her questions. She looked to Jeff Wilder, who gave her a subtle thumbs up. She placed her pad on the defense counsel's table and looked up at the judge.

The crowded courtroom was so prepared to her say the as yet unspoken words, "That's all, your Honor," that everyone acted as if they had been said aloud. Judge Lasko adjusted himself in his chair. Bruce Fuller gathered his notes for cross. He began to rise.

"Thank you, Dr. Philips, for your testimony thus far." *Thus far!!!* The heads of every lawyer and reporter in the room snapped toward Linda Gilchrist with a speed that screamed "whiplash." Sally Warren turned to Jeff Wilder, who shrugged, shook his head, and began to study the ceiling.

"Now, to summarize briefly, I understand you find no shortcomings or significant errors in Dr. Underwood's treatment of Melody Jarrett. Is that correct?"

"Yes."

"And that treatment dealt, in part, with events that Ms. Jarrett claimed she had experienced. Is that correct?"

"Yes."

"You have stated that Dr. Underwood's treatment fulfilled the standard of care irrespective of the veracity of Ms. Jarrett's memories of mistreatment. Is that correct?"

"Yes."

"In the course of your looking into the materials available, did you discover any information that allowed you to come to any conclusions as to whether the allegations shared by Melody Jarrett with Dr. Joan Underwood had elements of accuracy?"

"Yes."

"Are you saying that you were able to conclude some elements were inaccurate?"

"No."

"Were you able to conclude that you could not determine the accuracy of some elements?"

"Yes."

"Were you able to conclude that some elements of her account were accurate?"

"Yes."

"Objection!" shouted Fuller. "This is new information. It was not made available to plaintiff's counsel!"

Jeff Wilder began to rise. Lou Galvin sunk down in his chair. Gillian Bullock gave a grim smile.

"If it please the court, your honor, plaintiff's counsel has had the opportunity to depose this witness," said Linda. "Their deposition was rather brief. This was called to the attention of Plaintiff's counsel. . ."

"Objection denied. Please proceed, Ms. Gilchrist."

"Prior to the time of your deposition, had you had the opportunity to study materials other than medical records?"

"When I was asked to review this case, I was provided with materials that included earlier depositions and some drawings made by Melody Jarrett. . ."

"Objection!" shouted Fuller. "Ms. Jarrett's drawings of parties to this suit and other persons known and unknown have been declared inadmissible!"

"Sustained. Ms. Gilchrist! What are you trying to do?"

Linda's voice remained calm and reasonable.

"Your Honor, plaintiff's counsel is completely correct. May I approach the bench?"

"Counsels. . ."

"Your honor, defense has no intention of challenging your earlier ruling. The drawings to which Dr. Philips refers were provided to plaintiff's counsel during discovery. They were duly marked as exhibits 13 through 47. The drawings about which I am asking Dr. Philips to testify, exhibits 26 through 31, do not depict human figures or faces. I do not contest the issues to which plaintiff's counsel refers."

"Mr. Fuller?"

"Objection withdrawn, your honor."

"Back to work, counselors."

"I was preparing to ask you to tell us about some pictures drawn by Ms. Melody Jarrett. I will show you a picture marked Exhibit 24. If this is an exhibit that helped you form the opinions you have offered and will offer today, please confirm that this is the case."

"Yes, this was a helpful image."

Linda held up copies of the exhibit. "Your honor, may I distribute copies of this exhibit to the court?"

"Objection!"

"On what grounds?"

"Withdrawn."

"Go ahead."

Linda approached Dr. Philips once again. She carried no notes.

"Dr. Philips, what would you like to tell us about this picture?"

"This exhibit was made available to me for study prior to my deposition. It was stated to be a view out of the window of Dr. Travers' office."

"Objection! Irrelevant. It has already been proven that the office described by Ms. Jarrett does not exist! Dr. Travers' office has no window."

"Ms. Gilchrist?"

"Defense respectfully disputes that contention, your honor."

"This is outrageous, your honor."

"Ms. Gilchrist?"

"Dr. Philips is prepared to demonstrate that there is reason to raise the possibility that the office described by Melody Jarrett existed at the time of her treatment by Dr. Travers."

"I'll allow you to proceed, Ms. Gilchrist, but we need to see where this is going very quickly."

"Yes, your honor."

Jeff Wilder tried to beckon Linda over to the defense table. He received only a dazzling smile in return.

"Where the fuck is Gilchrist going?" Jeff whispered to Sally, now at his side.

"Damned if I know," she muttered.

Jeff rose. "Defense requests a brief recess, your honor."

"Let's hold off on that until we see where this line of questioning leads. Proceed."

"Dr. Philips?"

"Well, when I was told that this was a view out of Dr. Travers' office, I was puzzled. Dr. Travers' sixth floor office is too high up for that to be a view from his window. So, I had to consider whether that view was part of some inaccurate recollection. I even wondered whether it might be a view from Dr. Underwood's office. However, the building at her address is surrounded by low shrubs and a wide lawn. . . No trees.

"So, another possibility had to be considered. Was it possible that Ms. Jarrett, whose drawings are very realistic as a rule, was drawing a picture of a scenario that was meaningful to her? And, if so, what might she be drawing?

"One tree is several feet shorter than the other. It has been groomed not to the same full shape as the others, but to preserve maximal height. It seemed useful to look around HighPoint Centre to ascertain whether one of the groups of trees surrounding the building contained a tree like that. I undertook a few studies to look into that possibility."

"Please inform the court as to what you did, and as to what you discovered. . ."

"Objection!" from Fuller. "Dr. Philips withheld this information at deposition! It cannot be allowed at trial!"

"Just a moment," said Judge Lasko. "Dr. Philips. Did I hear you say that a copy of this drawing was made available to you prior to your deposition?"

"Yes, your honor."

"Did plaintiff's counsel ask you to specify the basis on which you came to the opinions that you reached?"

"No, your honor. They did not question me about Ms. Jarrett's drawings."

Fuller rose again. "Objection! Dr. Philips has not been deposed on these matters. We've had no opportunity to review Dr. Philips' findings."

Wilder and Warren looked to Linda.

"Your honor. With all due respect to the plaintiff's attorney, your honor," said Linda, "Dr. Philips was made available for deposition. Ms. Bullock and Mr. Fuller deposed him in my presence. They terminated the deposition abruptly in just over 45 minutes. The transcript is available. Mr. Mackey was concerned. He expressed his concern in a letter to Mr. Galvin and inquired whether he would like to depose Dr. Philips on any further matters. Mr. Galvin replied, and stated that plaintiff's counsels deemed no further examination of Dr. Philips was necessary. I am prepared to place copies of this correspondence in evidence."

"Mr. Galvin?"

"That is true, your honor, but. . ."

Judge Lasko stopped himself from breaking his pen. The gavel sounded loud as a gunshot. "Chambers! Bailiff, the jurors may take a twenty-minute break."

* * *

Judge Lasko kept his composure until he and the attorneys were alone in his chambers. "Make sense of this right now, ladies and gentlemen, or I can't promise that I won't have to find myself in contempt of my own court!"

"Your honor," Fuller began, "Dr. Philips is a disreputable hack. At the first break we took, we discussed what was happening in the deposition. It was clear that Dr. Philips was bumbling and stammering, just saying the same old, same old. We conferred with Mr. Galvin by phone. We agreed that it was pointless to spend the rest of the day eliciting exactly what he always says and would certainly say here as well."

Judge Lasko leafed through the transcript of Jay Philips' deposition. "Who wrote the questions you asked during that deposition? No, I withdraw that query."

He slapped the transcript down on his desk.

"I was puzzled when I first read this deposition. Once the preliminary questions had been completed, almost every subsequent inquiry gives the appearance of some sort to provocation or trap. They neither demonstrate nor explore Dr. Philips' credentials, observations, or opinions. They give the appearance of probing for ways to get under Dr. Philips' skin. Philips was clearly having a bad day, but he didn't bite. The deposition was terminated without attempting to elicit the information a deposition is designed to elicit. I am sure that there is some reason for the conduct of this charade, but the bottom line is this. . . You forfeit the opportunity to examine the witness for reasons of your own that seemed wise to you at the time. Whatever it was, your strategy threw away the opportunity for you to make adequate preparations for your cross-examination of Dr. Philips here today. Mr. Mackey offered you an opportunity to revise your unusual course of action, but you did not. And now, you are asking me to give you yet another opportunity to do what you have had two opportunities to do before.

"There will be no Mulligans in this courtroom. Your objection is denied. Any request to depose Dr. Philips further at this time will be denied. Dr. Philips is not a surprise witness. You knew he studied the pictures. What seemed like a clever strategy is turning out to look more and more like a miscalculation or a failure of due diligence on the part of plaintiff's counsel.

"To take this argument a step further, were I to grant your request in the face of what has transpired in your dealing with this witness it would go far beyond wrongful. It would be clearly prejudicial in favor of the plaintiff and probably would constitute grounds for reversal on appeal."

Judge Lasko rose. "See you in court in five minutes. This is addressed to both sides. I have seen far better lawyering. You made your cases. . . Now try them. . ."

CHAPTER 78

"Although I was very confused by Ms. Jarrett's pictures, and uncertain about what they signified when I began my testimony last Friday, an opportunity was afforded to me to examine the actual building in which Dr. Travers's office was located. I walked completely around HighPoint Centre. I found the one tree that was shorter than the others. Then, starting at the sixth floor, I looked out the windows at the ends of the hall and near the elevator banks midway on every floor, to assess the angle looking down from each floor. I took pictures from each floor. Five and six were way off. So were one and two. Four was pretty close, but three was best."

"Objection! Irrelevant!" from Fuller.

"Your honor, Dr. Philips is presenting only the first step of an investigation he has made, starting from that picture, already in evidence prior to Dr. Philips' deposition."

"Objection denied. But, Ms. Gilchrist, please do not misunderstand this as license to take us on some wild goose chase."

"Of course not, your honor. Dr. Philips, please continue."

"I stretched a line of cord from one end of HighPoint Centre to the other, on both long sides, those that would appear to be situated north and south on a map. I also stretched cord along the east and west sides, the shorter ones. I marked the place on the south-facing side at which the shorter tree was situated. I used a folding carpenter's rule to convert the lengths of cord into feet and inches. I subtracted the widths of the walls at each end and found the places on the second and third floor halls where that mark would fall. On the second floor, a door for the law firm of Carter, Bell, Luborsky, and Romano was in that place. On the third, there was a blank wall. . ."

"Objection!" shouted Fuller. "Ms. Gilchrist is wasting the time of the court. This is going nowhere!"

"With all due respect, your honor, this argument is reaching its conclusion."

"How long, Ms. Gilchrist?"

"Under five minutes, your honor."

"Very well."

"Please continue, Dr. Philips. Try to be as succinct as possible."

"Of course. We counted the frequency of scuffs and small tears in the wall coverings of each floor. There were fewer on the third floor. We assessed the cove base in a similar manner. . ."

"What is a cove base?" asked Judge Lasko.

"It's the vinyl covering over the lowest portion of the wall, your honor. The cove base on the third floor, all around, was far less worn and scuffed than elsewhere.

"We then assessed the portion of the hall wall on the third floor where the alleged suite 312 was likely to have been located. We did so with an instrument called a stud finder. It detects wooden or metal materials beneath the surface of the wall covering. Our efforts outlined an assembly of wooden and steel components consistent with the height and width of the doorways that were standard in the construction of HighPoint Centre. We documented our findings with photographs, and returned the following day to videotape our repeating these examinations."

"What did you learn as a result of these explorations?"

"I learned that a structure consistent with a doorway exists and was covered over at the point and on the floor from which Ms. Jarrett's picture could have been an accurate drawing."

"Objection! This is all wild guesswork. And let's remember that the pictures Ms. Jarrett drew do not point exclusively to Dr. Travers."

"Enough, Mr. Fuller!" said the judge. "Let's remember that your last remark is irrelevant. Let's review some basics. Dr. Travers is not on trial here. Dr. Underwood is the defendant. And I determine what is relevant. That was far less than five minutes, Ms. Gilchrist. Anything else?"

"Not from this witness, your honor. As much as I regret to ask to introduce an additional and a true surprise witness at this point, I ask leave to call to the stand a person prepared to place in evidence mail directed to suite 312."

"Objection! So, what if there are a few pieces of mail that were addressed incorrectly?"

"How much mail are we talking about, Ms. Gilchrist?"

"No more than a vertical foot or so, your honor."

In the dead silence fell upon the court, a soft muffled sob become barely audible. Eyes turned toward the defendant's table, where Dr. Joan Underwood sat weeping, making no effort to dry her tears.

"Court will be in recess. Twenty minutes!" said Judge Lasko.

"All rise!" cried the bailiff.

CHAPTER 79

After the break, Gillian Bullock did not return to the court. Bruce Fuller launched a heroic effort to provoke Jay Philips. Better men and better women had tried. Better men and better women had failed. Every now and then, the witness looked away from Bruce Fuller, Linda Gilchrist, Oliver Lasko, and the jury. He let his eyes rejoice as he found the face among the onlookers that cared, the face smiling back at him, and Jay Philips knew he had been looking for that one face for his entire life.

When Gillian Bullock returned, Fuller asked for a brief break.

* * *

"What did you find?"

"The building's floor plans are missing from official records. But I was able to reach the management company that leased out office space for the previous owner."

"And?"

"Suite 312 was on the plans. My husband is a do-it-yourselfer. I sent him over to HighPoint."

"No joy?"

"No joy. He confirms what Gilchrist and Philips found."

* * *

"No further cross, your Honor."

Judge Lasko looked to Jeff, who looked to Linda.

"Is you next witness in court, Ms. Gilchrist?"

"No, your Honor. We had told Dr. Grant to anticipate giving testimony Wednesday or Thursday. He returned to the United States from an ocean passage earlier today. We contacted him while yesterday. We expect him to arrive late tonight. If his Honor will allow us to start presenting Dr. Grant half an hour later than the usual hour, we will be ready."

"I hope that works for you, Mr. Fuller? If so, I am inclined to end early today and start a little late tomorrow. Motions from other pending litigation require my attention. Ms. Gilchrist, do you plan to request the opportunity to present a witness with regard to your statement about the mail that was discovered?"

"Your honor, the mail is fouled and filthy. If it please the court, rather than waste its time here, I am prepared to show photographs to his Honor in chambers and accept his judgment as to the merits of their being presented here."

"Ladies and gentlemen of the jury, we will stop here for today and resume 9:30 instead of 9:00 tomorrow morning. Please be in court by 9:15."

* * *

Judge Galvin and plaintiff's counsels studied the pictures. They were accompanied by a copy of the report of the officer on the scene, who confirmed that Ms. Catherine von Grosseschenkle, the aunt of Attorney Gilchrist, had noticed dogs entering and leaving a dog door at High-Point Centre. It described subsequent events, including allowing Catherine von Grosseschenkle to take the tainted mail away for disposal, including mail addressed to Suite 312.

Judge Lasko sat a few minutes in thoughtful silence. For once, Bruce Fuller was speechless. Finally, he spoke.

"Your Honor, I feel obliged to state that should this material be allowed into evidence, and my client be convicted, I would consider that grounds for appeal."

"Thank you, Mr. Fuller. This may seem as if I am reproaching you, Mr. Fuller, but let me assure you that what I am about to say should be taken seriously by one and all. The evidence presented this afternoon, and what might or might not be admitted into evidence tomorrow. . . I will have to consider the latter with great care. . . should cause all of you to discuss this evidence and its implications with your clients. There is a wise course of action that might be useful to consider, if you are able to see your way clear to do so."

* * *

Back at Mackey Markham & Wilder, Jeff Wilder, Sally Markham, and Linda Gilchrist sat with Joan Underwood in the Founders Room. A secretary knocked on the door.

"Sorry to interrupt. Brett Connery is *en route* back from Frankfurt. He should be here sometime tomorrow."

"Great news," said Sally. "But we can't count on getting him up to speed. OK. Where are we?"

"I don't really know," said Jeff. "Judge Lasko's message puzzles me, unless he's anticipating some move from Fuller and that bunch. Maybe he's telling us to consider some kind of settlement, to have some options in mind. Dr. Underwood?"

"I don't know how to look at this. I want it all to be over. I'll follow your advice. But I've had enough. I've spent the last umpteen years running," Joan Underwood began, her voice full of pain and fatigue. She stopped and rubbed her forehead. When she continued, her voice had gone calm, cold, and determined. "I'll follow your advice. But hear me. Now I know in every fiber of my being that Travers is a piece of shit, that this whole business was a nasty charade. I want to fight."

* * *

In the offices of Dunham and Brady, Bruce Fuller, Lou Galvin, and Gillian Bullock sat with Gordon Travers. Travers' brother attended by speaker phone.

"I can go after them for hours and challenge every alleged fact," said Fuller. "I can use the Grant cross to attack every argument the defense has made. I can raise hell in closing. But even though you continue to assert your innocence, Dr. Travers, and I am not doubting you. . . and even though I think Underwood's treatment of Jarrett was a travesty, this is going to be a very uphill battle.

"The evidence Philips and Gilchrist developed is unassailable. The original plans of the building indicate a Suite 312. The very fact that registered copies of the architect's plans for HighPoint Centre have disappeared suggest some collusion to conceal evidence related to a major crime. Ms. Bullock's husband confirms what Gilchrist and Philips found. Making an issue of the old Midvale office won't fly. Your brother tells me his practice there consisted mostly of older patients and men. That make it look like. . ."

The voice on the speaker phone came through rough, angry, demanding, and obscene.

"Sir, if you think so little of our efforts," said Fuller, "and believe the evidence against the plaintiff can be destroyed as easily as that, I invite you to come to court and offer your advice. I would recommend that you replace me as lead counsel. . . You certainly are a formidable litigator. . . But we both know Oliver Lasko would. . . Sir? He hung up.

"Dr. Travers, we will spend this evening considering available options. However, I strongly advise you and your staunch supporter to consider that we are just about out of running room. I think that was Judge Lasko's message."

"We will never give in. That simply cannot be."

"Dr. Travers," said Lou Galvin, "there is an old baseball story about the umpire who got a frog in his throat. It was a full count. As the pitch came over the plate, he couldn't make a sound. The batter started to scream, 'That pitch was outside. That was ball four. He walked me!' The catcher screamed back. 'Hell, no! He caught the corner of the plate. Strike three. You're out.' Back and forth they went, ball, strike, ball, strike, screaming at the top of their lungs, until the ump got his voice back again and screamed, 'It ain't nothin' till I call it.' You have to deal with the fact that no matter who you are, no matter who your brother is, no matter what both of you say, it ain't nothin' till Lasko calls it, and you can't count on calling it yourselves."

* * *

Late that night, Joan Underwood tried to calm her husband, Pat Coleman. Pat was not a man accustomed to express his feelings in words. She heard him in the yard, chopping firewood for an hour. When he finally came inside, filthy and drenched in sweat, he was still beside himself.

"I am going to kill that son of a bitch. No way around this. I am going to kill him."

Joan knew there would be no reasoning with Pat.

"You leave that bastard alone. At least until I'm done with him. Let's have a drink. We both could use a shower."

"OK."

That should pacify him till tomorrow, thought Joan. *What then?*

* * *

"What do you think, dear?" Linda's mother had come from the other side of the world for her, and for her sister Kate.

"I wish I knew, Mom. I'm just such a babe in the woods." Betty Gilchrist put her arms around her daughter and stroked Linda's hair as she cried softly.

"I'm so afraid."

"Tonight, tears and fears. Tomorrow, tigress and merciless."

"I hope so, Mom. I hope so."

"I know my girl."

CHAPTER 80

Linda Gilchrist completed her hasty preparation of Matthew Grant, excused herself, and sprinted ahead toward the courtroom. She burst through the door just after 9:30 and slid into a seat at the defense table alongside Dr. Underwood as decorously as she could. Jeff Wilder nodded and leaned toward her.

"You look like death warmed over. Are you OK?"

"Ms. Gilchrist," said Judge Lasko. "I expect attorneys to be present in a timely manner. Are you unwell?"

Before Linda could answer, she felt her stomach clenching like a fist, squooshing her stomach contents up and down. Her breakfast began to rise up in her throat. Clasping her hands over her mouth, she rushed from the courtroom, Dr. Underwood hot on her heels.

* * *

Linda tried to brush off Joan Underwood's attentions.

"I'm OK. I just want to get you through this trial. I don't even want to think about my stomach."

"Your stomach? Hmm! If you say so."

* * *

"Let me ask again. Are you unwell, Ms. Gilchrist?"

"It will pass, your honor. I believe I can hang in there."

"Very well. Yesterday evening Messrs. Galvin and Fuller contacted me and indicated that they would like to make a motion before we get underway today. I assume that this meets no protest from the defense?"

As Linda struggled to subdue her rebellious stomach and find her voice, she heard the sound of a nearby chair being pulled back from her table, scraping along the floor as someone prepared to take a seat alongside her. A familiar voice spoke out.

"The defense has no objection, your honor," said Bill Mackey. He squeezed Linda's shoulder as he seated himself, a cane by his side.

"Glad to see you back in action, Bill," said Galvin.

"The court echoes that sympathy. Let's get underway. Mr. Galvin."

"Thank you, your honor. Taking into consideration both recent events and the emergence of information that was not known to the representatives of either the plaintiff or the defendant, it has become clear that this case should not proceed. Our client has instructed us to bring this matter to an end."

"Am I to understand that your client is dropping any and all charges against Dr. Joan Underwood and Memorial Hospital?"

"Yes, your honor."

"Dr. Travers? Do you confirm that your attorneys are offering the court an accurate representation of your intent?"

"Yes, your honor."

"Mr. Mackey? Ms. Gilchrist?"

"We applaud the plaintiff's wisdom in taking this step, and request that all charges against the defendant be dismissed with prejudice," said Mackey.

"Dr. Travers. . . Do you understand that defense counsel is asking that you forfeit the option of any further similar actions against Dr. Underwood and Memorial Hospital? Would you like to consult further with counsel before replying?"

"Mr. Galvin and Mr. Fuller prepared me to anticipate that kind of request. I agree, your honor."

"Expenses?"

"Will be paid by plaintiff, Your Honor," said Galvin.

"Very well. Before I dismiss this matter, I would like to make some remarks to counsels for both plaintiff and defendants, and to the plaintiff and defendants themselves.

"These remarks would be easier to make if matters were less murky and confused. However, I hope that in the future all parties to this dispute will remember the importance of candor and circumspection. No one will walk out of this courtroom untouched, or shall I say, unscarred, by what has taken place here."

* * *

As the jury filed out and the bailiff began to usher spectators through the door, Joan Underwood collapsed in Pat's arms. She wept softly as he stroked her hair, crooning softly as he rocked her, "It's over. It's finally over."

"That looks like a happy ending," Betty whispered to her sister Kate. "No matter what it looks like, Linda won, and Linda won big. Two ways."

"I think they can forget the fertility clinic. All the women in our family have terrible morning sickness, and easy deliveries. I'm betting on twins."

"That Jay Philips. . ."

"I made a complete fool of myself. If he has any sense, he'll have nothing to do with me. In the meantime, it's me and Phoenix."

"I think he'll like the dog, too!"

* * *

On the courthouse steps, Mike Burgoyne and the opposing counsels were waiting for Travers and some of the witnesses to emerge.

"You kicked our butts, Ms. Gilchrist!" said Mr. Galvin. "Next time, I'll see you coming, or hire you away from Mackey Markham & Wilder."

"Linda, you and your team, really did one hell of a job," said Fuller. "I don't like to lose, but I can't feel too bad about this one. I'm not backing away from my position on these matters, but this. . . This was a whole different thing. Your client deserves her victory. I'd apologize to her myself, but I caught the 'Chi' thing. She'd probably try to kill me, and I wouldn't blame her. Where the hell is Travers? We better look after him."

Galvin and Fuller went back inside. Mike Burgoyne just smiled.

"Mr. Burgoyne?" asked Linda.

"I'll want to interview everyone involved, but not today. But I'd like a moment alone with Ms. Gilchrist."

As the others stepped away, he added, "I'm married to someone like you. Congratulations. Hope all goes well."

"What do you mean?"

"I was sitting behind your mother and your aunt. Ask them. About the case. . . Well done!"

CHAPTER 81

"So," asked Bill Mackey, "can I take everyone out for a victory drink, or do you all have other plans?"

"Are reporters going to track us down?" Joan asked.

"Probably, but we can swat them away. Or, we can get a private room at O'Rourke's."

"I love you all, and I owe you my life. But. . ." She turned to her husband. Pat Coleman was staring at Travers, his eyes focused like laser sights. Pat's fists were clenched, his knuckles dead white. Murder was on his mind.

"See what I mean, Linda? Pat, let's go home, right now. Let's try to work our way back to who we really are."

"Whatever you want," said Pat. He put one arm around Joan, and tried to speak. The words wouldn't come until the tears began to flow. "Sorry. My feelings got to me. I love. . . Joan is my life. I wish I had something to say that makes any sense, besides thanks. And if you find that Travers bastard dead, you know where to find me."

"Home, big guy! None of that. Now I need you more than ever."

Pat hugged Bill, Linda, and Jeff Wilder. Then he found Jay. "If I weren't so damn homophobic, I'd kiss you." He gave Jay a hug. "I'm not good with feelings. Let me say this before I stop myself. I love every one of you. Let's go, Joan. I feel like a fool."

"That's an improvement," said Joan. "I like you as a fool. I could get used to this."

Jay frowned and turned to Kate. "I hate to turn that offer down. But walking into a bar days after you decide to make a major life change just doesn't seem the way to go."

"Why don't you go, Jay?" said Kate. "I won't mind."

"I meant what I said. I'm all in."

"OK. Let's get some soft drinks and walk down the street. There's a park."

"Sold," said Linda. "But we have to wait for Jordan. He's making a pit stop."

Linda, Bill, Kate, Betty, and Jay waved as Joan and Pat walked away, their arms so tightly wrapped around one another that they seemed to be holding one another up.

"Two people laughing and crying at the same time," said Kate. "They are so good together." She whispered to her sister, "I hope someone kills that bastard before Pat gets to him. I want those two to live happily ever after."

They turned toward the courthouse door, looking for Jordan. They saw Fuller, Galvin, and Travers coming toward them. Gillian Bullock trailed behind, struggling with two heavy thick legal briefcases on wheels. Mike Burgoyne offered her his assistance. He gestured to a scruffy young man wearing a baseball cap and carrying a camera, both bearing the CNN logo. He turned his cap backward and squinted through the eyepiece. The camera was already rolling when Travers must have muttered something. Galvin and Fuller each reached to grab one of Travers' arms.

"Let's keep on going, doctor," Galvin instructed. Travers shook off his attorneys' grips and advanced toward Mackey and the others.

"You! Philips!"

Linda put herself between Travers and Jay.

"Dr. Travers!" Galvin raised his voice, "Come with us! Now!"

Linda felt a gentle pull on her arm. Speaking very softly, Jay said, "Linda, thanks. But I'll handle this." He let his voice become deeper, firmer. "Yes, Dr. Travers?"

Travers rushed forward and punched Jay in the stomach. Jay buckled, then pulled himself erect.

"I don't believe in violence, Dr. Travers."

Travers drew back his right fist to strike again, but Kate grabbed for his arm.

Travers pushed Kate to the ground.

"Jay, don't let him hit you!"

"You can hit me, but you can't touch her."

Jay moved toward Travers, his hands at his sides.

"Just for the lady, Philips, I won't hit you. I'll just shake the hell out of you."

Travers grabbed Jay's arms and started to whip him back and forth.

"Stop, Dr. Travers!" Galvin shouted. "Don't make a bad situation worse. Stay with him, Fuller! I'm going for help."

Galvin rushed back into the courthouse, almost bowling over Ben Jordan, blinking as he walked into the bright sunlight. There was a murmur in the crowd around Travers and Philips as a limo pulling up to the curb. Governor Chalmers and his personal attorney got out of a limo and strode quickly toward Travers. Ben raced toward Jay.

"No, Ben!" said Jay. "No violence."

"Your call," said Ben. "But if the mood strikes you, do it by the numbers."

"You're next, asshole!"

"Right," said Ben. "Travers, any man who punches out a pacifist and pushes a woman to the ground makes me quake with terror."

For a split second, Jay was sure he was going crazy. Everything around him became shimmering, grey, and unreal. Time slowed to a crawl. Jay floated above his body. He could see himself being shaken back and forth. He could see Kate, looking up at him from the ground, worried and tearful. *No!*

No! I just let that man hurt the woman I love. She's trying to protect me because I won't protect myself. No! That can't be right! No! Then Jay was back in his body.

Jay gripped Travers' upper arms and stared up at him, eye to eye.

"You shouldn't have hurt the lady."

"Do you think I care?"

"No. But I do." *I don't believe what I'm doing.* Jay selected his target. *OK, that's one.* Jay made a perfect fist. *That's two.* Jay conjured up a *Grey's Anatomy* picture of Travers' guts and organs. He planned to strike six inches below the skin overlying Travers' spleen. *That's three.* Jay pushed Travers back with his left forearm and threw his whole right arm and shoulder into the first punch he'd ever thrown. *That's four.* With Travers' grip loosened, Jay stepped quickly toward Travers, putting the whole right half of his body behind his arm and shoulder as he stepped to deliver the second. *That's five!* Travers' eyes went wide. His grip on Jay's left arm gave way. With room to power his strike with a strong stride forward backed by nearly the full weight of his body. . . *That's six.* Travers dropped arms to protect his abdomen. Super-Owl's words shot into Jay's mind. *It's always good form to. . . Seven* began two feet from Travers' body, arching upward with everything Jay could put behind it. A sickening crunch and a bridal veil spray of red droplets. . . Then pumping spurts of bright red arterial blood. Travers wavered back and forth, his nose mashed obscenely flat against his left cheek. Toppling like a fallen tree, Travers landed on his face. Jay left *eight* to whomever. . .

Jay knelt alongside Kate. "I'm sorry. I don't know how to tell you what a jerk I am for not. . ." An apology interrupted with a kiss. . .

A crowd of bystanders, sheriffs, police, and reporters had gathered round. CNN's cameraman did his job to perfection. He caught it all.

Governor Chalmers tried to take command. "Arrest that man. Look what he's done to Dr. Travers!"

"And that other guy was helping him," moaned Travers, "that Jordan. The camera got most of it."

Mike Burgoyne excused himself to Gillian Bullock and exchanged a few words with the cameraman before walking over to the defense attorneys.

Bill Mackey smiled. "I thought that was you. The living legend. Maserati Mike Burgoyne. Always a pleasure to see you when you're not kicking my ass."

"Our last encounter was a nail-biter, Bill. Could have gone either way."

The Governor and his companion strode up to Burgoyne, Fuller and Galvin close behind. "I'm glad you were here to see all this. Philips and Jordan should be charged. Mr. Phelps, here, is my personal counsel."

Maserati Mike's expression remained warm and friendly.

"I bore witness to a series of events."

"You saw Philips attack Travers," shouted Chalmers. "You heard Jordan egg him on."

"Mr. Fuller, you, Mr. Galvin, and I are extremely good litigators, as are you, Governor. You were an outstanding federal prosecutor and State's Attorney General before you became governor. When we lawyers are called sharks or snakes, all we can do is shrug. If we do our jobs well, we have to accept how others see us. It comes with the territory.

"Gentlemen, your Dr. Travers is a nasty piece of filth. He punched and shook Dr. Philips. He pushed a woman to the ground when she tried to help him. It seems like the much smaller man your Dr. Travers attacked fought back in self-defense and he looks surprised as Heli about how things went down. Jordan said five words. Just saying a few words hasn't made that much happen since the first six days of creation. Push this and you'll make public fools of yourselves. And you know it. . ."

Fuller tried to scowl. Then he sighed, shrugged his shoulders, and shook hands with Maserati Mike Burgoyne. Phelps tried to usher the governor away, but police and a school of reporters had already gathered around Jay Philips and Governor Chalmers.

Governor Chalmers shook hands with Burgoyne.

"Well, you just won another one, you sly bastard."

"Professional courtesy, Governor. I don't like our kind to look bad."

Chalmers turned to Jay Philips. "I'm sorry I lost my temper, Dr. Philips. I was wrong. You were just doing your job. But Dr. Travers is a friend of mine. I'm sure you can understand."

"No hard feelings, Governor. Maybe I can help you with a bit of damage control. The woman who was victimized claims there was more than one perpetrator. Maybe you could make a statement encouraging the public to come forward to identify any other people involved?" Jay pulled a childish primitive sketch out of his attaché case. "Not much to go with."

The governor sized up the plain, out of shape, little man standing before him holding a crude drawing. *He's pathetic! He's nothing!*

"Sure." He waved to the cameraman. "I have an announcement to make. The outcome of these proceedings has left many matters unresolved. I would not be surprised if down the road things look a lot different from the way they look today. It is possible that other individuals, members of the public, may have important information that would be useful to the authorities. Dr. Philips has a rather crude sketch he'll hold up for the camera. Now, it means nothing to me, but maybe it will help trigger some recollections in someone else, and help bring a bad man to justice."

"Thank you, Governor Chalmers." Jay held up the crude drawing. As the governor looked back toward the camera with a firm and resolute expression, Jay pulled aside the crude drawing aside to reveal a very detailed, almost photographic pencil sketch behind it.

Maserati Mike Burgoyne, a man rarely at a loss for words, stood slack-jawed. "Get that close-up!"

Ben Jordan tapped Linda on the shoulder. "More balls than brains! He may need protection. Oh, my God!"

The Governor noticed the shocked expressions of the bystanders. He looked back at the second drawing, snarled, and pushed Jay to the ground. He brought his right leg back to kick Jay, but a slender wooden rod thrust between his legs at a useful angle put the Governor face down on the pavement. When he looked up, photographer's strobe lights were exploding in his face. A strong foot pressed down on his back, fixing him in place.

That night the newspapers and evening news shows would feature the sight of three male images side by side on the ground: Jay Philips and the governor to either side, and between them, Melody Jarrett's drawing of an unnamed abuser, an almost photographic pencil-drawn likeness of Governor Chalmers. Above them stood Bill Mackey. One hand held his wooden cane. His right foot was planted firmly on the governor's lower back.

CHAPTER 82

"Gilchrist!"

"Yes, Sally?"

"Don't try to sneak past my door. Come on in. There's an important case we need to review."

Linda took the client's seat in front of Sally Warren's grandfather's imposing mahogany desk.

"I've been thinking. You know I've been very involved with women's rights issues, and that most of the pro bono cases I take on personally lean in that direction?"

"Yes, I do."

"In that connection, I've been thinking about that ballsy little terrier who held up a picture that looked like Governor Chalmers. In my guts, I'm sure it was Chalmers."

"Because. . ."

"Because long before people were talking about date rape, that man tried to get me drunk to get into my pants. If that ever comes back to me, I'll deny it and destroy you. Fair?"

"More than fair."

"I'm going to request your help on the latest pro bono case I volunteered to take."

"I don't know anything about it."

"That's because it's completely bogus. I created it and a fake file to give you time to do your Nancy Drew thing, so you can figure out why Governor Chalmers is so interested in Dr. Travers, why their offices are always side by side, and why Melody Jarrett drew such a detailed picture of the man. Are you game?"

"Absolutely, but why. . ."

"Because I hate the man. I already know he's guilty. There is no way I could ever be objective. Even if I found something, I might taint the evidence with my bias. No. Go get him. Go get him for all of us. And get the hell out of my office before I cry."

CHAPTER 83

Somewhere in Afghanistan Ranger Master Sergeant Doyle Clifford crumpled another piece of paper into a ball and hurled it toward his Kevlar helmet on the floor ten feet away. His headgear was already surrounded with dozens of balled-up sheets of paper compressed into tight little orbs by his powerful hands. None were inside.

How can I tell Helen I'm going to leave her? She goes to this Travers bastard after Doyle, Jr. died. Crib death, they said. I lose my son. . . and then I lose my wife to that asshole. She says he raped her. But nobody gets raped week after week, month after month, and goes back for more rape. No way she's leveling with me! No way that Travers asshole raped her.

"Hey, Doyle!" A buddy interrupted Doyle's meditations on double homicide

"Jeez! You can't even nail your brain bucket. Get over here! On my computer! There's something about your home town on CNN."

A voice was saying, "And now, more from our legal correspondent, attorney Michael Burgoyne, who's been covering the seemingly unending twists and turns of this amazing legal drama. Mike?"

"Thank you, Harry. For our viewers unfamiliar with this case, we are talking about a truly astonishing sequence of events. Dr. Gordon Travers sued Dr. Joan Underwood, claiming she created false memories in one of her patients, memories alleging Dr. Travers had abused her. It seemed as if the prosecution had destroyed the credibility of both Dr. Underwood and her patient. It seemed that the charges against Dr. Travers had to be wrong, because the office where the patient said she was abused had never existed. However, over the weekend Dr. Underwood's attorney, Ms. Linda Gilchrist, proved that amateur sleuths to rival Nancy Drew and Sherlock Holmes still walk among us. She and her team found proof that the mysterious office actually had existed, and that Dr. Travers' lawsuit was nothing more than a pack of lies to cover a horrible series of sexual assaults on not one, but on several of his female patients. Sadly, several of these women had reported Dr. Travers had molested them, but it appears that none of them had been believed.

"Harry, you have Dr. Benjamin Jordan in the studios of NBC 10 in Bala Cynwyd, Pennsylvania. You've has been kind enough to join with us in bringing you this interview. Dr. Jordan was an expert witness for Dr. Underwood's defense. His office is nearby.

"Dr. Jordan," said Mike. "I'm sure that many of our viewers will be asking themselves questions like these: How is it possible for a man to impose himself upon so many women? Did Dr. Travers have some unusual power? Was there something about the women involved? Were there sexual issues that made them more likely to succumb to whatever Dr. Travers was trying to do? Is psychotherapy really safe? Can hypnosis make a woman just give herself to a man?"

"It's a lot simpler than you might think, Mr. Burgoyne. Dr. Travers didn't need any unusual powers or abilities. The women he victimized probably suffered a wide range of problems, but we miss the boat completely if we try to pathologize his victims or condemn hypnosis. Hypnosis is just a facilitator of whatever else is going on. It can enhance positive and therapeutic suggestions much more easily than negative or hurtful ones. The essence of the problem is persuasive deception and misdirection. It's rarely just a matter of breaking someone's will or moral fiber. Usually aggressive sadist. . ."

"Wait, Dr. Jordan. Are you saying these events are primarily hostile rather than sexual?"

"That's exactly what I'm saying. Sex is just the place where the aggressive sadism occurs. Forcing sex on someone is a rape. That's a hostile and vicious abuse of power. It's a mistake to confuse it with any normal form of sexuality. And in scenarios like this, often the perpetrator's attack takes the form of convincing the victim that what the bad person wants is what the victim wants. To give you a simple example, if you can teach a person to see the image of that person's spouse or lover when they look at you, you move that person toward doing something that person would normally not be open to doing."

"Can you say more about that, Dr. Jordan?"

"Sure, but I won't. Telling people how to hurt other people is not my style. I'm sure most of your viewers are people of the highest principles, but there may be an exception or two out there."

"In defense of our viewers, I'm sure you are speaking in the hypothetical."

"Not unless you can prove that Travers character never watched CNN."

"Point taken. Thank you, Dr. Jordan."

CHAPTER 84

Linda knocked on the open door of Sally Warren's corner office.

"Remember Billie Mason?" she asked in a low voice.

"Yes, but I'm looking forward to forgetting her."

"She's got a new job in the governor's office."

"So?"

"Her references were from employees of Chalmers Brothers Investments. She was there under four weeks. She left us to work for the governor!"

Sally leaned back in her chair. "My God!"

"I've been going over phone logs for the day Bill got sick and had to leave court, the day Brett Connery was *en route* to Germany for that deposition that never was.

"I've been able to account for every call that came in for that date and the three days before that date. There are no calls we can link to any domestic or European number for Goliath Pharmaceuticals. Nor are there any outgoing calls from our office numbers to Brett's cellphone or hotel room in Europe. He certainly got no real message from Bill Mackey OK'ing his rushing off to Europe in the middle of a trial. Bill admits his memory for that day is none too good, but there is no record that he made any call to Brett from anywhere. Someone pretended to be him, or someone lied. Brett's secretary told me that she doesn't know how Brett got his messages that day, but when Brett or someone posing as Brett gave her the day off, Billie conveyed that message to her. And, when she got home, she realized that her cellphone wasn't working. She played with it for a couple of days before she brought it in for repair. The repairman told her there's something that tells you whether there's been water damage. . ."

"No!"

"I think I'll have to pay a visit to Ms. Billie Mason. Maybe I can persuade her to turn in exchange for immunity from prosecution. But I really don't have any experience negotiating immunity for a client."

"I'll mentor you through, but I want no direct contact with that Chalmers filth."

CHAPTER 85

What do I really know about Billie Mason? How do I find a way into her world? All I know about her is that when she walks by, she gives men whiplash! She's always flaunting what she's got, but she's got a classy way of doing it. She's quite a dresser. That's better than nothing. Maybe the other secretaries know something I don't know.

Linda invented a cousin in her early 20s. She cornered Brett Connery's young secretary and two other twenty-somethings as they were getting ready to leave.

"I need help."

"From us?" one asked.

"Exactly. I have a cousin who's going to be looking for her first job in a couple months, and she has a birthday coming. You're all younger than I am and you all dress so well. . . And though I hate to admit it, the way I have to suit up puts me pretty much out of the loop for what she might like, what she would be comfortable wearing. I don't want to get her something expensive that she'll just put in her closet and leave it there forever. You know?"

"You're cool, Ms. Gilchrist! I get a lot of 'classic' things from my aunts that I dig out to wear. . . Only when they visit!"

"You get it! So, where would you go for something really nice for work? But nice enough to wear to go out after work?"

"I call them my nice nearly naughty stuff," said Brett's secretary. "Forget the department stores around here. By the time you get to the stuff I like, I can't afford it."

"Right!" said another. "If you play the sales right, you can do pretty well at the mall. But that means scouting and waiting."

"There are some real neat boutiques downtown. But some are a lot more expensive than others."

"Give me a spread," said Linda, pulling out a pen and index card.

"Kittie's has some cute things, but a lot of junk."

"Totally 21 has less junk, but a lot of things that are so. . ."

"Boring?"

"That's the right word. Boring."

"Joan and Geri have good stuff, and good prices. But my sister tells me they sell what was big a year or two before in New York and LA. Like they bought left-overs from top places. . ."

"OK. Good ideas. But suppose you wanted the newest and best, and someone else was picking up the bill?"

"Oh! Lenore's, wouldn't you think?"

"Oh, yes! Great place, but way outside my budget."

"Consensus?" asked Linda.

"For sure!" came the chorus.

CHAPTER 86

Lenore's was open late that evening. The mannequins and fashions in the window were presented with a wit and panache Linda would have expected on Fifth Avenue in New York City. She was impressed in spite of herself.

As Linda walked in, the saleswomen who turned toward her were high fashion chic, high fashion sleek. Those not immediately engaged with clients followed a clever twisting course among the displays to soft rock music, presenting themselves and their clothing as if they were on a runway.

The only woman near Linda's own age greeted her warmly. *Her suit! Wasn't it on the cover of last month's Marie Claire?*

"Welcome! I'm pretty good with faces, and I don't think we've met. I'm Lenore." She extended her hand.

"Linda Gilchrist." Lenore had a warm, firm handshake and an open mischievous smile. *She's easy to like.*

"What can we do for you? Looks like you have a great sense of style. Some special occasion?"

"Actually, I'm here for my cousin. She's going to graduate college this spring, and she wants to work a couple of years before grad school. You know. The younger ladies at the office swear this is the place."

"Do you mind my asking where you work?"

"Mackey Markham & Wilder."

"A lot of the younger women at the better firms come here. I have a special fondness for yours. We have a part-timer who had a scholarship to a great private school. She got hurt and couldn't play basketball, so they were going to pull it. But your Mr. Bill Mackey rushed in, you know, like some superhero, and got it back for her. Too bad she's not here tonight. She's quite the student.

"So, you dress like a rising young associate, and those girls dress to make a good appearance and to be ready for whatever. . ."

"Bull's eye!"

"So, you figure your cousin will want to be ready for whatever until she decides where she's going and is too professional and mature for Lenore's."

"You said it, not I!"

"We might be able to surprise you."

"First things first. My cousin. . ."

"Of course. But let me ask, just so I can say thanks for telling you about us if they come in, who put out the good word?"

Linda told Lenore who had praised her.

"I'm surprised! I expected you to tell me it was Billie Mason. She's in and out of here all the time." She beckoned to one of the circulating ladies, "Linda, this is Harriet. Harriet, the dress you are modeling is the same one Billie Mason bought last week, isn't it?"

"Yes, but she bought it in a lovely plum. The color I'm wearing has a bit more red. We call it 'Perky Pomegranate.'"

"That would be our Billie, or, our former Billie. She's moved on to bigger and better things."

"I know. She's been waiting for months for that opening at the state house. Ambitious young lady, that Billie. Helen, help Linda find something for her cousin. And, since I'd be a fool not to show you what we have that might interest you, Linda. . . Harriet, please find Joyce and ask her to present some items that might tempt this discriminating woman."

An hour later, Linda left with pictures of two outfits to run by her "cousin," and wearing a smashing blazer that Helen, Joyce, and Lenore insisted had been designed specifically with Linda Gilchrist in mind.

"Especially in the next few months. . . We tried to tell Billie that working for the governor, she would need something like this for certain occasions," said Helen, "but she said it just wasn't her style. She felt too confined."

"I can see how she might have felt that way," Linda replied. Lenore rolled her eyes and nodded, but Helen and Joyce seemed puzzled, and finally shrugged.

CHAPTER 87

Linda spent a week following up hunches and simple facts that at first glance seemed to be an unconnected jumble. But something in her mind was working relentlessly to pull together that jumble, to find the pattern in that junk drawer in her mind. Her thoughts formed one configuration and combination after another, until those hunches, facts, and bits of chaos abandoned their kaleidoscopic whirl and settled inexorably into an unwanted but inexorable pattern. After a maddening weekend, Linda became convinced she was finally putting the pieces together. She called Billie that Monday evening.

"Billie, so much was going on at Mackey Markham & Wilder around the time you left the firm that a couple of forms related to your pension contributions were overlooked during your exit interview. We don't want to see you cheated out of anything you deserve. I've been assigned to make things right."

"Thanks, Ms. Gilchrist, but I don't care. I've moved on and I don't like looking back."

"I don't blame you. In fact, that's usually how I see things myself. Well, let me see here. Billie, it looks like you'd be throwing away a few hundred dollars."

"No big deal. Thanks, but no thanks."

"Let me take another look, Billie. No, actually it's $3,741.58. That sounds like serious money to me."

"Well, if it's that much, thanks for not letting me blow you off. Would tomorrow night work?"

* * *

Linda accepted Billie's offer of a cold drink and a tour of her apartment. Billie's balcony had an incredible view over the city. Her furnishings were expensive and tasteful. They showed the touch of an upscale interior designer. Billie did not come from money and had no immediately discernable set of skills. *There's only two ways a gal like this has an apartment like this. . . She's being kept, or she's the most expensive call girl in town. Or both!*

"Oh! I really like this Miro print, *A Surrealist Ballet*, his tribute to Degas. I have the same one in my exercise room, but you framed yours so exquisitely for this decor!"

"I'm glad you like it. I brought it from home."

Right! "Those modern Italian artists! They're wonderful, aren't they?"

"The best."

"Billie, I wish a lot of things were different. And I don't mean to hurt you. But Miro is Spanish, and that print is called *The Bird and Star*. It was a tribute to Picasso, and no way you brought a frame synched to the colors of your couch and rug from home. And I'm here about a somewhat different personnel matter. Do you remember what happened to Brett's secretary's iPhone?"

"No. I don't know what you're talking about."

"The one that crashed toward the end of your time at Mackey Markham & Wilder?"

Billie's forehead creased. Her eyes narrowed. "Oh, I heard about that. That she was real upset because somehow water got into it. Oh, yeah!"

"Billie, no one knew that until a few days after you left."

"I think you better leave."

"I will in a minute. But before I do, let me tell you a story. It's a story about a very pretty young girl who wanted more in her life than being a legal secretary could provide. She may have tried a few second jobs. . ."

Billie's hand went to her face. She began to shake.

"Somehow, she got herself connected with a few people, probably men. I don't know what happened, but I think that some people came along with offers that were a lot more lucrative than her job at Mackey Markham & Wilder. She may not even have known why she was supposed to pass on certain things to certain people, or to do some of the things she was told to do. But one of the things she did was to pass along information about our handling of the Underwood case to someone connected with Dr. Travers. And another of the things she did was to pass along a message that never came from a client, but from those people, a message that took a Mackey Markham & Wilder lawyer connected with the Travers case out of the country. Along the way she drowned that lawyer's secretary's iPhone, the only phone that secretary had. When that secretary was given the rest of the day off and her iPhone was trashed, the only two people who could have stopped that lawyer in time. . . Well, one was out of contact, and the other one had her lips sealed. That made it impossible to track down that attorney through normal channels until it was too late to prevent him from going overseas on a wild goose chase when he was needed here.

"And suddenly, that pretty young girl finds herself working for the governor, who seems to have some connection with a plaintiff. . ."

"I want to quit! I don't want anything more to do with that son of a bitch. You're right. I wish I was a smarter person. But. . . I never understood what it was all about."

She spread her arms and wheeled about the room. "Look at this! A hell of a lot better than a ratty, rusted-out trailer. And I don't have to do that much. . . Oh, my God! I don't want to go to jail again. What can I do? What do I have to do?"

CHAPTER 88

"Look. I've made two very powerful impressions on you," Kate began. "One good, and one I'd rather forget, but. . . I did what I did. You've made a very powerful impression on me. I'd like to hope we can get to know one another, but not while you're still grieving and I guess, while I am, too.

"I'm still too messed up about my own divorce. Until I get through that, I'm no good to anybody, including myself. I'm not going to lie to you. It nearly destroyed me. I'm all messed up about the cancer and mastectomies too, no matter what the doctors say. Sometimes I just don't know who I am any more. I've got serious surgery ahead of me. Betty, and Phyllis from AA. . . No, that's a lie. You. . . You've finally convinced me that I need to take a hard look at myself, and I need help to do it. I hope we can sit down and talk together say, a year from now."

"Well, I've never seen one of those rebound things work out too well, and. . . Let's just say you've become very important to me very quickly. And I have a lot of my own stuff to deal with. A year sounds good. Less chance to mess things up."

"Especially very important things. I have your number. Shall we say a year from today?" She looked at her watch. "Precisely?"

CHAPTER 89

"Bill, how did you come up with those instructions for Dr. Jordan? And how did you know he was such a gifted actor?"

Bill Mackey's colleagues and friends asked him that question dozens of times in dozens of ways. Bill just smiled. Those months of chemotherapy were patchy recollections at best. All Bill could do was smile, shrug, and say yet one more time that he just did not remember. The simple knowledge that he and his team hadn't failed his old friend and his family warmed his heart. That was all he cared to recall.

Linda couldn't give Bill much assistance. Ben Jordan had told her only that he had just left Bill's office, and that he had a request for her. That request set off a series of events that affected so many members of the jury that the other side had lost all hope of a smashing triumph, and maybe even had begun to see the writing on the wall before Linda and Jay Philips administered the *coup de grace*.

Jordan said his conversation with Bill was privileged. Bill said the same. For months, Linda could make no sense of the situation. Her inability to reason it through had slowly grown from mild curiosity to annoyance, and finally into an intense, obnoxious obsessive itch she could not scratch. Nearly half a year passed by before she could take a shot at putting it all together. When she did, she realized that no one would ever confirm the truth or prove the falsehood of what she had deduced.

Linda ran her thoughts by her sister Eve for the umpteenth time.

"I'm still trying to figure out how that all went down. It's driving me nuts. Bill says he doesn't remember giving Jordan instructions to pass along, and Jordan says only that he had been in Mackey's office, and their conversation was privileged. I think I've been looking at this all wrong. If the idea I have now is right, Ben Jordan is diabolical."

"He can be, uh, devious. I'll give you diabolical for the sake of argument. What makes you think you've been looking at this all wrong?"

"I've been assuming that before Bill went home, he gave Ben some instructions to pass on to me. I assumed that Bill wanted to set a trap for the other side just like they had set for us. With all the chemo, I thought that well, maybe he didn't remember doing that, or maybe it was such a sneaky plan he didn't want to admit it was his. But I just realized something. Bill was sick as a dog. I don't think he really had a chance to review the testimony that came out. He surely would have talked to me or left a message for me if he had, but he didn't. Yet Jordan spent some time with Bill and that other man early in the morning, and that man was Bill's doctor. Then Bill went home. Jordan said only that he had spent some time with Bill, and asked me to do something when he was on the stand. . . To leave a loose end."

"So?"

"Joan Underwood said something very interesting. She said she'd bet Ben was a fisherman, and a good one, since he always seemed to know what bait to use, and where to cast it."

"Well, he is a hell of a fisherman. But what do you mean?"

"I thought Bill came up with a plan. But now, I'm beginning to think. . ."

"That Ben did? No. . ."

"Eve! He said he'd just come from Bill Mackey, and that he wanted me to do something. He never said it was Bill Mackey who told him to tell me to do that something."

"Wow! And he said their conversation was privileged?"

"What does that mean to you?"

"That's what we say about doctor-patient confidentiality."

"So, I, as a lawyer, had professional tunnel vision. I assumed Bill was too sick to talk to me, and told Jordan to give me the message. . ."

"But since he was up and about that afternoon and vigorous enough to stomp on Travers the next morning. . ."

"Jordan may have been treating Bill, or trying to help him some way."

"My God, Linda. . . Say it out loud."

"Ben Jordan is really skilled with hypnosis. And my research taught me that doctors use hypnosis to reduce the nausea and vomiting that people can experience with chemotherapy."

"So?"

"Suppose Bill asked Ben to help him with his nausea and vomiting or Ben offered to do that. Suppose they met with Bill's own doctor at his office early that morning. Suppose Ben hypnotized Bill and taught him autohypnotic techniques to control nausea and vomiting. Suppose Bill went home and practiced his fool head off, and marched into court."

"Why drag in the other doctor?"

"Ben isn't licensed here, and you say he's a stickler for following the rules, if only to know where to bend them. Maybe he taught the other guy how to help Bill practice self-hypnosis, or to reinforce his suggestions."

"You're probably right. All that Nancy Drew stuff. It really took. Yep! This makes sense. I think you're right."

"How about you do me a favor? Next time you see Jordan, ask him what he really thinks of Dr. Rapier, the guy who took Joan Underwood over the coals."

CHAPTER 90

Linda poured over the contents of her "junk drawer." Billie Mason had been paid to undermine her firm's defense of Joan Underwood. At first, she had been paid with a line of credit at the most upscale shop in town. Now, she was on the Governor's staff and much, much, more. Something linked the Travers case to the Governor, and Billie Mason just might be the key.

Linda met Billie at the bar of a downtown hotel.

"I've never been here before," Linda said.

"I've been here too many times before," Billie replied. "Ouch! I guess that's as bad as it sounds."

"It hasn't been easy for you. Tonight, I just have a few questions, but I wanted to be sure we wouldn't be overheard. Billie, after you left Mackey Markham & Wilder, there was a month or so before you began at the Governor's office."

"Right. I was sort of between jobs."

"Sort of?"

"Well, the Governor began to pay me what I'd get in my new job."

"How did he pay you?"

"Well, it was. . . What do you call it? A no-show job, like politicians give their friends?"

"Sure, I understand that. What was your title?"

"I was secretary to the partners of Chalmers Brothers Investments."

"Chalmers Brothers?"

"Yeah. You know, a family partnership. The governor's family."

"What do they do?"

"They invest in commercial real estate."

"Around here?"

"Mostly out of town. Around here, they own the land that's being leased to Goliath Pharmaceuticals and something else. . . I saw it once. I hate to say it, but it's a real ugly building. . ."

"HighPoint Centre?"

"That's it!"

"OK, well, we see eye to eye on that one. Do you happen to know how many Chalmers brothers there are?"

"Well, the governor said four once. But another time he said three and a half. I don't know what he meant."

"Hmm. Were their names on the documents you handled?"

"Documents? I told you it was a no-show job."

CHAPTER 91

Chalmers Brothers Investments had a telephone number linked to Chalmers' law offices on the sixth floor of HighPoint Centre. Posing as a reporter doing a story on family businesses, Linda learned that Chalmers Brothers Investments preferred privacy to publicity.

"Is that the policy of all four Chalmers brothers?"

"Four? There are only three. And yes, they all agree."

"Oh? I was told there were four."

"There is a fourth partner. But the only name on our official communications was Beau Chalmers, the governor. The others prefer to enjoy their privacy. Since his election it's in trust, managed by Mr. Phelps."

CHAPTER 92

Shortly after Army Ranger Master Sergeant Doyle Clifford arrived Stateside on leave, he appeared at his home, unannounced. His arrival shocked and delighted his children. It terrified his wife, Helen. She believed he had come home to tell her their marriage was over.

After Helen and their children were asleep, he stole into each bedroom and stood watching his loved ones as they slept, lost in thought. He relived the way he had insulted and humiliated the woman he loved, the mother of his children. Was it a dream or a flashback from one dark night when he was a hair's breadth way from strangling Helen in her sleep?

The next morning, he awoke clear and determined. Late that afternoon he followed Dr. Travers home from his office. That night, he told Helen that since their dog hardly seemed to recognize him, the two would take a long, long walk and reconnect.

Doyle kissed his wife good-bye and drove off into the dark. He left his dog in the family SUV with water and food, and made his way to his enemy's home.

When he shook Dr. Travers awake, he identified himself. He informed Dr. Travers that he did not appreciate Dr. Travers' raping his wife while he was serving overseas.

When Dr. Travers began to lie, make excuses, and finally to blame Helen for coming on to him, driven by her sexual frustration because her husband was away so often and for so long, Master Sergeant Doyle Clifford continued his service to his country by slowly beheading Dr. Travers. He stuffed Dr. Travers into Dr. Travers' trash cans, left the garbage where it was, and walked away.

Master Sergeant Doyle Clifford and his team had never been detected during the covert operations they had performed in the course of their service to their country. The current mission was no exception.

When he had cleaned up and joined his wife in bed, she half-opened her eyes.

"Are you and the dog friends again?" she asked.

"Yeah. A night of getting to know one another all over again. Bought him some cheeseburgers."

"Mmm! Male bonding."

"Yeah. And since I was wandering around, I took out the garbage."

"But it's a day too early!"

"Damn! Here I was worried it might be much too late. Anyway, it's time for us to get to know one another all over again. I've let you down. That will never happen again."

CHAPTER 93

"Billie," asked Linda, "Can we meet up at that bar again? I have just a few more questions to ask you."

"Not there. Same chain as the place I was arrested in Atlanta the time I went to jail. I want to put all that behind me forever. What about Starbuck's?"

* * *

"Before you say anything, Linda, I'm not proud of what I was, and I'm not proud of what I am. If my brains were half as good as my body. . . I made some really bad choices. I wanted more. . ."

"Billie, I know I've been incredibly lucky. I can't begin to imagine what you've gone through, and believe me, I wish you the best. You may not know anything about what I'm trying to figure out. But I keep remembering. . . You said the governor said there were four Chalmers Brothers, and then he said there were three and a half. . ."

"Oh, God! I wish I'd never said that! But everything is going to come out anyway, right?"

"I'll do my best to protect you."

"I went to one of the governor's fund-raisers with some others from the office. The governor must have like what he saw. He sent an aide over to get my name and number. . . Look. . . He set me up in my apartment. No more living the life. . . Only two men to take care of instead of whatever. . . No real work. Great clothes and meeting important people. I was stupid enough to think that was a big step up in the world. I never should have left that trailer. . ."

"I'm not sure I understand. You were. . . with the governor? And someone else?"

"They love to spit-roast."

"To spit-roast?"

"You've been lucky. . . You wouldn't know. Low down stuff. Like a steer on a spit at a barbecue? Like one fucks your mouth and the other fucks you down below. They wanted my ass, though. Ucch! And then they'd switch places till they were through. . . Makes me want to vomit just remembering it. . ."

Linda, now heavily pregnant, struggled to control her rising nausea.

"Look. It's part of the life. But normal johns. . . Those two loved messing me up, smearing me with their filth."

"I'm so sorry. . ."

"Don't try, Linda. A world of sorry won't make it right. And they took pictures. . . Don't cry, Linda. We're in Starbuck's."

Billie's sad smile destroyed Linda. "I need to step out for a minute."

"Take your time. I've learned how to smile through anything."

* * *

"Back already?"

"I don't think I'm going to come back from this for a long time. I used to complain about my career going nowhere and cry because I used to think I would never have a child. I never knew how lucky I was."

"Me too," said Billie, "really, in a funny way. My sister died with a needle in her arm. I guess you want to know about the other man."

Linda wrote something on a napkin and passed it over to Billie.

"Yeah! That's the bastard. His half-brother."

"How did that happen?"

"I don't know. And I don't want to know."

CHAPTER 94

Dr. Travers' date of birth on the net. Linda got a copy of the obituary of the first Governor Chalmers, Governor Beau Chalmers's father, from the archives of a local paper. The late Governor Chalmers was remembered by his three sons, his two daughters, and his adopted son, Gordon Travers. Travers had been the son of his wife's sister, who had died in an auto accident while Gordon Travers was an infant.

Travers' father died in the same accident. His obituary listed a number of siblings. After striking out with three, she was able to reach the man's older sister.

"They killed him for sure," she said.

"What!"

"No matter what them rich sons of bitches say, they killed him. My brother ran out of money. He had to drop out of college. . . not smart enough for one of them scholarship things. But he was a good boy. Some rich folks offered to pay his way through college. All he had to do was marry this rich bitch who got herself knocked up and needed a name for her baby."

"That's hard to believe. . ."

"That's what I told him. . . Nothin' good will come of it. But he didn't want to come back here, back to nothin'. He wanted his dream."

"What happened?"

"They killed him. That's what happened. And when he died, they wouldn't bury him with their own. I still got his ashes. I guess when the rest of us go, we'll bury him with us."

"How did he die?"

"It was an accident, they said. Drinkin' and drivin', they said. Killed him and his so-called wife. Almost killed the kid, whosever he was. Don't know what happened to that kid. We talked it over and decided we wouldn't take him. He wasn't our blood. But they never asked us to. Their lawyer said his wife was the kid's god-mother, and they'd raise him."

"So, why do you think they killed him. . . Or them?"

"Well, Miss Gilchrist, we take our religion real serious. My brother never touched a drop of liquor. Never smoked, neither. No way that story is true. Somebody wanted to get rid of him, or them, or whatever. I pray for him every day. And for the souls of those no-good sons of bitches who killed him. Not as much, of course. . ."

"Do you have any idea about who would want to kill him?"

"Nobody. But when I think of why, it comes down to whoever got that rich girl in that way. Somebody wanted to hide some secret. Makes no sense no other way."

CHAPTER 95

Billie Mason, the exceptionally well-configured young secretary Governor Chalmers had lured away from Mackey Markham & Wilder with a remarkably generous raise and promises of a life with less wear and tear, knocked discretely.

"Governor? There's a gentleman here to see you."

"I told you to cancel all of my appointments and meetings today!"

"It's Senator Barton Laird. . . Senator!" Senator Laird breezed right past Billie Mason.

"I won't take up much of your time, Beau. I just drove in from DC and I can't take this pretty lady's 'no' for an answer. Our party chairman asked me to pay you a discreet visit."

"You can go, Billie. Why you, and not him?"

"Well, actually, Beau, he was going to send Representative Elias Stover. I stepped in and told him that we go back a long way. I don't think you want someone like Stover to drop in out of the blue. Better an old friend than an old SEAL and ordained Baptist minister."

"I can beat this, Bart."

"Beau. . ."

"I can. One more news cycle and it'll blow over."

"Beau. . ."

"Trust me on this, Joe. I'll get this behind me. I've got to focus on my reelection. . ."

"Beau. . ."

"Bart, I mean it!"

"Beau! Don't make this any harder than it has to be. The party is looking elsewhere."

"They can't!"

"Beau, later today members of your own party are going to introduce articles of impeachment in the state legislature. They've already run it by the national committee. The NC won't cover your butt. The chairman recommends you make a graceful exit."

"No way!"

"Beau, give it up. Your asshole half-brother. . ."

"I don't have a half-brother. . ."

"Some lady lawyer, I think her name is Gilchrist, took a close look at Chalmers Brothers Investments and put it together. Travers' offices always connect to one of your suites. You may not know that your buddy taped his adventures. You show up in a few."

"That's not true!"

"I'll say one more thing, and then I'm out of here. Cut out the bullshit! Stop lying to yourself. After your brother was murdered, the cops checked out his place. The only reason you and your dick that curves to the right aren't front page news everywhere is that a detective's daughter was one of his victims and that the attorney general has agreed to protect the confidentiality of one cooperating witness. He and the police chief sealed the evidence. Those particular tapes will probably vanish if they're not gone already. But the rest could leak out at any minute."

* * *

Just before five that afternoon, the speaker of the state house of representatives arrived at Governor Chalmers's office.

"Beau, I couldn't stop them. They introduced those damned articles of impeachment, and there's a lot of support from both sides of the aisle."

"I'll beat this!"

"I hope so."

"I could use a drink. What about you?"

"Sure."

The governor buzzed Billie and turned back to the speaker.

"Perky Tits will be right in. When she walks back out, savor every step she takes. What an ass!"

Billie brought in two glasses full of ice, a bottle of an exquisite small batch bourbon, a second of branch water, and two stirring rods on a silver tray. She poured and mixed a drink for the speaker.

"What about me?"

"Oh, I'm sorry." Billie Mason emptied the bottle of bourbon over his head, and then, "I forgot the branch water. . ."

"You're on the news, you smug bastard! Tapes of you and a bunch of Dr. Travers' patients. I thought we had something special! How could you. . .?"

She slapped the governor as hard as she could. "By the way, Ms. Perky Tits just quit, and Ms. Billie Mason is getting one hell of a raise until she gets another job with your incredibly great recommendation. You'll treat me with respect, or I'll call that squat little guy you called a loser and the lady you called a hag, and let the two of them scare the shit out of you. I'm no saint, but compared to you, I'm the Virgin fuckin' Mary.

"I apologize for causing a scene in front of you, Mr. Speaker."

The speaker rose. He opened and held the door for Ms. Billie Mason. He followed her out, shaking his head all the way. He was back in seconds.

"Beau," he said. "Some gentlemen are here to see you. They have badges."

* * *

Billie Mason walked into Governor Chalmers's office for the last time. Her now former employer stood cuffed, with a state trooper holding one arm, and a federal marshal holding the other.

Billie walked up to Governor Chalmers and planted herself only a foot away from his face.

"Before you leave this office and buy yourself the best lawyers you can find, I want you to know one last thing about me. . . I've been wearing a wire for the last month, you motherfucking son of a bitch." She spit in Governor Chalmers's face, and backed off a step or two for a final gesture.

"Nice one, ma'am," said the trooper on the right, as Billie made her exit.

"Guess we'll have to carry him out of here," said the federal marshal. "No way he's walkin'. That gal could kick field goals in the NFL."

* * *

Senator Barton Laird struggled with his conscience all the way back to his Alexandria home. He checked to be sure his wife was really asleep. Laird did not have a close relationship with the man his better angels were instructing him to call.

"Elias, just wanted to update you about Chalmers. Rest easy. I got there just before the cops. Really! So, no need for you to become involved. But there is something else. . . I'm not going to pretend I live my life like you live yours. But before I give in to temptation, I'm begging you to save a soul. She's breaking my. . ."

"I'll be right there."

Barton Laird had a rare moment of candor with Reverend Elias Stover. "I can't believe I'm calling you instead of finding her an apartment near my office. I just can't live with what I'm sure is going to happen to her. You don't need a crystal ball to see where she's headed. I can't face myself unless I try to do something. This is new territory for me. . . Damn! I can't believe I'm crying. You're crying too, you old bastard."

Elias Stover gave a sad smile. "Bart, these are tears of joy. For you. I'm all in. No, I don't know how what to do either, but we can't let that stop us."

"Us?" Barton Laird sat in silence, looking at the floor. "Damn, Elias! I don't believe what I'm saying. . . OK. You and me? That's one hell of an odd couple, even for Capitol Hill."

"I don't see it that way, Bart. Two confused, imperfect men trying to do better? That works."

CHAPTER 96

Two months later, Ben gave a talk in Boston. He and Elani spent an evening with Eve Gilchrist, Jim Cabot and their three young daughters before their planned family weekend.

"How's Jay Philips doing, Ben?" Eve asked.

"My heart goes out to him. His wife drops a bomb on him, tells him she's been betraying him for years. Then she goes and gets herself killed with her boyfriend. The kids didn't even tell him about the funeral until it was over. It gets worse, but that's enough."

"I never knew that."

"That's Jay. But he's on his feet. He's talking about trying to get that book of his published. In fact, an academic press is interested. I think he's really got a thing for your aunt. I'm afraid he'll get hurt."

"Not if she gets her head on straight."

"And how's Linda?"

"Huge and overjoyed. Any day now. You know it took her a long time, and now it looks like twins. And things are moving along for Hunter. I think they'll be raising those kids in California."

"And Bill Mackey?"

"Linda says he's looking good. Back to his normal weight and all."

"He's a damn good man."

"Yes, he is. Linda really admires him. Say, Ben. I meant to ask you. What's your professional opinion of Peter Rapier?"

"Not fit for your daughters' delicate ears. Or your husband's."

"OK. Well, another loose end from that sordid situation. . . Whatever made you say so much about yourself on the stand? Did Bill Mackey put you up to that?"

"Just got pushed into a corner."

"You? Pushed into a corner by this Gillian Bullock? Please!"

"That's my story and I'm sticking to it."

"Ben. Something went down."

"Eve. Have you ever heard me gossip? Or break a confidence?"

"No. Never."

"Then let's talk about you. You live in Boston, in a classy townhouse. Don't you ever wish you had room to garden?"

"Well, sure."

"If you could have a flower garden, what would you plant?"

"I don't know. . ."

Jim broke in, "Sure you do! Every time we pass a nice garden with great hydrangeas, you stop, you drink it in, and you say, 'But we really don't have room for the kind of plantings I like, a whole bunch of them with different colors. . .'"

"You're right, Jim. But now Ben is going to start interpreting, 'You can't have what you want, Eve, so you try to convince yourself you don't really want it.' And if you did, you'd be right. My mom loves them too. You've seen my folks' place on Martha's Vineyard. As a matter of fact, every woman in my family loves hydrangeas."

"Generation after generation," said Jim. "A couple of summers ago Eve's mom and a couple of her sisters went to town and created a whole bower of hydrangeas around that old pergola near the water."

"I bet that your Aunt Kate is a tiger in the dirt."

"That she is. It's like she and my mom compete to see who can get the most done, still trying to outscore one another."

* * *

As the Jordans gathered themselves to leave, Eve made a last valiant effort to complete the mission Linda had assigned her.

"Ben, are you telling me that all of your testimony just happened, just like that? If your friend Super Owl were there, I bet he'd be asking, 'Who writes your material?'"

"Eve, there's probably nothing I can tell you that would really answer your question. But if Super Owl were here, I think he'd say something else. . . Something like, 'It's always good form to punch a bully in the nose, one way or another.'

"And take this as a note to yourself. If you plan to use one query to set up or bait the trap for another, you have to disguise your second move with more sophisticated misdirection instead of springing it in the next sentence. Pass that along to Ms. Nancy Drew."

"Whatever are you talking about?"

"I wouldn't know. Just talking, I guess."

* * *

"Good lord, Eve! What time is it?"

"I know it's late, but I had to call you."

"Talk! Before I reach through the phone and kill you, beloved sister mine."

"This is worth it. The Jordans were over for dinner. I'm sure you're right. He'll never admit it, but you nailed it. Bill Mackey is a great lawyer, but he's not a warrior. And he's not a vindictive bastard. Ben Jordan is both."

"What did he say?"

"I told him what you told me about how he acted, that it didn't sound like spontaneous testimony. I said this genius friend of his would have asked, 'Who wrote your material?' Jordan told me that he had nothing to say, but if that friend of his was there, he'd probably say something like 'It's always good form to punch a bully in the nose, one way or another.'"

"Thanks. I hope it wasn't too much of an imposition."

"Linda, he caught me in the act. And he knew it came from you."

"No!"

"Yes! Just before he left, he said that if I plan to set up a trap, I should cover it up more carefully. . . And that I should pass that on to Ms. Nancy Drew. You were right again! Seeing through a Ben Jordan gambit is quite an accomplishment!"

"But it took me seven months."

"That's probably a new speed record."

CHAPTER 97

"Good to hear from you, Dr. Jordan."

"Call me Ben, Linda. Do you remember how after all that ruckus I was fretting about Elijah Springfield, the custodian at HighPoint Centre?"

"Yes. You said it didn't smell right."

"It still doesn't. Maserati Mike got me a copy of the police report on Springfield's drowning. Would you like to hear a crazy story about how Travers and Chalmers made him go away?"

* * *

"This is Chief Pendleton. Is this Dr. Jordan?"

"Guilty as charged. Thanks for sparing me a few minutes."

"I'm here with a Ms. Gilchrist and a Mr. Mackey. They say that you have a crazy story to tell me, but maybe you're not quite as crazy as you sound."

"They are being kind. Here is a time line. When Melody Jarrett was talking about filing charges against Dr. Travers, she consulted a lawyer named Phelps, who is a close friend of Governor Chalmers. She did not proceed, but Travers began to moan about being slandered. Elijah Springfield drowned early on a Saturday morning some time thereafter. The following Monday, a change of address form was filed, redirecting any and all FedEx mail for Suite 312 to Suite 618. Further, the door to the custodian's room was locked and HighPoint Centre contracted with a company that provides maintenance and repair services to office buildings and apartments. Later, regular mail was redirected. During the Underwood trial Ms. Gilchrist's aunt got through the dog door into that room. She found a substantial quantity of advertising and 'Current Resident' mail addressed to Suite 312."

"I remember."

"It was all from after Springfield died. I will guess that before he passed, he had collected and he or someone else destroyed that mail. After the room was sealed, some folks still slid the mail through the slot.

"Moving forward. When it became clear that the very existence of Suite 312 could be a problem, the lessors of the suites along that hall were offered inducements to relocate. After the removal of a door sign with the number, and the door itself, somehow the original plans disappeared. Then, the only problematic witnesses on the scene were the folks who delivered packages and mail, and Elijah Springfield. Since Travers didn't receive much mail there, he redirected Federal Express and other traceable deliveries ASAP once he began to worry. But he overlooked routine mail because it was mostly junk. When he realized his oversight, at first he feared calling attention to 312 by canceling mail delivery. Later on, and I don't know why, he decided the risk was worth it. That left Elijah Springfield. . ."

"Read the report. There was no evidence of foul play. His son told our people that the old man loved to fish, but he never learned to swim."

"I've been reading that report for two months. I'm not a trained detective, but it looks awful suspicious to me."

"Oh, no! Another smart-ass telling us dumb Southern lawmen that we're cartoon dummies?"

"No. Another smart-ass ready to praise the completeness of your men's report, and to draw an inference from it. Hear me out. Then snarl at will.

"Here goes. . . Elijah Springfield was a church-going, rule-following, non-drinker, non-smoker. Boating regulations stipulate carrying a certified floatation device for each person on board a vessel."

"So?"

"They recovered his tackle box, his anchor, his lunch-pail, and his hat. Those don't float. There is no mention of his floatation device. . . The one thing that could have saved his life is among the missing."

"The curious case of the dog in the night?" asked Pendleton.

"Who was that SOB who suggested Southern cops were dumb?"

* * *

"The pictures of Travers' boat at the time showed no damage. He sold it a while later to someone out of state. Your idea is clever, but it gives us nothing to work with."

"Chief, maybe that idea is dead in the water. But, like I told you, all you need is a big wake and you can do serious damage. Once two guys racing Cigarettes nearly turned my sailboat over on its side. I can imagine one high speed close miss to flip his canoe, and a second pass to pick up the life-preserver. But, back to the ramming option. . . Let me ask you something, as one clever SOB to another. I've got a buddy on Cape Cod, Portuguese fisherman, former SEAL. He's always singing love songs to his pretty boat. When he comes into port, his pretty boat wears protection. If you or I had a pretty boat, and we wanted to use our pretty boats to knock a fisherman out of a red canoe. . . Probably long gone by now, but if Travers was a cheap bastard. . ."

* * *

"OK, Jordan. I just walked by the slip where Travers kept his new boat. It's Chalmers' now. There's red paint ground into scuffs on three fenders. Apologies, Dr. Jordan. I'm calling for a search warrant."

* * *

"Pendleton is building a strong case. Thought you'd want to know."

"Thanks, Linda. I couldn't let a fellow fisherman go unavenged."

"I'm not sure whether you're joking, or dead serious!"

"Good question."

CHAPTER 98

"CNN legal commentator Mike Burgoyne and Attorney Linda Gilchrist, a member of the team that defended Dr. Joan Underwood, are with us tonight. Michael?"

"Thanks, Bill. I'm here with Attorney Linda Gilchrist, who played a crucial role in Dr. Underwood's defense. She followed up on a number of loose threads that led to the resignation of Governor Beau Chalmers, and ultimately to his incarceration for sex crimes and his indictment for the murder of Elijah Springfield, a maintenance superintendent who had information that might have revealed his participation in the predatory sexual practices of his adopted brother, Dr. Gordon Travers. Linda, can you help us bring some understanding and closure to this incredibly complicated and upsetting chain of events?"

"Many questions remain, Mr. Burgoyne, and several other people deserve as much if not more credit than I for getting to the bottom of this situation, but they prefer to remain anonymous. Long ago, the sister of the first Governor Chalmers became pregnant. The father was unknown. A young man was paid to marry her to give the child a name. That child was Gordon Travers. DNA evidence suggests that the real father was also a member of the Chalmers family."

"Gordon Travers was the product of incest?"

"So it would appear, and the governor was the only relatively young adult male in his family at the time. The records of the accident in which the parents of that child perished, but which the child survived, are incomplete. But the allegation that the father, who was driving, had been drinking heavily, is sustained only by unsubstantiated allegations. He was not a drinker, and the idea that the accident was due to his intoxication was put forward by the first Governor Chalmers, who was already on the record describing his brother-in-law as a non-drinker who forbade the presence of alcoholic beverages at his wedding to Governor Chalmers' sister. The accident and the explanation for it remain suspicious. The surviving child was adopted.

"The second Governor Chalmers and Dr. Travers grew up together. They were close friends. Apparently, both had lax attitudes toward sexual boundaries. Dr. Travers enjoyed the perks that came with the governor's power, and the governor enjoyed the grotesque and unethical entertainments Dr. Travers was able to arrange, and to videotape. They shared a very lovely mistress.

"Dr. Travers was able to exploit a number of his patients, and to let the governor participate. He saw most patients elsewhere, but saw vulnerable women in suite 312 at HighPoint Centre. Until his election, the governor could enter 312 from his own suite by a connecting door not opening into the hall. When the governor bought HighPoint Centre he relocated to the sixth floor and Dr. Travers moved his main office to a space in the governor's new suite.

"When Melody Jarrett filed a complaint, the governor and Dr. Travers decided to cover their tracks. They relocated the businesses near 312 to other properties on extremely advantageous terms, and only then 'renovated' the area. Suite 312 and those who passed it daily but were not beholding to Governor Chalmers disappeared from the scene.

The only person on site who knew about the renovation in detail was Elijah Springfield. Enough evidence has been found to suggest that his death was not accidental. Former Governor Beau Chalmers has been charged with involvement in his demise.

"Jarrett's actions made it imperative for Chalmers to discredit any and all charges against Dr. Travers, which might ultimately lead to his own door. His efforts took the form of attacking Dr. Underwood and attempting to show that any and all charges against Dr. Travers made by her former patient resulted from Dr. Underwood's ineptitude rather than the brothers' moral turpitude. The lawsuit against Dr. Underwood was no more than an elaborate diversion and cover-up. They were willing to throw her under the bus to protect themselves."

"Thank you, Ms. Gilchrist. I feel obliged to inform those listening that I covered the trial of Dr. Underwood, and Ms. Gilchrist has been extremely self-effacing about her role in shedding light on this matter. You and your unnamed associates have done a dandy job of detection. In doing so, performed a major public service by making it possible to remove a corrupt individual from high public office."

CHAPTER 99

Maserati Mike Burgoyne was halfway through his free weights routine when the first signs of a strange, vague discomfort spread across his chest. He tried to push on through, but it refused to yield. It intensified. It became a squeezing pressure. Then momentary dizziness, and a hint of nausea.

Shit! This is not good. Mike wavered. *Push through the pain or push through denial?* Rationality prevailed. *I didn't get where I am by ignoring evidence.*

Mike's call caught his friend and internist, Shelly Greenberg, halfway out his office door.

"Mike, I've been your doctor forever. You've never been sick or called me before. I'll call the paramedics and meet you at the emergency room."

"I thought you played golf Wednesday afternoons."

"Not until we figure out whether you're a hypochondriac or whether you just got a message from God."

* * *

Shelly reviewed Mike's test results with two top cardiologists. There was no getting around the elevated ST segments and flipped T waves on his EKG. When Shelly returned, Mike was hooked up to a monitor and an i.v., taking a nap. His wife Marci, a high-powered exec at a major studio, was holding Mike's hand and staring blankly at the wall. Shelly's voice startled Marci; her sudden movement awakened Mike.

"Well?" asked Mike. "Going to make your tee time? Or stuck here past tea time?"

"Mike!"

"If I wanted to wait for respect from this wise guy, Marci, I'd have to believe in reincarnation. Shall I start with the good news or the bad news?"

"Give me the good news and let me out of here. Not likely?"

"Marci. . . I'm not going to talk to Mike 'cause he'll try to out-argue me. . . Mike is strong as a horse and has the physiology of a man half his age."

"So, let's lose the i.v."

"But the two guys I trust most think your coronary arteries are probably constricted. They recommend angiography stat, with the likelihood of intervention to follow. Hopefully a stent, otherwise bypass surgery."

"You gotta be kidding."

"I thought you'd say that. Let's get the studies. Then you can argue with the images and my guys. Bill Hardy is ready for you. He's an interventional cardiologist. He'll help us visualize your coronary arteries and see what's what. I'll give you a few minutes with Marci before Hardy comes in to explain the procedures and get informed consent."

* * *

"I spared you all the cheap shots, like about how hard it was to find the heart in a lawyer as prominent as yourself," said Hardy, "and I told you what I was doing as I did it, but I'll summarize for you and your wife. You are in incredible shape except for two blood vessels that are unusually tortuous."

"Kinky," contributed Shelly.

"Unfortunately, they are two of the three arteries that take care of your heart itself. One was 90% blocked, and the other 85%. We were able to place a stent in each to enlarge the lumen of each artery, to give you much better blood flow. Even though you were feeling great until today, we'll want you to go to cardiac rehab after things settle down and gradually build up the strength of your heart. To answer what Shelly promised me you'd ask. . . No! You can't go right back to your usual level of activity, professionally or physically."

"The biggest challenge for you, Mike," said Shelly, "might be deciding how to proceed from here. The odds are that things will go well, and Bill can give you the best of care. But you'll still be at risk. You'll have to be monitored, and maybe even have to learn to take care of yourself in a different way."

* * *

Marci Burgoyne endured hours of Mike's fretful ruminations about the future. She knew better that to reason with him until he ran out of steam. Finally, she spoke.

"Mike, every week I listen to more hare-brained ideas than I can count. In Hollywood, everybody and everybody's idiot relatives and friends are running around pitching a project, a script, a client. . . My job, my skill, my talent, is to smile sweetly while separating the wheat from the chaff before running them by our CEO, our CFO, and our Board. You know I've never recommended a project up the line that didn't make money.

"Mike, nothing you've said passes any one of my tests. It's not just what you want. It's what will work. You know that line about writers? I face it with pitches. Sometimes I'll advise someone on how to make a project more likely to succeed. I have to help people kill their little darlings.

"It's only when you're considering more than one approach that's likely to succeed that you have the luxury of going with what you like best. As long as you keep trying to figure out how to keep the Maserati Mike Burgoyne show going as is, your best plans are pathetic non-starters.

"You need to bring in someone who can do some heavy lifting, a real colleague, someone who can fight the way you fight."

"People like that are as ornery as I am, Marci. And just about as easy to manage."

"True. But for half a year plus I've been hearing about this kid who did this or that smart thing, this kid who got into one impossible situation after another and found a way out. She and that crazy Jordan finally got Governor Chalmers under investigation for murder on top of everything else. You said she reminds you of you and your old buddy Lauder, but nicer."

"Marci, she is all those things, but she is a very beautiful woman."

"Mike, if you haven't grown up by now, I'll have you hit. How does that work for you?"

"You sure know the way to a man's heart, Marci. Is that the art of the deal, like what that Trump guy wrote?"

"No. Call it the art of war, Mike, like what that Sun Tzu guy wrote. He's my kind of man."

CHAPTER 100

During one interview with the media, Jay Philips' had mentioned his "going nowhere" book about the influences of hypnosis and dissociation theory in nineteenth century European and American literature. A sharp-eyed new hire at a struggling academic press teetering on the brink of financial meltdown invited the suddenly celebrated Jay Philips to submit a proposal, never suspecting that his oft-rejected project was no fantasy, but a completed manuscript, already professionally copy-edited and indexed.

Seizing the moment, the beleaguered press rushed Philips' book into print. It won immediate and impressive critical reviews in the *New York Times*, *London Times,* and the *New York Review of Books* and caught on quickly in certain intellectual circles. Jay was asked to give lectures at Yale and at the University of Chicago. Soon the feisty little press could be upgraded from "endangered" to "threatened" status, and Jay Philips was appointed Adjunct Professor in the English Literature Department of an ivy league university. His graduate course for next fall, on "Culture, Creativity, and Cure in Nineteenth Century English Literature," was filled the day it was announced.

"This may sound crazy, Ben, but I feel somehow that I've come back home, finally back from the wars, like Odysseus."

"You deserve all that credit, all that happiness, and much, much more," Jordan replied. "Yeah, you've already had enough with wars and whirlpools and witches and giants. No more side-trips! Godspeed your ship across the wine-dark sea, and with whatever looms before you. . . Oh, did I ever tell you that really classy ladies like hydrangeas, and that smart bower birds plant them in profusion?"

"I love hydrangeas myself. Does that make me a classy lady?"

"Close, but close only counts in horseshoes and hand grenades."

What the hell do you mean, Jordan? Looming before me? Looming? Odd choice of words. . . Odysseus had a wife waiting for his return. You can't be thinking that. . . And what the hell was that about hydrangeas?

A month later, Linda Gilchrist wrote, "I don't know what this means, but my father read your book. I promise I'll read it as soon as I deliver, and the little ones are sleeping through the night. Dad picked up on your references to the old classics, the Greek and Roman epic poems and all the stuff he says I should have read and made me promise to read. He said I should tell you that somewhere someone is knitting something, or was it weaving something, but that she keeps taking it apart so it's nowhere near finished."

Two men were sending him incredibly blatant messages that raised hopes Jay could hardly allow himself to hope, even though they dominated his every waking moment, and ruled almost every one of his dreams.

Many thought Odysseus had perished. Powerful men sought to win Odysseus' wife and Queen Penelope, and with her, his throne. They urged her to forget her long-absent warrior husband and choose his successor from among them. But faithful Penelope awaited the return of the man she loved. She promised her suitors that she would choose her new mate from among them when she finished weaving a shroud to honor her late husband. What Penelope wove by day, she unraveled under the cover of darkness.

That damn Jordan! Is that what he meant by "looming"?

She's such an amazing woman. They must know that with all the other men out there, I can hardly believe that she. . . Ben Jordan and Arthur Gilchrist may not know literature the way I do, but they understand the world and women far better than I. She's not my wife, but they talk as if she were. . . This is the kind of hope that unravels a man's mind. . . Or makes a woman unravel what she weaves. . . I can't make any sense of my thoughts, and my feelings are completely over the top. Why did I swear off alcohol?

Surviving love makes sailing past Scylla and Charybdis look like a lazy day cruise across the Chesapeake Bay! Jay mused. *If my heart is ready to burst and that's the best simile I can come up with, my future as a poet looks grim! I better keep my day job.*

Jay established dense clusters of Nikko blue and medium pink hydrangeas around the margins of his yard, hoping Kate really loved them as much as he did. He established two small Wim Rutten's Red hydrangeas at either side of his front door. And he dared to hope. . .

CHAPTER 101

Wallace Goldman, the crack New York attorney consulted by Jay Philips' children and their spouses, had no answers for the questions they raised about his ex-wife's estate. He referred them on to his go-to psychiatric consultant, Nate Donaldson.

Jay's son Evan presented their concerns. He described how his mother had always been openly critical of the man he thought was his father. She realized from the first, she'd said, that her marriage had been a mistake. Knowing she could never love a child conceived with Jay Philips, she had continued a covert liaison with the love of her life and repeatedly became pregnant with him, not with Jay. In the year before her death, she had expressed concerns about Jay's sanity. She finally could marry her lover when his own wife passed away.

However, in the joy and happiness of her freedom from Jay and the satisfaction of finally living with the man she loved, she had forgotten to change her will. Written when their children were young, the Philips' wills stipulated that should one of them die, everything would pass to the survivor. But with so many prominent people challenging their father's judgment, and even his sanity, were there grounds upon which the legitimacy of their mother's will could be challenged?

Super-Owl nodded his understanding, and asked the others to confirm their agreement with Evan. He asked a great number of questions, inquiring in detail whether the object of their concern had shown any number of serious psychiatric symptoms or made any irrational judgments or expenditures.

"No, none of these," summarized Evan. "It's the judgment of his professional peers. Is my father crazy? Is he competent?"

"Before I answer, can you tell me about how you all understand Mrs. Philips' behavior in these matters?"

"My father's ideas and his questionable reputation has been a burden to our mother, and to all three of us," said the son.

"I see. And what do you think would happen to Dr. Philips if you were to prove him insane, incompetent?"

"Well, someone would have to be appointed to oversee his affairs."

"Would he be allowed to remain in his home?"

"Probably not. It's much too much for him."

"Has he ever shown poor judgment in caring for any of you or in providing for any of you or your mother?"

"No."

"Well, it's rare that people come to me with a question that can be resolved quite straightforwardly."

Six young bodies inclined toward Super-Owl.

"Mr. Goldman has already informed you that the will you find so frustrating is valid. Now, it becomes my task to inform you that nothing you have said in any way challenges Dr. Philips' sanity or competence."

"But Dr. Chaudvent described my father as irrational, as a dangerous psychiatrist!"

"So he did. But I'm sure you can find the archived CNN footage that describes how in a recent court battle, this Dr. Chaudvent was denied standing as an expert, in part because he criticized your father without having read his papers. Further, a second expert on the same side admitted that he had been forced to acknowledge that he had underestimated the quality of your father's work. Further still, your father's recent book has been well-received, so well-received that I actually read the darn thing. So, I don't think calling your father crazy is any more than a nasty insult.

"Moving on to your second concern, competence. . . Competence relates to specific situations and circumstances. A person can be competent to do many things, but incompetent to do others. It is impossible to build an argument for your father's incompetence in the management of financial matters without evidence that he does not understand what he has, what he wants to do with it, and what the consequences of his choices are likely to entail with regard to financial matters.

"What I am hearing is that Dr. Philips' children neither like nor love nor respect him. Further, his wife has been unfaithful to him, that his wife divorced him and apparently alienated the affection of his children from him, and further, that his children have severed their relationships with him. While it is remotely possible that this long and intriguing narrative of secret assignations and strategic pregnancies is completely accurate, I have to tell you that it does not ring true. You can always check it with genetic testing, but without that, it has no credibility. It comes across as a clever ruse to rationalize infidelity and betrayal in a manner as to capture your affection, to cause you to react with sympathy for a long-tormented secret love finally free to be seen in the light of day."

"I won't let you say things like that about my mother!"

"I already did. And if I choose to repeat them," Super-Owl sat erect and leaned forward, "I doubt you could stop me. However, I would like to call your attention to all you have said about your father, and to invite you to contemplate whether or not he is deserving of these demeaning insults that you apparently accept as truths, without any data to support them."

Evan Philips rose. "We're through here. You don't understand anything. What do we owe you?"

"Don't pay this fraud a thing," said a brother-in-law.

"You must hate women!" said one daughter.

"We came to you for help," said the second, "and you've given us nothing. What do you think we should do? Apologize?"

Super-Owl stood, silent. The son wrote out a check. Super-Owl took it, tore it into small pieces, and stuffed them into the breast pocket of the son's suit.

"Have a nice day," said Super-Owl.

* * *

Several hours later Super-Owl picked up a message from a weeping young woman. He couldn't recognize her voice or make out her words, but he wrote down her number from his caller i.d.

"Hello. I'm Dr. Donaldson. I'm sorry, but I couldn't make out your name or your message. Were you trying to reach me?"

"I must have been a real mess when I called. I'm Margaret Heinz. I was in your office earlier today."

"Sure. Your father is Dr. Philips. Your brother Evan spoke for the rest of you earlier today."

"Evan has a way of taking all the air out of a room. You know?"

"I've met one or two like that. How can I help you?"

"For years my mother has been telling us that Dr. Philips wasn't really our father. She said that by the time she realized he was a lunatic whose own colleagues made fun of him, she stayed with him for us because the love of her life, our father, had made the same kind of mistake. They broke up, married others on the rebound, and had good reasons to keep up this elaborate charade.

"But you didn't seem to accept that notion. Why not?"

"Margaret, I never met your mother. For all I know, this secret soulmate thing might be real. But I am familiar with your father's work, and how badly he's been treated by many of his colleagues. I don't know how to assess him the way you, your brother, and your sister may be doing, but you've been given a very warped view of him as a professional and a scholar. And you may want to check out his activities in Travers v. Underwood and Memorial Hospital and form your own opinions. Please call me again if you feel I can be of further help."

* * *

The message on Jay Philips' voice mail was short.

"Dad, this is Margaret. I'm confused. I don't know what to think. But I want to talk to you. Face to face. I'm shaking. I'll get George to drive me. Just name the time and place. We'll make it happen. . . I'm sorry, Dad. No matter what, I love you."

Jay couldn't make his body move. He would never remember how long it took before his tears began to subside, or how much longer still before he could make it to his bed. Had he been under surveillance, the tapes would have revealed that Jay Philips had fallen asleep crying. . . With a smile on his face.

CHAPTER 102

"Dr. Underwood?"

At first, Joan Underwood couldn't recognize the voice.

"Melody? Melody Jarrett?"

"Yes, Dr. Underwood. Please don't be angry at me. My friend called me. She's another woman Dr. Travers hurt."

"I saw that Governor Chalmers resigned. Is that true? That Dr. Travers is dead?"

"Yes, Melody. Both those things are true."

"I'm so sorry, Dr. Underwood. My family is no good, but they're all I've got. I just couldn't face everybody knowing my story. I know I put you in an awful situation. Even if you don't say so, you've got to be angry. Don't even try to deny it."

"Fair enough. How are you?"

"I've been terrible! I just went on the run. I've been going from friend to friend, cousin to cousin, waitressing all over, and getting into trouble with too much wine. But I think I'm turning a corner."

"I'm glad to hear that. But what about the treatment you need?"

"I don't think you ever believed how important my faith is to me."

"You may be right. Whenever something came up that you didn't want to discuss, you tended to start talking about God."

"Yeah! My new therapist told me that first session. Looked me in the face and said, 'Melody, your faith should bring you strength. It's not something to hide behind. There nothing holy about not confronting your problems.' I'd rather come back to you, but I've realized I can't get well where I was hurt, where everything triggers me and pushes my buttons."

"I hope that it's someone who knows about your condition. . ."

"You think he does."

"What?"

"He was one of your expert witnesses. So, I guess he's some big deal, wrote a lot of things about DID. He's as kind as you are, but not as pretty."

"How did you find him?"

"One of my cousins is seeing some real famous guy Donaldson, and he told her I should go to this fellow. He agreed to see me for next to nothing, if. . . If I called you and came clean."

"I'm surprised."

"He said, 'You can't build a new life on a foundation of fear and bullshit.' Not exactly a poet."

Joan chuckled, "Well, I can't see you in the Midwest, and one of my experts doesn't treat that much DID, so give my regards to Dr. Philips. I'd send him my own family. . . Well, the ones I like!"

CHAPTER 103

From the newest secretaries to the most senior partners, the entire firm of Mackey Markham & Wilder rose as one to applaud and cheer as Bill Mackey entered the Founders Room. Jeff Wilder asked everyone to be seated.

"Well, Bill. It's good to have you back on board full-time. You've cut a lot of tough opponents down to size, but that last bad boy, the big CA, was the nastiest of them all. You're a role model for all of us, and I have to admit, one hell of a hero as well."

Wilder pointed to a new frame hidden behind dark burgundy cloth at the far end of the room, positioned where no portrait had hung before.

"Bill, if it's alright with you, I'll ask Linda Gilchrist to do the honors. She did the cover, and I don't want anyone to undrape it wrong and pull the whole thing off the wall. Linda?"

A heavily pregnant Linda Gilchrist carefully removed the drape that covered an ornate frame, and once again all rose to their feet and applauded. A news photographer had caught the precise moment when Bill Mackey, after sliding his cane between the governor's legs to trip him to the pavement, applied an elegant and highly polished black wingtip shoe to the small of Governor Chalmers's back, forcing him to stay in place while Philips seized the moment and held up Melody Jarrett's drawing of the unknown abuser just inches from the governor's face as they lay side by side.

"We were thinking of entitling it, 'The Long Leg of the Law,' but we thought it might be unseemly for a dignified gent like yourself. Perhaps we should see it metaphorically, as an updated portrait of St. George slaying the dragon. Who knows?"

"I'm speechless."

"I doubt it, Bill. I'd bet that the first dozen things that crossed your mind you dismissed as tactless under the circumstances, or not fit for the delicate ears of our younger associates.

"But today, as we celebrate your return and the quality of professionalism you bring to everything you do, and everyone who has been touched by your influence, whether they wanted to be or not. . ."

Wilder paused for the titters of everyone present who had experienced the Mackey style of mentorship.

"And an anonymous donor has endowed the William Mackey Professorship of Jurisprudence at the new law school SouthEast will open next year."

When the clapping and shouts subsided, Wilder raised his hands for silence.

"We have two other matters to celebrate. We welcome Brett Connery to the ranks of our partners. Bill, Brett was due a while back, but he refused to accept the promotion unless you were here for the occasion." Bill and Brett shook hands, and then hugged.

"Will wonders never cease?" Sally marveled.

Jeff resumed, "And we are also saying good-bye to one of our best and brightest. As most of you know, Ms. Linda Gilchrist's husband has been offered an endowed professorship in California. He found the position attractive, but he was reluctant to relocate and interrupt Ms. Gilchrist's professional career yet again. Fortunately for this couple, although unfortunate for Mackey Markham & Wilder, a colleague in California, known best by a rather colorful appellation, has invited her to join his practice. After she becomes accustomed to being called 'Mom,' she will join a firm that will do business under the name, Burgoyne and Gilchrist Associates. And no. . . None of you can afford her retainer!"

CHAPTER 104

The evening's logs had dwindled down to ash and a galaxy of glowing embers. Nate Donaldson and Ben Jordan, ballet bachelors for the evening, relaxed by fireplace of the Donaldsons' brownstone.

"Have you read that Jay Philips book?" asked Super Owl. "Kind of interesting."

"Sure. I'm surprised you read it," Ben replied.

"So am I. He popped into my mind one day. So, I did a little searching, and there it was."

"The guy is impressive. He jumps into a completely different field and hits a home run. In addition to everything else, he'll be teaching literature. And, by the way, he's raving about your last book."

"You mean 'Down With Assholes'? That's the invisible ink title for *Understanding the Bully and Bullying: A Study of Narcissistic/Sadistic Compensation for Personal Inadequacy*."

"That's the one."

"When are you going to write a book of your own, Ben?"

"Maybe someday."

"I've heard that before. More than once, I think. So, changing sore subjects, in that case you and Jay Philips were involved with. . ."

"Linda Gilchrist is trying to figure out how to deal with twins."

"She sounds like an amazing gal, Ben, but about that case. . ."

"Over and done with, Nate."

"Just like that?"

"Just like that. Linda Gilchrist, her aunt, and Jay Philips turned the tide. Fantastic bit of detective work, just like I told you. I was just along for the ride."

"I was going to offer you some really exceptional Armagnac, but when you try to finesse an obvious prevarication like that past me, I begin to think you don't respect me and don't deserve my Armagnac. I'm OK with subterfuge to protect confidentiality in professional situations. . . But you've got no excuse."

"OK. I'm undone. You dangle a really great Armagnac in front of me and I start to whine and grovel. Yes! I did a crippled minnow."

"Ah. . . I see." Super Owl poured the Armagnac with the care and reverence most reserve for a cherished lover. They sat in silence, appreciating every nuance of its bouquet and taste, savoring every subtle change as the Armagnac opened to the air and temperature.

"A most versatile bait. You son of a bitch! You pumped up the shame! You let them think you were wounded, humiliated and circling the drain, and then you were mean."

"Why else cast a lure like that to a barracuda, even a rather nice barracuda?"

"Good point."

"Someone once told me that it's always good form to punch a bully in the nose, one way or the other."

"I can't imagine who would say such a thing."

"Perhaps I was mistaken."

"Let's hope for better times for Dr. P."

"Amen to that!" They clicked glasses.

CHAPTER 105

It was 365 days later. Precisely.

Jay Philips' cell phone rang.

"Ready to try to avoid messing things up?"

"No. The heck with try. Ready to avoid messing things up. Ready to make things work, whatever it takes."

"Confident?"

"I wish. Let's say, scared but determined."

"When would you like to start?"

"As soon as possible."

There was a knock at Jay's door.

"Someone's knocking on my door."

"Interruptions already? Do you really care?"

"I'll be right back."

"Stay on the line."

Jay had to push hard to begin to open his front door. There was a gruff bark, a shuffling sound, and then it opened easily. A massive but familiar dog looked up at him. It sat at the feet of a woman. Jay saw a lovely face with a smile that reached into his chest, opening his heart with an inexpressible tenderness. Wise gray eyes, as full of tears as his own. Kate held a cellphone in one hand and a toothbrush in the other.

"What lovely hydrangeas!" she said. "I hope I didn't overpack."

The End

ACKNOWLEDGMENTS

During the tempestuous years of the "Memory Wars" I served as an expert witness in the classic "false memory" and "iatrogenic creation of multiple personalities" cases of the era. Once I traveled south to testify on behalf of an excellent young colleague. Upon my arrival I learned that her adroit attorney, Phyllis Lile-King, Esq., had uncovered the plaintiff's deceptive efforts to undermine the credibility of the patient around whom and about whose treatment the trial revolved. The plaintiff had taken steps to obscure the existence of the office in which events crucial to the case had taken place, casting doubt on the patient's account of what had transpired, in part, in this office that "did not exist." But Ms. Lile-King is a great fan of Nancy Drew mysteries, and a keen thinker. She discovered and unveiled the ruse just before my arrival. By the time I appeared in court, my testimony was mere window-dressing. I was incredibly impressed. She was kind enough to give me permission to write a mystery inspired by her amateur sleuthing.

As an expert on trauma and dissociation, I was thrown into the cauldron of the memory wars. Ultimately, I became the defendant in a "false memory" case. My experiences exposed me to "the good, the bad, and the ugly" of attorneys and expert witnesses at work.

I want to acknowledge the skill, dedication, and most surprisingly, the caring, that I received from Jeffrey Lerman, Esq., Marianne Bechtle, Esq., and their team of professionals and support personnel at the law firm of Montgomery McCracken Walker & Rhoads LLP. I acknowledge as well the expertise and support of my personal attorney in that litigation, William J. O'Brien, Esq., of Conrad O'Brien Gellman & Rohn, PC.

Thanks as well to other gifted and ethical attorneys among my longtime friends, Robert N. Axelrod, Esq., Stephen H. Green, Esq., the late Barden Levavy, Esq., and preeminently, my son, David A. Kluft, Esq., of Foley Hoag; also Robert L. Rubenstein, accountant and Adjunct Professor of Law Firm Management at the William & Mary School of Law.

Profound thanks to Renee Parker, M.D., and Mary Sylvia for their comments on earlier drafts of this manuscript, and to Lynn Crook, preeminent historian of the "Memory Wars." Lynn spared time from her own eagerly-awaited book to offer me feedback on my project. I am profoundly grateful to Alan W. Scheflin, J.D., L.L.M., M.A., retired Professor Emeritus of Santa Clara University School of Law for his reviews, commentaries, and suggestions concerning the accuracy of legal aspects of *A Sinister Subtraction*.

I have learned a lot from the individuals whom I acknowledge. Any and all errors or inaccuracies in the legal or historical aspects of *A Sinister Subtraction* that go beyond the realm of poetic license are the responsibility of the author.

RPK

CPSIA information can be obtained
at www.ICGtesting.com
Printed in the USA
BVHW042308260719
554492BV00003B/4/P

9 781949 093278